OUIJA
FOR THE RECORD

OUIJA
FOR THE RECORD

A True Story
By
D. Lynn Cain

Copyright © 2007
D. Lynn Cain
Paperback edition: 978-0-557-15871-3
Hardcover edition: 978-0-557-15872-0

All rights reserved. No part of this book may be reproduced, stored, or transmitted by any means—whether auditory, graphic, mechanical, or electronic—without written permission of both publisher and author, except in the case of brief excerpts used in critical articles and reviews. Unauthorized reproduction of any part of this work is illegal and is punishable by law

OUIJA
For the Record

Introduction	ix
1. It Begins	1
2. Mary Frances and Walter Levoy	13
3. Ouija	23
4. Elijah	39
5. God and Angels	47
6. The Saving of Levoy	61
7. The Mission	73
8. The Revelation	89
9. Getting Ready	109
10. Embarking on the Mission	125
11. The Last I Will Send	143
12. Dolmer's Legacy	151
13. Grand Theft	165
14. Barbara's Mountain	173
15. Jeane Dixon	193
16. The Extortion	203
17. Destination Kabul	211
18. Kabul	219
19. Ouija's Back	231
20. Settling In	237
21. Kargha Lake	249
22. The Gift of the Nabirs	259
23. Abdul Wassy	269
24. The Fleece	287
25. A Question of Faith	305
26. The Exorcist	317
Epilogue	331

Dedication

I could not have written this story without the unwavering support of my husband Ken. He was the one who encouraged me to write the story in 1980 on my Silver Reed typewriter and he stood by me during the final four years of obsessive writing that culminated in this book in 2007. When it came time to publish it, he said "just do it" while driving down Lake Shore Drive.

I have to thank my children for listening to the story and for telling me I had to write it down. My son Jason entered my scarred life only four years after our family's saga was over, but his presence in my life has helped me become a better person. My daughter Sarah believed in my story and invested her time and energy to make it real. She has inspired me to be more than I ever thought I could be.

To my brothers and sister, thank you for understanding my overwhelming compulsion to faithfully tell our amazing story.

And, finally, thanks to Taryn Phillips-Quinn who convinced me that the story was worth telling and that I was capable of telling it.

This story is for all of you.

Introduction

We can either control our destiny or it will control us. It has taken me more than half a century to understand that I can control my destiny. I have faltered in every aspect of my life, standing still for years, moving forward in others—forward to what I didn't know.

The only certainty in my life has been that a chain of events occurred between 1968 and 1970 that have had a profound effect on me and my family. Who would I have been without these events? Should I miss the person I would have been, or should I simply accept the person I am?

I tried to forget everything that led up to our sojourn in Afghanistan, but it seems the words of a woman I met in 1970 have imprisoned me in the memories for almost forty years.

What follows is our small story set against a chaotic backdrop of peace, love, and war. Although some names have been changed and some events dramatized, this is a faithful telling of our story.

Chapter 1

It Begins

The Goodwill store had air conditioning.

"Lord have mercy, it's hot," Mommy said with a hint of her lingering Mississippi twang. She lifted her glasses and squinted at the thermometer hanging from a mulberry branch in our back yard. "Good God, it's 110 degrees in the shade."

She pulled a blue and white polka dot handkerchief from her housedress pocket and dabbed at the sweat that was glistening on the folds of her neck. She weighed nearly 270 pounds, and she was *sweltering*.

"You knowed it, Mary Frances," Ila Dee replied as she fanned her face lazily with the TV guide. "Why don't we load up the kids and head to Goodwill?"

Mommy and Ila Dee had been friends since before I was born. Ila Dee was an Okie and Mommy was "born in Corinth—thirty miles from Tupelo, Mississippi. Elvis' birthplace." They had met at the soda fountain in Litchfield Park nearly twenty years earlier.

Mommy tells the story that in 1946 she felt a need to start a new life away from Mississippi. So, at twenty-six, she divorced her husband Louis and left her three boys with her momma in Corinth. Then she moved to Memphis with her sister, Edith. When neither could make enough money to support themselves and Edith's kids, they put Edith's kids in an orphanage and hopped on a bus for Arizona.

Mommy met Daddy in 1950 outside the soda fountain in Litchfield and they'd been together ever since. Daddy is Walter Levoy Cain and he was a staff sergeant in the Air Force up until '66, when he retired at the age of forty-three. That was two years ago.

Daddy's a janitor at Unidynamics and Mommy works part-time as a maid at the Wigwam Resort in Litchfield. She spends every cent she earns at the Goodwill store, which angers Daddy to no end. But Mommy always said, "Where else can you take two dollars and buy three dresses, two shirts, four pairs of pants, and a set of pans?" Daddy couldn't argue with that.

We live in Avondale, which is south of Western Avenue. It's near, but not quite in, the poor side of town. Goodyear was north of Western and it's where all the "high falutin" people lived.

Today was Mommy's day off and her money was burning a hole in her pocket like it always did. "Let's get outta here," she said as she grabbed her purse and headed to the front door. "Tricia, Dinie," she yelled to me and my sister. "You gals wanna go to Goodwill?"

"Yes, yes," we yelled back. "Wait for us." We slipped on our rubber thongs hurriedly and ran squeaking down the hall, pushing each other along the way.

I'm Dinie—it's really Diana Lynn. Mommy named me after a movie star. Tricia is really Patricia Faith, named after Aunt Faith, Daddy's sister. I'm thirteen and Tricia's fourteen—Irish twins according to Daddy.

As we ran past our brothers, Mike and Timmy, I pushed Mike off the homemade stilts he was trying to master in the front yard. "Can we—" Mike started.

Mommy shook her head violently and walked past them without saying a word. She recoiled in pain as her fingers touched the searing hot door handles of the '59 Plymouth station wagon. "Damnit, I'll never get used to this infernal heat," she muttered.

"Don't I know it?" Ila Dee agreed as she used her skirt hem to open her door.

I inhaled sharply as I pushed open the door of the Goodwill store. I held my breath as long as I could. As soon as I drew my next breath, I was overpowered by the stench of starch and body odor.

"Puh-wee," I gasped involuntarily.

The smell reminded me every time of the ironing I did for Wigwam guests. The hot steam from the iron melted the starch into the sweat stained armpits and nearly made me vomit more than once. Mommy said a clothes pin on my nose might help, but I got used to the smell 'cause I sure liked the ironing money.

We took our time strolling through Goodwill, enjoying the cool of the air-conditioning. As I pulled a yellow empire waist dress from the rack, I slipped off my thongs and stood on the cold linoleum. "Ahh," I sighed. Then I heard Mommy in the far corner of the store.

"Well, I'll be." she exclaimed. "It's a Ouija board. You ever seen one, Ila?"

"Nope," she tapped the box and turned it over. "Is it a game?"

"Yep, it's kinda like a gypsy. It tells the future—but you gotta be careful with these things," Mommy warned. "Oh, what the hell. It'll keep the kids out of my hair this summer."

"Mary, yep, that's what you need," Ila said cynically as she absently rooted through piles of clothes.

I bought the empire dress with my ironing money, and Mommy bought the Ouija game for twenty-five cents. When we got home, she put it on the top shelf in the hall closet with Monopoly and Life.

School finally let out just before Memorial Day, and the neighborhood kids descended on the desert in back of our house in search of the right spot for our fort. We worked together to dig a hole at least five feet deep and ten feet in diameter and covered it with scraps of wood from Daddy's work shed.

Mommy had a rule that we couldn't come in the house during the day "because one, your Father is sleeping; and two, because you're filthy." So, we spent the hot summer days in our fort or playing board games on the picnic table in the back yard. She would unlock the door for bathroom breaks, but only if it was an emergency.

When the heat became unbearable, we'd turn on the sprinkler and run through it to cool down. But, the water coming from the outside spigot was too warm to drink, and it tasted like plastic. We much preferred the icy cold water that continually drained from the swamp cooler.

Monopoly was our favorite game. Mike usually won because he was older, and he insisted that he was the only one who could be banker. Mike always ended up with Park Place and Boardwalk, and then he'd play the rest of us into bankruptcy. We accused him of cheating—but maybe we were just bad players.

Life was our other favorite, but it took a lot less time to play and almost no strategy was involved. Occasionally, Mommy would let us join her weekly neighborhood gin rummy game, but only if we could keep up with the play.

Finding a new game one evening in June was a real treat.

"What's this?" Mike asked as he peered into the dark hall closet. Michael Levoy—Big Mike as opposed to Little Mike, our nephew—was sixteen, six foot five, and weighed 130 pounds soaking wet. He reached for the Ouija box and held it above his curly head to inspect it. The box was tattered and yellow, and the lid was held together with silver duct tape at the corners. He shook it.

"There's nothing in it," he said as he slammed the box back onto the shelf.

Mike was a colicky baby, according to Mommy. According to Daddy, he was growing up to be a trouble maker. Mike had a silver cap put on one of his permanent front teeth after a bad bike accident. The dentist said to come back in a few weeks and he'd replace it with a white cap. That was four years ago.

"Get it down, get it down," Timmy cried as Mike pulled the box out from under Monopoly and took it to the kitchen table.

Timothy Ray was a year younger than me and was Mommy's "baby." In his eighth year, Timmy returned from a camping trip with ringworm. Every kid I knew had had ringworm at least once, and it was no big deal. Timmy wasn't that lucky.

Daddy insisted that he could heal the ringworm with a concoction of rubbing alcohol and hydrogen peroxide. Over the next two months, the ringworm ate a three-inch round scar on the back of Timmy's head. Mommy finally had enough and took Timmy to the Luke Air Force base doctors. They killed the ringworm, but they said there was nothing they could do about the scar.

The patio door slid open just then and Mommy stepped inside, backwards. She balanced a laundry basket on her right hip and closed the door with her free hand. In the basket were stiff, clean clothes she had just removed from the clothesline in anticipation of a dust storm.

"Do you two know how that works?" she asked when she noticed the box on the table.

Mike and Timmy shrugged their shoulders and looked at each other. "Nope" they said in unison.

"It's a Ouija board," Mommy said mysteriously. "It tells the future." She dumped the clothes on the kitchen table and began folding them on the other end of the table. I had been sitting in Daddy's vinyl recliner, watching television and half-listening to what was going on in the kitchen. Now I was intrigued.

Mike opened the box and held up the only game piece. He looked quizzically at Mommy.

"That's it," she said. "It takes two people to play."

The Ouija board looked pretty simple to me with its tan background and black lettering. A sun was in the upper left hand corner, with the word "YES" next to it. In the upper middle was "Ouija—The Mystifying Oracle" and in the upper right was the word "NO" with a moon next to it.

In the middle were the letters of the alphabet arched in two rows—A through M on the top row and N through Z on the bottom row. And, under that were the numbers 1, 2, 3… through 9 and then a 0. At the very bottom of the board was "Good Bye" and the maker's name: William Fuld, Baltimore, MD.

The indicator was the only game piece. It was teardrop shaped and had three stubby legs with felt on the bottom of each. In the center of the teardrop was a round hole with a magnifying glass in it.

Mike and Timmy sat down at the table—facing each other and on opposite sides of the board. Mike asked, "Now what?"

"Both of you touch the indicator on opposite sides with your fingers. Ask a question and it will spell out an answer," Mommy said absently as she continued folding clothes. I sat down at the table and watched in anticipation.

"This is weird," Mike said shaking his head. "What am I supposed to ask?"

"Here, I'll ask a question," Mommy said. "Who will Mike marry?"

We stared at the indicator, waiting for movement. Nothing.

"It's supposed to start spelling out the answer," Mommy said as she leaned closer to Mike and peered over her glasses. "Hmmmm."

Our eyes grew wide as the indicator suddenly lurched across the board. It stopped over the letter "S." Then it slowly moved to the "T", then "U" and "P" "I" "D."

Timmy interpreted, "Stupid?"

Mommy put her hands on her hips and glared at Mike. "You're moving that, aren't you?" she accused him.

"Yeah, 'cause this is stupid," he bellowed.

I took Mike's place at the table as soon as he got up. "I want to try," I said.

I rested three fingers from each hand on the edges of the indicator. Then I asked, "Who will Timmy marry?"

Nothing.

I pushed the indicator intentionally just to make sure it wasn't stuck to the board. Still nothing.

"This is a stupid game," Mike repeated as he drank grape Kool-Aid.

Tricia had been watching *Bonanza* in the living room and was suddenly interested, "Can I try?"

When none of us would join her at the Ouija board, Mommy turned from the sink, where she had begun washing pinto beans. She wiped her hands on her apron and offered to sit with Tricia. They had barely placed their fingers on the indicator when it started gliding across the board to quickly spell a word.

"H-E-L-L-O"

Mommy and Tricia pulled their hands back from the indicator as soon as the word was spelled. "Oh my Lord," Mommy said. "I never seen one move that fast."

"You moved it," Mike accused, jabbing his finger at Tricia's face.

"Like I can spell upside down and backwards," Tricia responded.

"It so is you," Timmy repeated.

I just shook my head. It amazed me that Timmy always sided with Mike in any argument. How could he do that, knowing that Mike took pleasure in physically torturing him and taunting Timmy about his ringworm scar? Idiot brothers.

Tricia was angry now. "I didn't move it," she said, sticking her tongue out.

Mommy sat thoughtfully for a minute and then came to Tricia's defense, "She couldn't have moved it. It's upside down for her, and it moved too fast. Nobody can spell that fast upside down."

I looked from Mommy to Tricia and then back to Mommy. I was skeptical about this game, but I wanted to see more.

They gently placed their fingers back on the indicator and Mommy asked, "Who are you?"

"I A-M O-U-I-J-A" it spelled quickly.

I was suddenly chilled and unconsciously rubbed the goose bumps on my arms. I couldn't take my eyes off the board.

"Ask it something," Timmy prompted, when no one spoke.

"Will I live to be 100?" Mommy asked.

The indicator moved quickly to the upper right corner to NO.

The questions came faster then.

"Will Tricia live to 100?" Mommy asked.

"YES"

"Will she get married?"

YES was the answer.

"Who to?"

"O-L-D-E-R M-A-N"

"How old?" Tricia asked, concerned.

"3-0"

"Thirty years old?" Tricia repeated, disappointed.

The indicator moved to YES.

I couldn't help myself, "Who will I marry?"

"B-L-A-C-K M-A-N"

Mommy winced and reacted quickly, "I'm sure you're not marrying a nigger." I cringed whenever she said that word. She had no qualms about calling people niggers because she said it was not derogatory in the South—it just meant field worker. I was pretty sure my black friends, Ivory and Daisy, would disagree with her. It just wasn't worth arguing with her anymore, though.

"And when will I die?" I asked defiantly, ignoring her comment.

"2-9"

"From what?"

"C-A-N-C-E-R"

At that point, Mommy took her hands off the indicator and looked at me. "Diana, don't believe everything it says. It's just a game."

Mike laughed and said, "I don't believe *anything* it says. I think Tricia's moving it."

"Yeah, me too," I said suspiciously. It seemed mighty strange to me that Ouija's news for me was all bad, but Tricia got only good news.

Tricia's eyes had turned to slits, and she was fuming. Before she could answer, Mommy cut her off and told us to set the table for dinner.

* * *

Monsoon season was just getting started in June, and we were housebound in late afternoons because of dust and thunderstorms. On one particularly dark and ominous afternoon, Mommy brought out the Ouija board again.

It was pointless for anyone but Tricia and Mommy to sit at the board, so the rest of us just watched. As soon as they placed their fingers on the indicator, it started moving.

"H-E-L-L-O   A-G-A-I-N" it spelled. "I   H-A-V-E   B-E-E-N   W-A-I-T-I-N-G"

"What were you waiting for?" Mommy asked.

"W-A-N-T   T-O   T-A-L-K" it spelled quickly. "A-S-K   M-E   Q-U-E-S-T-I-O-N-S"

"Where are you?" Mike asked.

"I   A-M   H-E-R-E"

"I've got a good question," Timmy said. "Who will be the next president of the United States?"

"N-I-X-O-N" was the reply.

"Who's he?" Timmy asked Mommy.

Mommy shrugged. She frequently commented on how handsome the Kennedy men were whenever there was a news story about them. I think she did it to provoke Daddy, who absolutely despised the family, for some reason.

"No way, man," Mike said. "Kennedy's gonna win. Everybody knows that."

The indicator moved slowly to NO.

"The only way Kennedy will lose is if he's dead," Mike pronounced defiantly.

We waited expectantly for at least a minute, but there was no movement from the board.

"Ouija?" Mommy finally prodded. "Why isn't Bobbie Kennedy going to be President?"

"C-A-N-T   S-A-Y"

"Why?" I asked stubbornly.

"N-E-X-T Q-U-E-S-T-I-O-N"

We were easily diverted to the next question and sat with the Ouija board for another hour or so before dinner.

Daddy had just started working the graveyard shift and slept all day, but he'd wake in time for dinner. Then he'd watch television with us until he had to go to work at ten o'clock. After dinner that night, Daddy turned on the television to watch the news. Tricia and I washed and dried the dinner dishes while everyone else settled in the living room.

When I heard that someone named Andy Warhol had been shot, I ran to the living room, dishtowel and plate still in my hand. "Who's Andy Warhol?" I panted.

"He's some drugged up, hippy longhair," daddy said, shaking his head. Then he changed the channel abruptly to watch a rerun of *Get Smart*.

Ouija had been forgotten in the closet. It seemed like a pointless game to me and I much preferred being outside and playing with my friends. That is, until June 6th, 1968.

On the morning of the third day after Warhol was shot, our cartoons were interrupted by a special news report: "Robert Kennedy was mortally wounded at the Ambassador Hotel in Los Angeles shortly after midnight. A Palestinian is suspected—"

I didn't hear the rest. The spoon in my hand stopped midair, and then I lowered it slowly into the bowl of cereal I was eating. It was 1963 all over again. I was in third grade when President Kennedy was assassinated. The teachers called us in from recess that day and told us the President had been killed. I remember sitting on the sidewalk and crying. Then they let us go home, where Mommy was crying hysterically.

"Dear Lord, not again," Mommy said tearfully at last. "When's the violence gonna stop?"

She was engrossed in the news story unfolding on the television, but kept muttering to herself, "First, the President, then Martin Luther King, now Bobbie. The whole world's falling apart—race riots, war protestors, nuclear war—when's it all gonna end?"

We stayed in the house all day, watching the news with Mommy. When we woke Daddy to break the news of Bobbie's death, he said "Good riddance," and then rolled over. "Wake me for dinner."

"You're the cruelest man I've ever known," Mommy yelled. Then she slammed the bedroom door.

The nightly dust storm had cooled the temperature in the valley by at least thirty degrees that night. After dinner, Mommy grabbed her old guitar and motioned for us to follow her outside. She carefully slid her bottom into the aluminum chaise lounge and started strumming "Jimmy Crack Corn," a favorite of the neighborhood kids. Within a few minutes ten kids were sitting on our front lawn, listening to Mommy sing and play.

She told the kids they would have to go home and she finished with my favorite song.

> *Hang down your head, Tom Dooley.*
> *Hang down your head and cry.*
> *Hang down your head, Tom Dooley.*
> *Poor boy's abound to die.*

I think she sang it for Bobbie.

Chapter 2

Mary Frances and Walter Levoy

Mommy said she wasn't waking Daddy for dinner. She said he didn't deserve dinner for what he said about Bobbie Kennedy. So he was pretty angry when he finally woke up right before time to go to work that night.

"What's this slop?" he grimaced, pointing to the glass of milk and cornbread Mommy had placed on the table in front of him. "You call this dinner?"

"Yes, Levoy," Mommy sneered. "We can't afford *real* food."

"Stop spending every dime you make at Goodwill, and maybe we could have decent meals," he screamed, sucking air into his lungs between each word. He shoved her aside and pulled the sliding patio door open violently. He kicked the screen door off its rollers and stepped over it.

He cursed at himself under his breath as he settled back into his smoking chair on the back porch. Next to him, on a small patio table, was an ashtray overflowing with cigarette butts, and on the floor was a garbage can filled to the brim with crumpled Winston cigarette packs.

"We'd have more money if you'd stop smoking and breaking things," Mommy screamed. "I guess we can add the screen door to the list of things you broke," she stopped to count on her fingers.

"Let's see, the hole you punched in the closet door, the TV lamp you broke, the—"

Daddy reached for the patio door and slammed it shut in her face. She ranted all the way down the hall and then kicked her bedroom door shut.

She cursed for a few more minutes, and then all I heard was the tappety-tap of typewriter keys.

I sighed with relief when they were finally in separate areas. Why couldn't my family be more like Judy Gebhart's? I'd stop at her house sometimes after school, and it was so pleasant. No one ever raised their voice at her house.

I read the TV Guide absently and was comforted by my mom's typing. Mommy was a big Zane Grey fan. She joined a book club just so she could collect all of his novels. There must have been at least thirty of them on the hall bookshelves.

After finishing his last book *Boulder Dam* one day, she announced that she was going to become a writer. So, she commandeered the 1948 Remington typewriter that Daddy had "borrowed" from the Air Force before he retired. She told us that Zane Grey had self-published his first novel and look where he got. She was sure she could do it too.

I read her first twenty-page manuscript called *Poor Boy*—the story of Frankie Barns and his quest to escape a life of poverty in the South. It was okay. Now she was working on *Yesterday,* about a horsewoman named June Weldon, who was struggling to save her logging business.

Mommy had asked Daddy to read *Poor Boy* and give her his opinion, but I guess she didn't want his honest opinion. After he told her there were a lot of grammatical errors, she hurled his favorite paperweight at him, barely missing his head. She swore that he'd never read another book—until it was published and he had to buy his own copy.

Daddy stayed on the back porch for thirty minutes smoking one cigarette after another. On his way out the front door, he asked me, "What's your momma doing?" I was pretty sure he could hear the typing, so I couldn't figure out why he was asking.

"She's writing," I replied nonchalantly.

He shook his head and reached for his Dristan. "She's a goddamned idiot," he said in between sprays up his huge nostrils. "She's got better things to do than write trashy novels."

"What's wrong with writing?" I asked. "You don't know anything about writing. Maybe she will get published." I hated it when he put Mommy down.

"Punkin', there ain't nothing wrong with writing," he smiled. "But your momma didn't finish the ninth grade. She doesn't know how to write."

"But she could be a writer if she practiced," I defended her obstinately.

Just then, Mommy appeared in the hallway.

"I heard everything you said Levoy." Tears welled up in her eyes, and she blurted out angrily, "Would you rather I spend my time on a barstool? Would that make you happy?"

"Why change your spots *now*?" he retorted vehemently.

"Maybe I should have just died in that canal, huh?" Mommy shouted.

"Maybe." He was surprised by what he said—almost like he knew he should take it back.

"What kind of man would say that about his wife in front of his kids?" she cried.

I had been laying on the cool tile, watching TV and trying to ignore their current battle, which was really hard since it was going on over my head. As Daddy passed me on his way to the front door, I sat up reflexively.

"Good, get out of here," I thought to myself.

I was yelling at Mommy inside my head, "Don't follow him, don't follow him." She didn't listen.

She followed him to the door and screamed, "Why don't you just say it, Levoy. You wish I was dead."

"I didn't say that," he said as he climbed into his Chevy pickup.

"Oh yes you did," she slammed the front door shut. "I can't live like this." She stepped over me and stumbled down the hall to the bedroom. No more tappety-tap from the bedroom that night.

Although no one told me the story of the canal accident, I had pieced it together with my brothers and sister over the years. Sometime around Christmas of my third year of life, the four of us kids had the mumps and whooping cough all at the same time. Mommy wasn't taking care of us—old Miss Diefenderfer was.

We asked her where our Mommy was, but she wouldn't tell us. And then Daddy appeared at our front door on Christmas Eve. We were surprised to see him because he was supposed to be away for a long time—in a very cold place called Alaska.

We heard them talking about the accident, about how Mommy had been drinking at the Wishing Well bar and was so drunk when she left at four o'clock in the morning that she drove off the road, flipped the car, and landed upside down in the canal. Miss Difenderfer had been taking care of us ever since that night—that is, until Daddy came home.

Mommy broke both legs, hips, and arms and was hospitalized for months. She was thirty-eight years old and the base doctors told her she might never walk again. She was determined to prove them wrong and gave up the crutches a year after the accident. Her right leg is shorter than her left by a good two inches, but she's still able to get around pretty well.

After Mommy recuperated, Daddy got stationed to Greenland. Mommy moved us into a tiny three bedroom apartment in the Avondale Circle. It was where the "poor folks" lived, she said. She converted the walk-in closet into a bedroom for the boys so we could have a dining room table. A swamp cooler saturated the apartment with the sweet smell of wet hay and kept the apartment at a humid, but bearable, 95 degrees during the hottest months.

By then, Mike was in first grade. A lot of days, Mommy would send Mike to school and within minutes, she was sitting on a barstool at the Oasis. She took us three younger ones with her and told us to stay in the car. If we got out, we'd get a whipping. But the car was like an oven, and we were baking within five minutes. Being the oldest, Tricia knew how to open the doors and would let us out. She'd wait until she was sure Mommy had downed a few drinks, and then she'd venture into the bar for a glass of water.

With a little water, we could play in the parking lot for hours. Our favorite pastime was herding wooly worms into makeshift holding pens under the eucalyptus tree. When the sun was straight overhead, we'd scramble back into the car and be there waiting for her when she came out.

If Mommy didn't go to the bar during the day, she'd go at night. She'd tuck us into bed and leave after she was sure we were asleep. As soon as she left, Mike would wake us and turn on her phonograph. She would have killed us if she knew we played her Gene Autry records or that we played "Mutual Admiration Society" over and over. First the boys would sing with Eddy Arnold, and then the girls would sing with Jaye Morgan:

> *You and me belong to the-e-e-e*
> *mutual admiration society.*
> *I say that you're the greatest one,*
> *You say, "No you're the greatest one"*
> *And we'd go on like that from night 'til dawn.*

One morning, I woke up early and ran to Mommy's bedroom to ask for some cereal. I threw open the door and then stood there with my tiny four-year old hand glued to the doorknob. Whose feet were in Mommy's bed? She sat up, shocked at my intrusion and immediately shooed me from her room.

We pretended that these things never happened. We certainly never told Daddy about anything Mommy did while he was gone. It was safer that way.

* * *

With all the fighting, I had forgotten about the Ouija board and its prediction about Bobbie Kennedy. Mommy sent us to summer recreation at the grade school early the next morning, and when we arrived home a little after lunch, she was waiting for us at the front door—which she never did.

The Ouija board was on the kitchen table. "What took you so long?" Mommy asked Tricia angrily. "We gotta talk to the Ouija board."

"Can't I even get a drink of water?" Tricia asked, annoyed.

"No. Sit down right now," Mommy seemed anxious. "I've been waiting all day to talk to Ouija."

"But, don't you want us to go *outside* and play?" Mike asked sarcastically.

"Shut up, Mike," Mommy replied.

"I W-A-S W-A-I-T-I-N-G" the Ouija board spelled as soon as Mommy and Tricia's fingers touched the indicator.

There was a protocol emerging during the Ouija board sessions. Mommy would call out the letters because she sat on the side where the letters were right side up. She'd place her fingers on the wide part of the indicator, while Tricia's fingers barely touched the pointy side of the teardrop.

I was entranced by the graceful movement of the indicator across the board. Their fingers reminded me of the concert pianist I had seen at Grady

Gammage Auditorium in sixth grade. His fingers glided gracefully over the piano keys touching each key with just the right pressure to bring out the melody of a piece. Like the pianist, if Mommy and Tricia applied too much pressure, the indicator screeched to a halt. Too little, and their fingers would be left behind as the indicator flew from letter to letter.

"Is the assassination what you couldn't tell us about?" Mommy couldn't contain herself any longer.

The indicator moved to YES.

"Was Sirhan Sirhan the only shooter?" Mike interjected. "If there's more than one shooter, we can tell the FBI."

Again it was YES and then "O-N-L-Y O-N-E"

"Why didn't you tell us about it before it happened?" Mike demanded. "We could have stopped it."

"E-X-A-C-T-L-Y"

"But shouldn't we have tried to stop it?"

The indicator moved to NO quickly, and then spelled "Y-O-U A-R-E N-O-T G-O-D"

Mommy hadn't said a word during this exchange. Then she blurted out, "Ouija, are you the devil?"

The indicator moved slowly to NO.

Mommy shrugged her shoulders, "I've heard of Ouija boards being possessed by devils, and I was just testing it," she nodded knowingly. "The devil has to answer honestly." I wasn't sure how she knew this, but I believed her.

"That's stupid," Mike interrupted. "The devil is a liar. Why would he have to tell the truth?"

"T-H-E B-I-B-L-E S-A-Y-S S-O"

"Who are you?" Tricia asked out of the blue.

"I A-M O-U-I-J-A" came the answer just as quickly.

"Why are you talking to us?" Mommy asked.

"D-U-E C-O-U-R-S-E"

"Ouija, can you tell us *anything* we want to know?" Timmy asked.

"N-O-T E-V-E-R-Y-T-H-I-N-G"

"Mommy, can we invite other people to talk to Ouija?" I wanted my friends to see this amazing game.

"I don't think that's a good idea," Mommy said shaking her head. "People won't under—"

Ouija interrupted, "I W-I-L-L T-A-L-K T-O O-T-H-E-R-S"

"Can Beverly talk to Ouija?" I asked. Beverly was Ila Dee's daughter and my best friend. When Ouija answered affirmatively, I pushed, "How about other friends?"

Mommy nodded her head to show Ouija's assent.

After summer rec the next day, Mommy and Ila Dee were waiting for us at the front door. We had brought my friend Beverly; Mike's pal, Mike Gonzales; and Tricia's friend, Alicia.

"Keep it down," Mommy whispered. "Your Daddy's asleep." Ouija was lying on the kitchen table, and the nine of us crowded around it—some standing, some sitting, talking to each other excitedly in hushed voices. Mommy and Tricia took their places at the board. Our eyes darted back and forth, expectantly waiting for someone to speak to Ouija.

Ouija started it off, "H-E-L-L-O"

I noticed that there were raised eyebrows on the newcomers' faces. They responded directly to Ouija. "Hello," they said in unison.

"S-H-E W-I-L-L I-L-A"

"What?" Ila was surprised. "I didn't have a question."

"Y-O-U T-H-O-U-G-H-T I-T"

"Did you think something?" Mommy asked Ila Dee.

Ila Dee was half shaking her head when her eyes lit up, and she realized, "Oh, my God. I was just thinking that Carol and Jack have been dating for six months, and I'll bet they get married soon." Carol was Ila's oldest daughter, and this would be her third marriage.

"Well, I'll be," Mommy said incredulously.

Ouija had everyone's attention after that, and the questions came too fast for Ouija to answer. Mommy hushed everyone repeatedly, and she made a rule that each person got three questions. The questions were the usual, 'Who will I marry? Where will I live?' I didn't take a turn—I much preferred to watch everyone else's reaction to the predictions.

We talked to Ouija for the rest of the afternoon, barely stopping to get food and drinks. Finally, Ouija ended it by moving the indicator to GOOD BYE. It was over for the day.

Summer recreation lasted another week, and each day we'd bring home a different group of kids to talk to the Ouija board. Mommy had always made it clear to us that friends were not welcome at our house. Her reasons were many—kids were too noisy, or too messy, or whatever. We knew better than to bring people to our house. She didn't have to tell us.

Suddenly, we were normal kids who could have friends over. That is, as long as Daddy was asleep.

Chapter 3

Ouija

Mommy frowned as she looked up from the Brownie camera. "Patricia," she said, "quit hunching over. You look like Grandma Cain." Hearing this, Tricia instinctively pulled her shoulders back and smiled. She didn't want to look anything like our grandmother. Mommy despised Grandma Cain.

"For God's sake, how many times do I have to tell you not to smile? You look hideous with your front tooth showing," Mommy shook her head and turned her attention back to the Brownie.

"Who cares if she looks hideous?" I finally said. "Would you push the stupid button so we can go to Sunday school?" After school let out, Mommy had cut our hair short and permed it with tiny rods so that it frizzed uncontrollably.

I was mortified that I now looked just like my Mother and sister. We looked like there were brown poodles perched atop our heads. Adding insult to injury, Mommy now insisted that Tricia and I wear matching dresses so she could take a photo of her "twin girls."

After she released us from our pose, I looked my sister up and down. We didn't look anything alike. The similarity ended with the poodle cuts and the horn-rimmed glasses. She was five foot nine—almost four inches taller than me. She had Daddy's huge nose, and I had Mommy's. She had two bright red burns on her throat from when she was three and ran into Daddy's lit cigarette.

She had bowed legs, and I had knock knees. And then, of course, there were the teeth. One of her front teeth was actually in front of the other one—giving the illusion that she had but one tooth. Somehow, miraculously, I had perfectly straight teeth. Daddy blamed my siblings for their crooked teeth, insisting that if they had let him pull their loose teeth like I did, they would have straight teeth too.

Tricia noticed me staring at her and scowled. "What are *you* looking at?"

"Nothing," I said. How could *anyone* think we looked like twins?

Daddy dropped us off at the curb in front of the First Southern Baptist Church in Avondale and made a U-turn on Central Avenue. We sauntered into the church wing where Sunday school classes met. Mommy always expected us to go to Sunday school and the church service. That meant we'd be inside a stupid buildingg for four whole hours. Brother Valley's sermons were interminably long, and I didn't understand them. I waited anxiously for his last words each week, "Amen and God Bless," which meant I could go home.

As I sat in the back pew of the church with my siblings, my thoughts wandered back to the day five years ago when I was baptized. I could still feel the warmth of Pastor Valley's strong hand on the nape of my neck as he leaned my eight-year-old body backward in the water. Balancing me precariously on my heels, he closed his eyes and raised one hand to God and triumphantly shouted, "I baptize you in the name of the Father, the Son, and the Holy Ghost." He whispered to me to hold my nose, and then he dipped me into the chlorinated water of the baptismal. When he wrenched me from the water's grip, he told me I was born again and was safe from hell.

I knew Daddy wasn't safe. He was proud to be atheist. Daddy left religion behind at seventeen, when he joined the air corps to escape his

Mormon relatives in Colorado. Mommy hated the Mormons too, because they believed Daddy was still married to Clara, his first wife.

I guess Mormons don't believe in divorce, so Daddy was going to be with Clara in heaven—or, in his case, hell—for eternity no matter what Mommy did. Mommy forbade us from ever saying Clara's name.

Mommy didn't care whether Daddy was atheist or not. She said he was just anti-everything, and I had to agree with her. He really liked the word *antidisestablishmentarianism* and commanded that we spell it as fast, and as often, as possible.

Tricia always won the spelling contest for that word. She was always the best at everything, which irked me to no end. She went to the regional spelling bee in sixth grade and came close to winning the whole thing. When she was seven, she wrote a letter to the *Wallace & Ladmo* television show and all four of us ended up on the show. She even went to the Arizona State Fair at the Coliseum for her peanut butter cookies.

I'd had about enough of constantly being compared to Tricia by my family and all my teachers. So, last year Tricia wanted to enter a drawing contest that was advertised in a *Betty & Veronica* comic book. Art was my thing and I was determined she wasn't going to be a better artist than me, so I scratched a big "X" through her drawing. She went crying to Mommy that I had ruined her drawing, and I got a whipping. I didn't mind because Tricia didn't enter the contest, which was all I really cared about.

Suddenly, I was brought back to the present by the words "Ouija board." I turned to see my sister whispering to Aunt Edith in the pew in front of us. I was glad Tricia told Aunt Edith about the Ouija board, but I didn't think Mommy would be happy.

Mommy hated hypocrites, and she considered her sister to be a big fat one. "You wouldn't believe some of the things she's done," Mother would say. "And she has the nerve to show her face in that church."

Aunt Edith was on her third marriage. She had three girls from the first marriage whom I barely knew. Betty was the youngest. She was married to a preacher named Glen, and they lived just outside Avondale near the White Tank Mountains. One of their daughters drowned in the canal a couple years earlier. She was my age.

Barbara and Jimmy were her next set of kids and they're in their 20s now. They're the ones who went to a Memphis orphanage when Aunt Edith moved to Arizona. I think Aunt Edith must have sent for them after she married Uncle Mac.

Her last set of kids were with her in church today—Aubrey and Tommy—and they were teenagers, like us.

After church, Aunt Edith told us to get in her car because she was taking us home. As we pulled up in front of our house on Holly Lane, she slipped out of the front seat and slammed the door. "Mac, go on home," she said leaning on the window ledge. "I want to talk to Mary for a minute."

This was an interesting turn of events. Aunt Edith never came to our house—her and Mommy talked on the phone every day, but our families didn't socialize, *at all.*

I followed Aunt Edith into the house and sat down at the kitchen table so I could hear what they were talking about. Mommy had two huge oven mitts on and had just pulled a juicy ham out of the oven that made my mouth water. She slid the pan onto the stovetop and asked her sister, "What are you doing here, Edith?"

"That ham smells mighty good, Mary," Edith stalled.

Mommy ignored the comment. "I don't know why you're here, but I got some sweet iced tea, if you want."

"No, thanks," Edith stalled again and then blurted out, "Patricia told me about the Ouija board."

"Is that right?" Mommy said. I could tell Tricia was going to get it later.

"Do you have a Ouija board in your house?" Aunt Edith finally asked.

"What business is it of yours?"

"Mary, you remember those folks in Corinth who messed around with that Ouija board when we was kids?" She asked. "They were killed in a train wreck after they got rid of the thing."

"Lord have mercy, Edith," Mommy laughed, kind of scarily. "I can't believe you're so superstitious about a board game."

"Mary, board games don't talk to you," Edith said sharply. "You *know* that Ouija boards are a medium for evil spirits to come back into our world."

Mommy was unusually nice. "I'll tell you what," she said, sneaking a glance through the patio door to where Daddy was puffing away. "Why don't you come back tomorrow when Levoy's asleep and talk to it for yourself?"

Aunt Edith's eyes turned to slits, and she glanced at Daddy. "Does he know about this, Mary?"

"No," Mommy warned. "And you'd better not tell him."

"I'll come back tomorrow and talk to the thing," she agreed. "If I get an inkling that it's an evil spirit, I won't have nothin' more to do with it." She started to walk away and then turned back to Mommy, "And I'd recommend that you don't neither."

After Aunt Edith left, Mommy found Tricia in our bedroom. "Don't you ever go telling my sister what's going on in *my* house," she slapped Tricia hard on her face. "You got that? It ain't none of her business."

Tricia set her jaw tight and stared at Mommy through squinty teary eyes. "Yeah, I got it," she said.

They didn't talk to each other throughout lunch, which made Daddy curious. "What's gotten into you, sister," he said to Tricia. "Why the glum face?"

Mommy intercepted the question, "She didn't get to do something she wanted, and now she's in a mood," Mommy dumped a big pile of mashed potatoes on Tricia's plate and whispered, "I've got news for you, young lady, I'm the Mother in this house, and as long I draw breath, you're not going to run it."

As Timmy reached for the plate of ham, his elbow knocked Daddy's glass of iced tea over, spilling its contents onto Daddy's lap. Daddy jumped up and screamed at Timmy, "You damn moron. What is wrong with you?"

Timmy recoiled, thinking Daddy was going to hit him, "I didn't mean to do it. I'm sorry, Daddy."

Daddy looked at Timmy for a second and then left the table, shaking his head.

"You're such an ignoramus," Mike said angrily.

Timmy dropped his hands onto his lap and lowered his head. He stiffened his back as he steeled himself against his own self-loathing. He was really smart at schoolwork, but he always seemed to do stupid things when Daddy was around, so Daddy reserved 'moron' only for Timmy. No matter what stupid thing the rest of us did, Daddy never called us morons.

"He's not a moron," I said to Mike. "You are."

It was a relief to go to my bedroom that night after dinner. I closed the door so I would have some privacy. Tricia was reading a book in the family room and wouldn't bother me for awhile. I lay on the sofa bed, eyes fixed on the ceiling. I would be an eighth grader next year—and then high school—and then? I didn't care what happened to me after high school as long as I wasn't anywhere near my family.

The next morning I awoke in the bed by myself. Tricia was up and showered. It was nine o'clock already. I was late for summer recreation—they must have left without me. Then I remembered that summer recreation had ended last week. What would I do for the next eight weeks?

My answer was on the kitchen table. There sat the Ouija board with Tricia and Mommy engaged in a conversation with it. Timmy and Mike were on their way to the table with their bowls of cereal. I was the last one up.

"G-O-O-D M-O-R-N-I-N-G D-I-A-N-A"

I waited for Mommy to finish calling out the letters before I answered, "Good morning, Ouija."

"W-H-A-T D-O Y-O-U W-A-N-T T-O A-S-K"

"I want to know why the people in my family can't be nice to each other." I cried. I stared at the indicator—avoiding my family's eyes.

"T-H-E-Y C-A-N"

"Then why aren't they?" I demanded.

"What's the matter with you?" Mike yawned. "Did you wake up on the wrong side of the bed or something?"

"I just want a normal family."

"W-H-A-T I-S N-O-R-M-A-L"

"There are families that are nice to each other," I said. "They *show* that they love each other. They do things together—like swimming, or something. I want one of those families."

"Actions speak louder than words," Mommy chimed in. "It would be nice if my kids showed me a little appreciation and love—"

Ouija interrupted. "L-O-V-E S-T-A-R-T-S W-I-T-H Y-O-U M-A-R-Y"

Mommy obviously wasn't expecting that, and she removed her fingers from the indicator. "Well, I guess I've been told," she said. She sat for a minute and thought. Then she put her fingers back on the indicator and spoke to Ouija, "Levoy is the most difficult man I've ever met. If I say black, he says white. It doesn't matter what I say, he says the opposite. It's not possible to have a 'normal' family life with him."

The indicator slid to YES. "I-T S-T-A-R-T-S W-I-T-H Y-O-U"

"I could try to be nicer, I guess," Mommy conceded.

I was stunned. Was this *my* Mother? I rubbed my eyes to make sure someone hadn't switched in a substitute mom.

Just then, there was a knock, knock, knock on the front door.

I opened the door, and there stood Aunt Edith. The second time in two days. Amazing.

From the kitchen, I heard Mother's voice calling out the letters.

"H-E-L-L-O E-D-I-T-H" Ouija spelled.

Aunt Edith didn't waste any time after she was settled at the kitchen table. "Are you the devil?" she demanded.

The indicator slid to NO.

"I already asked that question," Mommy said. "Do you think I'm an idiot? It's not the devil or an evil spirit."

"Who are you?" Edith asked.

"O-U-I-J-A"

"But what kind of spirit are you?" she asked.

"O-N-E T-H-A-T H-E-L-P-S T-H-E L-I-V-I-N-G"

"Were you every alive?" Mike rushed to the next question, "Were you a man?"

The indicator moved slowly to YES. Then it didn't move for a minute.

Mike persisted, "When did you die?"

"1-9-2-2"

"Where were you from?" Aunt Edith asked.

"S-O-U-T-H   C-A-R-O-L-I-N-A"

"Did you fight in the Civil War?" Timmy said abruptly.

The indicator moved to YES.

"Were you a soldier for the north or south?" he continued.

"S-O-U-T-H"

"What was your name?" Tricia asked.

"L-A-W-R-E-N-C-E   D-A-V-I-D   F-U-R-T-I-C-K"

"Oh, my god!" Mother and Aunt Edith squealed in unison. "It's granddaddy."

Ouija answered YES.

I had goosebumps.

"Diana, I can't keep track of what he's saying," Mother signaled for me to retrieve a piece of paper and a pencil from Daddy's desk. "You write down the letters and tell us what it spells, ok?"

I felt so important.

Aunt Edith recalled for us that their Grandpa Furtick had died when she was seven. She remembered him only vaguely.

"Should we call you granddaddy?" Mommy asked a little reverantly.

"C-A-L-L   M-E   O-U-I-J-A"

"But why?"

"L-A-W-R-E-N-C-E   F-U-R-T-I-C-K   I-S   N-O   M-O-R-E"

"Are you the only spirit we can talk to through the board?" Aunt Edith asked, very interested at this point.

"T-H-E-R-E   A-R-E   O-T-H-E-R-S"

"Will they talk to us?" Mommy asked.

"I   W-I-L-L   L-E-T   S-O-M-E   S-P-E-A-K"

"Are you in charge of the communications through this board?" Mommy asked.

"F-O-R N-O-W"

"When will someone else be in charge?"

"W-I-L-L T-E-L-L Y-O-U"

"Where are you now?" Mike asked.

"H-E-R-E"

"But we can't see you," Mike said, looking around the room.

"Y-O-U C-A-N S-E-E M-E S-P-E-A-K"

"But, do you have a body?"

The indicator moved swiftly to NO. "I A-M A S-P-I-R-I-T"

"How do you know the future?" Mommy asked.

Aunt Edith snapped her head around at that. "What do you mean, how does it know the future?" she asked.

"It predicted that Bobbie Kennedy was going to die," I said reverently.

"Oh, my God," both hands went to her chest.

Mommy repeated, "How do you know the future?"

"N-O-T F-U-T-U-R-E F-O-R M-E"

"It's the future for us?" Timmy asked.

"T-H-E-R-E I-S N-O F-U-T-U-R-E O-R P-A-S-T I-N M-Y W-O-R-L-D"

"Are you in heaven?" I asked.

"N-O-T I-N H-E-A-V-E-N"

"Will you be in heaven someday? I asked.

"H-O-P-E S-O"

"Yeah, so do I," Mike laughed.

"Can I ask some questions about my future?" Aunt Edith asked timidly.

Ouija said YES.

"Will I live a long life?" she asked, wincing and crossing her fingers in the air.

The indicator spelled "8-3"

"That's a long life," Aunt Edith laughed. "And will my children outlive me?"

Ouija didn't move.

"Should I repeat the question?" she asked Mommy.

"S-O-M-E W-I-L-L O-U-T-L-I-V-E"

A look of horror came over her face. "Who will die?"

Mommy interrupted her, "It won't answer that question."

"C-A-N-N-O-T I-N-T-E-R-F-E-R-E"

"Is that a rule or something?" Mike asked.

The indicator moved to YES.

"Why did you choose to talk to us?" Mommy asked.

"Y-O-U W-E-R-E L-I-S-T-E-N-I-N-G"

"Listening? Don't other people listen, too?" she asked.

"L-I-V-I-N-G D-O-N-T W-A-N-T S-P-I-R-I-T-S A-R-O-U-N-D"

"Why?" she asked.

"F-E-A-R"

"Should we be afraid?" she asked.

The indicator moved to NO. "W-A-N-T T-O H-E-L-P Y-O-U"

"So, are we the only people that you are talking to?" Mike asked.

Ouija said YES.

I couldn't believe my ears. In all of the world in 1968, we were the only people listening for spirits?

"Can you help us get rich?" Mike asked.

"R-I-C-H I-N M-O-N-E-Y"

Mike nodded emphatically.

"M-O-N-E-Y D-O-E-S N-O-T M-A-K-E Y-O-U R-I-C-H"

"It could sure help."

"M-O-N-E-Y K-E-E-P-S Y-O-U F-R-O-M B-E-I-N-G R-I-C-H"

"You're talking about spiritual riches." Aunt Edith answered smugly. Mommy turned her head to me and rolled her eyes meaningfully. "That's in Matthew 19, verse 21, and then she quoted from memory, "If thou wilt be perfect, go and sell that thou hast, and give to the poor, and thou shalt have treasures in heaven; and come and follow me." She smiled and continued, "It goes on to say that 'it is easier for a camel to go through the eye of a needle, than for a rich man to enter into the kingdom of God."

The indicator moved to YES.

"Do you miss having a mortal body?" Tricia asked.

"A-L-W-A-Y-S"

"The Bible says you'll get your body back," Aunt Edith said.

"H-O-P-E S-O"

"What do you miss the most?" I asked.

"G-R-A-S-S U-N-D-E-R F-E-E-T"

"What's best about being in your world?" Mike asked.

"N-E-V-E-R H-U-N-G-R-Y"

"And no pain, right?" Timmy asked.

"N-O P-H-Y-S-I-C-A-L P-A-I-N"

"Do you still have other pain?" he asked, concerned.

"P-A-I-N O-F W-H-A-T I D-I-D T-O O-T-H-E-R-S"

"What did you do?" I asked.

"K-I-L-L-E-D S-O-M-E"

"In the war, right," I realized. "Do you remember everything from your life?"

"M-O-S-T T-H-I-N-G-S"

"Do you remember us?" Aunt Edith asked, hopefully.

"O-H Y-E-S"

"What do you think of the world now?" Mommy asked.

"S-O-M-E T-H-I-N-G-S D-O-N-T C-H-A-N-G-E"

"Like what?" Mike asked.

"P-E-O-P-L-E" Ouija stopped. "W-A-R"

"Yeah, except now we have atomic weapons," Mike said sarcastically. "We can wipe out the Soviet Union."

Ouija moved sadly to YES.

"Will there be a nuclear war?" Mike was excited at the thought.

"C-A-N-T S-A-Y"

I was disgusted by his excitement. Why do boys want wars? Because they're stupid, I decided. Even Daddy had tried to convince Mommy to go to Las Vegas for a nuclear test at the Nevada Test Site back in '62. She refused to drive through the desert for seven hours just to see a mushroom cloud that you could see on television any day of the week.

Mike interrupted my thoughts. "Will Armageddon be a nuclear war?"

"C-A-N-T S-A-Y"

"What's Armageddon?" Timmy asked before I could.

"Read the Book of Revelations, you moron," Mike ranted. "Armageddon is supposed to be the final war."

Suddenly, with no warning, the indicator moved to GOOD BYE.

"Oh well, it's time to make lunch anyway," Mommy said, looking at her watch. "Where did the time go? Levoy's going to be up soon."

"It's like we enter the Twilight Zone when we talk to Ouija," Mike echoed.

"I better get going," Aunt Edith said. "I can't come back until Wednesday, Mary. But, I will be back." She hugged Mommy tightly and then left.

We were up by eight o'clock the next morning. With cereal bowls in hand, we sat down at the kitchen table with Ouija.

"G-O-O-D   M-O-R-N-I-N-G"

"Good morning, Ouija." we responded in unison.

"Are we going to talk to someone else today?" Tricia asked.

"M-E"

"Have you always watched over our family?" Mommy asked.

"S-O-M-E-T-I-M-E-S"

"Do you watch over my Daddy?" Mommy continued.

"V-I-S-I-T   H-I-M   T-O-O"

We talked to Ouija for the next three hours. Mommy asked about family she hadn't seen since she moved to Arizona. Ouija answered all of our questions.

"What are you trying to help us do?" Mike asked.

"R-E-A-L-I-Z-E   Y-O-U-R   P-U-R-P-O-S-E"

"Our purpose?"

"W-H-Y   Y-O-U   E-X-I-S-T"

"Why do we exist?" Tricia asked.

"A-L-L   I-N   G-O-O-D   T-I-M-E"

"Do you know what our purpose is?" I asked.

The indicator slid to NO.

"Who does?"

"I   C-A-M-E   T-O   M-A-K-E   Y-O-U   C-O-M-F-O-R-T-A-B-L-E   W-I-T-H   T-H-I-S   M-E-D-I-U-M   F-O-R   C-O-M-M-U-N-I-C-A-T-I-N-G"

"But who does know our purpose?" I persisted.

"A-N-O-T-H-E-R   S-P-I-R-I-T"

"Who?"

The indicator froze.

"Ouija?" Mommy whispered.

Still no movement.

"Ouija? Ouija?" Mommy cried. "Don't leave."

Nothing. Was the spirit of our grandfather gone as fast as it had come?

Mommy kept repeating, "Ouija?"

Then, suddenly, the indicator moved forcefully.

"I A-M N-O-T O-U-I-J-A"

"Then who are you?" Mommy asked.

"E-L-I-J-A-H"

Mommy and Tricia removed their hands from the indicator simultaneously.

Just then, Daddy emerged from the bedroom whistling. Mommy threw the board on top of the kitchen cabinets just as he rounded the corner into the kitchen.

Chapter 4

Elijah

"Wake up, Patricia," Mommy said shaking Tricia's shoulder. "We have to talk to Ouija first thing this morning."

"What?" Tricia drawled.

I rolled over to see what time it was—seven o'clock? This was getting ridiculous. It's summer. Aren't kids supposed to sleep until noon or something?

I hated sharing a room with Tricia at that moment, but I hated the sofa bed I shared with her even more. Mommy thought a sofa bed would give us more space to play with our dolls. She said that closing it up every morning would be no worse than making a bed. She was wrong.

She bought the stupid thing at Gil's Used Furniture on Western Avenue. Mommy was at Gil's at least once a week—whether we needed furniture or not.

She dragged me to the store with her every once in awhile. It was really embarrassing the way she flirted with him, so I'd tell her I was bored and walk home by myself. She'd stay and talk to Gil for hours. He was tall, like Daddy, but not as skinny. With Gil, it was "goddamn this" and "goddamn that." I tried not to get too close to Gil for fear of getting sprayed with nasty yellow tobacco spit.

Since Tricia was pulling the covers off me as she slid out of bed, I decided to get up too. Mommy didn't wake the boys, so it was just the three of us at the kitchen table. As I retrieved a bowl and the box of Corn

Flakes from the cabinet, Mommy and Tricia took their positions at the Ouija board.

Mommy started cautiously, "Are you Elijah?"

The indicator moved deliberately to YES. I shuddered. I couldn't take my eyes off the board after that.

"Why are you here?" she continued.

"W-O-R-L-D N-E-E-D-S M-E" was the reply.

"Are you here to help the world or to help me?" Mommy asked.

"B-O-T-H"

"How are you going to help us?"

"G-U-I-D-E Y-O-U"

"Guide us to what?"

"T-R-U-T-H"

"What do we have to do?" Tricia asked.

"R-E-C-O-R-D A-L-L"

"Record all for what?" Mommy asked. I could tell she was getting frustrated with Elijah. I didn't think she really knew who he was—other than a character from the Bible. As I was about to warn her, the indicator started moving quickly.

"D-I-A-N-A M-U-S-T R-E-C-O-R-D A-L-L"

"Did you get that?" Mommy asked.

"Yes, I have to get a notebook and record everything," I repeated urgently.

"Go," mom said as she scooted me from the kitchen.

I ran down the hall, slipping on the rug and crashing my body against the boys' bedroom door. I pounded on the door with my knuckles and whispered urgently, "Get up, it's Elijah."

My school notebook had some lined paper in it, and I thought it would be perfect for writing a record of what Elijah said. By the time I got back to the kitchen, both Mike and Timmy were standing by the table, rubbing their eyes.

"B-R-I-N-G B-I-B-L-E M-I-K-E"

"Wha—," he started.

Ouija didn't wait for him to finish his protest. "G-O N-O-W"

"Hurry up, Mike," Mommy echoed.

Mike returned with his tattered King James Bible, and he laid it on the table in front of him. I'd never seen my brother move that fast.

"C-A-L-L E-D-I-T-H"

"What?" Mommy asked, petulantly.

"S-H-E N-E-E-D-S T-O B-E H-E-R-E"

The indicator was moving so fast that none of us could keep track of the words in our heads anymore. The indicator stopped ever so briefly after it spelled each word, so I could tell where words ended. As soon as the indicator stopped moving completely, everyone looked to me to read back what was said.

"Write neatly, Diana," Mommy said after she saw my sloppy handwriting. "Use block letters."

"Ok," I answered eagerly.

As soon as we had complied with Ouija's commands, Mommy called Aunt Edith and told her that Ouija wanted her there immediately. Within five minutes, she was sitting at our kitchen table too, and she had Aubrey and Tommy with her.

"Mary, what in God's heaven is so urgent that I had to get here this early?" Edith asked.

"Another spirit is speaking to us from the board. It's Elijah," Mommy said excitedly as she placed her fingers on the indicator. "He told us that you need to be here."

"Have you lost your senses?" Aunt Edith said slowly. "It's one thing for it to be the spirit of our dead grandfather. But, for it to say it's a prophet from the Bible—that's crazy, Mary."

"E-D-I-T-H B-E-W-A-R-E"

"This is heresy," Edith whispered to herself.

"I A-M E-L-I-J-A-H"

"Mary—do you know who Elijah *was*?" Aunt Edith looked from the board to Mommy.

"I K-I-N-G-S 1-7"

Before any of us could speak, Aubrey reached for the Bible in front of Mike and turned the pages to the chapter and verse. He read aloud, "And Elijah the Tishbite, who was of the inhabitants of Gilead, said unto Ahab, As the Lord God of Israel liveth, before whom I stand, there shall not be dew nor rain these years, but according to my word."

"So, what does that mean?" Timmy asked.

"Elijah said there'd be a drought and there was—for three years." Aubrey said not looking up from the pages. He read the rest of the chapter to us, and we listened intently as he recounted Elijah's miracles for the widow and her son. Ouija was silent as Aubrey continued reading Chapter 18 about Elijah's test of sacrifice on Mount Carmel.

Aubrey's voice became Elijah's voice, and he couldn't stop reading, and we couldn't stop listening. I read these passages before, but they were meaningless before this day. Now, Elijah was in the room with us, and we were hearing *his* story for what seemed like the first time.

Aubrey continued reading II Kings, until he got to chapter 2, verse 11, and then he read very slowly: "And it came to pass, as they still went on, and talked, that, behold, there appeared a chariot of fire, and horses of fire, and parted them both asunder; and Elijah went up by a whirlwind into heaven."

"You never died," Aubrey said, sitting back in his chair.

The indicator moved slowly to NO.

According to the Bible, only one other person had not died. My mind whirled—I couldn't think straight.

"M-A-L-A-C-H-I 4 5 A-N-D 6"

As soon as I read back the scripture citation, Aubrey turned to page 954 in the Old Testament and read the last two verses.

"Behold, I will send you Elijah the prophet before the coming of the great and dreadful day of the Lord; and he shall turn the heart of the Fathers to the children, and the heart of the children to their Fathers, lest I come and smite the earth with a curse."

"I A-M E-L-I-J-A-H"

The indicator moved powerfully to GOODBYE.

"What's he talking about?" Aubrey asked.

"That passage is talking about the Day of Judgment—after Armageddon, it's believed," Aunt Edith said smugly. I could tell she liked being the only person who knew the Bible. Then, she laughed nervously, "You can't seriously believe this."

"I don't know what to believe," Mommy answered honestly. "I'm gonna have to hear more."

"Don't you think it's highly unlikely that Elijah came to Avondale, Arizona, to talk to *you* through this Ouija board?" Aunt Edith slammed her fist hard on the table for emphasis.

"Ouija said we were the only people listening." I countered.

"But, why would he come to *you*?" she insisted.

"Why wouldn't he?" Mommy was getting defensive.

"Mary, you and Levoy are not Christians and you don't even pretend to be religious," Aunt Edith said. "Besides, you're no angel, if you recall."

"Neither are you." Mommy accused. "Do you think he should have come to you?"

"At least I go to church, Mary."

"So, you think only people who go to church should be able to talk to spirits?"

Aunt Edith's voice was getting louder, "Well, it would make a whole lot more sense than Elijah talking to you through a Ouija board. A *Ouija board*, of all things."

"Please keep your voice down." Mommy warned, equally loud.

"What? Do you think *the board* can hear me?" Edith laughed.

"It probably can, but I was more worried about Levoy," Mommy said nodding her head towards the hallway. "Anyway, a spirit can still be here even if we're not talking to the Ouija board."

"God's still here even when you're not in church," Aubrey chastised his mom. "Right?"

"How do you explain that it knows the scriptures, Aunt Edith?" Tricia asked.

"Scriptures can be memorized, Tricia," Aunt Edith responded sarcastically. "Even the devil can quote scriptures." She looked at her watch and hurried towards the door. "I have to go to work. I'll talk to you about this later, Mary." As she shut the door, she yelled back, "Go home, boys."

Aubrey and Tommy ignored their Mother's last words and stayed the rest of the afternoon. We read passages in the Old Testament until about an hour before Daddy awoke. Aubrey read so beautifully that we designated him the official reader. Besides, Mike wasn't very good at it.

"Can I try the Ouija board now?" Aubrey asked sheepishly. "You know, to see if it works for me."

"Take my place," Mommy said as she got up from the table to start dinner. "Who knows if it's ready to talk."

Aubrey sat down and placed his heavy fingers on the indicator. It didn't move.

"You have to be light-fingered," Tricia reached over and lifted his fingers slightly. "Like this."

"So, I just ask a question, and it answers?" he muttered to himself. "Elijah, why did you come back to earth now?"

"T-O P-R-E-P-A-R-E T-H-E W-A-Y"

"Prepare way for what?" Tommy asked.

"Y-O-U W-I-L-L K-N-O-W S-O-O-N"

"We'll know what soon?"

"I-N G-O-O-D T-I-M-E"

"Have you been in heaven all these thousands of years?" Aubrey continued, changing the subject.

The indicator moved swiftly to YES.

"Can you tell us what it's like?" Tricia asked.

"W-H-A-T Y-O-U W-A-N-T I-T T-O B-E"

"What did *you* want it to be?" Aubrey asked.

"T-O S-I-T A-T T-H-E F-E-E-T O-F G-O-D"

I said those words with emphasis. They were so powerful for me and everyone in the room that we couldn't speak. Only Mike had the courage to ask the next question.

"And do you?" he asked politely.

The indicator moved to YES.

As Aubrey read the YES, mom slowly turned from the sink filled with black-eyed Suzies and looked at all of us full on.

"I've got chill bumps," she said, rubbing her forearms. She glanced at the clock on the wall and said, "It's four o'clock—time for Levoy to wake up. Put the board away. You boys go home now."

"Goodbye Elijah." we all said.

GOODBYE.

Tricia gingerly folded the board and placed it under the coffee table in the family room.

"Can't we keep talking?" I asked. It seemed rude somehow just to put the board away when *we* were finished talking. I mean, it was Elijah after all. Eating dinner was such a mundane thing to do in the presence of a couple thousand year-old prophet who had something really important to say to us.

"No, we've been talking to it for eight hours," Mommy said. "Tomorrow's soon enough, Diana."

Aubrey and Tommy left reluctantly and promised that they would be back the next morning—bright and early—to talk to Elijah.

Chapter 5

God and Angels

Only Aubrey was true to his word. He returned the next morning and every morning after that for two weeks. Like us, he couldn't get enough of the Ouija board.

We talked to Elijah all day long, sometimes stopping for meals, but most of the time we talked straight through mealtime. We kept the board hidden from Daddy. He didn't care about religion, and we knew he wouldn't be impressed just because Elijah was talking to us.

We agreed that no one else could talk to Elijah—he was ours. It just wouldn't be right for kids to be asking dumb questions of a prophet who sat at the feet of God.

When we weren't talking to Elijah, we were reading the Bible. We'd flip it open and just start reading—until we had read an entire book. When none of us understood what we had read, Elijah would interpret.

We finished reading in Matthew about the chief priests and elders who delivered Jesus to Pontius Pilate because he claimed he was the Son of God, which was blasphemy.

Mike pronounced smugly, "The Jews killed Jesus."

"I W-A-S O-F J-E-W-I-S-H D-E-S-C-E-N-T"

Mike froze—realizing what he had said.

"I didn't mean you killed him," he apologized awkwardly. "I meant the Jews who came after you."

"T-H-E   H-I-G-H   P-R-I-E-S-T-S   C-O-N-V-I-N-C-E-D T-H-E-I-R   P-E-O-P-L-E   J-E-S-U-S   W-A-S B-L-A-S-P-H-E-M-I-N-G"

"So, it was really the Romans who killed him?" Timmy asked.

The indicator moved deliberately to NO.

"N-O-T   J-E-W-S" Elijah stopped briefly and continued, "N-O-T R-O-M-A-N-S"

"Then who did it?" we asked together.

"E-V-I-L   P-E-O-P-L-E"

"It doesn't matter why you kill." Mike whispered. "Killing makes you evil?"

"E-X-A-C-T-L-Y"

"What about in war?" Timmy asked.

"K-I-L-L-I-N-G   I-S   E-V-I-L"

"What if you're fighting evil armies?" Mike reasoned. "Like Hitler?"

"K-I-L-L-I-N-G   I-S   E-V-I-L"

"So the reason doesn't matter?" Tricia asked.

"C-O-R-R-E-C-T"

"And that was Jesus' message?" I asked. "Turn the other cheek?"

The indicator moved swiftly to YES. "M-A-T-T-H-E-W   5   3-8"

Mommy hadn't said a word during this exchange. She had been focused on keeping her fingers on the indicator as it swooshed around the board.

"But it doesn't seem right to let someone kill you," she said. "We should defend ourselves from people who want to kill us."

"Y-O-U   M-A-K-E   T-H-E   C-H-O-I-C-E"

Mommy thought for a second. "That's why I sent my kids to church—I didn't send my first set of boys, and I think it was a mistake. I wanted these kids to learn about what Jesus taught."

"Y-O-U D-O N-O-T G-O"

Mommy was taken aback. "Uh—no. My Daddy was a preacher, and I figure I heard enough from him."

"T-H-E-R-E I-S N-O-T-H-I-N-G E-L-S-E F-O-R Y-O-U T-O L-E-A-R-N"

"Well, sure, there's always more to learn," she said tentatively. She squirmed a little in her chair. "I just don't think I should go."

"A-F-R-A-I-D"

"The whole town knows what I done in the past," she whispered. "They'd call me a hypocrite if I went to church now."

"L-I-K-E Y-O-U C-A-L-L Y-O-U-R S-I-S-T-E-R"

Mommy didn't respond.

"B-E-T-T-E-R T-O L-O-O-K L-I-K-E H-Y-P-O-C-R-I-T-E T-H-A-N T-O B-E I-G-N-O-R-A-N-T"

Mommy smiled, despite herself. "You got me there," she finally surrendered. "I'll tell you what. I'll think about it."

"T-H-E-Y W-I-L-L W-E-L-C-O-M-E Y-O-U"

"That remains to be seen."

I couldn't believe my ears. We had begged and begged for Mommy to go to church with us, and she had steadfastly refused. Now, Elijah had convinced her—with very little effort.

Aunt Edith stopped by shortly after that to retrieve Aubrey. She was ecstatic that Mommy was thinking about going to church.

"I guess I'll take back what I said about that board," she admitted. "If it can get you to go to Church, it must have good intentions."

* * *

We were in good spirits when Aubrey arrived on our doorstep at eight o'clock the next morning.

"W-A-K-E L-E-V-O-Y"

My eyes grew wide at that. Tricia and Aubrey removed their hands from the indicator and turned to Mommy. Why would the Ouija board want us to disturb the rhythm and peace we were enjoying by getting Daddy involved in this? Why?

"He ain't gonna talk to you," Mommy countered. She motioned Tricia and Aubrey to put their hands back in place.

"H-E W-I-L-L"

"I'd rather not wake him," Mommy answered stiffly.

"I H-A-V-E A M-E-S-S-A-G-E F-O-R H-I-M"

"Who from?"

"G-O-D"

I shuddered. "*The* God?" I heard myself saying.

"Y-E-S D-I-A-N-A"

"But why would God want to talk to *him*?" Mommy asked belligerently. "Give me the message. I'll tell him."

"M-E-S-S-A-G-E I-S N-O-T F-O-R Y-O-U"

"Go ahead, Diana," Mommy finally motioned for me to wake him.

The notebook slid off my lap as I jumped up and ran down the hall. Daddy had just gone to sleep. He was not going to be happy if I woke him, but I really had no choice. If Elijah wanted to talk to him, then so be it.

"Daddy, get up." I slammed my fist against the door. I yelled again, "Get up, Daddy."

From inside, I heard mumbling and the bed squeaking as he rolled out. A second later, the door opened just wide enough for his nose to protrude. "What's the matter, punkin'?" he slurred.

"We need to talk to you right away," I said urgently. Then I ran.

"Ok," I said as I plunked down on the couch. "He's up."

And then we all just sat there. Nobody talked and nobody moved—not even Ouija. Daddy emerged a few minutes later. We cringed collectively as he caught sight of the Ouija board. Mommy had replaced Aubrey at the board and was waiting for Ouija to say something.

"What's going on?" Daddy demanded.

Ouija didn't move.

"It's a Ouija board—a medium for talking to spirits." Mommy answered breathlessly, trying to fit the words in before she drew her last breath, I was sure.

"I *know* what a Ouija board is," Daddy replied sarcastically.

"Levoy, over the past month, this board has predicted things that none of us could have known. It was the spirit of my granddaddy at first, but now it's Elijah. You know, from the Bible, and it's been talking to us ever since. It told us to wake you up because it wants to give you a message from God." She stopped abruptly and looked away, her hands still resting on the indicator.

"I can't believe you've stooped this low, you b—," Daddy shouted.

"H-E-L-L-O L-E-V-O-Y"

"You have lost your mind." he said, ignoring me reading the words back to him. Just then, he noticed that there were five of us sitting around the table with Mommy. "You got your own kids involved with this thing?"

"It's not me, Levoy," Mommy cried.

We all chimed in, "It's not Mommy—it's a spirit."

"Q-U-I-E-T" Ouija shouted. "I   H-A-V-E   A   M-E-S-S-A-G-E F-O-R L-E-V-O-Y"

Mommy shouted out the letters over Daddy's protests. When she was finished, I read the words back urgently.

"This is crazy," he replied.

"G-O-D W-A-N-T-S Y-O-U T-O A-C-C-E-P-T C-H-R-I-S-T"

As soon as Ouija stopped, I blurted out the message.

"You're out of your goddamned mind, Mary." He stood over Mommy, finger thrust within inches of her glasses. She didn't flinch.

"D-O-N-T B-E A-F-R-A-I-D L-E-V-O-Y"

"I'm not afraid." he yelled back.

"Daddy, this is a special Ouija board. Please listen." I screamed, tears streaming down my face and falling from my chin onto my shirt.

Daddy looked at me with concern and replied, "The only way I'd become a Christian is if God himself asks me—to my face."

He charged from the room and slammed the front door behind him.

"O-K"

Mommy seemed angry with Elijah. "Why does *he* have to be a Christian?" she asked.

"A-C-T-S 1-6 3-1"

Aubrey read, "And they said, believe on the Lord Jesus Christ, and thou shalt be saved, and thy house."

The indicator slid to GOODBYE.

Daddy came home the next morning and went straight to bed without speaking to any of us. Dinner was uncomfortably quiet that night.

After dinner, the neighborhood kids gathered under the streetlight on our corner for a game of Red Rover, Red Rover. As I walked through the living room towards the front door, I couldn't help glancing at the Ouija board sitting on the coffee table. Its voice beckoned to me to stop and guilt nuzzled me when I didn't. I hesitated only briefly and then willed my body out into the warm summer evening.

The Red Rover game had already started as I emerged from the house. Mommy was close behind me and yelled, "Diana, you want to earn some extra money?" I watched as she gathered her housedress about her and lowered her great girth onto the grass in the front yard.

"Sure," I answered. Mommy paid ten cents to any of us who helped with the endless task of weed pulling. I needed the money, desperately, for a Monkees album that had just been released.

I much preferred pulling weeds to picking Mommy's corns for five cents. It seemed like Mommy had more corns than a corn field. Where they all came from I didn't know—the woman never wore closed shoes.

She patted the ground next to her. "Sit here."

We sat together on the grass and lazily discussed our yard invaders. The new crop of dandelions, tumbleweeds, and milkweeds defiantly peeked through the blades of Bermuda grass despite our relentless campaign to remove them. Instinctively, my thumb and forefinger knew exactly where to pinch the stems, ensuring an intact removal from the earth. Mommy said I was a good weed puller.

Near dusk, Mommy looked up from her work and shielded her eyes from the sun with her hand. "We're done now," she said and pointed over my shoulder. "Storm's a'comin."

I turned to see the storm growing in the southern sky. The kids had scattered back to their collective homes, but I stood defiantly in the yard and waited for its approach. I kept my eyes on it, watching as it pulled the topaz sky into its bowels.

As the sky reddened around me, I closed my eyes and mouth and let the hurtling sand scrape against my skin and ravage my body. It caked me and filled my nostrils. As the dust fog thinned, I stretched out my arms and threw up my face to the sky, daring the lightning bolts to strike me. They declined.

As the storm ebbed, I begged for every drop of rain it could spare, but there was not enough to quench my skin's thirst. No matter. I claimed victory over the desert in its war against me—at least on this day, anyway.

"Diana, get in this house before lightning strikes you," Mommy screamed.

* * *

Mommy was nowhere to be found the next morning and Ouija was missing. Tricia and I searched high and low for the board, without success. Could Mommy have taken it to a friend's house to talk to them? Wouldn't she need Tricia to do that? Did she throw it away? No, it wasn't in the garbage can.

The doorbell interrupted our search and rescue mission. Ila Dee stood on the other side of the screen door with another Ouija board box clutched tight to her bosom. We stared at her.

"Hey," she said nonchalantly. "I bought this here Ouija board last week, but it don't work." She shoved the box into Tricia's arms and without saying another word, turned to walk back down the street to her house. We watched her and then turned to each other. "That was strange," Tricia said shrugging her shoulders.

Four hours later, Mommy came home with two paper bags filled with groceries. She kicked the door closed behind her and dropped the bags loudly onto the kitchen counter. She popped her head around the family room door, where we were hovered around the Ouija board.

"I need help with the gro—" her jaw dropped as she looked first at the board, then at Tricia and Aubrey, whose hands were on the indicator.

"Hi, Mommy," Timmy said, beaming.

"Go home, Aubrey." Mommy yelled. "I threw that damn thing into a dumpster at Gil's," she said with her hands on her hips. "How did it get back here already?"

"One mystery solved," I thought.

Tricia must have been thinking the same thing. "Ila Dee gave it to us because it didn't work for her," she explained quickly. "But, it works just fine for us."

"M-A-R-Y Y-O-U C-A-N-T H-I-D-E"

"God in heaven." Mommy squealed hysterically.

The indicator moved slowly to NO.

"No, what?" she asked.

"I A-M N-O-T G-O-D"

Mommy stumbled out of the room backwards and fell into Daddy's outstretched arms.

"You said you weren't going to mess with that thing, Mary." he bellowed.

Mommy shoved him aside as she ran for the patio doors and fresh air. We told Daddy about the missing board and how we came to acquire a new one. When we finished, he motioned to Tricia and Aubrey to place their fingers back on the indicator. "I want to talk to it," he commanded.

"H-E-L-L-O L-E-V-O-Y" it spelled immediately.

"Which Elijah are you?" Daddy squinted.

"I A-M E-L-I-J-A-H P-R-O-P-H-E-T O-F G-O-D"

"Which God?" Daddy asked.

"T-H-E L-O-R-D O-F H-O-S-T-S" Ouija paused. "G-O-D O-F I-S-R-A-E-L"

Daddy sat motionless for at least thirty seconds and stared into space. We said nothing. Then he abruptly stood up and walked away.

What were we supposed to do now? Somehow, it just didn't seem respectful for a bunch of teenagers to be talking to Elijah—without adult supervision. But, politeness dictated that we not leave if Elijah wished to talk. Tricia and Aubrey placed their hands back on the indicator.

Nothing.

Tricia hid the Ouija board under our sofa bed so mom couldn't throw it away again. For the next few days, we talked to Ouija only when Mommy and Daddy weren't around.

Two nights after Mommy started ignoring the board, Elijah demanded to see her.

"D-I-A-N-A T-E-L-L M-A-R-Y T-O C-O-M-E"

I hesitated, but Tricia gave me the evil eye. I tiptoed past the bathroom, where Daddy was taking a shower and headed for the kitchen. Mommy was mopping the kitchen floor.

"Mommy, Elijah wants to talk to you," I pleaded.

"You can tell Ouija I won't talk anymore," she said defiantly.

I kept trying, "But—"

"No," she said flatly.

Tricia and Aubrey held the board precariously on their laps as they sat on desk chairs across from each other in our bedroom. Mike and Timmy were nowhere to be found, so the house was unusually quiet.

"She won't talk," I said as I lowered myself into a lotus position next to Tricia. Just then, the water stopped running in the shower, and we heard Daddy finishing the last chorus of "She'll Be Coming Round the Mountain," notoriously off-key. As we snickered, the indicator started moving.

"G-E-T Y-O-U-R F-A-T-H-E-R"

"Daddy," I yelled from my seated position, despite Tricia's huffing sounds over my head.

Daddy emerged from the bathroom in a cloud of white steam. He stopped at our doorway for a second and saw the Ouija board.

"Elijah wants to talk to you," Tricia said.

Aubrey looked suddenly uncomfortable. He took his hands off the indicator and stood up to leave. "Man, I forgot I have to go to King's with my mom," he said as he squeezed past Daddy.

Water dripped from Daddy's huge ears onto the towel that was draped around his neck. We kidded him relentlessly about his 'Elmer Fudd' ears. In response, he'd good-naturedly wiggle his right ear and then his left. As a show stopper, he'd wiggle both together. No matter how many times he did it, we clapped uproariously.

"What do you want, sister?"

"Daddy, Elijah wanted to talk to you. But, without Aubrey, we need you to talk to him." Daddy stood without answering, staring at his oldest daughter. Then he sat down across from her and placed his enormous hands precariously on the indicator.

"He's here, Elijah," Tricia prompted anxiously when the indicator didn't move.

"N-O-T E-L-I-J-A-H"

"So, who are you now?" Daddy asked sarcastically. His hands lifted off the indicator as he spoke, but Tricia pushed them back on just in time for Ouija to speak.

"G-A-B-R-I-E-L"

"Gabriel?" I asked.

"T-H-E A-R-C-H-A-N-G-E-L"

"So, you're Gabriel—Gabriel the Archangel?" Daddy repeated in obvious disbelief.

The indicator moved swiftly to YES.

Daddy didn't say a word.

"Why have *you* come?" I prompted.

"A-M M-E-S-S-E-N-G-E-R"

"A messenger from where?" Daddy asked belligerently.

"I S-T-A-N-D I-N P-R-E-S-E-N-C-E O-F J-E-H-O-V-A-H A-L-M-I-G-H-T-Y G-O-D"

"You're an archangel?" I asked, mystified. "Are there many like you?"

"S-E-V-E-N"

"Let's get on with this," Daddy interrupted. "Who has a message for me?"

"G-O-D"

"So, why did God send *you*?" Daddy asked.

"H-A-V-E B-R-O-U-G-H-T M-E-S-S-A-G-E-S T-O O-T-H-E-R-S"

"Who?"

"D-A-N-I-E-L," Ouija paused, "Z-A-C-H-A-R-I-A-S A-N-D M-A-R-Y"

"Mary, the Mother of Jesus?" I asked, recalling my Bible stories. An angel who had talked to Mary was talking to me? This was hard to believe.

The indicator moved to YES.

"Why would God have a message for me?" Daddy asked.

"Y-O-U A-R-E C-H-O-S-E-N"

Daddy jerked his fingers from the indicator and scrutinized Tricia for a good fifteen seconds. Out of curiosity, he placed his fingers back on the indicator. "Why would God choose me? I'm an atheist," he answered. "This doesn't make sense."

"But Elijah asked you to become a Christian," Tricia responded, without taking her eyes off the board.

"Who said it was Elijah?" Daddy asked.

An overwhelming sense of urgency overcame me, and my heart pounded against my chest. Why were we talking amongst ourselves when an angel had a message from God? "Shouldn't we talk to Gabriel?" I said, pointing dramatically at the board.

Slowly, Daddy moved his hands back to the board. Just as his fingertips touched the edge of the indicator, it moved quickly.

"Y-O-U   S-A-I-D   Y-O-U   W-O-U-L-D   B-E-C-O-M-E   A   C-H-R-I-S-T-I-A-N   I-F   G-O-D   A-S-K-E-D   Y-O-U"

Daddy sat motionless.

"S-O-M-E-O-N-E   W-A-N-T-S   T-O   T-A-L-K   T-O   Y-O-U"

It stopped moving and then continued "W-A-I-T"

I closed my eyes and envisioned Gabriel in flowing purple robes floating above us, returning to heaven. He disappeared into an intensely bright light.

The board was silent as we waited. The swamp cooler whirred on the roof above our heads, and I couldn't help savoring the smell of its sweet, wet hay.

Tricia didn't move a muscle. Daddy twitched from the strain of keeping his hands on the small indicator for so long a time. Several minutes passed like this, and then the indicator jerked slightly as if it wanted to say something. It stopped.

"Who are you?" Daddy asked cautiously.

The indicator slid boldly from letter to letter.

"I   A-M   A-L-P-H-A   A-N-D   O-M-E-G-A

T-H-E   B-E-G-I-N-N-I-N-G   A-N-D   T-H-E   E-N-D

T-H-E   F-I-R-S-T   A-N-D   T-H-E   L-A-S-T"

The shaking of my lap made it difficult to read the words I had scrawled on the lined paper.

Daddy looked like he was having a similar experience, but he asked again, "Who *are* you?"

"G-O-D"

"Which God?"

"T-H-E L-O-R-D G-O-D I-N H-E-A-V-E-N"

"Why have you come to earth now?" Daddy's gruff voice was barely audible.

"Y-O-U K-N-O-W"

"Daddy's an atheist," I interjected.

Daddy looked at me like I had stabbed him and then shook his head slowly.

"Why does Daddy need to be a Christian?" Tricia asked bravely.

"I H-A-V-E S-O-M-E-T-H-I-N-G F-O-R H-I-M T-O D-O"

It was obvious that Daddy still didn't believe, but he answered politely, "I have to think about this."

"D-O-N-T T-A-K-E T-O-O L-O-N-G," and then it slid to GOODBYE.

That was June 30, 1968.

Chapter 6

The Saving of Levoy

Being Southern Baptist meant we couldn't do a lot of things our friends could do—like dance, or wear makeup, or wear short dresses. I had never been to a movie theater, not even a drive-in. My movie exposure was limited to movies on the *Wonderful World of Walt Disney* on Sunday nights and the annual airing of the *Wizard of Oz* and *The Ten Commandments*.

The one glitch in our religious training was when our Sunday school teacher convinced the pastor to let her take a busload of us kids to see *Bonnie and Clyde* at the local drive-in. She sold it to the pastor as a scare tactic to keep us from turning to a life of crime. We loved it.

Church was our domain. I secretly hoped that Mommy wouldn't come to church for fear of what she might do, or say. Since she refused to talk to Ouija, I was certain she wouldn't be there. So, it was quite a surprise the next Sunday when she showed up for services. She saw us enter the sanctuary and motioned for us to join her on the back pew.

Pastor Valley's fire and brimstone sermon seemed to delight Mommy. She clapped and raised her hands and even recited the Lord's Prayer with the congregation.

At the end of the service, I watched as Mommy's eyes followed the pastor down the aisle towards the front door, where he waited to greet the congregation. After he passed our pew, Mommy told us to go ahead outside and wait for her in the car. She lingered at our pew until she had maneuvered herself to be the last person in the reception line.

I watched as old Miss Diefendorfer emerged from the church. She was in line in front of Mommy, but seemed to be ignoring our mom and intentionally took her time congratulating the preacher on his sermon. Mommy tapped her foot as she waited for Miss Diefendorfer to finish, and then she positioned herself in front of him at the top of the church steps.

She shielded her eyes from the sun with her Bible and rested her other hand on the pastor's bent arm. The way the wind sculpted her robust body from her pale yellow dress reminded me of one of Renoir's paintings that I had learned about in art class last year.

When she finished talking, Pastor Valley nodded and dropped his arm. Mommy's hand slid off as they parted.

"What were you talking about?" Tricia asked when Mommy had settled behind the steering wheel.

"You'll find out soon enough," Mommy smirked. She swore as she touched the blistering hot steering wheel. "Dammit," she cried. "You'd think after 18 years, I'd be used to this heat."

As soon as she slid into the seat and put the car in reverse, sweat started to bead on her forehead. "You know, I never realized how handsome Pastor Valley is," she said as she studied her reflection in the rearview mirror. "He's the finest dresser I ever met."

She said she didn't believe the vicious rumor about him and the church secretary for one minute. What rumor?

The next afternoon, the loud pounding on the front door rattled the living room windows. I jumped up from the cool floor and opened the door before the ruckus could wake Daddy.

Brother Valley, knuckles in mid-knock, was standing on *our* front porch. Deacon Jones and the church secretary Miss Babcock were with him. This was not good.

"Hello Sister Diana," he clasped my hand tightly and flashed the experienced smile of a TV evangelist. "Your Mother asked me to come over."

He stepped inside and removed his hat. "Is she here?" he asked, spinning his hat in his hands, and examining the room deftly with his hazel eyes.

Before I could say anything, Mommy rounded the kitchen wall and answered him, "Pastor Valley, thank you for coming," she finished wiping her hands on her apron. "Oh, hello, y'all," she said, not recognizing the others.

"This way," she said, motioning them to follow her into the family room. "I want you to talk to—" her voice trailed off as she saw the smiles melt from their pious faces.

They stopped abruptly at the sight of the Ouija board on the coffee table. Tricia and Aubrey sat across from each other, a little paler than usual, I thought. They didn't say a word.

"You brought me here to talk to your Ouija board?" Pastor Valley asked incredulously of Mommy as he turned on his heels.

"Yes, Pastor, I need you to talk to it and tell us if it's God or—" Mommy started.

"I will not talk to the devil," he said, turning his head and blocking it from his view with one hand. "It is Satan—I know that. Your souls will be condemned to hell if you mess with an instrument of the devil." His face had turned a fierce crimson during his tirade and his evangelist smile had been replaced by a vicious snarl that exposed dingy yellow teeth.

"I   J-O-H-N   4-2" The indicator surged from letter to letter and Aubrey yelled out each one. The pastor recoiled at his commanding voice.

"Diana, what does it say?" Mommy was rushing me as I flipped the pages to find it.

Pastor Valley's hand swept in front of my eyes across the Bible lying on my lap, "You don't have to look it up, Diana. I know what it says. Hereby know ye the Spirit of God: Every spirit that confesseth that Jesus Christ is come in the flesh is of God."

"M-Y S-O-N C-A-M-E I-N T-H-E F-L-E-S-H"

The Pastor's eyes darkened. I was transfixed by the rhythmically pulsing vein on his temple. "Sister Mary, you must get these innocent children away from this demon."

At that, Sister Babcock grabbed Tricia by her poodle haircut and jerked her away from the Ouija board. Tricia's size ten foot struck Aubrey's jaw and catapulted him across the room. As I jumped from my chair to avoid Aubrey, the Bible slid off my lap.

Seeing the imminent desecration of the Bible, Deacon Jones gasped and dove to stop its fall. He landed in a heap at my feet, proudly thrusting the Bible skyward like it was a football. I grabbed it from his clammy little hand.

"You get your goddamned hands off my kids," Mommy screamed as she shoved Miss Babcock into the wall. She swung around to strike the pastor, who grabbed her wrist just as she was about to strike his face.

"You pious little shit," Mommy shouted. "It passed the test. It's God."

Before the pastor could answer, Daddy appeared in the doorway. "What the hell is all the commotion?" he yelled as he quickly surveyed the bodies sprawled around the room.

"Levoy, they said it's Satan," Mommy shrieked helplessly, still in the preacher's clutches.

"Get your damn hands off my wife," Daddy said as he grabbed the preacher by his shirt. His other hand was clenched as he readied a punch. The pastor released her wrist and pushed past Daddy to help the deacon to his feet.

"If you follow that thing, you will be damned." He shoved his index finger into Mommy's face as he passed her, "I'm warning you." As the three stormed out, he made one final pronouncement, "You mark my words. No good will ever come of this," he said.

I was horrified at what had just happened. The Bible was safely pressed against my bosom, protected by my crossed arms. Mike and Timmy righted the chairs and helped Tricia and Aubrey to their feet. Mommy picked up the indicator and the board and placed them on the table.

All the while, Daddy was frozen, eyes fixed on his trembling hands. He hid them behind his back when he caught my gaze.

"What are we supposed to do?" Mommy pleaded. "We won't be able to show our faces after they're finished with us." With these words, the fear that had been rising in my throat escaped and seemed to spread and infect my brothers. Unconsciously, my hand moved to comfort my aching throat.

Tricia and Aubrey regained their composure and sat back down at the board.

"R-O-M-A-N-S 1-2 1-9"

I read quickly, "Dearly beloved, avenge not yourselves, but rather give place unto wrath: for it is written…" I stopped reading and closed my eyes to keep the tears from escaping.

"Is there more?" Tricia prompted.

"…Vengeance is mine;" I choked, "I will repay, saith the Lord."

And then Ouija signed off.

When Aubrey didn't show up the next morning, Mommy phoned her sister. "He's not coming over there no more, Mary," Aunt Edith's voice was icy.

"What?" Mommy couldn't believe her ears.

Edith didn't mince words. "You know, Mary, when I'm at your house, I believe in the Ouija board, but when I get home, I realize it's just too fantastical to be true. And, after the preacher said it was evil, it would be foolishness to let my son be involved. It's over." She hung up.

Needless to say, we were more than a little surprised when Aubrey came knocking on our door 20 minutes later. "I had to come because I believe," he was crying. "We can't tell my mom that I'm here, though."

For the next few days, Aubrey would arrive at around eight o'clock each morning, and we'd talk to Ouija for the rest of the day. He insisted that we close the curtains in the family room so Aunt Edith wouldn't see Aubrey when she drove by on her way to work.

Daddy sat with the Ouija board for a few minutes each day and asked questions about Bible passages he had read the night before. After he was satisfied with Ouija's answers, he left for work. Then Aubrey would leave.

Early on the fourth morning after the preacher denounced the Ouija board, our phone rang. Mike answered, and holding his hand over the mouthpiece, whispered that it was Aunt Edith. We shushed Aubrey and giggled quietly when Mike handed the receiver to Mommy.

"I didn't *think* you could—" Mommy's smile faded as she listened. "Lord have mercy," she finally said. She closed her eyes and subconsciously rubbed the blood blister above her right brow so hard, I was sure it would burst and squirt blood all over us. The quarter-inch blister had been on her forehead since Tricia was born. Although the doctors couldn't explain it, they told her it was nothing to worry about, and she could have it removed if she wanted.

Something bad must have happened.

I mimed to Mike that he should lean closer to hear what Aunt Edith was saying. He leaned slightly and shrugged his shoulders.

"How?" Mommy asked. Her finger had moved from her brow to her mouth, and she was chewing on a nail. "Are they ok?" Again, "Lord have mercy."

After a few more seconds, Mommy said, "Vengeance is God's, Edith." I couldn't tell from Mommy's face what Aunt Edith was saying, but Mommy hung up without saying goodbye.

"What happened? What's wrong?" Aubrey stood up.

Mommy looked past Aubrey to Patricia, who was standing stiffly in the corner of the room. Her eyes were fixed on the board. Mommy moved to her side and wrapped her fingers around Tricia's thin arm.

As she coaxed her daughter out of the corner and back into the chair, she reminded Tricia that she was needed, "Put your fingers back on the indicator, sister." Tricia did as she was told, and Mommy took Aubrey's place across from Tricia.

As soon as she placed her fingers gently on the indicator, it started moving, slowly at first and then faster.

"V-E-N-G-E-A-N-C-E I-S M-I-N-E"

"Lord, did you do this?" Mommy asked cautiously.

Ouija did not move. Then, slowly, "D-I-D N-O-T S-T-O-P I-T"

"Stop what?" hysteria was creeping into Mike's voice.

"A-C-C-I-D-E-N-T"

"Whose accident?" When the indicator didn't move, Mike jumped up and yelled, "If you're not going to tell me what's going on, I'm leaving."

"B-E V-E-R-Y C-A-R-E-F-U-L M-I-K-E"

"Michael Levoy Cain," Mother's voice warned him. "Sit down, and I'll tell you what happened."

Mommy inhaled deeply, "Pastor Valley's wife and daughter were driving to Del's Orchards to minister to the migrant workers when their car veered off the road and crashed into an orange tree. The car rolled over, and his little girl flew out of the car. His wife was trapped behind the steering wheel." She paused to take a breath. "The doctors don't know if they'll live," Mommy swallowed hard. "The police don't know why she ran off the road."

"I K-N-O-W"

My hands covered my mouth to keep me from speaking.

"Lord, we didn't want anything to happen to these innocent people. How could you have let this happen?" Mommy's tears were meandering to her chin, where they pooled, and then crashed in a big glob onto the board.

"T-H-E-I-R S-O-U-L-S A-R-E R-E-A-D-Y"

"Are they going to die?" Mommy asked.

The indicator didn't move.

"How could you let this happen?" Mike's anger was replaced by incredulity.

"S-O-M-E W-O-U-L-D H-A-V-E Y-O-U B-E-L-I-E-V-E T-H-A-T O-N-L-Y T-H-E-Y C-A-N T-A-L-K T-O G-O-D"

"You mean like the high priests in Jesus' time?" Timmy asked.

"R-I-G-H-T"

"So, you were punishing Pastor Valley for denouncing you?" Mommy asked.

"I C-H-O-O-S-E W-H-O I T-A-L-K T-O"

"And you want to talk to us through this board?" I asked after reading Ouija's answer.

"Y-O-U W-O-U-L-D N-O-T L-I-S-T-E-N A-N-Y O-T-H-E-R W-A-Y"

"But, why do you want to talk to us?" Mommy pulled a tissue from the box on her lap and dabbed at her cheek in between questions.

'Y-O-U A-R-E M-Y C-H-O-S-E-N F-A-M-I-L-Y"

"Chosen for *what*?" Mommy asked.

"I-M-P-O-R-T-A-N-T   M-I-S-S-I-O-N"

"We're going to be missionaries?" Excitement crept into my mind.

"S-O-O-N   E-N-O-U-G-H," and then the indicator slid to GOODBYE.

It was well past dinnertime, but food was the last thing on our minds after this session with Ouija. We were too excited for television, so Mike turned on the RCA and adjusted the tuner knob until we heard a scratchy voice: *And, now, listeners, you've been asking for this song all day. Hereis Gary Puckett and The Union Gap with Young Girl.*

Timmy grabbed the flyswatter from atop the fridge and held it to his mouth. With it as his microphone, he sang so off-key that we laughed uproariously and tried to drown him out with our own voices.

Young girl, get out of my mind
My love for you is way out of line
Better run, girl,
You're much too young, girl

With all the charms of a woman
You've kept the secret of your youth
You led me to believe
You're old enough
To give me Love
And now it hurts to know the truth, Oh,

Halfway through, our voices trailed off because none of us knew the other verses, but we sang extra loud on the chorus to make up for it.

For the rest of the evening, we listened to the radio and talked nonstop about being chosen for an important mission. With the world globe as a prop, we tried to guess where we would be sent—Africa? Argentina? Vietnam? India?

We never talked about the pastor again.

Out of habit, we went to church the next Sunday. One of the deacons gave the sermon for Brother Valley. Aunt Edith was not at her usual pew in front of us. In fact, no one sat in that pew. Mommy spoke to no one, and no one spoke to her.

When the sermon was over, we left by a side door. On the way out, I overheard two women nodding towards Mommy and whispering, "She's got a lot of nerve." I couldn't hear the rest. Mommy must have overheard too, because she didn't make us go to evening service that night. Instead, we stayed home and talked to God.

Between sleeping and working, Daddy didn't have much time to talk to Ouija. We updated him each day from my meticulous handwritten record and then he'd give us any questions he wanted to ask. He wasn't expecting what happened the next time he sat with Ouija.

"I N-E-E-D Y-O-U-R D-E-C-I-S-I-O-N L-E-V-O-Y"

"What decision?" It looked like Daddy wouldn't be able to stall anymore.

"I A-S-K-E-D Y-O-U T-O B-E-C-O-M-E A C-H-R-I-S-T-I-A-N"

"I'm still thinking about it," Daddy replied.

"Y-O-U A-R-E R-E-C-E-I-V-I-N-G P-E-R-S-O-N-A-L I-N-V-I-T-A-T-I-O-N"

"I'm not ready to make a decision," Daddy said stubbornly.

"W-I-L-L I-T T-A-K-E D-E-A-T-H O-F P-A-T-R-I-C-I-A"

Daddy jumped out of the chair, knocking it over as he rose. "What kind of devil are you to threaten me with the death of my own daughter?"

Mommy and Tricia held their fingers on the indicator. Daddy looked desperately from one to the other hoping one of them would answer him. Mommy was staring at Tricia, and Tricia was staring at the board.

"H-E-R S-O-U-L I-S R-E-A-D-Y"

"You would kill an innocent child to force me to become a Christian?" Daddy couldn't believe what he was hearing. It struck me as odd that he would say that. He must not have read the Old Testament. I was so relieved they weren't talking about my death.

"I C-A-R-E O-N-L-Y F-O-R Y-O-U-R S-O-U-L-S"

Mommy reached up and held Daddy's forearm tightly as she pleaded, "Levoy, please, please do this for your family."

He glared at Mommy as anger, and then fear, crept into his moist eyes. He backed out of the room and slammed the front door on his way out. The truck's engine revved in the driveway a few seconds later, and then its roar eerily choked to a stop. The Ouija board was silent until Daddy's face slowly re-emerged through the front door.

"All right," Daddy surrendered. He collapsed into the chair.

"P-R-O-F-E-S-S T-H-I-S A-T T-H-E R-E-V-I-V-A-L T-O-N-I-G-H-T"

The Ouija board was talking about the revival meeting at the Coliseum that night in Phoenix. We arrived early enough to claim six seats in the third row. The evangelist said that six thousand weary souls filled the Coliseum that night. He was angelic-like, having silver white hair and dressed head to toe in white.

Before he began, he deliberately removed his jacket and draped it across the back of a chair. I could see that his underarms were sweat stained already. Sweat poured from his hairline and rolled down his face before he even began his sermon. He had no notes, but held his black Bible in his right hand and a white handkerchief in the left.

"Are you ready to receive the word of God tonight?" he screamed as he brought the Bible down hard onto the pulpit. When his voice became too gravelly, he gulped water from a glass left for him beside the pulpit. Then he'd wipe his full face with the handkerchief.

He alternately screamed, gulped and dabbed for the next three hours. Whenever the audience grew too quiet for him, he'd scream into the microphone, "Can you say 'praise God'?" The audience roared back, "Praise God," and a sea of white hands rose to the ceiling.

I couldn't help looking at Daddy a lot that night. Was he going to keep his word and go down to the altar at the end of the sermon to profess his belief in Christ?

The evangelist finally signaled to the organist to play and lowered his voice. "Is there anyone here who wants to accept Jesus Christ as their personal savior?" The organist played quietly, and the audience sang,

Amazing grace, how sweet the sound,
That saved a wretch like me.
I once was lost, but now am found,
Was blind, but now I see.

Hundreds of people made their way slowly to the altar and knelt, but not Daddy. On the last verse, Tricia took Daddy's hand and gently nudged him into the aisle. He didn't resist. They walked side-by-side to the altar, where Daddy knelt stiffly and closed his eyes.

When the last soul knelt at the altar, the evangelist raised his hands to God, "Accept these souls, Dear Jesus. Hallelujah. Hallelujah. Can we all say, Amen?" Amen.

Daddy was saved.

That was July 9th.

Chapter 7

The Mission

I watched as Mommy cautiously slipped her hand into Daddy's big paw. He flinched, but he didn't withdraw from her advance. They smiled at each other, almost embarrassed. We began the long shuffle up the aisle of the massive building and finally exited the parking lot at one o'clock in the morning.

Everyone in our family was safe from everlasting damnation. I was sure of it. So sure, that I ignored a voice stealthily chipping away at my mental bliss. The voice demanded: 'When, exactly, did *Mommy* become a Christian?' She didn't go to the altar with Daddy, and she had never claimed to be a Christian. Oh well, I reasoned. God knows things I don't. I wasn't going to upset the proverbial apple cart by mentioning this to anyone. I was sure we were on the road to being a normal family.

"Lord, what would you have us do?" Mommy asked of Ouija the next morning.

"L-E-V-O-Y M-U-S-T B-E B-A-P-T-I-Z-E-D"

Daddy stood near the patio door with his first cup of steaming coffee in his hand, a pack of Winstons in the palm of the other. Ouija had caught him off guard.

"What?" he asked.

"L-U-K-E 1 1-6"

Aubrey read, "He that believeth and is baptized shall be saved; but he that believeth not shall be damned."

The Cheerios I had just eaten churned in my stomach at the thought of asking anyone from the Baptist Church to baptize Daddy, especially after Daddy threatened to punch him out.

Mommy must have been thinking the same thing. "And who's going to do this baptism?"

"P-A-S-T-O-R V-A-L-L-E-Y"

"He's not going to baptize him," Mommy said. She hadn't even sent a card to the family after the accident.

"M-A-T-T-H-E-W 2-8 1-9"

Aubrey read, "Go ye therefore and teach all nations, baptizing them in the name of the Father, and of the Son, and of the Holy Ghost: Teaching them to observe all things whatsoever I have commanded you; and lo, I am with you always, even unto the end of the world. Amen."

Daddy had not said a word during the exchange. He pleaded with the board, "Please don't make me do this. Can't another preacher baptize me?"

The indicator moved quickly to NO. "C-A-L-L H-I-M N-O-W"

"I'll call him after I have a cigarette."

"N-O-W"

"But—" Daddy started.

"N-O-W"

"This can wait until I have a cigarette."

"L-E-V-O-Y" Ouija moved forcefully. "Y-O-U A-R-E C-A-L-L-E-D O-F G-O-D"

Daddy sipped the steaming coffee.

"Called for *what*?"

"M-I-S-S-I-O-N"

"What mission?" Mommy interjected.

"I-N G-O-O-D T-I-M-E" after a brief pause, Ouija continued, "C-A-L-L N-O-W"

Mommy reached for her address book and opened it to the page for the church. Daddy hadn't moved. She wrote the number down on a slip of paper and handed it to him.

He weighed his options. Ignore the board and end up like the pastor's family, or do what the board wanted and call the man, which seemed like a far safer choice. Without warning, Daddy picked up the phone, index finger shaking as he dialed the number. He stretched the phone cord through the patio door and closed it behind him. He lowered himself into the lawn chair and lit a Winston.

We held our collective breath as we watched him suck in a gob of smoke while the phone rang on the other end. He turned his back to us. He spoke and listened for no more than a minute.

"Bastard," he mouthed as he turned back to face us again. He opened the patio door and seeing us, swiped at the smoke that had stung his eyes.

For an instant his face reminded me of how vulnerable it looked when he started at Unidynamics. "I'm a jet engine mechanic," he had complained. "Not a janitor." Mommy took pleasure in adding insult to his injury, "Well, if you could get along with people, you'd still be in the Air Force, and I wouldn't have to be a maid at the Wigwam."

"What did he say?" Mommy prodded.

"That son of a bitch said that it will be a cold day in hell before he'll baptize me. He said we have to denounce the board." Daddy swatted purposely at a fly buzzing around his ears and continued, "By the way, we're no longer welcome at his church."

"But that's our church," Timmy blurted out.

"Not anymore it ain't," Daddy laughed.

Timmy jumped up, sending the chair backwards into the corner cabinet filled with dishes. He tripped over Aubrey's feet on the way out of the kitchen, knocking the Bible off Aubrey's lap. I picked it up.

Daddy pointed his finger at Timmy as he passed. "Watch what you're doing, you moron."

"L-E-V-O-Y" Ouija shouted. "B-E C-A-R-E-F-U-L"

Daddy turned on Ouija, "Why did you make me call him? You knew what he would say."

"H-E W-A-S B-E-I-N-G T-E-S-T-E-D"

"Why did you have to humiliate me to test him?"

"Y-O-U A-R-E A-L-S-O B-E-I-N-G T-E-S-T-E-D"

Daddy sat down in Timmy's empty chair. "Why is being a Christian so painful?"

"N-O-T S-U-P-P-O-S-E-D T-O B-E E-A-S-Y"

"But you're God." Mike yelled. "Why don't you make people do what you want?"

"F-R-E-E W-I-L-L"

"You are testing us for a reason?" Mommy asked.

The indicator moved slowly to YES.

"What's the reason?"

"I-N G-O-O-D T-I-M-E"

"Will we pass the tests?" I asked.

"D-O-N-T K-N-O-W Y-E-T"

"But you're God," Mommy said. "You know everything."

"Y-O-U H-A-V-E F-R-E-E W-I-L-L"

"But why do we have to be hated?" I asked.

"R-E-A-D I J-O-H-N 3 1-3 A-N-D R-O-M-A-N-S 8 2-8"

I turned to the verse and read humbly, "Marvel not, my brethren, if the world hates you." I flipped to the second passage, "And we know that all things work together for good to them that love God, to them who are the called according to his purpose."

I read on, "For whom he did foreknow, he also did predestinate to be conformed to the image of his Son that he might be the firstborn among many brethren. Moreover, whom he did predestinate, them he also called; and whom he called, them he also justified; and whom he justified, them he also glorified. What shall we then say to these things? If God be for us, who can be against us?"

"I A-M F-O-R Y-O-U"

* * *

The next morning Ouija had good news.

"N-A-Z-A-R-E-N-E-S W-I-L-L B-A-P-T-I-Z-E"

Ouija was right.

Mommy called the Church of the Nazarene on Central. She told them Daddy had become a Christian, received a calling from the Lord, and that God had told Daddy to convert to Nazarene and be baptized. Then she warned us not to mention the Ouija board to anyone. "Just tell them he received a calling through prayer." Daddy was baptized the next Sunday.

For the next week, we woke up, ate breakfast, and talked to the Ouija board for fifteen hours a day. We didn't stop talking until Ouija said GOODBYE. Aubrey was the only person Ouija would talk to outside of our immediate family.

Then out of the blue, Ouija told us to start swimming every day at the public pool next to the A&W Root Beer Stand on Buckeye Road.

"You want the kids to swim?" Mommy asked. "But how will I talk—?"

"Y-O-U A-N-D L-E-V-O-Y T-O-O" Ouija interrupted.

"We don't swim," Mommy said flatly.

"Y-O-U W-I-L-L L-E-A-R-N"

"Let me get this straight," Mommy reasoned. "You want us to wear skimpy swimsuits to a public pool?"

"A-P-P-R-O-P-R-I-A-T-E S-W-I-M-W-E-A-R"

My heart jumped. This was outstanding news as far as I was concerned. My right hand cramped constantly after recording every word Ouija uttered, day after day.

This would end our days of canal swimming forever. Unlike a swimming pools' sparkling turquoise water, canal water was brown and fish-infested. Its swift flow crashed violently through gates that diverted the water to desperate cotton fields along its steep banks. I had stayed away from canals ever since Dennis Miller drowned in one three years earlier. When I close my eyes, I can see his familiar pale freckled face and copper red hair resting peacefully in the casket. Poor Dennis had missed everything all because he wanted to cool off on a hot summer day.

Mommy took us to Goodwill the next morning to buy new swimsuits, and we were at the pool by ten o'clock. We stopped swimming long enough to eat the peanut butter sandwiches Mommy made, and then we swam for another two hours. We were home by three o'clock—the hottest part of the day—and we talked to Ouija for another eight hours.

Daddy joined us at the pool on Saturday. My Daddy *always* wore Levi jeans and black cowboy boots and it was strange to see him in a swimsuit. He jumped into the deep end and sank immediately to the bottom of the pool. For the rest of the day he watched mostly from the shade of the lone olive tree. At the end of the day, he lifted his watch in the air and pointed to it to signal that it was time to go.

When Daddy wasn't there, Mommy flirted shamelessly with the lifeguard. Geronimo was a Pima Indian in his late twenties with black-brown leather skin and watery blue eyes. Mommy stared at Geronimo as she whispered that he lived on the reservation with his parents until he was twelve. That's when his mother left his father and moved to the white man's world. Geronimo quit school to work the fields and still lived with his mother in Tolleson.

"He's such a nice boy," Mommy cooed one afternoon. "We should have him over for lunch or something."

My eyes grew wide at that thought. Daddy was not going to like having another man at our house. Mommy had to know that. Tricia suggested that we ask Ouija first.

Ouija told us to invite him for homemade ice cream the next day. Aunt Edith had given us a manual ice cream maker the Christmas before. After Daddy left for work, Geronimo came over and we took turns cranking the ice cream for two hours.

"Have you ever heard of a Ouija board?" Mommy asked Geronimo suddenly. I couldn't believe my ears. This was the woman who told us not to mention the Ouija board to anybody. What was she doing?

"I've never heard of this thing," Geronimo said. "What is it?"

"A Ouija board lets you talk to spirits."

"These are good spirits?" he asked.

"Yes," Mommy nodded. "They are good. They help you live like Christ. Do you know what that means?"

Geronimo's eyes lit up. "Yes, I am a Christian. Missionaries came to the reservation. I was baptized," he said proudly.

"Praise God," Mommy smiled broadly and clapped her hands together tightly. "Geronimo, we don't just talk to a spirit. We talk to God."

Geronimo squinted and cocked his head. His smile caused deep crevices to run from the corner of each eye all the way to his chin. "You do this instead of praying?" he asked thoughtfully.

"Oh, no, we still go to church and pray. God told us that he has an important mission for us."

"What mission?"

"We don't know yet. We're hoping to find out soon," Mommy said as she motioned Tricia to bring the board to the kitchen table. "Do you want to talk to God?"

"Oh, yes."

"H-E-L-L-O G-E-R-O-N-I-M-O"

"Hello, sir," he responded as he touched his hand to his forehead, chest and shoulders in the sign of the cross.

"W-E-L-C-O-M-E" Ouija paused. "I H-A-V-E B-E-E-N W-A-I-T-I-N-G"

"What?" Mommy asked.

"G-E-R-O-N-I-M-O I-S A-L-S-O C-H-O-S-E-N"

"For *our* mission?" Aubrey asked incredulously.

The indicator slid to YES, "G-E-R-O-N-I-M-O W-I-L-L G-O W-I-T-H Y-O-U"

"Did you want us to swim so that we would meet Geronimo?" Tricia asked.

The Ouija board answered YES.

"This is an honor for me," Geronimo's long black eyelashes caressed his cheek, and he bowed his head. It didn't take much to convince him.

We talked to Ouija for the next eight hours. Ouija insisted that Geronimo sit next to Tricia most of the time. I noticed that Tricia stared at Geronimo when he wasn't looking, and he did the same when she looked away. Geronimo stayed until one o'clock the next morning, and it was Tricia, not Mommy, who walked him to the door.

"Levoy, don't go getting' mad," Mommy said the next morning. "God chose another person for our mission. His name's Geronimo—he's the lifeguard at the pool," she said motioning over her shoulder. "He's right behind me."

In a flash, Daddy flew into a jealous rage, "You asked another man to come into my damned house?" Daddy's fist swung and hit the table lamp, sending it crashing to the floor where it broke into hundreds of pieces.

"You asshole. Do you really think I have him coming *here*? This was Ouija's idea." Mommy and Daddy were standing toe-to-toe, screaming at each other.

"This is your M-O, you bitch."

"Daddy, it was the Ouija board's idea," I cried. I didn't know what M-O meant, but I recognized a war in the making.

"Who do you think is behind the Ouija board?" Daddy turned on me, screaming.

"It's God. It's God," was all I could say.

Mike and Timmy joined in, "It's not Mommy," they said in unison.

"Why don't you ask the Ouija board?" Tricia said nonchalantly as she walked in the door ahead of Geronimo. Geronimo must have heard the yelling. He stood just outside the door and asked Tricia, "Should I leave?"

"No, Daddy just didn't know you were coming. We're going to talk to Ouija now," she said flatly.

She took Geronimo's hand and led him to the board, where they both sat down. As we watched, she instructed him to put his hands on the indicator lightly. He kept his eyes on her face. As his fingers touched the indicator, it flew angrily off the board and hit the wall near Timmy. It landed on the floor on its three peg legs.

Daddy hadn't moved and seemed ready to pounce on Geronimo at any moment. His red face paled to pink.

Timmy retrieved the indicator and placed it back on the board.

It immediately jerked from letter to letter, "T-H-I-S   I-S   N-O-T   H-O-W   C-H-O-S-E-N   F-A-M-I-LY   B-E-H-A-V-E-S"

"I didn't do anything," Mommy defended herself.

"Y-E-L-L-I-N-G   S-W-E-A-R-I-N-G   A-R-E   N-O-T   F-O-R   C-H-R-I-S-T-I-A-N-S"

"Well, I wasn't the only one doing it," she answered defiantly.

"Y-O-U   K-N-O-W   B-E-T-T-E-R" and then, "E-X-O-D-U-S   2-0   3   1-7"

"What is that, Diana?" Mommy asked.

I turned to the page in Exodus and read silently for a minute. "It's the Ten Commandments," I finally said out loud.

"V-E-R-S-E   7"

I read, "Thou shalt not take the name of the Lord thy God in vain; for the Lord will not hold him guiltless that taketh his name in vain."

Mommy had no answer for that. She muttered something about starting dinner.

"G-E-R-O-N-I-M-O   I-S   T-O   H-E-L-P   O-N   M-I-S-S-I-O-N"

Daddy watched his daughter and Geronimo without saying a word. Suddenly, he thrust his hand toward Geronimo's body and said stiffly, "I'm Levoy."

Geronimo hesitated for just a second, but then took Daddy's hand. "Thank you for letting me be here," he choked back tears.

"I don't make the decisions around here. It does," Daddy said, pointing to the board. Then he asked the board, "When will we know what our mission is?"

"N-O-W"

"Mommy, come quick," I yelled to the kitchen. "God's going to tell us about our mission."

"I can hear you from here," Mommy yelled back.

"M-I-K-E G-E-T G-L-O-B-E"

"Why do I have to?" Mike didn't look up from his handiwork. He was drawing a comic strip hero. "Let someone else do it."

"I A-S-K-E-D Y-O-U"

"Get off your sorry ass," Daddy threatened. "Before I get my whip out."

"Here," Mike sneered as he dropped the globe onto the board. Tricia scowled at him and moved it off the board onto the table.

"V-E-R-S-E 1-2 I-S F-O-R Y-O-U M-I-K-E"

"Honor thy Father and thy Mother: that thy days may be long upon the land which the Lord thy God giveth thee," I read smugly.

"D-I-A-N-A S-P-I-N G-L-O-B-E A-N-D S-T-O-P W-I-T-H F-I-N-G-E-R"

"Ok," I said. The globe was cool to my touch, and I enjoyed feeling the raised continents under my fingertips. I closed my eyes and started it spinning. I stopped it suddenly with my finger and opened my eyes.

"S-A-Y N-A-M-E O-F C-O-U-N-T-R-Y"

Its name was long, but the country was tiny. "Which continent?" Timmy asked impatiently.

"Asia," I answered and then sounded out the name, "Afghanistan?" I had never heard of it.

"Y-O-U A-R-E G-O-I-N-G T-H-E-R-E"

"On a trip?" Daddy asked.

The indicator slid to NO.

"To live?" Mike asked, looking up from his drawing.

The indicator slid to YES.

"Why?" Daddy asked.

"Y-O-U W-I-L-L K-N-O-W S-O-O-N"

"Afghanistan?" Daddy murmured to himself in disbelief.

"I-S-A-I-A-H 4-2 9 T-O 1-3"

I read loudly, "Thou whom I have taken from the ends of the earth, and called thee from the chief men thereof, and said unto thee, thou art my servant; I have chosen thee, and not cast thee away. Fear thou not, for I am with thee; be not dismayed; for I am thy God; I will strengthen thee; yeah, I will help thee; yeah, I will uphold thee with the right hand of my righteousness.

"Behold, all they that were incensed against thee shall be ashamed and confounded; they shall be as nothing; and they that strive with thee shall perish. For I the Lord God will hold thy right hand, saying unto thee, fear not; I will help thee."

"F-E-A-R N-O-T"

"We can't move to Afghanistan," Daddy said sarcastically. "How would we get there?"

"M-A-T-T-H-E-W 1-7 2-0"

I read, "And Jesus said unto them, because of your unbelief: for verily I say unto you, if ye have faith as a grain of mustard seed, ye shall say unto this mountain, remove hence to yonder place; and it shall remove; and nothing shall be impossible unto you."

"A-L-L T-H-I-N-G-S A-R-E P-O-S-S-I-B-L-E I-F Y-O-U B-E-L-I-E-V-E"

"We know nothing about Afghanistan or missionary work," Daddy shook his head. "How would we live?"

"F-A-I-T-H"

"How do we get ready?" Mike asked suspiciously.

"S-T-U-D-Y B-I-B-L-E" Ouija paused. "R-E-A-D A-B-O-U-T A-F-G-H-A-N-I-S-T-A-N L-E-A-R-N L-A-N-G-U-A-G-E"

Mike was disappointed—not his idea of a fun summer.

Daddy looked around the room at his wife and children, his wife's nephew and this new person, Geronimo. We stared at him, anxiously waiting for him to speak.

"This is incredible," he said. And, then he surrendered, "I guess we're moving to Afghanistan."

My hands were clapping before I could stop them. Daddy smiled his big goofy smile. He left reluctantly for work shortly after that.

Mommy stayed away from the board for the rest of the afternoon and talked to us only to tell us to put it away before dinner. She sent Aubrey home, but let Geronimo stay. As we sat down for dinner, Mommy seated herself in Daddy's chair at the head of the table. A slip of paper fell out of her paper napkin as she unfolded it.

"What's that?" Tricia asked.

Mommy opened the paper and read the words printed on it, "Mary, an angel is watching you." She laughed, "Ok, who wrote this?"

When nobody fessed up, Mike asked, "Let me see it. Whose writing is it?"

"I don't recognize it," Mommy seemed stunned.

Mike scanned the faces around the table. "I'll bet you anything Tricia wrote it," he sneered.

"I didn't write it," she said, sticking her tongue out.

"I'll bet Mike has one too," Timmy said. "He doesn't believe in the Ouija board."

"It better not write me any notes," Mike said as he raised his plate and found nothing. He shook open his napkin. No notes.

We finished dinner in the usual fifteen minutes and Mommy teased Mike, "Are you sure you don't have a note?"

"Yep," Mike laughed, silver tooth gleaming. Tricia raised his plate before he could stop her. A folded piece of paper now lay on the table. She snatched the note just as Mike grabbed for it. She read it aloud, "There is also one watching you, Mike."

I stopped breathing when I saw the note—it wasn't there before. How did it get there? I exhaled slowly and looked at each face around the table. Geronimo's face was frozen as he stared at the note in Tricia's hand.

Mike gave voice to my own thoughts, "This is weird."

After dinner, Mommy insisted that we talk to Ouija again. "Lord, did you write those notes?"

The indicator slid to YES.

"Do we really have guardian angels?"

"A-L-L M-Y C-H-I-L-D-R-E-N H-A-V-E G-U-A-R-D-I-A-N A-N-G-E-L-S"

"What do they do?" Tim wanted to know.

"W-A-T-C-H A-N-D P-R-O-T-E-C-T"

"Are they here now?" I shivered as I said it.

The indicator slid to` YES.

"W-H-E-N Y-O-U G-E-T C-H-I-L-L-E-D I-T I-S G-U-A-R-D-I-A-N A-N-G-E-L"

The hair stood on my arms and the back of my neck as I read it back.

I caught Mommy digging through all the drawers and closets the next morning. She said she was just spring cleaning, which I found odd since it was August. I knew what she was looking for. It was the same thing I was looking for. The paper and pen used for the notes from Ouija earlier in the week.

She must not have found them, though, because she was completely contrite and deferential when Ouija spoke after that.

There was so much to do to get ready for Afghanistan. First, we had to learn everything about the country, its people, and their language. Ouija told us to go to the Avondale library and check out as many books on Afghanistan as possible. There weren't many.

Next, we had to study the Bible so that we knew it inside and out. Ouija gave us a timetable for finishing each book in the Bible.

Finally, Daddy would need to be trained as a preacher, so Ouija gave us passages for him to study and use for his first sermon.

It was about that time that I mentioned I was running out of room in my binder. "What should I do?" I asked.

"I-M-P-O-R-T-A-N-T T-H-A-T Y-O-U R-E-C-O-R-D A-L-L"

"I'll buy another notebook and paper," Mommy promised.

'W-I-L-L N-E-E-D T-H-R-E-E M-O-R-E B-I-N-D-E-R-S"

Three more binders? What, were we writing another Bible?

I watched the news with Daddy that night, and the anchor talked about the Soviet Union invading a place called Czechoslovakia. "Damn Reds," Daddy muttered between teeth clenched around an unlit cigarette. I wondered if Czechoslovakia was anywhere near Afghanistan.

That was August 20th.

Chapter 8

The Revelation

"Hallelujah, praise God." Mommy screamed as she flung open our bedroom door and slammed it against the wall. "I'm healed."

Mommy's shrill screaming pierced my eardrums. We had talked to Ouija until one o'clock in the morning again, and I tried to open my eyes, but the sleep had hardened to concrete and I couldn't get my eyes open.

"Get up." She clapped her hands sharply for emphasis and, when we didn't respond fast enough for her, she clapped again, harder.

Tricia bolted upright in the bed, and I sat up lazily. Seeing our movement, Mommy continued down the hall. "Get up, you two," she yelled as she slammed open the boys' bedroom door. "Everybody up." she yelled. "I need to talk to Ouija *now*."

Tricia's eyes were barely open as she sat down at the board across from Mommy.

"Lord, is this my fleece?" Mommy's huge breasts heaved under her blue gingham housedress. "Did you heal me, Lord?"

The indicator moved slowly to YES, and Mommy started sobbing. She raised one hand above her head, and with her face to heaven, she cried, "Thank you, God."

I rubbed my eyes and blinked as I tried to clear the sleep. What was going on? Did I miss something? "What's a fleece?" I asked. Mommy swiveled in her chair to face me.

"I prayed that God would give me a fleece—a sign—that he is speaking through the Ouija board. The sign is that he healed me of arthritis," Mommy's hazel eyes were red-rimmed.

She continued breathlessly, "I woke up at two o'clock this morning in a pool of sweat. My body shook like I had Parkinson's." She saw our puzzled faces and explained. "Grandma Doshie's disease." We understood.

"It felt like someone was in the room with me. Then a pressure on my shoulders forced me to my knees. My hands and hips got so hot, I screamed from the pain. It went on for an hour or more, and then it just suddenly stopped."

She shook her head and continued, "I was so weak—I couldn't get back into bed, so I lay down on the floor and, when I awoke, I moved my fingers, and they didn't hurt anymore; and my hips didn't hurt when I tried to get up off the floor. This morning was the first time in ten years that I didn't have to take Bufferin before I could even get out of bed. God cured my arthritis."

She put her hands back on the indicator.

"Y-O-U K-N-E-L-T B-E-F-O-R-E M-E T-O A-C-C-E-P-T T-H-E H-E-A-L-I-N-G"

"Oh, thank you, Lord," Mommy sobbed.

"D-O Y-O-U B-E-L-I-E-V-E N-O-W"

"Yes, Lord. Whatever you want me to do, I am your servant."

"P-R-E-P-A-R-E Y-O-U-R F-A-M-I-L-Y F-O-R M-Y W-O-R-K"

"I will."

Daddy walked through the door just then, and Mommy jumped up and ran to him. To his surprise, she hugged him tight and sobbed into his chest as she told him the story. Mommy and Daddy joined hands and motioned for us to join them in a circle on our knees. We prayed. It was so weird.

For the next ten days, we held a family morning prayer, read our assigned Bible chapters and went swimming. After swimming, Geronimo would come home with us, and we'd talk to Ouija.

After dinner each night, we read our books on Afghanistan.

"They speak Farsi," Tricia read aloud from the book. We learned about the strict Muslim traditions—most of the desert nomads lived in tents, and the women wore chadres or burkas that covered them from head to toe. But in Kabul, the capitol, most of the people wore western clothes and lived in modern homes with running water and electricity. Qandahar was the other city to the south. Ouija said we would live in Kabul.

"Mommy, are we going to learn Farsi?" Timmy asked after we finished reading the final chapter of the book. Timmy and I still used Mommy and Daddy to address our parents. Tricia and Mike, being older, had started calling them 'mom' and 'dad' that past spring. Teenagers don't call their parents mommy and daddy they had said.

Mommy nodded her head, but before she could say anything, Ouija interrupted, "C-A-L-L   T-H-E-M   M-O-T-H-E-R   A-N-D   F-A-T-H-E-R"

"Why?" Mike snapped.

"I-T I-S E-X-P-E-C-T-E-D I-N A-F-G-H-A-N-I-S-T-A-N"

I didn't think it sounded strange at all. That's what my friend Judy called her parents.

"I like that better anyway," Mommy said. "It makes you sound more grownup."

We nodded our heads in unison and at her prompting said, "Yes, Mother."

Mother abruptly changed the subject, "Lord, I don't mean to question you, but how are we going to get to Afghanistan?"

"P-L-A-N-E"

We laughed at Ouija's joke.

"No, I mean, how are we going to pay for it?" Mother continued.

"N-A-Z-A-R-E-N-E   M-I-S-S-I-O-N   B-O-A-R-D   W-I-L-L   S-E-N-D   Y-O-U"

"They'll send our whole family as missionaries?" Timmy asked in disbelief.

The indicator slid to YES and continued, "M-U-S-T   W-R-I-T-E   L-E-T-T-E-R   S-O-O-N"

After Sunday service, Father asked Brother Wilson how we would go about becoming missionaries. Brother Wilson was in his fifties and had the softest silver hair I'd ever seen. I wanted to pet his head. If he had any reaction to Daddy's request, his face didn't betray him. He asked us to join him in his office, where he leaned over his desk and flipped through a book as big as the Book of Life. He suddenly stopped and ran his index finger down a page until he found what he was looking for.

"Ahh, here it is," he said looking up. "You need to write to Dr. Phillips. He's the head of the Foreign Mission Board." He wrote the address on a piece of paper and smiled as he handed it to Father. He removed his reading glasses and said, quite genuinely, "Mr. Cain, it's so good to have a family in our congregation who is so committed to God's work." Father's face flushed as he clumsily thanked Brother Wilson.

When we got home, Ouija dictated a letter to Dr. Phillips.

Dear Dr. Phillips,

Brother Wilson of the Church of the Nazarene in Avondale gave me your name. I received a calling to work as a missionary in Kabul, Afghanistan, shortly after I became a Christian last month. God spoke to me personally and told me he wanted my family to go on this mission.

These are the members of my family who will be going with me (I am 45): my wife Mary Frances (48) and our children, Michael Levoy (16), Patricia Faith (14), Diana Lynn (13), and Timothy Ray (11). To prepare for this mission, we study the Bible every day; prepare sermons; study the Afghan people and their culture; and are learning their language.

We are ready to go to Afghanistan at a moment's notice. Thank you for your help.

God bless you.
Walter Levoy Cain
Called of God

Mommy mailed it on August 28, 1968.

The news on television incited our Father nightly. If it wasn't more bad news about the invasion of Czechoslovakia, or the hippies in San Francisco, it was the police beating protestors outside the Democratic National Convention in Chicago. "What's this world coming to?" was his favorite line. "It wasn't like this in my day."

"What do you mean?" Mike would scold. "All we've got is a police action in Vietnam and a couple of protesters. You had Hitler and World War II." We could always count on Mike to put things in perspective.

A few days before I was to start the eighth grade, Mother took us to Goodwill for school shopping. The faded pink mini-dress I slyly placed at the bottom of the clothes stack somehow made it past Mother's scrutiny. I was glad of that—the dress would go perfectly with the white go-go boots I'd gotten at K-Mart the day before. Although Mother would buy used clothes, she drew the line at shoes and undergarments.

While we waited in the checkout line, Ila Dee asked a question that had been lingering in my mind as well, "Mary, what you gonna do when Patricia's at school all day?" She whispered then, "I mean about Ouija?"

"I'll just fritter away my time like I always did," Mother said unconvincingly. "I'll be writing and reading the Bible. It'll go fast."

I guess it didn't go as fast as she thought. After the first day of school, she was waiting for Tricia at the kitchen table with the Ouija board in front of her. Neither said a word as Tricia dropped her books on the floor next to the TV and dutifully took her seat at the table.

What was a relaxed schedule in summer became hectic when school and homework were added into our routine. Sometimes dinner consisted of peanut butter spread thinly on saltines washed down with a tall glass of milk. We prayed and read the Bible during breakfast, and after school we'd talk to Ouija, study the Bible and Afghanistan, and do our homework. In that order.

As I spent less time with the board, my mind started to doubt that it was God. Some of the things it said reminded me of my sister. She tried some of Diane Gebhart's Doritos at school one day, and that night the Ouija board told us to buy a bag. She had started locking me out of our bedroom so she could study for hours at a time. I became suspicious that she was studying the Bible so she could give us verses to read.

But how could she have known what the Ouija board knew? What about Bobbie Kennedy and the pastor? She couldn't have seen the future, I was sure. I tried desperately to squeeze these thoughts out of my mind when we sat down with Ouija. I wouldn't want it reading *my* mind.

We all knew that our school friends would never understand what was going on at our house, so we agreed to tell them only that we had applied to the missionary board and were hoping to leave for Afghanistan soon.

At the beginning of the second week of school, Tricia awoke with a terrible headache. "I feel like my head's going to explode," she cried. "Every time I open my eyes, it pounds even more. Light hurts it." Mother gave her two aspirin and sent her to school anyway. Her headache lasted five days. On the sixth day of the headache, she couldn't even sit at the Ouija board. That's when Mother called the base doctor.

"She has horrible headaches," Mother said into the telephone receiver.

After a brief silence on Mother's end, she answered the nurse's question. "She sleeps ok; but she's sleepwalking."

Mother listened intently and answered, "We have an aquarium, and lately the fish have been disappearing one by one. Last night, I woke up one night and found her standing near the aquarium. I asked her what she was doing, but she didn't answer—"

The nurse said something and Mother continued, "Her eyes were open. She plunged her arm, up to her elbow, into the water. She had an angel fish in her hand and it looked like she was going to put it in her mouth," she paused briefly for effect and continued. "It slipped out of her hand and slid across the floor. Then she went back to bed."

Mother chuckled at what the nurse said. "I was flabbergasted. I didn't know if she was going to eat the fish or not."

The nurse scheduled an appointment, and the three of us drove to the base the next afternoon. After examining Tricia the base doctor asked, "Is she under any extra stress?"

"Just school," Mother lied.

The doctor wrote in the file and without looking up said, "Mrs. Cain, I can't find any medical reason for her headaches, so I'm inclined to believe they are due to stress or nerves. I think her headaches will diminish if you reduce her stressors."

He continued, "If she has a headache, keep her home from school. Give her two aspirin every four hours. A lot of patients report that lying in a dark room helps relieve their headaches. Try that. Bring her back if the headaches persist."

Mother seemed relieved.

After that, if Tricia didn't want to go to school, Mother didn't make her. They talked to Ouija all day long, and they'd tell us what it said while we were at school. I was very jealous that Tricia got to stay home and talk to Ouija. Why couldn't I have headaches?

* * *

Ouija told Father that he would give his first sermon on Sunday, September 15th. Father had been studying scriptures and outlining his sermon for weeks. I couldn't imagine him giving a sermon—especially in our back yard. Father told us to invite only our closest neighbors—the Gonzales and Englishes. Even Ila Dee's husband, Dwayne, showed up. Geronimo asked if his mom and sister could come. Mother invited Aunt Edith and Mac.

On the 15th, we set up folding chairs in our back yard, and Tricia made some of her award-winning peanut butter cookies. A gallon of cherry Kool-Aid was already chilling in the fridge.

We were seated and ready to receive God's word by eleven o'clock. The shade of the mulberry tree made the 100 degrees almost tolerable. The hot metal of the folding chair seared the skin on my legs when I sat down and within minutes my dress was sweat soaked.

A thought strayed into my mindscape that this must seem comical to our friends. Father had never spoken to a group of people before—not about anything. How would he be able to do this? I was sure I would vomit any minute.

Father stood flat-footed in front of us with his Bible open and draped over his hands. He wore black cowboy boots, tan Lee jeans, a freshly pressed rodeo shirt, and a turquoise and silver bolo tie. He stared at his notes as the sweat beaded on his forehead. When he was ready to start, he looked up and nodded uneasily to each family, "Welcome to our service. Today, I'm going to be talking about Christ and how he came to earth to die for our sins."

It was a pretty safe subject as far as I was concerned. Father told the story easily and quoted appropriate scripture to highlight his points. We opened our Bibles to the scriptures he quoted and read silently with him. He spoke for thirty minutes and then asked Mommy if she'd lead us in a song, "What a Friend We Have in Jesus". Father asked us to stand, and then he prayed, and we concluded with Amen.

Not a complete embarrassment. I could tell that my brothers and sister were as relieved as I was. Our friends shook Father's hand and congratulated him as they went inside for refreshments.

After they left, Ouija congratulated Father, too, "W-E-L-L D-O-N-E"

The indicator stopped for a few seconds, then started moving again, "A-R-E Y-O-U R-E-A-D-Y T-O L-E-A-R-N A-B-O-U-T Y-O-U-R M-I-S-S-I-O-N"

"We're going to be missionaries, right?" I asked, a little disappointed it was up for discussion.

The indicator moved slowly to NO.

"What?" Daddy asked.

"Y-O-U W-I-L-L B-U-I-L-D T-H-E T-E-M-P-L-E F-O-R M-Y S-O-N"

Mother and Father knew what it said before I could read it back. They looked at each other and then at the board.

"But the temple is going to be rebuilt in Jerusalem." Mother said.

The indicator went to NO.

"But, everyone believes—"

"T-H-E-Y A-R-E W-R-O-N-G"

"How can all these people be wrong?" Father asked.

"P-R-O-P-H-E-T-S S-O-M-E-T-I-M-E-S M-I-S-I-N-T-E-R-P-R-E-T"

"When will your son come back to earth?" Mother interrupted.

"O-N-L-Y I K-N-O-W"

"Will you tell us?" Mother pushed.

The indicator moved swiftly to NO. "M-Y T-I-M-E I-S N-O-T S-A-M-E A-S Y-O-U-R-S"

No one said a word as Ouija continued, "R-E-A-D M-A-L-A-C-H-I 4 5"

Aubrey turned quickly to the chapter and verse. He read, "Behold, I will send you Elijah the prophet before the coming of the great and dreadful day of the Lord."

"I S-E-N-T E-L-I-J-A-H T-O Y-O-U"

The great and dreadful day of the Lord referred to Armageddon and the millennium rule of Christ. How could we be a part of it? This was not possible. We were going to build a temple?

"You're talking about Armageddon." Mike said tentatively.

The indicator moved ominously to YES.

Except for Mother's gasp, the room was silent.

Mike finally asked, "When will it start?"

"I-T S-T-A-R-T-E-D I-N 1-9-4-8"

"What do you mean?" Mother asked.

"I-S-R-A-E-L R-E-T-U-R-N-E-D H-O-M-E"

"That's the year Israel became a country," Mike was annoyed that Mother didn't know that.

"I-S-A-I-A-H 1-1 1-1 TO 1-2"

Aubrey read, "And it shall come to pass in that day, that the Lord shall set his hand again the second time to recover the remnant of his people, which shall be left, from Assyria and from Egypt, and from Pathros, and from Cush, and from Elam, and from Shinar, and from Hamath, and from the islands of the sea. And he shall set up an ensign for the nations, and shall assemble the outcasts of Israel, and gather together the dispersed of Judah from the four corners of the earth."

"E-Z-E-K-I-A-L 3-6 2-4"

Aubrey quickly turned to Ezekial and read, "For I will take you from among the heathen, and gather you out of all countries, and will bring you into your own land," and then Aubrey added his own comment, "God is talking about the Israelites."

Ouija encouraged Aubrey to read on, "C-H-A-P-T-E-R 3-7"

Aubrey continued reading and stopped at verse 21. He emphasized each word, "And say unto them, Thus saith the Lord God; Behold, I will take the Children of Israel from among the heathen, whither they be gone, and will gather them on every side, and bring them into their own land: And I will make them one nation in the land upon the mountains of Israel; and one king shall be king to them all: and they shall be no more two nations..." When he finished reading Chapter 38, Mother put her hands back on the indicator, and it moved quickly from letter to letter.

"1 T-H-E-S-S-E-L-O-N-I-A-N-S 4 1-6 T-O 1-7"

Aubrey read, "For the Lord himself shall descend from heaven with a shout, with the voice of the archangel, and with the trump of God, and the dead in Christ shall rise first: Then we which are alive and remain shall be caught up together with them in the clouds, to meet the Lord in the air; and so shall we ever be with the Lord. Wherefore comfort one another with these words." As soon as he finished reading, the indicator moved again.

"1 CO-R-I-N-T-H-I-A-N-S 1-5 5-2"

Aubrey turned to the passage, "In a moment, in the twinkling of an eye, at the last trump: for the trumpet shall sound, and the dead shall be raised incorruptible, and we shall be changed."

"That's the rapture, where Christians are taken," Mother said matter-of-factly. "It comes first."

"A-L-L O-F M-A-T-T-H-E-W 2-4"

Aubrey read the first two verses silently, and then he unconsciously started reading aloud, "… and what shall be the sign of thy coming, and of the end of the world? And Jesus answered and said unto them, take heed that no man deceive you. For many shall come in my name, saying, I am Christ; and shall deceive many. And ye shall hear of wars and rumors of wars; see that ye be not troubled; for all these things must come to pass, but the end is not yet. For nation shall rise against nation and kingdom against kingdom; and there shall be famines, and pestilences, and earthquakes, in diverse places. All these are the beginning of sorrows…" Aubrey's voice trailed off.

'R-E-A-D A-L-L" and Aubrey read the next 42 verses out loud.

As soon as he stopped reading, Ouija said, "R-E-V-E-L-A-T-I-O-N-S 1-3"

Aubrey read the entire chapter and concluded with, "here is wisdom. Let him that hath understanding count the number of the beast: for it is the number of a man, and his number is six hundred threescore and six." Aubrey calculated the number in his head and finished, "that's 666."

"What does that mean?" Mike asked Ouija.

"P-E-O-P-L-E W-I-L-L H-A-V-E N-U-M-B-E-R-S F-R-O-M B-I-R-T-H"

"What do the numbers mean?" Aubrey asked.

"6-6-6 I-S O-N-L-Y P-A-R-T O-F N-U-M-B-E-R"

Mike couldn't stop himself, "Is 666 for the Soviet Union?"

The indicator moved slowly to NO.

"But the Soviets are our enemy." Mike yelled. "It has to be for the Soviet Union."

"S-O-V-I-E-T U-N-I-O-N W-I-L-L N-O-T S-T-A-N-D"

"Then which country is it?" Mike asked.

"C-A-N-T S-A-Y"

Aubrey read farther into the Book of Revelations. He read about the seven years of tribulation; plagues that kill three-quarters of the world's population; the battle of Armageddon, where the beast and the false prophet were cast into the lake of fire; about Satan being bound for a thousand years; and about those who do not take the mark of the beast who will live and reign with Christ for a thousand years.

Then Satan will be loosed and go out to deceive the nations in the four quarters of the earth, Gog and Magog, to gather them to do battle. Fire will come down from God and devour Satan and his followers and they will be cast into the lake of fire and then, Judgment Day, followed by a new heaven and a new earth.

"I-T W-I-L-L S-T-A-R-T A-N-D E-N-D I-N A-F-G-H-A-N-I-S-T-A-N"

"What are we supposed to do?" Father asked meekly.

"B-U-I-L-D T-H-E T-E-M-P-L-E"

"How?" Father pleaded.

"I W-I-L-L G-I-V-E P-L-A-N-S"

"But who will physically do it?" he continued.

"T-H-E A-F-G-H-A-N-S"

Father dropped his head in his hands and hid his face. "It will take forever to build," he cried.

"N-O-T F-O-R-E-V-E-R"

"Remember Noah, Levoy," Mother prodded.

"F-A-I-T-H O-F A M-U-S-T-A-R-D S-E-E-D"

"When will you give us the plans, Lord?" Mother asked.

"T-O-M-O-R-R-O-W"

We talked to Ouija for a few more hours about Afghanistan and asked questions about what we had read in Revelations. Then Ouija said GOODBYE.

Aunt Edith stopped by the house early the next morning to drop off some ironing for me from the Wigwam. She said she'd wait for me to iron the basket of laundry and take it with her to work. I set up the ironing board in the family room and started ironing. I strained to hear a hushed conversation between her and Mother in the kitchen.

"Mary, don't you think it's strange that you are going to be missionaries even though you just started going to church?" Edith asked.

"I don't think it's strange at all. God called us, we didn't call him," Mother responded.

"You are not qualified to be missionaries. How do you think this is going to happen?" Edith asked with a note of genuine concern in her voice.

"I think the Lord will make a way for it to happen," Mother answered.

"If anyone on that mission board has the brains of a piss ant you won't be accepted," Edith said firmly.

My ears strained unsuccessfully to hear Mother's rebuttal. I sprayed starch on the sleeve of the white shirt I was ironing.

Then I heard Aunt Edith ask how Geronimo fit into this scheme. Mother told her that Geronimo was chosen to go with us.

Aunt Edith slammed her fist down hard onto the kitchen counter. "I can tell you this, Mary, no 14 year-old daughter of mine would be allowed to date a 28 year-old Indian from the wrong side of the tracks."

"They're not dating," Mommy answered.

"Well, what do you call it when they leave in the car together and don't come back for four hours—and you don't know where they've been?"

They lowered their voices after that, and I couldn't hear what was said. I finished my ironing within fifteen minutes and tied the hangers together so Aunt Edith could carry them more easily. She thanked me and told me she'd drop off the three dollars I'd earned after school.

Mother didn't mention this conversation during our session with Ouija that afternoon, but she did ask Ouija when the letter from the mission board would come.

"S-O-O-N"

Father said he had some questions for Ouija. Before he could ask them, Ouija interrupted.

"Y-O-U M-U-ST S-T-O-P S-M-O-K-I-N-G"

From the look on his face, Father was not at all prepared for this. When he retired from the Air Force the year before, his doctors told him that he had emphysema. They told him to stop smoking immediately, but he told us the doctors didn't know what they were talking about. He'd smoked five packs a day since he was thirteen, and he was not about to stop.

With his eyes fixed on Mother, Father asked Ouija, "Why?"

"1 C-O-R-I-N-T-H-I-A-N-S 3 1-6 T-O 1-7"

Timmy turned to the passage and read, "Know ye not that ye are the temple of God, and that the Spirit of God dwelleth in you? If any man defile the temple of God, him shall God destroy; for the temple of God is holy, which temple ye are."

"S-T-O-P D-E-F-I-L-I-N-G Y-O-U-R T-E-M-P-L-E"

"I'll think about it. I have some important questions to ask you," Father had successfully eluded the command.

The indicator slid to YES.

"You said we are to build a temple. Why?"

"A-M-O-S 9 1-1"

"In that day will I raise up the tabernacle of David that is fallen and close up the breaches thereof; and I will raise up his ruins, and I will build it as in the days of old." After reading this verse, Timmy read the whole chapter about the house of Israel being sifted among all nations, 'like as corn is sifted in a sieve.' Timmy finished, "and I will plant them upon their land, and they shall no more be pulled up out of their land which I have given them, saith the Lord thy God."

"Israel went home in 1948," Mike confirmed. "But the tabernacle of David hasn't been rebuilt in Jerusalem," he said.

The indicator moved to NO.

"A-C-T-S 1-5 1-5 T-O 1-7"

Mike read now, "And to this agree the words of the prophets; as it is written, After this I will return, and will build again the tabernacle of David, which is fallen down; and I will build again the ruins thereof, and I will set it up: That the residue of men might seek after the Lord, and all the Gentiles, upon whom my name is called, saith the Lord, who doeth all these things."

"T-E-M-P-L-E   W-I-L-L   N-O-T   B-E   I-N   J-E-R-U-S-A-L-E-M" Ouija stopped. "R-E-V-E-L-A-T-I-O-N   2-1   R-E-A-D
A-L-L"

Timmy read the first verse and then, "And I John saw the holy city, new Jerusalem, coming down from God out of heaven, prepared as a bride adorned for her husband. And I heard a great voice out of heaven saying, Behold, the tabernacle of God is with men, and he will dwell with them, and they shall be his people, and God himself shall be with them, and be their God. And God shall wipe away all tears from their eyes; and there shall be no more death, neither sorrow, nor crying, neither shall there be any more pain: for the former things are passed away.

The following verses described the new Jerusalem and then Timmy read, "And the twelve gates were twelve pearls: every several gates was of one pearl: and the street of the city was pure gold, as it were transparent glass. And I saw no temple therein: for the Lord God Almighty and the Lamb are the temple of it. And the city had no need of the sun, neither of the moon, to shine in it: for the glory of God did lighten it, and the Lamb is the light thereof."

"I A-M T-H-E T-E-M-P-L-E"

"Then what are we building?" Father queried.

"T-E-M-P-L-E F-O-R T-H-O-U-S-A-N-D Y-E-A-R-S O-F P-E-A-C-E"

"How can we do this?" Father asked shaking his head slowly.

"Z-E-C-H-A-R-I-A-H 6 1-5"

Again, Timmy read, "And they that are far off shall come and build in the temple of the Lord, and ye shall know that the Lord of hosts hath sent me unto you. And this shall come to pass, if ye will diligently obey the voice of the Lord your God."

"We can do it—if we obey?" Mother interpreted.

"M-A-L-A-C-H-I 3 1"

"Behold, I will send my messenger, and he shall prepare the way before me: and the Lord, whom ye seek, shall suddenly come to his temple, even the messenger of the covenant, whom ye delight in: behold, he shall come, saith the Lord of hosts."

"M-Y S-O-N W-I-L-L C-O-M-E" Ouija paused. "Y-O-U M-U-S-T B-U-I-L-D"

"Are you ready to give us the plans?" Father asked.

"Y-O-U R-E-A-D-Y T-O S-T-O-P S-M-O-K-I-N-G"

"Yes," Father said as he lowered his head and submitted.

"T-I-M T-A-K-E A-L-L C-I-G-A-R-E-T-T-E-S D-E-S-T-R-O-Y"

Father reached into his shirt pocket and pulled out a pack of Winstons. He handed them to Timmy. Then he straightened his leg and reached into his front pants pocket, where his fingers found the silver Zippo lighter he had owned for almost thirty years. He handed it begrudgingly to Timmy. Father cringed as Mother told Timmy to get the carton of cigarettes from the fridge and destroy them. Timmy gathered the ashtrays on the back porch and threw them in the trash.

Ouija was quiet, and as Timmy sat back down, it continued, "T-E-M-P-L-E I-S 6-0-0 F-E-E-T L-O-N-G 3-0-0 F-E-E-T W-I-D-E 3-0-0 F-E-E-T H-I-G-H"

"Wait a minute," Mother interrupted. "Diana, write the plans on a separate page and keep them apart from the rest of the notes." I nodded my head and complied.

"1-2 W-I-N-D-O-W-S E-A-C-H S-I-D-E" Ouija paused. "W-I-N-D-O-W-S 2-6-0 F-E-E-T H-I-G-H 2-0 F-E-E-T W-I-D-E"

"Those are huge windows," Father interrupted. "Are there window panes?"

"O-N-E P-I-E-C-E O-F G-L-A-S-S"

"Can that be done?" Mike asked, turning to Father.

The indicator went to YES.

I tried to envision this building, but it was bigger than my imagination.

"S-E-V-E-N W-I-N-D-O-W-S A-T T-H-E F-R-O-N-T" Ouija paused again.

"W-A-L-L-S O-F L-I-M-E-S-T-O-N-E 1-2 F-E-E-T L-O-N-G 6 F-E-E-T H-I-G-H"

Ouija paused so that I could catch up.

"L-I-M-E-S-T-O-N-E F-L-O-O-R-S" Ouija paused. "F-L-O-O-R-S G-O 1-0-0- F-E-E-T O-U-T-S-I-D-E W-A-L-L-S"

"There's a porch all the way around the building?" Father squinted as he tried to envision this.

The indicator moved to YES and Ouija continued, "I-N C-E-N-T-E-R I-S R-O-U-N-D F-O-U-N-T-A-I-N 1-4-4 F-E-E-T I-N D-I-A-M-E-T-E-R"

"Where does the water come from?" Father asked.

"F-R-O-M A-B-O-V-E" Ouija continued, "I-T I-S W-A-T-E-R O-F L-I-F-E"

"How are we going to run wires for electricity if the building is made of stone?"

"N-O E-L-E-C-T-R-I-C-I-T-Y N-E-E-D-E-D"

"Are there doors?" I asked.

"F-O-U-R D-O-U-B-L-E D-O-O-R-S A-T B-A-C-K E-A-C-H 2-0 F-E-E-T H-I-G-H"

"Are there pews?" Mother asked.

The indicator moved to NO.

"T-H-E-R-E I-S W-R-I-T-I-N-G O-V-E-R D-O-O-R-S"

"What is it?" I asked.

"E-N-T-E-R T-H-O-S-E W-H-O L-O-V-E P-E-A-C-E"

"What is the roof made of?" Father the practical asked.

"T-I-M-B-E-R-S C-O-V-E-R-E-D W-I-T-H S-H-E-E-T-S O-F G-O-L-D G-L-A-S-S"

"Will Levoy preach in this church?" Mother interrupted.

The indicator moved to NO.

"What denomination will it be?" Father was relieved.

"N-O-N-E"

"No religion?"

"R-E-L-I-G-I-O-N I-S W-H-A-T H-U-M-A-N-S D-O"

"I don't understand," Father said.

"T-H-I-S T-E-M-P-L-E I-S F-O-R A-L-L P-E-O-P-L-E"

"But, there are so many religions—how can they all worship in the same place?"

"N-O-T F-O-R W-O-R-S-H-I-P"

"What's it for?"

"P-E-A-C-E"

"So the people who come to this temple come for peace," Father said. "That's what they have in common?"

Ouija said YES.

Chapter 9

Getting Ready

Ouija refined the plans for the temple throughout the rest of September. We asked if there would be gold or silver anywhere in the temple, and God told us there would be no need for earthly riches there. We continued to practice Farsi on each other, and we waited for the letter. Every day we asked when it would come, and every day Ouija told us "soon." It felt like we were in purgatory—somewhere between heaven and hell, just waiting for others to decide our fate.

I told only one of my school friends about our pending move to Afghanistan. Soon, I was wishing I hadn't.

"So when are you leaving for Afghanistan?" my science teacher asked one day as he handed my homework to me. The question caught me off guard. How did he know? It hadn't occurred to me that my friend Judy would tell anyone about our mission.

"Soon," I repeated what Ouija had told us that morning. I hoped if I treated it as 'no big deal,' he would drop it.

"Who is sending you to Afghanistan?" he asked as he handed homework back to the boy in front of me. He had turned and was smiling down at me.

"The Nazarenes," I said. I knew it was a lie, but I couldn't tell him about Ouija.

"What do you have to do to be a missionary?" he held the papers against his chest as he looked full on into my face. I couldn't tell if he was taunting me or not.

"Study the Bible, the language," my voice trailed off, "you know."

"What's the language?" a voice yelled from the back of the class. Mr. Boone turned to see who had asked the question. It was Mark Hutchison, the kid I'd had a crush on since sixth grade.

"They speak Farsi," I said, "Salaam alaykum. It means hello, and goodbye. Mark smiled and responded, "Salaam alaykum." My heart jumped.

"Very good, Diana," Mr. Boone congratulated me and handed out the rest of the homework papers. Then he walked to the front of the classroom, where he began talking about volcanoes. My inquisition was over.

As Tricia and I stood side-by-side washing dishes that night, one of our favorite songs came on the transistor radio on the shelf above the sink. I turned up the volume, and we sang together.

Do you know the way to San Jose?
I've been away so long. I may go wrong and lose my way.
Do you know the way to San Jose?
I'm going back to find some peace of mind in San Jose.

L.A. is a great big freeway.
Put a hundred down and buy a car.
In a week, maybe two, they'll make you a star
Weeks turn into years. How quick they pass
And all the stars that never were
Are parking cars and pumping gas

Do you know the way to San Jose?
They've got a lot of space. There'll be a place where I can stay
I was born and raised in San Jose
I'm going back to find some peace of mind in San Jose.

Fame and fortune is a magnet.
It can pull you far away from home
With a dream in your heart you're never alone.
Dreams turn into dust and blow away
And there you are without a friend
You pack your car and ride away

I've got lots of friends in San Jose
Do you know the way to San Jose?
Can't wait to get back to San Jose.

We laughed uproariously as the DJ came back on. Tricia blew soap bubbles into my face and I snapped the dishtowel on her butt in retaliation. Mother yelled from the living room that we needed to quiet down. As I turned back to the dishes, I confided to Tricia about the inquisition at school, "Mr. Boone asked me in front of the whole class today when we were going to Afghanistan. I hope we get word soon."

"Me, too. Everybody keeps asking me when we're leaving," Tricia frowned as she folded the dish rag and hung it over the sink. "I wish I hadn't told them."

Mother told Aubrey and Geronimo that she didn't want them to come over that night because Father had been extremely irritable ever since he quit smoking. She made Father's favorite dinner—green chili burros—to help improve his mood. After we finished the dishes, we automatically assumed our positions around the Ouija board. As soon as Mother and Tricia's fingers touched the indicator, it started moving.

"I-T I-S T-I-M-E"

"Time for what?" Father asked happily as he grinned from ear-to-ear. None of us were prepared for what came next.

"T-I-M-E T-O S-E-L-L H-O-U-S-E"

Father's grin melted into a frown. "You have *got* to be kidding."

"I D-O N-O-T K-I-D"

"We have to sell our house?" Mike's jaw hung open.

"D-O Y-O-U P-R-E-F-E-R T-O G-I-V-E A-W-A-Y"

"But, this is crazy. We haven't even heard from the mission board. We can't sell our house," Mother said directly to Father.

"A-R-E Y-O-U C-A-L-L-I-N-G M-E C-R-A-Z-Y"

"No," Mother whispered.

"H-E-B-R-E-W-S 1-1 1"

Father opened his Bible and turned the pages gingerly to the verse, "Now faith is the substance of things hoped for, the evidence of things not seen."

"D-O Y-O-U B-E-L-I-E-V-E T-H-A-T I W-I-L-L S-E-N-D Y-O-U"

Father nodded his head slightly.

"P-R-O-V-E Y-O-U-R F-A-I-T-H"

Father closed his eyes and submitted, "What must I do?" As he did, he closed the Bible, holding his place subconsciously with his finger.

Ouija told us to sell the house to Ila Dee's sister and her husband for $1,000 down. When Father protested that we could get more money than that, Ouija scolded him, saying that Sissy and Sonny needed a house, and they could only afford to pay one thousand.

Mother called Ila Dee the next day and told her what Ouija had said. Ila was ecstatic—she had been trying to help her sister find a house to rent, and now she would own one. She thanked Mother profusely before they got off the phone.

Sissy and Sonny showed up that afternoon and worked out the details—they would give us a check and when their credit was approved, they would take over our mortgage. Mother and Father asked just one thing—that we be allowed to rent the house for $110 per month until we got our letter from the mission board. They eagerly agreed to our terms.

Ouija told us the letter would come soon, and that we needed to start selling our furniture, but keep our bedding and dishes. Sissy and Sonny had plenty of furniture of their own, but they had friends who needed some. So, each day after school, I would come home to less and less furniture. One day in early October, I came home and the sleeper sofa in our bedroom was gone.

"What are we going to sleep on?" I asked incredulously. She threw a quilt to me and pointed to the floor. Mike and Timmy laughed when they saw we had no bed, but they weren't laughing the next day when their bunk beds were missing.

Ila Dee called every day after we sold the house to her sister, wanting to know if we had gotten the letter yet. Mother told her that as soon as we got it, we'd leave. But, we sold most of our furniture, and the letter still hadn't come. The empty rooms and linoleum floors amplified every sound, an effect we enjoyed, but one that seemed to irritate Mother.

Ouija surprised us again shortly after that. "Y-O-U   M-U-S-T   B-U-Y   P-I-A-N-O"

Mother thought it was a joke. "Sure," she chuckled. "We sold all of our furniture, and now we gotta buy a piano—when no one in our house plays one."

"T-H-I-S   I-S   N-O-T   A   J-O-K-E"

"But, who's going to play it?" Mother was still laughing.

"P-A-T-R-I-C-I-A" Ouija paused and started again, "B-U-Y   U-S-E-D   P-I-A-N-O   F-O-R   1-0-0   D-O-L-L-A-R-S"

"But who's going to teach her to play?" Mother asked.

"I   W-I-L-L" it paused slightly, and then, "S-H-E   W-I-L-L   P-L-A-Y   I-N   T-E-M-P-L-E"

"Can I play too?" I asked. I had wanted to play the piano ever since learning how to read music in sixth grade chorus.

The indicator moved to NO. "J-U-S-T   P-A-T-R-I-C-I-A"

"That's not fair," I whined to Mother.

"Y-O-U   W-I-L-L   P-L-A-Y   O-T-H-E-R   I-N-S-T-R-U-M-E-N-T"

"What instrument?" I asked suspiciously.

"A-C-C-O-R-D-I-O-N"

Despite his misgivings about spending money and knowing what was ahead of us, Father told Mother to go ahead and buy a piano. She reached for the silver flour canister from the top shelf in the kitchen cupboard and whispered to me that it was the house and furniture money. She unscrewed the lid, counted $100, and then returned the canister to the shelf.

She found a piano in the newspaper the next day and sent Father and Mike to buy it sight unseen. They rolled the ancient piano up a ramp and onto the bed of the pickup truck and brought it home that afternoon. Besides the piano, all we had left was the TV and some lawn chairs. Tricia bought some beginning piano books and practiced diligently for two hours every day after that.

And then on October 12th two things happened.

Mother and Father were watching the evening news in their lawn chairs with the four us sprawled on the floor at their feet. The announcer started the broadcast by talking about the disruption at the Olympic Games. Tommie Smith and John Carlos, U.S. athletes in the 200-meter dash, were shown with bowed heads, with one fisted hand raised, while the "Star-Spangled Banner" played.

The announcer said it was the black power salute, and the athletes said they were doing it in sympathy for the Africans who boycotted the games because of South Africa's participation.

"What's wrong with South Africa?" I asked.

Mike sat up and thumped me on the shoulder. "Don't you know anything ignoramus?"

"Stop it," I punched him in retaliation.

"South Africa is segregated. The whites took the land from the native Africans and then made them slaves."

Now I understood. Last year, after Father retired from the Air Force, we moved to Mississippi for seven months so Father could help granddaddy

Furtick build an A-Frame house for some people. We registered at Kossuth Middle School, which was segregated then.

"So, what's wrong with that?" I asked about the athlete on the television screen.

Father's face turned crimson and he scowled, "Goddamned communists, that's what they are. They have no respect for America." Mike opened his mouth to respond when a banging on the front door stopped him.

Mother opened the door and there stood the sheriff.

"Mrs. Cain?" he asked. Mother nodded and stared blankly at him. "Consider yourself served with this eviction notice," he said matter-of-factly as he handed the papers over. "You have twenty days to remove you and your family from these premises." He turned abruptly and walked back to his patrol car.

Mother stared at the sheriff's back as he walked away. Father snatched the folded papers out of Mother's hand and sat back down. We turned off the TV and sat on the floor at her feet as he read out loud.

"It says that Sissy and Sonny own this house, and they want to take possession by October 31," he read shakily.

"What are we going to do, Levoy?" Mother pleaded.

"Why don't we ask God?" Tricia was already sitting at the kitchen table. Tears welled in Mother's eyes as she joined Tricia.

"Lord, why are you letting this happen?" Mother cried.

"F-R-E-E W-I-L-L"

"But, Lord, did you know this was going to happen?" Mother asked.

The indicator moved slowly to YES.

"Why didn't you tell us?" she demanded angrily.

"D-O Y-O-U B-E-L-I-E-V-E Y-O-U W-I-L-L G-O T-O A-F-G-H-A-N-I-S-T-A-N"

"Yes," Mother nodded her head adamantly.

"T-H-E-N W-H-A-T D-O-E-S I-T M-A-T-T-E-R"

I waited for Father's inevitable fiery explosion, but it never came. He sat with slumped shoulders in the lawn chair and looked at the linoleum beneath his boots.

"Lord, what are we going to do?" Mother asked.

"S-E-L-L T-R-U-C-K R-E-N-T U-H-A-U-L M-O-V-E T-O—"

"To where?" Mother was shocked.

"S-A-N F-R-A-N-C-I-S-C-O"

"But, Levoy doesn't have a job, and we've got only two thousand dollars. What are we going to do for money?"

"H-A-V-E F-A-I-T-H"

"But why can't we stay here until the letter comes?" Father interrupted Mother as she was about to answer.

"S-A-N F-R-A-N-C-I-S-C-O I-S J-U-M-P-I-N-G O-F-F P-O-I-N-T F-O-R A-F-G-H-A-N-I-S-T-A-N"

Mother and Father talked all night in their bedroom. I strained in my bed to make out what they were saying, but they were barely audible. The next morning, Mother was up at dawn and told us we didn't have to go to Sunday school. She wanted to tell Ouija that we were going to move to San Francisco on faith. We would leave town on October 30th.

After we talked to Ouija, Mother called Ila Dee and asked her how Sissy could have done this to us after all we did for her.

Ila Dee didn't mince words with Mother, "What the hell, Mary. You sell them your house, and then you want to live in it indefinitely? They can't wait until some day in the future when you might get a letter. What if you never get a letter? Then what?" She hung up on Mother.

Aunt Edith was even less sympathetic when Mother phoned her. We could hear Edith's yelling from across the kitchen. "Mary Frances, it serves you right for selling your house to a white woman and a nigger. How could you have done this to me—and the rest of your neighbors? We don't want no mixed race yungins' around here."

"Edith, we are all the same color in God's eyes," Mother countered.

"Well, not in my eyes. Oh, and Mary," she paused for effect. "Aubrey told me what's going on over there. He won't be coming to your house anymore. And, you can just forget taking *my* son anywhere with you. We want nothing to do with you as long as Satan is running your lives." Then she hung up on Mother.

Mother slowly replaced the receiver on its cradle. "I guess you heard that. She doesn't want Sonny in her neighborhood because he's colored. And she calls herself a Christian."

It suddenly dawned on me that everyone in town must know about the Ouija board—even the kids at church and school. The same thought must have occurred to Mother because she told us we didn't have to go to school anymore. Father told Unidynamics that he resigned effective October 30th. One of his old Air Force buddies bought his pickup for three hundred dollars. The day he drove it away, Father stood in the driveway with his arms folded across his chest for a minute and stared at the road where his truck had been. Mother dropped him off at work for the next week.

We sold or gave away everything that wouldn't fit in the back of the station wagon and a ten foot U-Haul trailer. Ouija instructed us to buy a footlocker at Penney's for our sheets and towels, and other items that we wouldn't be able to buy in Afghanistan.

Penney's was in Phoenix. We had never shopped at a fancy department store before, so we took our time roaming up and down the aisles, touching all the pretty clothes. We finally found a green footlocker and brought it home.

Ouija told us we would need jackets in Afghanistan because it was colder there, so Mother took us to Goodwill. I picked out a white vinyl double-breasted car coat. She gave each of us one suitcase for our clothes. It was up to us to get everything we owned into the suitcase.

Packing and getting rid of our belongings consumed most of our time up until the 28th. On that day, Father expressed concern about the move and the safety of his family.

"Y-O-U H-A-V-E G-U-A-R-D-I-A-N A-N-G-E-L"

"Well, it would sure make me feel better if I could see my angel," Father laughed.

"A-L-L R-I-G-H-T"

We smiled at each other and turned in our chairs to look for an angel when Ouija continued.

"Y-O-U-R A-N-G-E-L I-S A-T T-H-E D-O-G P-O-U-N-D"

Mike spit the milk out of his mouth and laughed, "Our angel is a *dog*?"

The indicator moved to YES. "A-N A-N-G-E-L I-N T-H-E D-O-G"

"We have to get a dog?" Mother mumbled. "We have never had a pet, and now we have to get a *dog* when we're moving?"

"T-O P-R-O-T-E-C-T Y-O-U"

"Will they even allow a dog in Afghanistan?" Mother was grasping for any reason not to get a dog. She hated dogs.

The indicator slid to YES again.

"What will the dog look like?" Timmy asked, smiling.

"Y-O-U W-I-L-L K-N-O-W W-H-E-N Y-O-U S-E-E H-I-M"

Father leaned back in the lawn chair and rested his elbows on the chair arm. His mouth was covered by his right hand, and he raised his eyebrows as Ouija talked, but said nothing.

When we finished talking to Ouija, we went to the Avondale dog pound across the tracks. It stank of dirty dogs, urine and poop, and formaldehyde. There must have been 50 dogs in the chain link pens—sometimes five or six in one pen.

I walked behind my family, eyes fixed on the concrete floor. I couldn't make myself look at the pitiful dogs. The foul stench was making me sick to my stomach. How would we be able to find our angel from among these poor animals? Just then, I heard Timmy's voice a few pens in front of me.

"This is the one," he shouted as he squatted and threaded his fingers through the chain links.

"Get your hand out of there," Father commanded. "He'll bite you."

"No, he won't," Timmy answered. He was petting a long-haired red dog. The dog licked Timmy. He had bright brown eyes and a smile as he looked at each of us. The keeper told us that it was a male collie and spaniel mix probably not older than three.

"He's a quiet one, this dog. We picked him up this morning. He hasn't barked since he got here," the keeper scratched his head. "He's mighty lucky."

"This is the one," Tricia pronounced. Mother smiled and petted the dog's nose.

"We'll take this one," Father said to the keeper. After shots and care instructions from the keeper, the dog was ours. He willingly jumped into the back of our station wagon. On the way home, he drooled on my shoulder and panted in my ear. Then he licked my neck. It tickled. What a great dog, I thought. As soon as we got home, Timmy and I gave him a quick bath. We asked Ouija if he was the right dog.

"O-F C-O-U-R-S-E"

"Let's name him Laddie," Timmy said as he hugged the dog's soft fur.

The indicator went to NO. Timmy and I exchanged worried glances. Then Ouija continued, "I-S-A-I-A-H 4-1 8"

Mike read, "But thou, Israel, art my servant, Jacob whom I have chosen, the seed of Abraham my friend."

"Are we naming it Abraham?" I asked.

The indicator went to NO again. "F-R-I-E-N-D O-F G-O-D"

"That's a mouthful," Mother said.

"H-E I-S M-Y F-R-I-E-N-D" Ouija paused. "H-E W-I-L-L P-R-O-T-E-C-T"

Timmy and I volunteered to take care of Friend of God. We got a bowl from the box of dishes and immediately filled it with tap water. He lapped it up and stood smiling at us when he was finished. Since we had no dog food, we gave him table scraps after dinner. Timmy was in charge of poop.

Father picked up the U-Haul trailer from the dealership and brought it home the next morning. We assembled everything that was going with us in one room, and Father surveyed its mass. He meticulously planned how he would pack the trailer—around the piano, of course.

In all of the excitement, someone left the front door open, and Friend escaped. Timmy and I chased him down the street, but he was too fast for us. We lost sight of him at the intersection of Holly Lane and Central Avenue.

I couldn't believe it. Our guardian angel ran away from home. When we got back home, Mother was standing in the front yard, hands on hips, shaking her head, "What kind of a guardian angel is this who leaves his family?" she asked looking skyward.

We drove around the neighborhood, calling "Friend" from the open windows. We extended our geographic search, but never even got a glimpse of him. Later, we asked Ouija why Friend left.

"H-E H-A-D S-O-M-E-T-H-I-N-G T-O D-O F-R-I-E-N-D W-I-L-L B-E B-A-C-K"

"He's a *dog*." Mike scowled. "What could he have to do? He's not coming back."

"Y-O-U C-O-N-T-I-N-U-E T-O D-O-U-B-T M-I-C-H-A-E-L"

"He doesn't know where we live," Mike insisted. "He's a *dog*."

"H-E W-I-L-L"

That night, Mother picked up hamburgers for dinner from A&W. Father had packed the trailer and hitched it to the station wagon by the time she got back. The station wagon was riding low from the weight of the trailer.

We sat on the floor cross-legged and started to eat our hamburgers when we heard a loud scratching on the front door. Mike opened the front door and there sat Friend, looking hungry and tired.

"I can't believe it," Mike laughed.

"Did you finish your business?" Mother cooed to Friend as she tore her hamburger in half and offered the bigger half to the dog.

"D-O Y-O-U B-E-L-I-E-V-E N-O-W" Ouija asked Mike after we finished dinner.

Mike laughed and nodded his head.

"Y-O-U W-O-R-K-E-D H-A-R-D" Ouija congratulated us. "N-O-W H-A-V-E F-U-N"

"What do you mean?" Father was suspicious.

"G-O T-O D-I-S-N-E-Y-L-A-N-D"

Mother clapped her hands together, "Buford lives near there. We can stay with him."

Father's face froze. Buford was Mother's oldest son. He had just served three tours of duty in Vietnam, where he had been shot twice and contracted malaria. Now he lived in Chula Vista, California, and was a drill sergeant at Camp Pendleton.

"Disneyland is expensive, and we're going to need our money to live in San Francisco."

"M-Y F-A-M-I-L-Y N-E-E-D-S R-E-S-T B-E-F-O-R-E M-I-S-S-I-O-N"

Ouija was insistent, so Mother called Buford to ask if we could stay with him and go to Disneyland. He told her that we should plan on spending at least three hundred dollars at Disneyland for a family of six, what with food and all. That's a lot of money.

"This is not wise," Father voiced his objection later that night. "We've already spent five hundred dollars getting ready to move. This will leave us with only twelve hundred."

"H-A-V-E F-A-I-T-H"

Father finally got excited about the move after dinner that night. The electricity had already been turned off, so we all curled up on our blankets in the living room and went to bed when the sun went down.

I laid there staring at the ceiling for the longest time. Ouija had told us to do something that was bothering me. It just didn't seem very 'Christian.' Ouija had told us to leave the house dirty and leave a key hanging from the ceiling that they could see through the window.

"But they'll have to break the window to get to the key," Mother said.

The indicator moved to YES.

Ouija dictated a letter that I placed in an envelope and taped to the outside of the front door.

Dear Miss Graham,

Thank you for letting us live in the house these past few weeks. It would have been better for you if you had not behaved so badly, though. God is offended that you treated his family this way.

Mary and Levoy Cain

"But, Lord, why are you addressing the letter to her as a 'Miss?'" Mother asked. "She's married."

The indicator moved eerily from letter to letter, "C-A-N-T S-A-Y"

Chapter 10

Embarking on the Mission

I was awake when the sun peeked over the eastern mountains the next morning. Dressing quickly, we rolled our blankets and wolfed down doughnuts. Then we waited for Geronimo. Promptly at five-thirty, his '52 Lincoln rumbled onto our street. I was surprised that he drove himself. He was supposed to ride with us—how was his car going to get back to his house?

He gingerly closed his car door so as not to wake the neighbors, I guessed. Then he walked across the grass to where Tricia was standing with blankets in her arms, smiling at him.

"I'm not going," he said kindly as he got close enough for her to hear.

"What do you mean?" she pleaded. "I thought you wanted to go."

"No, *you* wanted me to go," he said as he rubbed her shoulder with his hand. "My Mother needs me here. I can't leave her. Do you understand?"

"God wanted you to go," Tricia corrected him as she gazed into his eyes.

"I can't," he said. "Call me when you get settled, and I'll come visit you." He kissed her on her mouth lightly and backed away, touching his lips with three fingers to blow her a kiss. Then he turned and walked back to his car. He hesitated before turning the key. Then he started the engine and was gone.

Tricia's eyes filled with tears as she ran sobbing into the house. Father and Mother had just come out and hadn't witnessed the exchange. They looked at Mike, who shrugged his shoulders. "The Indian's not going," he said callously as he threw a pillow into the back of the station wagon.

I told them what happened and they consoled Tricia for the next fifteen minutes outside the bathroom door. She finally came out, and we loaded ourselves and our dog into the car. When the last car door slammed shut, Father turned the key and nothing happened. He slapped the steering wheel and cursed it.

"Just what I need now," he said as he tried again. The engine roared to life, and the car idled while Father held his foot on the brake. He and Mother exchanged teary-eyed glances without saying a word. I was suddenly suffocated by the feeling that we were being run out of town because we had done something wrong. I choked back tears and said goodbye to our house and to Avondale.

The eight-hour drive across the desert was mercifully without incident, and we pulled up in front of Buford's house at around two o'clock. Buford and Aida told us they would join us at Disneyland the next day with their children, Little Mike and Brenda.

After dinner, Buford casually brought up a subject he had never discussed with Mother, "Mom, you've never been religious. When did you and pop get the calling to be missionaries? I mean, how did it happen?"

"Have you ever heard of a Ouija Board?" Mother responded.

"No," Buford said. "What's that got to do with it?"

Mother gave Buford the condensed version of our story. He and Aida listened intently and then looked at each other when Mother had finished. "You think it's God?" he asked incredulously. "And you're going to travel all the way around the world because it told you to?" His smile faded into cynicism.

"It proved it's God," Mother said. "Do you want to talk to the spirit?"

Aida spoke for both of them then, "No, we don't want to talk to no spirit, mom."

"Pop, do you believe this?" Buford asked Father, whose head was bowed, and who up until that point had stayed out of the conversation.

"Most of the time I do," Father grinned and nodded. "A lot of strange things have happened because of Ouija, Buford. Sometimes I have doubts, but I wouldn't have sold my house if I didn't believe."

We switched to a safer topic of conversation after that, one I was very interested in—what we would do at Disneyland. We decided to split up into groups and meet at pre-arranged times and locations.

We arose early the next morning for the two-hour drive to Disneyland. When we pulled into the parking lot, I was overwhelmed. I was sure that the parking lot alone was bigger than all of Avondale. As we stood by the car, Father handed each of us forty dollars—for ride tickets and food throughout the day. He made us synchronize our watches and confirmed our next meeting time and location. Then we split up. Little Mike went with the boys and Brenda came with Tricia and me. The grown-ups stayed together. That was the last time we saw each other that day.

Tricia and I missed the first meeting time because we underestimated the line time for It's a Small World. We finally got to the gates at Frontier Land almost an hour after we were supposed to be there. None of our family showed up for the next 30 minutes, so we decided to continue riding. We had never been to a large amusement park before and were a little nervous, but our sheer joy of being there overcame our fear. Then we missed the second meeting time because of long lines.

We agreed to keep a sharp eye out for relatives. Since we never saw them, we decided we would just meet them at six o'clock—the time we knew we were leaving. It sounded like a good plan to us.

We started looking for the car at six o'clock, but finding it was not as easy as we thought it would be. Neither of us had paid attention when Father parked, and now it was dark. We had no choice but to systematically walk up and down rows of cars until we spotted our blue and white Plymouth. We were relieved when we saw Mother and Father standing at the end of one of the rows. Relief turned to apprehension, however, as we drew closer to them.

They spotted us and before we could say anything, Mother screamed, "Where the hell have you been?" She walked up to Tricia and slapped her shoulder. "We've been looking for you all day. Why weren't you where you were supposed to be?"

At the same time, Buford twisted Brenda's hand out of mine and screamed at me, "Brenda is only four years old. Didn't you think we'd be worried? This is the last goddamn time you'll take care of my daughter." He handed his daughter over to his wife as he glared at me.

Father's twisted face was screaming as he jabbed his forefinger into Tricia's face and yelled, "You two don't have a goddamn brain between you."

Streams of sweat poured down Mother's face and neck and her clothes were sweat-soaked. I didn't think it was that hot. She stood next to Father and screamed at Tricia, "We've been standing in this god-awful heat for two damn hours. We were just about to call the police."

Father spun on his heels and jammed his hands into his back pockets, "We never should have come here," he bellowed at the sky. "We don't have money to waste on this shit." And then he pointed his finger in Mother's face, "This is all your fault."

"How dare you." Mother screamed back. "I had nothing to do with this."

"You're behind the board, you know it," his twisted face was an inch from hers.

Buford stepped between the two and started, "Pop, just a—"

"Buford, don't." Mother's face was determined as she pushed Buford aside and stood in front of her husband. "I can take care of myself. Levoy just shut up about the goddamned money. That's all you've talked about all day. In case you forgot, I didn't want to come here either."

It was then that I noticed people were standing by their cars—watching and whispering. My throat closed and hot tears burned my eyes. I couldn't breathe. Forgotten in all the commotion, I slid down the side of the car and dropped onto the hot pavement, where I covered my ears with my hands and sobbed uncontrollably. My mind screamed, "Please God, make this stop."

Buford must have noticed the crowd gathering and lowered his voice, "Mom, let it go. People are watching."

"I don't care who the hell sees us," Mother yelled at her son. Buford threw his hands up in the air and ushered his family as far away as possible. Mother and Father continued screaming at each other, rehashing their entire lives in front of what I thought was the world.

Buford watched from a distance, and when the fight seemed to die down, he returned, "Can we leave now?" He didn't wait for a response as he waved his family into their car.

As soon as we got back to Buford's house, it started again. Friend had gotten out of his pen, chewed the hose into pieces, and scratched gaping holes into the patio screen door. By the time we walked into the back yard, Buford was herding Friend back into the pen.

"What possessed you to get a dog when you are going overseas?" he was frustrated from his exertion at chasing Friend around the yard.

"Buford, we'll pay for the damage he's done," Father offered lamely.

"You don't have the money," Buford said. "Just leave tomorrow."

That night, Mother and Tricia reluctantly sat down on the bed in Mother's room and placed their hands on the indicator.

It didn't move for a few seconds, and then it crept from letter to letter, "A-S-H-A-M-E-D"

"It was all Levoy's fault—" Mother started.

"Y-O-U W-E-R-E T-E-S-T-E-D Y-O-U F-A-I-L-E-D"

"But we're only human," Father replied.

The indicator slid to GOODBYE.

Buford and Aida said very little the next morning. They wished us luck and politely said their goodbyes in the driveway. I turned in the seat to wave goodbye, but I decided not to when I saw the disgusted look on Buford's face as he shook his head and turned his back on us.

Eventually, we apologized to each other on the drive that morning. We had given in to the devil. It was not one person's fault. We were just human, after all. I tried especially hard to be good the rest of the way to San Francisco. We spent one night at a motel near Carmel, where we asked Ouija for instructions for the next day.

"G-O T-O B-E-R-K-E-L-E-Y"

"But isn't that where the hippies are?" Mother asked.

"All right!" Mike approved. "We're going to Haight Ashbury. I can't wait."

"Y-E-S M-I-K-E"

Father mapped out our route that night, and we set out early the next morning. With any luck, we'd arrive in San Francisco by noon. Of course, as luck would have it, we ran out of gas somewhere south of San Jose.

"How could we run out of gas?" Mother squealed. "Isn't the gauge working? Are you sure we ran out of gas?"

"The gauge says we have gas," Father was calm as he opened the hood of the car and checked the hoses and belts. "We should have had enough gas to drive a hundred miles." He stood next to the car and looked first in front of the car and then behind it. "The last exit was twenty miles behind us. I'm going to hitch a ride to the next exit," he said as he opened the trailer doors and grabbed the emergency gas can.

"Well, the devil's really tempting us today," Mother said as she dabbed sweat from her forehead with a tissue.

Father nodded as he walked to the front of the car and held the gas can in one hand and held up his thumb to hitch a ride. After a few minutes, a Chevy truck pulled over, and the driver pointed to the pickup bed. Father jumped in and waved goodbye to us. We waited restlessly for him to return for more than an hour. Finally, on the other side of the freeway a red pickup stopped, and Father jumped out. He crossed six lanes of traffic and a concrete barrier to get back to us. He had enough gas to take us to the next gas station.

Mother was unusually nice to Father after he poured the gas into the tank. "Thanks, Levoy." Father nodded distractedly as he entered the mayhem of the San Francisco highway system. We were back on the road again and only a hundred miles from our destination. As traffic got thicker and faster on the freeway, Father's shoulders stiffened. I thought his huge hands would crush the thin blue steering wheel.

We exited the freeway at University Avenue and realized that we were in the heart of Berkeley—right at Haight and Ashbury Streets. It was nothing like Avondale. I pressed my face against the car window and stared in awe.

College students were everywhere—at least I assumed they were college students. It was a cool 70 degrees; and the girls wore peasant shirts or dresses; and the boys were shirtless and wore cutoff jeans. Most wore sandals, but some were shoeless. I watched one couple holding hands as they walked. They were elated when they saw another couple approaching. They all hugged and kissed, and then the girls joined hands and the four continued walking.

I rolled down my window so I could better hear the street sounds. Musicians played on every corner, and small crowds gathered around them, dancing and laughing. Tambourines jangled to the sounds of strumming guitars and saxophones. The street smells blended together, but I could make out the smell of incense, curried food, cigarettes and what I thought was marijuana smoke, and sewage. The smells overpowered me, and I drew in my breath. I finally exhaled when I spotted a girl carrying a flower. "It's a flower child," I said wide-eyed. Tricia and I broke out into song, "Are You Going to San Francisco." As far as I was concerned, Berkeley was better than fireworks. Mother and Father didn't seem to share my enthusiasm.

"I'm not living with these hippies," Mother spat.

We drove up and down hills on two-lane streets for hours, looking for what I didn't know. I guess we were searching for a rental sign, but school had started, and there was not an apartment to be found within ten miles of Berkeley. Father clenched the steering wheel so tightly that his knuckles had turned stone white. I felt wretched after being in the car for fourteen hours. At around eight that evening, Mother said, "Levoy, if you don't get me out of this car soon, I'm gonna have a breakdown."

Father spotted a run-down motel just ahead and pulled into its parking lot. He left us in the car and went to the registration desk. He triumphantly returned five minutes later, dangling a key in his left hand. "We've got a room," he said as he closed the car door. A room?

With only one bathroom, it took an hour to get everyone showered and ready for bed. A shower never felt so good. Mother and Tricia were already at the Ouija board when I finished my shower.

"Lord, what are we going to do?" Mother asked. She seemed truly frightened. Our situation was weighing heavy on her, I could tell. Even I recognized that we were in a precarious situation. We had no home, furniture, or food. We had very little money and no income in sight.

"F-E-A-R N-O-T"

"There are no places to live here," Father said. "Where should we go?"

"O-A-K-L-A-N-D O-R V-A-L-L-E-J-O"

Father's eyes lit up. "Daryl is stationed on Mare Island in Vallejo," he said. Daryl was Daddy's second son by Clara, she who shall not be mentioned, and I had never met him in all my life.

"G-O T-H-E-R-E"

Ouija told us that it would be easier to search for an apartment in Vallejo if we dropped the trailer at a gas station first. Then it signed off, and we went to sleep—Mother and Father took the bed, and we slept on the floor. Friend curled up at Timmy's feet.

We crossed the toll bridge into Vallejo around noon the next day. Several gas station owners turned us down when we asked to leave our trailer. We happened upon a gas station that was a U-Haul dealer, and the owner agreed we could leave the trailer there for the day.

It must not have occurred to Mother and Father that apartments might be difficult to find because of Vallejo's close proximity to the naval station on Mare Island. We stopped at more than ten apartment buildings inquiring about the availability of a two-bedroom apartment. At six o'clock, we had run out of options when Mike spied a 'for rent' sign in one of the smaller buildings. Mother and Father came out of the building clapping their hands excitedly.

"She was all set to rent us a two-bedroom, but when I told her we had a dog, she changed her mind," Mother said. "But then she told us there was a hotel in downtown Vallejo that has an apartment building right next to it."

She looked at Father and said, "I don't think we should tell them about Friend. We have got to find a place by dark or I'm going to go crazy."

As we pulled into the parking lot at the Casa De Vallejo Hotel, the car bottomed out. "Everyone, stay in the car," Father ordered as he slammed the door behind him.

We took it as a good sign that he was gone for half an hour. "We've got a one-bedroom furnished apartment," he said triumphantly as he finally approached the car. "He said it was too small for six people, but I talked him into it. I told him we wouldn't be here long."

The apartment was on the third floor of one of the buildings adjacent to the hotel. I stood at the bottom of the stairs at the back of the building and looked up in awe. I had never lived anywhere with stairs before. Mother stood beside me and followed my stare, "I sure hope we don't have to be here long," she quipped as she turned to Father. "How are you planning to get a piano up three flights of stairs?" Father grinned and shrugged his shoulders. "I have no idea," he said.

I ran up the stairs, anxious to see our new home. A small kitchen overlooked the parking lot in the back. The living room was a good size and had everything but a TV. A bathroom was off a small hallway that led to the only bedroom at the front of the apartment. A door opened onto a balcony above Sonoma Boulevard. It was small, but we wouldn't be there long.

I stood at the top of the stairs looking at the parking lot below. Everyone was carrying a load from the trailer, and Timmy stood at the bottom of the steps, tugging on Friend's leash. "He won't go on the stairs," he shouted to Father as he looked up the three flights of stairs.

"Then carry him," Father yelled back.

Mother stood in the middle of the living room and directed the placement of boxes and luggage. "Where are we all going to sleep?" Mike said as he surveyed the small apartment.

"The girls will sleep on the sofa bed, and you two boys will sleep on cots in the bedroom," she said pointing down the short hall. "It's only for a little while."

Later that day, Mr. Beck, the hotel manager, told Father we could store the piano in a little room in the hotel garage.

Mother called the Nazarene Mission Board early the next morning and gave them our new address. Father returned the U-Haul the next day and called Daryl from a pay phone in the hotel lobby.

"I'd like to see you, Daryl," he said as he twisted the cord around his finger. I could hear his conversation from where I sat in the lobby. He listened as Daryl talked, and then answered, "Because I want to get to know you. I haven't seen you since you were a baby, Daryl. I want you to meet your brothers and sisters." Daryl must have agreed because Father responded, "When will you be off duty? I'll pick you up." They arranged to meet the next Saturday afternoon at the guard gate on Mare Island.

Tricia was anxious to practice piano, but Mother said the garage was too dark and unsafe for her to go alone. So I had to go with her. Each afternoon, we crossed the street to the hotel and went to the piano room in the garage. I usually sat on the cold concrete floor and listened as Tricia strained to see the notes on the page in the poorly lit room. After she perfected each hymn, we sang it together.

Every morning and evening, Timmy and I would take our guardian angel for a walk. Friend refused to go anywhere near the stairs, so we took turns carrying him up and down. We tried everything to get him used to the steps, but he would just cock his head to one side until we gave in and carried him.

Father left the apartment by seven o'clock each morning to go to the hotel coffee shop, where he'd have three cups of coffee and buy a local paper. He used the hotel pay phone to call on jobs he found in the paper. On the fifth day of this routine, he came back early and announced proudly that he had gotten a maintenance job at the hotel.

"I T-O-L-D Y-O-U I W-O-U-L-D P-R-O-V-I-D-E"

"Thank you, Lord," Mother gushed.

"T-H-E C-H-I-L-D-R-E-N M-U-S-T G-O T-O S-C-H-O-O-L"

"What?" Mother was dumbfounded. "I thought we were leaving soon?"

The indicator slid to YES.

"Then why enroll them in school?" she asked again.

"T-H-E-Y N-E-E-D T-O B-E I-N S-C-H-O-O-L"

What a relief, I thought. There were no other children in the hotel, and we were getting bored walking the dog and watching TV.

"Well, all right," Mother acquiesced and called that afternoon to enroll Mike in Vallejo High School. Tricia, Timmy and I rode the bus in the opposite direction to Franklin Junior High School.

Mother found a Nazarene Church across town that we began attending. Father worked days, and so we saw him a lot more than we did in Avondale. He worked on Sundays so he couldn't go to our new church. Mother spent Saturday afternoons "witnessing" to anyone who would listen at the Sonoma Boulevard Laundromat.

We settled back into a routine with Ouija. Out of boredom—and to escape the isolation of the apartment, Mother made daily visits to the public library. In between witnessing to the librarian and other unsuspecting readers, she checked out every available book on the history of Persia. She was fascinated by Genghis Khan, and she made us listen to her read her books after dinner.

Timmy and I spent most of the weekends at the park with Friend, where we'd dawdle for as long as possible, doing anything we could to stay away from the tiny apartment. We watched as Navy ships came and went. On many occasions, we'd sit on the bay's embankment, with feet dangling, enjoying the salty sea breeze that never tired of blowing.

We sat for hours sunning ourselves and listening to Mike's worn transistor radio. I smiled as Otis Redding's "Sitting on the Dock of the Bay" made its way to my ears in between crackling sounds from the radio. I realized how far I was from the desert, and I missed it.

* * *

Meeting Daryl for the first time was intimidating. His six foot seven inch body towered above me. He took my small hand in his as he introduced himself. I was transfixed by his brown eyes—so different from the blue eyes that dominated my family. Daryl was nineteen when he joined the Navy, and he had been at Mare Island since the summer before.

"Why did you move to Vallejo, dad?" he asked suddenly as we waited for Mother to put dinner on the table that first Saturday.

Father shushed us with his eyes and told the story to Daryl, leaving out the Ouija board. He told Daryl that we were going to be missionaries and had been told to move to Vallejo by the Nazarenes.

"How long will you be here?" he asked.

"Not long," Father said as Mother set a dish of pinto beans in front of him.

We genuinely liked Daryl and Mother asked him to come for dinner again the next weekend. On the third weekend, Father picked him up on Friday night, and he spent the weekend with us. By then, we knew we had to tell him the truth about Ouija. We couldn't go that many hours without talking to Ouija.

"Daryl, remember how I told you the mission board was going to send us to Afghanistan?" Father began. Daryl nodded and Father continued, "Well, that's true, but God speaks to us through a Ouija board. Do you know what that is?"

Daryl squinted his eyes and looked from Father to Mother. "Yes," he said slowly. "But I never heard of God speaking through one."

"We weren't going to tell you, but God wants you to know the truth. He wants to talk to you," Mother said. She reached under the sofa and pulled the Ouija board out. Daryl was surprised to see her do this. She placed it between her and Tricia and the indicator immediately started moving.

"H-E-L-L-O D-A-R-Y-L"

"Hello," he replied warily.

"H-O-W I-S Y-O-U-R S-O-U-L"

Daryl seemed surprised by the question, but he answered honestly, "Fine, I think. Who are you?"

"J-E-H-O-V-A-H"

"So, why are you talking to me?" Daryl seemed puzzled, as if he didn't belong in this story.

"Y-O-U H-A-V-E Q-U-E-S-T-I-O-N-S"

"Yes," Daryl said sheepishly looking at us. "Will I marry?"

The indicator slid to YES. "Y-O-U W-I-L-L M-A-R-R-Y S-O-O-N"

"Are you seeing someone?" Father asked Daryl.

"Yes, Sue," Daryl answered quietly. From then on, he seemed comfortable talking to the Ouija board. He asked many questions about his own life and about our mission. Ouija answered all of Daryl's questions that night and every night after.

The Saturday after Thanksgiving, Timmy returned with the mail from the hotel. He bounded up the stairs, two at a time, and clutched a letter in his right hand, "It's here. It's here." he screamed as he tripped on the last step. My heart jumped in my chest.

"Give it to me," Mother said as she snatched the letter from Timmy's hands. A smile crossed Father's face and stretched from ear to ear. Mother tore open the envelope and read quickly at first, and then slower.

```
Dear Mr. Cain,

Although we believe that God has called you
for a mission, The Church of the Nazarene is
unable to offer your family a post as
missionaries in Afghanistan as you requested.
It is our policy to send young, single,
college graduates on overseas missions.
Additionally, even if you met our criteria, we
would not be able to send you to Afghanistan
because of strict government restrictions on
Christian evangelism. It is a Muslim country.
God bless you.

Your friend in God, Dr. Phillips
```

The letter slipped from her hand and floated hopelessly to the floor. We sat stunned at first. Mother broke the silence, "What are we going to do?" she shrieked as tears welled up in her eyes.

Timmy and I cowered near the stairwell in anticipation of Father's reaction. He looked dazed, frozen with fear. In an instant his fear was replaced by anger. He pushed Mother away from him with both hands. Friend immediately responded by snarling at Father. Father kicked at him, which made him even more ferocious. Timmy kneeled next to his dog and held him back, "No, Friend. It's ok."

Father ignored the dog and bent over in front of Mother, who by then had sunk back into the couch in dismay. He scowled as he counted on his fingers in front of her face, "We believed. We studied the Bible. We sold our house. I quit my job. We moved to San Francisco. We did our part," he was yelling loud enough by then for the neighbors to hear. He paused and then pronounced, "God didn't do his part."

"I think it's a test of our faith," Mother said resolutely.

"Don't you get it?" Father screamed at her as he jammed his index finger into his temple, "It's not God." He looked from Mother to Tricia and pronounced calmly, "I don't know what it is, but it's not God." He turned and stomped down the stairs and out of the apartment.

"I don't think it's God, either," Mike crossed his arms and scowled at Mother and Tricia, standing his ground.

Timmy and I exchanged worried glances. My heart's pounding was so loud I was sure everyone could hear it. Then I felt it rise in my chest, past my stomach and get stuck in my throat. I couldn't swallow. Fear was welling up in my tear ducts and stinging my eyes.

My mind grew frantic. What was going to happen to us? Would we stay in California or move back to Avondale? There was no way I could go back to Avondale after having told everyone we were going to Afghanistan to be missionaries. They would think I was the biggest liar in town.

In the midst of my despair, Mother sat down deliberately at the Ouija board and motioned for Tricia to join her. It struck me that Tricia seemed more stunned than I was. She hadn't spoken or moved the entire time dad was yelling. In response to Mother's command, she robotically placed her fingers on the indicator, staring at nothing.

"F-E-A-R N-O-T"

"But, Lord, you said the Nazarene Mission Board would send us to Afghanistan."

"W-R-I-T-E T-O T-H-E-M I S-A-I-D"

"You said they would send us…" Mother repeated.

The indicator slid to NO.

"But if they don't send us, how are we going to get there?" I asked.

"Y-O-U W-I-L-L K-N-O-W S-O-O-N"

"Why can't we know now? Levoy doesn't believe you're God." Mother cried.

"L-E-V-O-Y I-S B-E-I-N-G T-E-S-T-E-D"

"But why, Lord?" Mother asked.

"D-O Y-O-U R-E-M-E-M-B-E-R J-O-B"

"Yes, Lord," Mother sighed. "But I don't think Levoy wants to go through what Job went through."

"R-E-A-D B-O-O-K O-F J-O-B"

Timmy opened the Bible to the first page of the Book of Job and started reading, "There was a man in the land of Uz, whose name was Job; and that man was perfect and upright, and one that feared God, and eschewed evil."

He read for an hour and we sat quietly, each of us lost in our own thoughts, each trying to ignore the letter on the floor.

Chapter 11

The Last I Will Send

Ever since the letter, images of Charlton Heston roaming through the desert circled endlessly in my mind. How would we go to Afghanistan if Father stopped believing in the Ouija board? Would we be forced to wander through our own spiritual desert for forty years until we had all been punished for the sins of our Father?

The flashing red light on the switchboard lifted me abruptly from my thought fog. "Franklin Junior High School," I said distractedly. "Who can I connect you to?"

The principal's wife was on the other end. "I need to talk to my husband," she said urgently.

"Just a moment," I said as I pulled out the red cord and jammed the plug into the hole for the principal's phone. As I disconnected from the call, I glanced over at Melissa, my new best friend. She sat next to me and was operating the other switchboard. She deftly dispensed of her own calls and turned to me, "Do you know when you leave for Kabul, yet? It's been nearly a month. Shouldn't you have heard by now?"

Melissa was exasperated—she was as anxious as me for our adventure to begin. She said she wanted to tell people that she knew someone overseas. Of course, I never told her about Ouija. I had learned.

"We'll hear soon," I lied, turning my attention back to the switchboard. I didn't need to be reminded that Thanksgiving had come and gone and Christmas was fast approaching. We were supposed to be in

Afghanistan by now. I wanted desperately to change the subject before she could ask more questions. I searched my brain for a diversionary question.

"Do you know who sings *In the Year 2525*? I want to buy the album." I knew that was just the ticket to get her off my subject and on to her favorite group. She loved Zager and Evans and told me that she could listen to that 45 over and over on her record player. I didn't hear her off-pitch singing—I was congratulating myself on another successful diversion. All I could see was Moses.

Mother and Father barely spoke after the letter arrived and Father was noticeably absent whenever we brought the Ouija board out. I felt like I was in purgatory—waiting for someone, anyone, to make a move.

After two days of stony silence about our future, Ouija finally made a move. "W-R-I-T-E T-O T-H-E P-E-A-C-E C-O-R-P-S"

Mother was skeptical. "Lord, why would the Peace Corps take a family?" She shook her head slowly and continued, "I mean, if the missionary board wouldn't send us, why would the Peace Corps?"

"D-O Y-O-U B-E-L-I-E-V-E"

"Well, Lord, I believed the missionary board was going to send us, but that didn't happen, did it?" Mother huffed, obviously forgetting she was talking to God. Mike looked up from his books at the other end of the kitchen table and raised his brows at her sarcasm. We were all waiting.

Ouija spelled angrily, "P-R-O-V-E-R-B-S 8 1-3 A-N-D 1-4" and then it stopped moving abruptly. Mother and Tricia sat with their hands on the indicator for a moment, anticipating more, but Ouija was silent.

Timmy reluctantly opened the Bible after a minute or so and read the verse, "The fear of the Lord is to hate evil; pride, and arrogancy, and the evil way, and the froward mouth, do I hate."

Mother pursed her lips and slowly removed her fingers from the indicator. "Well, I guess I've been reprimanded, huh?" She laughed nervously and turned in her chair to motion for me to hand her my pen and paper and then she drafted the letter to the Peace Corps—without Ouija's help.

That night after dinner we tried to fill Father in on what Ouija had told us. He feigned mild interest, but it was obvious that he was struggling to even comment, "So, the Peace Corps will send us. I'll believe it when I see it." With that, he got up from the table and grabbed Friend's leash for his nightly walk.

As the back door slammed shut behind him, Mother pushed her chair away from the table and moved quickly to follow him. She peeked out from behind the curtains and waited. Then she followed him out the door.

I couldn't imagine why she was sneaking out of the apartment like that. Within fifteen minutes, the front door slammed and the dead bolt clicked into place. Then nothing. I moved to the banister rail in time to see Mother lean against the door below me and begin to sob. After a few seconds, she straightened her back and wiped her tears determinedly from her face with both hands. As she moved to climb the stairs, I leaned back to where she couldn't see me.

"Patricia, I need to talk to Ouija," she wheezed as she climbed the last step. "I gotta know something." She grabbed the board and indicator on her way to the kitchen. Tricia dutifully pushed her books to one side of the kitchen table and placed her hands on the indicator.

"What is Levoy doing that I need to know about?" Mother demanded.

"S-M-O-K-I-N-G"

"Why didn't you tell me? What a fool I've been. I just caught him—he smoked two cigarettes in less than five minutes. He saw me watching from under the steps and threw the cigarette down in the parking lot. Then he left with Friend. I'm afraid for him, Lord."

"L-E-V-O-Y M-U-S-T F-I-N-D H-I-S O-W-N W-A-Y"

"What do you mean?" Mother broke down then and started sobbing uncontrollably. Between sobs, she asked the question I had been asking myself, "He's not going to Afghanistan, is he?"

The indicator paused and then crawled to NO and slid slowly to YES.

"Which is it?" I urged the board to answer.

"H-I-S D-E-C-I-S-I-O-N" and Ouija paused. "F-E-A-R N-O-T"

Mother's shoulders heaved suddenly.

"A-L-L W-I-L-L C-O-M-E T-O P-A-S-S," and then the indicator slid to GOODBYE.

We were asleep by the time Father and Friend returned from their walk. After that night, no one questioned Father about his sudden desire to walk the dog. We knew he had backslid, but we thought there might be hope for him still—especially if we got our letter from the Peace Corps.

The week after Mother mailed the Peace Corps letter, she decided to try out another church—Faith Tabernacle, a Pentecostal church on Georgia Street. Mother had seen a flyer hanging on the message board at the Laundromat about a revival there and insisted that we "try out the church." Without discussing it with Ouija.

On the morning we were to attend services at Faith Tabernacle, Tricia gently suggested to Mother that we consult with Ouija first. After all, Ouija had told us to go to the Nazarene church.

"No, I don't think Ouija would care where we go to services, Patricia," she replied as she patted Tricia on the back. "I'm pretty sure I can try out another church without asking Ouija's permission."

Faith Tabernacle was the biggest church I'd ever seen. "They must have a lot of members," Mother said as she slid her hand under her dress before settling at the end of the pew. There were *two* aisles running from the back of the five-sided church to the front—I was sure they must have been 100 yards long. Each pew held at least 35 people seated on bright red velvet cushions.

The vaulted ceiling rose 50 feet over our heads and was oak paneled in a pentagon pattern. The stage spanned the width of the church, was fronted by a padded altar, and had two rows of pews for the choir. To the left of the stage was a grand piano and to the right was an organ. A dark oak pulpit took center stage and on it was a pitcher of water that glistened from the light of the chandelier suspended above the stage.

Mike and Timmy seemed unimpressed with the church. They had brought a small pad of paper and had begun playing tic-tac-toe as soon as they sat down. Tricia leaned forward in her seat between me and Mother and shook her head slowly, obviously disapproving of her brothers. Mother didn't see what they were doing. She was mesmerized by the sight of the handsome young preacher who had just walked onto the stage after the choir. My eyes followed her gaze, and I understood why her mouth was hanging open so foolishly.

Brother Johnny Monroney's slim and fit body was outlined by the white three-piece suit and wide turquoise tie. He had dark blonde hair sleeked back over his head. The white of his suit contrasted nicely with his tan. I was a little letdown when I saw something glinting on his left ring finger as he poured himself a glass of water. After gulping the full glass of water, he placed his hands on both sides of the pulpit and claimed it as his own. His only flaw that I could see was a wide gap between his two pearly white front teeth. And when he spoke for the first time, his words were hypnotic.

"Welcome to the house of God, good people of Vallejo," he said looking over the 600 people in front of him. "Are you happy in Jesus?" The thought crossed my mind that we would probably be spending a lot of time at this church.

"Why don't we get this here service started with a song from our brothers and sisters in the choir?" he turned and waved his hand to the choir director to start. Immediately, the choir stood together, the organ and piano started playing in unison. The choir hummed at first, swinging in their robes and clapping, and then they broke into a loud song:

"Oh happy day, oh happy day,

when Jesus came,

when Jesus came,

he took my cares away."

The congregation rose as one when the choir started the second chorus. Mike beat me to his feet, and Timmy wasn't far behind. Everyone around us closed their eyes and clapped and sang with the choir. After twenty minutes of singing and clapping, Brother Monroney walked back to the pulpit and faced the choir. On the final chorus, he turned back to the congregation. He thrust his right fist into the air and patted his heart with his left hand. And when the last note was played, he yelled, "he took my cares away." He moved to the side of the pulpit and bowed elegantly. We clapped wildly. I couldn't help feeling that I had just attended my very first rock concert.

Brother Monroney wiped his brow with a white handkerchief as he turned to the choir, and then raised his hands and clapped once more for them. After the congregation had settled, he poured another glass of water and drank it slowly. Then he started his sermon.

"Tonight, brothers and sisters, we are going to turn to Romans, my favorite book in the New Testament. Please turn in your Bibles to Romans 8 so that we can receive the word of God from our brother Paul." His Bible magically opened to the verse and chapter, and he began to read. He stopped between each verse to explain what it meant in the context of the times and to modern Christians.

I was mesmerized, but jolted back into reality by his reading of verse 14: "For as many as are led by the Spirit of God, they are the sons of God. Is God leading you and your family? Have you given yourself over to him? Are you a son or daughter of God? Let's go to verse 24. For we are saved by hope: but hope that is seen is not hope; for what a man seeth, why doth he yet hope for? But if we hope for that we see not, then do we with patience wait for it."

Out of the corner of my eye, I could see that Mother and Tricia turned to look at each other, and then I turned and looked at Mike and Timmy. Was this a message from God to us? That we should have hope even if we don't see what will happen?

He kept reading, "And we know that all things work together for good to them that love God, to them who are the called according to his purpose. For whom he did foreknow, he also did predestinate to be conformed to the image of the Son, that he might be the firstborn among many brethren."

Brother Monroney stepped off the stage and walked down the aisle toward our pew. He turned the page in his Bible and looked Mother in the eye as he continued reading, "Moreover whom he did predestinate, them he also called; and whom he called, them he also justified; and whom he justified, them he also glorified. What shall we then say to these things? If God be for us, who can be against us." He raised his voice and his Bible to the ceiling, and as he lowered the Bible, he looked Mother in the eye and shouted, "Sister, what say you?"

For once, Mother had absolutely nothing to say. He turned and walked back to the pulpit.

"Let's read the final two verses in Romans 8 together," he said as he looked over the crowd. "For I am persuaded, that neither death, nor life, nor angels, nor principalities, nor powers, nor things present, nor things to come, nor height, nor depth, nor any other creature, shall be able to separate us from the love of God, which is in Christ Jesus our Lord." He closed the Bible, "Can you say Amen?"

"Amen," I heard myself shouting with the others. Somehow my arms had raised over my head without my knowing it. I chanted "Hallelujah" over and over.

Brother Monroney spoke above the den of Amens, "Let us pray together. Lord, help us be ever ready for your call. Let us hope for things not seen and believe that if you have called us, you will prepare the way for us. Amen." He opened his eyes and said, "Please be seated."

The only person left standing was a red-haired young woman two rows in front of us who was swaying with her hands held above her head. She began to speak loudly in another language. Tricia turned to me and shrugged her shoulders. She whispered, "It's not German."

I whispered back, "It's not French."

She spoke and swayed uninterrupted for several minutes. She clenched her fists above her head to emphasize certain words and then stopped as suddenly as she had started speaking.

Then, a round bald man across the aisle from us began speaking in English, "Listen, my children. My messengers are among you tonight. Receive them, and you will be blessed. They are the last I will send." He went on for another five minutes, but I didn't hear a word after that.

Mother had fainted and fallen headfirst into the aisle.

That was Sunday, December 8, 1968.

Chapter 12

Dolmer's Legacy

"Lord, how could I have doubted you?" Mother said as she moved her hand from the indicator to her bosom. "Was it you speaking through that woman in a foreign language?"

"T-H-E L-A-N-G-U-A-G-E W-A-S N-O-T F-O-R-E-I-G-N T-O M-E"

"Why didn't you just make her speak English so I could understand the message?" Mother probed.

"I-T W-A-S A-N-C-I-E-N-T T-O-N-G-U-E," Ouija stopped. "R-E-A-D I C-O-R-I-N-T-H-I-A-N-S 1-4 2-2"

The Bible lay in front of Timmy on the coffee table. He instinctively turned the pages to the chapter and verse and read aloud, "Wherefore tongues are for a sign, not to them that believe, but to them that believe not; but prophesying served not for them that believe not, but for them which believe." After Timmy finished, there was complete silence.

"So it was for us because we were starting not to believe," she confirmed.

Ouija answered her, YES.

"Are we the last you will send?" I asked abruptly.

The indicator slid quickly to YES.

And then Ouija said something that simply made no sense.

"M-I-K-E A-N-D M-A-R-Y G-O TO P-E-T S-T-O-R-E B-U-Y H-A-M-S-T-E-R F-O-R D-A-R-Y-L"

Mike, who had been ignoring the entire exchange with Ouija, dropped his book to his lap in disgust. With his long legs still stretched between the sofa and coffee table, he mocked the board, "I'm not going to no pet store—and why would Daryl need a hamster?"

"B-E   C-A-R-E-F-U-L   M-I-K-E" Ouija threatened. "D-O   A-S   I   S-A-Y"

"Mike, I wouldn't argue with Ouija, if I was you," Mother smiled knowingly. She pushed the board away and knocked Mike's legs off the coffee table when she passed. "Come on, Mike."

While they were gone, Tricia and I started dinner. The Ouija board had given us a new recipe for Chinese cabbage. We combined the cabbage, canned tomatoes, grated cheese and eggs in oil in a covered frying pan and cooked it for an hour. I placed the last plate on the table just as Mother and Mike returned from the pet store with a small brown hamster in a cage. They looked like they had seen a ghost.

"You will never believe what happened," Mother exclaimed as she placed the cage with the obviously frightened hamster on the coffee table. Before we could ask what had happened, she continued, "We walked into the store and let the door close behind us. As we did, a bell rang softly that was hanging on the door knob. A black raven sitting on a perch near the door spoke to us—I thought it was a crow, but the shopkeeper said it was a raven. Anyway, as soon as we walked by it, it said, 'Hello, Mike. Hello, Mary.'

Tricia and I gasped simultaneously. She instinctively grabbed my forearm and closed her fingers like a vice. As I wrenched my arm free of her clutch and starting rubbing it, I noticed chill bumps on her arms. "But, how did it know your names?" I asked, spellbound.

"That's the strange part," Mother took a breath as she lowered herself onto the couch, "The man said the bird had arrived just this past week and hadn't spoken a single word. In fact, they weren't sure it could talk. So, he was as surprised as we were that it knew our names."

Mike seemed shaken, but stubbornly denied its meaning, "You're making a big deal out of nothing. Those are just the names the stupid bird knew. It doesn't mean anything."

"Well, why don't we just ask Ouija," Tricia chided Mike. She placed the board and indicator on the table in front of Mother and placed her fingers at the ready. "Was that you, Ouija?" she asked after Mother was seated. "Was that you talking through the bird?"

The indicator moved slowly to YES and then spelled, "M-I-K-E A-L-W-A-Y-S N-E-E-D-S P-R-O-O-F" Ouija stopped. "D-O-U-B-T-I-N-G T-H-O-M-A-S"

"A lot you know, Mike," Tricia laughed.

"You did that, Tricia, not the board," he clenched his teeth and hissed.

"Just drop it, Mike. If the Ouija board says it was him, then it was him," Mother put the board away and stood to finish dinner preparations.

The next day, Daryl dropped by the apartment on his way to Mare Island. Mother handed him the hamster and told him we were instructed to buy it for him. As she tried to push the cage into his hands, Daryl pushed it away. "I don't want a hamster."

Mother was aghast, "What?"

"I'm never talking to that Ouija board again," Daryl shook his head violently, "Me and Sue been talking about this Ouija board thing. We agree that it's the devil and we want nothing to do with it."

"Why are you so angry?" Tricia asked.

"I think you're all crazy. So does dad. He says you're possessed or something."

"Why you ungrateful son-of-a-bitch," Mother started. "After everything we've done for you and Sue." Before she could finish, Daryl turned away. "Don't turn your back on me, you bastard."

He turned back to face her wrath, towering above her. He very calmly said, "What did you do for us? You rushed us into a marriage that we weren't ready for. Now, you're buying us a hamster that is probably possessed, just like you."

"Get out of my house." she yelled. "Don't ever come back."

"You can be sure of that."

Tricia stood frozen in the middle of the living room with a dinner plate of half-eaten food in one hand and an empty glass in the other. She seemed unable to move, unable to stop what had transpired before her eyes.

Daryl stomped down the stairs two at a time. Tricia yelled, "Wait. Stop. Don't go." But it was too late. He slammed the door behind him.

Mike and Timmy stood next to each other near the banister. "Why did you make him go?" Mike yelled at Mother. "He was our brother. Now he's gone." Mike struggled to control his rage. He turned to the wall behind him and slammed his fist into it. Luckily, the wall gave way to his powerful swing, leaving a hole in the plaster the size of his fist. He pushed past Mother and followed Daryl out the front door onto Sonoma Boulevard.

Mother didn't mention any of this to Father when he came home from his walk with Friend. In fact, unless absolutely necessary, she wouldn't talk to Father at all after that night. Mike was even more rebellious against Ouija after that incident.

Two days later, Vallejo High School's principal called Mother to come pick up her son. He had been in a fight, and apparently he lost. The details from Mike were sketchy at best. He said he had been in the bathroom minding his own business when three football players came in and for no reason, cornered him and pummeled him with their fists.

Mike was a strange looking, gangly creature. He never gained weight no matter what he ate. Between his slight build, thick glasses forever repaired with electrical tape, and his sterling tooth, he was the brunt of many a bully's jokes and, in this case, their physical attacks.

Mother brought him home from the hospital with five stitches above his left brow, two black and swollen eyes, broken glasses in hand, and red marks that turned quickly to bruises all over his body. There was no doubt in my mind that he had been punched and kicked repeatedly—and by more than one person. My heart ached for him.

He would say no more about the beating and after his wounds had healed, he refused to go back to school. He said that since we were leaving soon, there was no point in him going back to that school. Mother agreed.

We hid the fact that our lives were falling apart. We hid it from our friends, from the people at Faith Tabernacle, and from our family members who were in cities scattered across the country. Christmas came and went. Ouija told us to save our money for traveling and setting up a house in Kabul.

Our collective slide into depression was halted momentarily when we got a call from Aunt Edith shortly after New Year's Day. Mother had listed her as a reference in our application for the Peace Corps. She called to let us know that someone from the Peace Corps had called her. She promised Mother that she gave us a glowing reference and didn't mention anything about the Ouija board.

As soon as Mother hung up the phone, she grabbed Tricia by the arm and pulled her to the kitchen where Ouija was laying on the kitchen table. Mike and Timmy were nowhere in sight. They usually left when we started talking to Ouija anyway.

"Lord, this is a sign, isn't it?" She said gleefully. "Are they going to take us?"

"Y-O-U W-I-L-L K-N-O-W S-O-O-N"

Mother's gleeful expression dissolved into sadness. "Levoy's not going to Afghanistan, is he?"

The indicator moved to NO.

"Lord, how will we build the temple if Levoy doesn't go?" She took her hands off the indicator without realizing that Ouija couldn't answer. "How will we do anything without him? I thought you were calling *him*, not me. There is no way I can do this without a man. We won't be safe without a man."

Tricia sat patiently with her hands on the indicator, waiting for Mother to join her. When she didn't, Tricia cleared her throat and said quietly, "Mother?"

Realizing what she had done, Mother quickly placed her fingers back on the indicator.

"Y-O-U W-E-R-E C-H-O-S-E-N T-O-O," Tricia read the letters out loud.

"But, Lord, I'm a woman," Mother whined.

"W-O-M-E-N A-R-E C-A-L-L-E-D"

Mother, Tricia and I exchanged surprised expressions.

"Who?" Mother asked.

"M-A-R-Y M-A-G-D-A-L-E-N-E"

Mother's lower jaw dropped, and she seemed unable to speak. The second time I had witnessed such an unlikely reaction from her recently.

Ouija continued, "M-A-R-Y W-A-S A-P-O-S-T-L-E L-O-V-E-D B-Y M-Y S-O-N H-E A-P-P-E-A-R-E-D T-O H-E-R F-I-R-S-T A-F-T-E-R C-R-U-C-I-F-I-C-T-I-O-N" Since this was a long one, I wrote it all down and read it back slowly.

Mother finally recovered, "But Mary Magdalene was a prostitute."

The indicator slid to NO, "S-H-E W-A-S B-E-L-O-V-E-D A-P-O-S-T-L-E"

Now I was curious, "But why doesn't the New Testament say that?"

"B-I-B-L-E D-O-E-S N-O-T I-N-C-L-U-D-E E-V-E-R-Y W-O-R-D W-R-I-T-T-E-N"

Mother nodded.

"Y-O-U A-R-E C-A-L-L-E-D"

Mother pulled her shoulders back and set her jaw determinedly, "And I will answer, Lord."

From that moment forward, Mother excluded Father from all discussions about Afghanistan. We never told the boys about this conversation with Ouija. We assumed they would have no interest in it. In fact, we weren't sure they would even *go* to Afghanistan without Father. I was starting to think that it would be three women who would prepare for Christ's second coming.

If only we could get to Kabul.

We expected a letter from the Peace Corps any day especially since they had checked Mother's references. The letter arrived three days later. Tricia and I jumped up and down excitedly in front of the hotel clerk who had handed us the letter. He walked away shaking his head and mumbling something about crazy teenagers.

"Open it," I urged. Tricia shook her head and clutched the envelope in her left hand out of my reach.

"Mother would kill us if we did that," she said breathlessly as I chased her out the hotel's front door and raced across the street to our apartment building. She paused at the front door and gushed, "She's going to want to read this herself."

As we tripped up the stairs to the apartment, we screamed together, "It's here. The letter from the Peace Corps. It's here." Mike and Timmy met us at the top and Mike grabbed it from Tricia's outstretched hand.

"Give that to me, Michael Levoy," Mother said as she relieved him of the letter. She tore open the envelope and started reading quickly:

```
Dear Mr. and Mrs. Cain:

Thank you for applying to the Peace Corps. We
are definitely interested in having your
family serve in the Peace Corps. However, we
have no immediate assignments in Afghanistan.
There are many countries that need people.
Please contact us to discuss your options…
```

Mother's voice trailed off to a whisper before she could finish reading.

Mike was smiling ear to ear. "We've been accepted," he stopped mid-sentence and looked from Mother to Tricia, to me, and finally to Timmy. "This is good news. We're going overseas."

"It's not good news, Mike," Tricia said flatly. "It's not Afghanistan."

"What's the difference?" he snarled.

"Patricia, get the Ouija board out," Mother said calmly. She sat down on the kitchen chair, with her hands folded neatly in her lap until Tricia returned with the board. They placed their hands on the indicator and waited for motion. Finally, Ouija moved.

"F-A-I-T-H O-F M-U-S-T-A-R-D S-E-E-D"

"I don't understand where the money will come from to pay for us to get to—" Mother started.

Mike interrupted, "If you're God, then why don't you make money for us? Or even better, maybe you could just snap your fingers, and we'd be in Kabul."

"W-H-E-N W-I-L-L Y-O-U L-E-A-R-N"

Mike shook his head and walked out of the kitchen muttering, "I can't believe this. What idiots."

Mother remained focused on her mission, "Ouija, where will the money come from to get us to Afghanistan?"

Ouija didn't move and neither did Mother.

Finally, Ouija ominously spelled out, "C-A-L-L   Y-O-U-R   U-N-C-L-E"

"You want me to call Uncle Dolmer?" Mother recoiled in disbelief. "There is no way I'm going to call Uncle Dolmer to ask him for money. Don't ask me to do that. I still have my pride, Lord."

"P-R-I-D-E   G-O-E-T-H   B-E-F-O-R-E   A   F-A-L-L"

Dolmer Horn was Mother's uncle, on her Mother's side. He owned a plantation outside of Corinth. Mother and her siblings had spent time with him in their youths, mostly helping out during the harvest. Mother talked fondly of those times on his farm.

Dolmer had never married in all of his 79 years. He was the second youngest of the seven Horn children born to David and Laura Horn. My grandmother, Dulcye Odessa Horn Furtick, was his younger sister. Dolmer had done well for himself and it was rumored—mostly by Mother and Aunt Edith—that he was worth a lot of money.

"C-A-L-L   H-I-M   S-O-O-N"

As Tricia slid the board under the couch, Mother muttered to herself, "Dolmer is the stingiest man I've ever met. He has the first nickel he ever earned. He will never give us any money. We're screwed if our only hope is Dolmer Horn."

Mother put off calling Uncle Dolmer for the rest of that Saturday. She didn't mention any of this to Father. Mother finally worked up the courage to call him on Sunday. She dialed the number and waited for three rings. As she was ready to tap the hook, Dolmer answered. Tricia and I sat nervously next to Mother on the couch as she talked and listened.

"Hello, Uncle Dolmer. It's Mary Frances," her southern drawl crept back into her voice for Uncle Dolmer's benefit, I'm sure. They exchanged pleasantries, Mother at her most charming. "Well, I'll be," she said a couple of times. Then she got to the point.

"Uncle Dolmer, do you think you could loan me about $3,000?" There, she had said it. How could he refuse her? Mother had always said she was his favorite niece. After a few seconds, she answered a question he must have asked, "It's for airfare to go to Afghanistan."

Uncle Dolmer spoke for a few minutes and then Mother asked, "Who told you that?"

After he answered, Mother chided him, "Now Uncle Dolmer, you know God commanded Christians to spread the word. We are only—"

It was difficult interpreting what was being said based on this one-sided conversation we were hearing. She looked at us helplessly as she shook her head to silently disagree with what he was saying after that.

"I know, Uncle Dolmer. But, we were chosen by—" He stopped her mid-sentence.

By now, her eyes were wet and red-rimmed. She sat rigidly holding the phone to her ear with her right hand. Her left hand was raised to keep us shushed while she listened to his tirade. After three or four minutes, it ended abruptly.

Mother smiled into the phone and said defiantly, "Goodbye, Uncle Dolmer. God bless you." She carefully placed the receiver back in its cradle and patted it like it was a child.

"Well, that's done. He won't give us money to preach to no heathens. Apparently, Edith called him months ago and told him all about our situation," she laughed weakly. "It's up to the Lord now, girls."

She didn't want to talk to Ouija that day. It was Sunday, January 12, 1969.

Tricia hounded Mother all the way to school the next day. She said we should have talked to Ouija that morning before we left. Mother was dismissive and said that we would later that night. I made sure I was close by for that conversation. Mike and Timmy were at the park with Friend, as usual.

"Well, Lord," Mother sighed heavily and continued with just a trace of sarcasm in her voice, "He won't give us the money. What's the plan now?"

"H-E W-I-L-L G-I-V-E Y-O-U M-O-N-E-Y"

"No, I don't think he will," she retorted.

"P-A-T-I-E-N-C-E"

"He's not giving us the money."

All hope was lost to me. We were being punished, I was sure. Moses and I roamed the desert together in my dreams.

At least our daily routine remained unchanged. I went to school. I fought with my siblings and tried not to listen to my parents argue about money and the future. Mother complained to Father at dinner that Mike was 16 and needed to finish high school or get out of the house. She said she was worn out by his endless defiance.

The rest of the week went by without many sessions with Ouija. We were discouraged.

On Friday, January 17, the phone rang in the middle of the night. I picked up the receiver and groggily answered. "Hello?"

It was Aunt Edith. "Let me speak to your Mother right now," she said urgently. I called for Mother a couple of times. She finally came to the living room and sat down on the edge of the coffee table before taking the receiver from me. She rubbed her eyes and asked, "Hello?"

She gasped, "Oh my God." And then, "When?" and then "How?" She was listening intently as Aunt Edith talked on and on about something important, I could tell.

I sat up in the sofa bed and reached over to shake Tricia awake. She leaned on one elbow and whispered, "What's going on?" I told her it was Aunt Edith, and it was something important.

"Who gets the money?" Mother asked. After Aunt Edith finished talking, Mother gasped, "Oh my God" again. By this time, Father had his jeans on and was rubbing his eyes as he came into the living room. Mike and Timmy followed close behind.

"Call me tomorrow, Edith. I'll talk to you then," she finished and hung up.

She impulsively ran to Father and hugged him around his waist, but he didn't respond. He just looked over her head, arms hanging at his side and asked, "What was that all about?"

Mother told him that Ouija told us to call Uncle Dolmer for the money. Father pushed Mother away from him then and opened his mouth to speak, but before he could say anything, she continued, "Levoy, Ouija told us that Uncle Dolmer would give us the money."

"But he *didn't*, did he?"

"Uncle Dolmer died this evening in his sleep, Levoy. They don't know what he died of yet, but they think it might be a heart attack."

Father was taken aback, but continued the attack, "That doesn't mean you're going to get any money. How naïve can you be?"

Mother's hands moved slowly to her hips and she finished, "He died without a will, Levoy. And since he never married, his brothers and sisters inherit his estate."

Mother folded her arms across her chest and continued proudly, "And since his sister, *my* momma, is dead, the three of us children get a share of the inheritance. I get one-third of her share. So, in the end Uncle Dolmer will pay for us to go to Afghanistan. Just like Ouija said."

Friday, January 17, 1969.

Chapter 13

Grand Theft

"Don't you want to watch *The Avengers* tonight?" Tricia asked me a few days later.

We were alone in the apartment with control over the TV. A rare occurrence. Tricia and I had always been devoted fans of *The Avengers* and *The Man from U.N.C.L.E.* and never missed an episode of either. *U.N.C.L.E.* had gone off the air the prior year, much to our dismay. The world would never be the same without Napoleon Solo and Illya Kuryakin. Tricia loved Napoleon and I loved Illya.

Truth be told, I thought Robert Vaughan was too old for either of us. He must have been at least 35. Tricia and I had an agreement that Tricia always got the old actor, and I got the younger. She got Peter Turk and I got Davy Jones on *The Monkees;* and on *Bonanza*, she got Adam and I got Little Joe. Neither of us wanted Hoss.

There was a lot of chemistry between Steed and Peel on *The Avengers*. Steed was old, but he was British and that alone earned him a high rating on my sex-o-meter. When Steed and Mrs. Peel were on the screen together, it was electrifying to watch, especially when she donned her black, skin-tight leather outfit and jumped on the back of Steed's scooter. But, alas, Mrs. Peel was no more. Diana Riggs had been replaced by a very young Tara King in the previous season, and I was losing interest in the show. Tara made Steed look even older, and it kind of turned my stomach.

"Nope, I don't like it since Mrs. Peel left," I sighed without looking up from my homework. Tricia nodded her agreement and continued turning the channel selector and intermittently adjusting the rabbit eared antenna to tune in one of the few channels we could pick up.

It didn't matter to me what was on TV anymore. My mind had been on our mission ever since we learned that Uncle Dolmer had died without a will. I didn't understand what "intestate" actually meant, but Mother explained that it came down to the fact that we were getting money from him—enough to pay our airfare to Afghanistan. To me, it was pretty clear that we'd be leaving for Kabul soon. I felt perfectly justified in excitedly telling Melissa during gym class that we were leaving in the next month or so, which *was* true I was sure.

"That is so exciting," she said breathlessly as she ran next to me on the track during gym class. "How long does it take to get there on a plane?"

"I think it takes two days," I guessed. "It's on the other side of the world. It's a long trip." We talked excitedly about living overseas for the rest of the class. When Timmy and I got home that afternoon, Tricia and Mother were already sitting at the Ouija board. Amazingly, Mike was listening too. My balloon of happiness instantly popped as I heard what they were talking about.

"Lord, Edith said it will take months to probate the estate," Mother cried. "Can you tell us when we will leave for Afghanistan?" Beads of sweat dotted her forehead, just at the hairline. Feeling the sweat roll down her forehead, she reached for a tissue with one hand and swiped it away.

"S-O-O-N M-A-R-Y"

Mother pressed Ouija for an answer, "Lord, I need to know when." More sweat beaded on her forehead, and she absently wiped it with the back of her hand.

"A-R-E Y-O-U D-O-U-B-T-I-N-G"

"No, Lord. I'm just trying to plan ahead," Mother denied. "The kids are in school, Levoy's working. We have to pack, make plane reservations, and get passports. All that stuff."

"I-N G-O-O-D T-I-M-E"

And then Mike verbalized a question none of us had the guts to ask, "Ouija, did you kill Uncle Dolmer?" Mike clenched his jaw waiting for Ouija's response.

Ouija moved to NO. "I-T W-A-S H-I-S T-I-M-E T-O L-E-A-V-E"

Timmy interjected lamely, "Was his soul ready to go to heaven?"

The indicator moved to NO.

I stared at the board for a few interminable seconds and then tore my eyes away to look at Timmy. He looked to be as scared as me—we both knew what this meant. Uncle Dolmer was burning in hell because he refused the Ouija board. It had happened again.

"Then you let him die?" Tricia asked quietly, teary-eyed, fingers shaking slightly as she pressed the indicator.

"I D-I-D N-O-T I-N-T-E-R-V-E-N-E"

* * *

For the next few weeks, nothing changed. We attended services at Faith Tabernacle and got to know Brother Monroney and his family. They took Mother up on her offer to let me babysit for them and so I had a little spending money.

At school, Melissa hounded me incessantly about Afghanistan. I kept telling her that it would be any day now. On days when I just couldn't take it anymore, I'd feign an upset stomach and stay home from school, which I did at least once a week.

Father was completely immune to Ouija and ignored all of us as well. He and Mother argued most of the time, about almost anything, even safe subjects like the weather. When the bickering escalated to screaming, the neighbors rapped violently on the shared wall, which usually quieted the argument down.

Eventually, Mother and Father stopped talking to each other and instead slung barbs at each other via one of us kids. Dinner was the only time Father was in the apartment, and we spent it in sullen silence. As soon as Father cleaned his plate, he grabbed the leash and secured it to Friend's collar. Together, they skulked out the door without a word or backward glance. We preferred Father's absence to the fighting, that's for sure.

About that time, Mother received a Power of Attorney in the mail from her brother James. It named Hoyt as the executor of Dolmer's estate. Hoyt was Mother's cousin. She didn't much care for him and balked at making him the executor. Ouija overrode her objections and commanded her to sign it and return it to Hoyt if she wanted to go to Afghanistan, which she did.

February had come and gone and we were still in Vallejo at the beginning of March 1969. I was perpetually cold—64 degrees was not warm enough for my thinned Arizona blood. By mid-March, Phoenix would be experiencing daytime temperatures of 100 degrees or more and I missed it. I should be wearing shorts and sleeveless shirts by now, and here I was still wearing my white vinyl car coat to school every day with long pants. Dressing for cooler weather was a novelty at first, but it was beginning to wear on all of us. We complained to Ouija constantly that we were tired of being cold.

"I-T W-I-L-L B-E C-O-L-D-E-R I-N K-A-B-U-L"

"How much colder?" I asked suspiciously.

"5-0 D-E-G-R-E-E-S I-N M-A-R-C-H"

I moaned. Mike looked up from the model airplane he was working on and asked excitedly, "Is there skiing?"

The indicator moved to YES. Ouija continued spelling, "Y-O-U M-U-S-T L-E-A-V-E F-O-R K-A-B-U-L N-O-W"

Mother clapped her hands together and held them to her lips. "Hallelujah, thank you, Jesus," she said over and over as she raised her hands above her head. Then we were all clapping and jumping up and down. Mother shushed us and motioned for us to sit on the couch.

"Lord, what should we do now?" Mother said with all the fake reverence she could muster.

"G-O T-O T-H-E M-O-N-E-Y"

She blinked rapidly and shook her head. She lifted her fingers from the indicator, but Ouija started moving suddenly and she had to catch up, "G-O T-O M-I-S-S-I-S-S-I-P-P-I"

"Who should go to Mississippi?"

"E-V-E-R-Y-O-N-E"

"Even Levoy?" she puzzled.

Ouija answered NO.

"But how will I get the money to go to Corinth? I don't have any money," she pressed. I was hoping Ouija would make money appear on the coffee table at this point, but somehow I knew that was not how it worked. Mother continued, "You want me to drive two thousand miles to Corinth in a ten year-old car? This seems crazy to me."

"N-O-T C-R-A-Z-Y," Ouija answered. "Y-O-U K-N-O-W H-O-W T-O G-E-T M-O-N-E-Y"

Mother's head was moving slowly side-to-side as Ouija spoke. "Lord, I have no idea how to get money," she paused as she realized what Ouija was saying. "You want me to take Levoy's Air Force retirement check?"

Before the indicator could land on YES, Mother interrupted, "That's just not right. How will he live without it?"

"H-E W-I-L-L B-E O-K"

"No, no, no," Mother couldn't stop herself. "We can't do that to him."

"H-E I-S N-O-T B-E-L-I-E-V-E-R"

That night, Father had an emergency at the hotel—a water pipe broke—conveniently keeping him at work until nearly midnight. Mother had resigned herself to Ouija's course of action and began directing us to pack our bags before he got back and to hide them where he wouldn't see them.

I didn't sleep much that night. I was guilt-ridden. Leaving Father without saying goodbye didn't seem quite right even though he was a non-believer. I also didn't get a chance to say goodbye to my friends, but I would write and let them know what had happened to us. I was going to miss Melissa.

Father's $270 retirement check arrived on schedule in the mail the next morning. And, as Mother usually did, she forged Father's signature on the check and cashed it. This time, though, she didn't buy money orders to pay bills. She took the cash and jammed it into her wallet. We would use it to pay for gas and motels on the drive to Corinth.

We knew we couldn't stay with granddaddy because he had told Mother to stay away as long as she was "fooling with a Ouija board."

Mother called one of Aunt Edith's daughters, Barbara, to see if we could stay with her. Barbara lived about twenty minutes outside of Corinth in a small Tennessee border town called Selmer. She had two small children and lived on a farm. She told Mother she could use our help on the farm for a few days since her husband was on the road with his motorcycle gang.

Barbara was Mother's favorite niece and she had loaned us $167 to move from Corinth back to Avondale the year before. Barbara was loaded according to Mother because of the insurance from her husband Dee's motorcycle accident.

As soon as Mother returned from the bank with Father's cash in her hand, she rushed us to get our suitcases loaded into the back of the station wagon. She put Ouija in a shopping bag and put it on the front seat between her and Tricia. You never knew when you would need to consult Ouija during the trip, I guess. Mike, Timmy and I sat in the backseat with Friend tucked in a small space on top of the suitcases.

I sat behind Tricia in the backseat and immediately positioned a pillow between me and Timmy. I definitely did not want his cooties on me for a three-day trip. The Plymouth's muffler scraped as we turned onto Sonoma Boulevard.

As I took one last look at the Casa de Vallejo, I saw my Father standing at a second floor window, arms folded across his chest, and a scowl etched on his face. We locked eyes and then he shook his head and turned away.

Mother never looked back. I guess she was preoccupied with driving.

That was Monday, March 31, 1969—my parents' nineteenth wedding anniversary.

Chapter 14

Barbara's Mountain

"We ain't stopping, Mike," Mother shouted for the third time. "You can just forget about it."

Mike was persistent, "Why can't we just detour to Avondale to say goodbye to everyone? It's not that far out of the way."

"We already said goodbye," Mother snapped. "Besides, Ouija told us to drive straight to Barbara's. No stopping anywhere. Period."

Mike opened his mouth, "But—"

"That's it, Michael Levoy Cain" she raised her right fist and glowered at him in the rear view mirror. "I don't want another word out of you," she warned, "Do you hear me? Not another word."

"This car won't make it to Mississippi," Mike scowled, just loud enough for me to hear. I shook my head in disgust, turned my back on him and Timmy, and continued my vigil at the side window.

"Why did you even come?" I asked the window.

Mother had been driving for eight hours straight, stopping only once for gas. We weren't even to the Arizona border yet. Mike had his permit, but Mother didn't trust him to drive. She said he was careless, and she didn't want to die on her way to being a missionary. So, I was crammed in the backseat with Mike and Timmy—two of the rudest human beings on earth.

They laughed hysterically whenever one or the other of them belched or farted. I wasn't laughing. I nearly wore out the window crank from opening and closing the window in a never-ending quest for fresh air.

In between farts and belches, Timmy worked determinedly on his design of a ship on his Etch-a-Sketch. Just as he would get the outline of the ship where he wanted it, Mike would reach over and shake the Etch-a-Sketch, and then the circus would start all over. What a jerk, I thought to myself.

I stared out the window as mountains and deserts melted behind us on Interstate 5. At Bakersfield, we scooted over to Barstow on California 58, where we joined Route 66, finally. What did Steinbeck call it? Ah, the Mother Road. It would take us all the way to Oklahoma City. I couldn't wait to get out of California. Where was that border sign, anyway?

Eight hours was way too long to sit in the backseat of a car with rotten brothers, and a dog that panted in my ear and drooled on the back of my neck. I escaped the circus periodically by closing my eyes and trying to imagine what life would be like in Afghanistan. Despite my best efforts to conjure that image, the only sight I saw was Father standing dejectedly at the hotel window.

Mother had asked each of us if we wanted to stay with Father or come with her. We all said we wanted to go to Afghanistan and serve God. I had my doubts about Mike, but I knew why I was going. So, even though most of us were going for the right reason, it still felt to me like we had abandoned Father. A part of me pitied him and another part knew that he probably wasn't all that sad to be rid of us.

As the first Arizona saguaro blurred past the car, my mind mulled over what Ouija had told us to do before we left. We were told to burn everything written by or about Ouija. I had kept copious notes of what Ouija had said for the past year. Hundreds of pages of notes neatly printed letter-by-letter on lined school paper.

I was the record keeper, but last night Ouija relieved me of that duty.

Despite my pleas to preserve the binder, Mother obeyed Ouija in the end. She lit the corners of the pages with Father's Zippo lighter. As the pages ignited, she dropped them one-by-one onto the small bonfire glowing in the kitchen sink. She burned every shred of evidence that Ouija had ever existed, and then she threw away the binders. Only the plans for the temple were safe from the inferno. We would need them once we reached Kabul, she had said.

Twelve hours after we started out from Vallejo, Mother decided she couldn't drive one more mile. She exited Route 66 in Williams, Arizona, and parked on a side road. "I need to sleep," she yawned. Pointing to the diner across the street, she said as she nodded off, "We'll have breakfast there in the morning, and then we'll get back on the road." There wasn't enough money to stay in motels.

The next morning we cleaned up in the diner's bathrooms and then downed a delicious breakfast of eggs, bacon, and biscuits. The biscuit gravy wasn't as good as Mother's, but I ate every bite. Mother told us to eat up, because there wouldn't be another meal until dinner.

As we piled back into the Plymouth, Mother turned the ignition key and the expected roar of the engine was replaced by a halting, grinding noise.

"Oh, Lord, please don't let this car break down," Mother pleaded as she dropped her forehead to the steering wheel. She turned the key three more times, chanting the whole time. On the fourth try, the engine turned over and sputtered anxiously. "Thank you, Jesus." she exclaimed. What a relief.

Despite Mike's prophesy, the car ran beautifully after that. The only other trouble we had was a flat tire on the outskirts of Oklahoma City. Inconveniently, the spare was under the mat in the back of the station wagon. With all of our worldly goods sitting on the shoulder of the road, Mike jacked up the car and changed the tire. He didn't do too bad a job, despite never having changed a tire before.

We spent another night in the car at a well-lit gas station east of Oklahoma City. It was April 1st, Edith's birthday. Mother debated calling her sister to wish her a happy birthday, but said she really didn't want to hear Edith calling *her* an April fool. She decided to call after we reached Barbara's.

In the morning we skipped breakfast and at sun-up joined Interstate 40, which took us through Little Rock and on into Memphis. And then, for some reason, with 30 hours behind us and Selmer within sight, Mother took an unplanned detour from Route 64 and headed to Shiloh National Military Park.

Tricia was beside herself. "Mother, I stink, and I want a bath," she crossed her arms determinedly and pouted. "Ouija told us not to stop anywhere, and now we're going to a cemetery?"

Mike lent his voice to her lament, "I don't want to see no cemetery."

"Shut up, both of you," Mother snapped. "Patricia, just so you know. Ouija doesn't make all my decisions. I want you kids to see this cemetery. We'll get to Barbara's before dark even if we stop here."

It was at least 100 degrees, and my shorts were melted to the back of my legs. I was pretty sure I smelled bad. I was with Tricia. All I wanted was a nice cool bath and a seat that wasn't moving at 50 miles an hour. But Mother could not be swayed no matter how much we groaned and complained. She was going to show us Shiloh cemetery, come hell or high water.

As we passed through the gates of Shiloh, Mother used her best tour guide voice, "Shiloh was where one of the worst battles was fought during the Civil War," she explained. "The south fought the north here for two days on April 6 and 7, 1862." She slowed down and pulled the car off the road near a field where thousands of white markers lined up row after row under magnificent magnolias and black walnuts.

"So what's so special about this cemetery? Just a bunch of dead people," Mike sneered from the backseat.

She stopped the car and turned in her seat to face him. "Show some respect for once in your life. More than 24,000 union and confederate soldiers were killed here. There's acres and acres of these markers for northern soldiers. I'll show you what they did for the southern soldiers."

She pulled slowly back onto the road and stopped near a memorial with confederate soldiers frozen in bronze. She pointed to the memorial and continued her story, "The confederate soldiers are buried in mass graves." She choked up.

"So, who won?" I asked.

"The Yankees," Mother blew her nose with a tissue, raised her glasses and dabbed at her eyes and finished her story. "After this battle, they marched to Corinth, killing everybody in their way, and took control of the railroads."

"The spirit we talked to—your great granddaddy—was a sergeant in the South Carolina militia. After the war he settled in Mississippi and married Mary Magdalene Huffman.

She stopped a second as her lineage unfolded in her memory.

"His parents were David Furtick and Eliza Ann Jackson; David's parents was George Furtick and Mary Magdalene Zachael. And, George's parents was John George and Celia Fertig—that used to be our name."

She turned down another cemetery lane, "According to my daddy, John George and Celia came to the new world from Germany and were given a land grant in South Carolina in 1758 from King George II."

She swerved suddenly back onto the road and squinted at highway signs until she found Highway 142, which headed in the direction of Selmer. Safely in the right lane, she continued with her Mother's lineage.

"My momma, Dulcye Odessa Horn, was the daughter of David Burton Horn and Laura Frances Emmons," She paused to collect her thoughts. "Now, Laura Emmons' daddy owned land along the Mississippi and Tennessee state line—somewhere near here. He refused to fight in the Civil War 'cause he had relatives on both sides. The story goes that a friend warned him that confederate soldiers was going to burn his house down, so his wife sewed all their gold in the hem of her skirt, and they hid in the woods.

They moved to Texas after that and that's where their daughter Laura met David and they moved back to Mississippi in 1876 to their parent's old farm and raised their seven children—Miss Nove, William Oscar, David Arthur, Bertha Beatrice, Dolmer Barnhill, Vinne Lee, and your grandma, Dulcye Odessa."

She chuckled, "Did anybody write that down? That's all I remember and who knows how long I'll remember it?"

After we crossed the Tennessee border, Mother's twang was even more pronounced. She had been transplanted in Arizona for so long that I didn't realize her roots, my roots, were in the south, and just like Rhett Butler in *Gone with the Wind*, my great, great granddaddy refused to fight in a war that pitted one American against another.

An hour out of Shiloh, we exited Route 142 at Tennessee Route 15. Our instructions were to turn left at South Railroad Street and follow it to the first dirt road on the left, which we did. A small shack was teetering on the edge of the hillside and to our right, atop the hill, was the roof of another house—Barbara's house.

"Lord have mercy," Mother exclaimed as we passed what looked like an outhouse on the neighbor's property. "I sure hope Barbara's got running water."

Mother coaxed the Plymouth up the narrow, dusty drive that disappeared on the other side of the hill. At the top of the hill was a rambling white house surrounded by ramshackle sheds, a double seater outhouse, some rusted farm equipment, and a small chicken coop. A red-haired woman in her mid-20s stood near the coop with a diapered baby on her hip.

As the Plymouth rounded the final bend, she saw us and waved excitedly. She tossed the remaining feed to the clucking chickens and dusted her hand on her shorts.

As the car slid to a stop on the gravel in front of the young woman, all four doors sprang open in unison. Friend jumped over my shoulder and started sniffing the ground for the perfect place to pee. Just then, a small black-and-white spotted bulldog raced from the woods, barking and growling ferociously.

"Look out," I screamed, anticipating a fight.

Friend turned on the dog instantly and before any of us could move, had the dog pinned to the ground, with the smaller dog's neck in his mouth. Timmy stumbled to the dogs and pulled hard on Friend's choke chain. Finally he released the other dog, but continued a muffled growl.

"Get the hell out of here, Buster," Barbara said, kicking her dog out of her way with her left foot. "I can see we're going to have to keep these two apart." The bleeding dog squealed and retreated under the house.

Barbara ignored Buster's whining and slid the baby absently from one hip to the other. She beamed and motioned expansively, "Welcome to my mountain, Aunt Mary."

"So help me, hannah." Mother exclaimed as she hugged Barbara and the baby at once. "You look younger every time I see you. And here you got yourself a family and a farm." Mother looked around expectantly and asked, "Is Dee home yet?"

"This here's Macky," Barbara ignored Mother's question and nodded at the towhead in her arms. "He's almost nine months. Oh, here comes DJ," she smiled brightly and pointed her shoulder to the two-year old bounding down the front steps. DJ stopped short as he caught sight of us and started fiddling nervously with his drooping diaper.

"Is Dee here?" Mother repeated intently.

"Naw, he'll be home in a couple a days," Barbara said dismissively. She ushered us into the small house and told us to make ourselves comfortable. She gave us a tour—three small bedrooms, living room, kitchen, and to Mother's relief, a bathroom.

"Macky's crib is in my room," Barbara said as she opened her bedroom door. "I figured DJ and the boys can share a room. You and the girls can share a room, Aunt Mary." Mother nodded and thanked Barbara profusely for her hospitality.

After the tour and a snack of peanut butter and crackers, we unloaded the car and started our shower routine, which felt heavenly after three days of bath deprivation. Within two hours, we had crawled into our makeshift beds. Blankets and pillows spread neatly on the floor. We fell immediately asleep.

Over the next few days, we settled in and started a new routine on Barbara's mountain. We tried a couple of times to let Friend and Buster play together, always with a disastrous result. So, Friend was chained to the front porch, and Buster was in a fenced holding pen. He rammed the fence so hard that the fur on his small pug face was constantly blood-soaked.

Mother insisted that we help out on the farm to earn our keep. She convinced Barbara that she should take advantage of the wild strawberries growing on the hillside. So, each day we had to pick and clean strawberries so that Mother and Barbara could start cooking and canning preserves, assembly-line fashion.

Mike and Timmy mowed the grass, fed the chickens, and cleaned the coop. They were also supposed to keep the two dogs apart, if possible. Tricia and I were charged with cleaning the mountains of dirty laundry in the wringer washer on the back porch. So, anytime we weren't picking strawberries, we were rotating clean clothes to and from the clothes line.

In the midst of all the work, I developed my first full-blown crush on a real life boy—as opposed to a movie star. Lucas, the blonde 16-year old who lived with his grandparents in the shack down Barbara's mountain was the object of my lust. We had met one day while picking strawberries alongside the road.

"Who are you?" he asked bluntly, never stopping his quest for strawberries. "I never seen you afore."

"I'm Diana," I said, waving shyly. "We're visiting my cousins for a few weeks." I suddenly realized that my hand was filthy, and I jerked it down.

"Where ya'll from?" he asked. "You ain't from 'round here. I bet you're from the north, ain't ya?" He was flirting with me. I was sure of it.

I suddenly noticed that he had no shirt on under his overalls. My eyes went instinctively to his muscles moving gracefully under his tanned skin as he pulled strawberries from their stems. I looked away suddenly.

"No, we're from Arizona—that's out West. You ever been there?" He shook his head and kept gazing into my eyes while his hands plucked strawberry after strawberry and dropped them gently into his bucket. We gazed into each other's eyes without speaking and then looked away suddenly, embarrassed. I smiled to myself.

After meeting Lucas, I spent more time at the bathroom mirror admiring my sun-kissed cheeks, tanned skin, and gold highlighted hair.

That's when I realized that I was kind of pretty, especially if I took off my god-awful ugly black glasses.

Since I had no make-up to primp with, I decided to focus on my hair. The poodle cuts had grown out by now and my hair was shoulder length. Tricia told me that brushing my hair a hundred times would make it shinier. So, I'd hang my head upside down and brush repeatedly until I was lightheaded and static-ridden.

I spent as much time as possible out of the house and at the bottom of the hill with Lucas. Mother called the executors of Dolmer's estate every day without fail. Les and Hoyt were brothers and lawyers. I had met them only once or twice when we lived in Mississippi in '67. When she finally talked to them a week or so after we arrived, they told her it would be months before the estate was settled. That didn't sit too well with Mother.

"Well, Les, that's just not gonna do," she said. "I need that money now." Les must have asked her why.

"Well, that's none of your business, Les." She listened for just a moment and then interrupted, "It doesn't matter what Edith told you. I'm an heiress, and I want my money." I strained to hear what Les was saying, but couldn't make it out.

Mother was shaking her head, "No, Les. I want it now." She pulled the earpiece away and shouted, "Well, we'll just see about that," and then she slammed the phone down.

Barbara, who had been washing lima beans at the kitchen sink, had cocked her head to one side to hear the conversation better. She straightened up when Mother slammed the phone down and turned to see Mother's expression.

"Aunt Mary is there a problem with the money?" she asked.

"Nothing the Lord can't handle," Mother bragged.

"Aunt Mary, you know I'm happy y'all come to visit," Barbara paused and seemed to be searching for the right words. I was willing her not to say anymore. "But I thought you'd be leaving after a couple of days. This here's a small place."

"Well, Barbara, I'm surprised at you," Mother was taken aback, "We've been helping out to earn our keep."

"Of course, Aunt Mary," she paused again, "it's just that since you run outta money, I been buying the food, and I can't keep doing that."

"I know that, Barbara," Mother answered sharply. "I promise you we'll be leaving soon. Just bear with us, please."

Barbara looked around her small and crowded living room. "I'll try to be patient."

I got up off the couch and quietly slinked out the front screen door. I decided I'd spend my evenings on the front porch from that day on. Maybe the house would be bigger for Barbara if I wasn't in it. Apparently, the thought never crossed my brothers' pea brains.

Tempers flared on and off for the next few days, that is until Dee and his gang showed up on their motorcycles late one night. The roar of the Harley Davidson motors rumbled like thunder through the holler below. As the thunderous roar drew closer and louder, Barbara raced out the back door to meet them. Six motorcycles roared up the gravel driveway and lined up next to each other in front of the house where they were suddenly silenced. We stood on the porch as Barbara ran to her man.

Dee dropped the kickstand, raised his leg over the seat, and just as he was pulling his helmet off his strawberry curls, Barbara landed in his arms and cried, "Oh, Dee, thank God you're home. It's been so hard without you."

Dee pushed her back gently and dropped his black helmet on the seat. "Don't get too excited, babe. I'm only here for the night." I hadn't seen

Dee for two years, but I would have recognized him anywhere. His muscular body was nearly six feet tall and his nose was straight and his jaw was square. He threw his leather jacket over his shoulder, lit a cigarette, and threw his other arm over his wife's shoulders. "What d'ya got to eat, woman?" he asked flirtatiously.

He caught sight of us on the porch and nodded to Mother, "Howdy y'all. Didn't know ya was still here." He waved to us slightly and looked down into Barbara's admiring eyes as they walked arm-in-arm into the house, "Where are my boys?"

"Doesn't he look just like James Dean?" Mother fawned.

Mike wasn't impressed, "Isn't he the one who died in a fiery car crash?"

"Shut up, Mike."

Dee was true to his word. After his wife fed and bedded him, he slept for a few hours, and he and his friends roared back down the drive by dawn. He said he was just passing through and wanted to say hi to his family.

After the roar of the motorcycles had faded into the distance, Mother turned and faced Barbara, who couldn't take her eyes off the driveway.

Mother said snidely, "Well that was quick, wasn't it? He barely said two words to us and now he's gone."

"He wasn't here to see you," Barbara retorted and turned to go back in the house.

I could see Mother's hackles were raised, and I knew that was not a good sign. Tricia and I exchanged worried glances. If only one of us could think of a diversion quickly.

"I hate to tell you this, girl, but that boy is up to no good," Mother just couldn't shut up. "And why is he traveling with women? Don't you think that's just a little bit peculiar?"

Barbara's nostrils were flaring, but before she could answer, Tricia came to the rescue, "Mother, I think you're supposed to call Les now, aren't you?"

"I almost forgot," Mother was distracted. "Let's call now—that should surprise him."

Barbara must have known about Ouija. I heard her talking in hushed tones to her mother in her bedroom each night. But Barbara never mentioned Ouija to us, and we didn't talk to Ouija in front of her. We waited until she went to bed, and then we'd close our bedroom door and talk.

"Lord, I'm feeling cooped up here with all these kids," Mother complained after Dee left. "When are we ever going to leave for Afghanistan?"

"D-R-I-V-E T-O M-E-M-P-H-I-S T-O-M-O-R-R-O-W"

"Memphis?" Mother asked, "But why?"

"T-I-M-E T-O M-A-K-E R-E-S-E-R-V-A-T-I-O-N"

The three of us looked at each other, wide-eyed. We knew we would have to give them a departure date to get tickets. "When are we leaving?" I asked.

"J-U-N-E 2-1"

"What?" Mother was stunned. "We don't have any money. How can we do that?"

"D-O-N-T N-E-E-D M-O-N-E-Y F-O-R R-E-S-E-R-V-A-T-I-O-N"

Mother asked me to find a piece of paper and write down what Ouija wanted us to do the next day. We were to go to Memphis International Airport and reserve seats to Kabul on Pan American Airways. We were to reserve seats for five people and a dog on June 21, 1969. Then Ouija instructed Mother to start the passport process. A group passport would cost less than individual passports we were told.

After placing Ouija under the bed in its hiding place, we stumbled excitedly down the hall past all the baskets of clothes until we reached the boys' room. Mother shook Mike and Timmy and as they rubbed their eyes, she explained the plan.

Mother wasted no time the next morning getting on the road to Memphis. We had never been to an airport, let alone been on airplane, so seeing the tower and terminal, crazy lanes of traffic and sudden turns into parking lots took a lot of nervous maneuvering on Mother's part.

Once inside the terminal, Mike and I stopped suddenly to stare at the lone television at the end of the ticket counter. We hadn't seen a television set since we left Vallejo. Mother and Tricia left us standing there and we raced to catch up with them at the Pan Am ticket counter. They were already talking to the ticket agent.

"Yes," Mother was nodding. "I'd like to make reservations for one-way tickets to Kabul, Afghanistan on June 21st."

"One way? Are you sure?" the ticket agent asked.

"Yes, ma'am," Mother repeated.

The ticket agent smiled, "Well, that's far away, isn't it now? Y'all movin' there?"

Mother smiled, "Yes ma'am."

The agent continued her typing and asked absently, "Why are you moving?"

Mother responded without hesitation, "I'm a journalist."

What? Did I miss something?

"Well, ma'am, we'll book you on American Airlines to New York. From there, you'll take Pan Am. Let me see what we can do for you." She flipped through a book and typed intermittently on the computer reservation system. Several minutes passed before she looked up at us again.

"Ma'am, it looks like you'll fly from Memphis to New York and then to Paris. From there, you'll fly to Beirut on to Teheran, and then into Kabul. Oh my," she stopped and glanced up at Mother. "It's a propeller plane from Teheran to Kabul—might be a bit bumpy. You'll arrive in Kabul on the morning of June 23rd." She kept typing. "Too bad you're not flying with Pan Am in December—they'll have their new 747s then."

Mother nodded absently and suddenly remembered Friend, "Oh, we have a dog, too."

The ticket agent cocked her head, "You're taking a dog?" Mother nodded and the agent continued, "That must be one special dog. You can take a dog to Afghanistan, but you can't bring a dog back to the United States. Quarantine issues."

"You could say he's special," Mother mused to herself. "We don't have to worry about quarantine. We're not planning on coming back," Mother said flatly. As the agent ticketed Friend and reserved a kennel, Mother asked, "I know we have to get a passport and an Afghan visa. Is there anything else we need to do?"

The agent handed Mother the itinerary she had printed and reached over for another sheet of paper. "This will tell you everything you need to do. It's from the State Department. You're going to need shots. Your dog too."

Mother asked timidly, "When do we have to pay for these tickets?"

"At least fifteen days prior to your flight, ma'am." She rested her elbows on the countertop and asked sweetly, "Is there anything else I can do for you?"

"No, thank you," Mother said nervously. Her hands trembled as she carefully folder the papers and placed them in her handbag.

"Well, that's that," she said as we crossed the street to the parked car. "We're going to Afghanistan in two months."

I couldn't contain myself anymore, "Why did you tell them you were a journalist?"

"Well, we can't tell people we're going to be missionaries, remember? Missionaries ain't allowed in Muslim countries."

We celebrated my fourteenth birthday with fried chicken and Mother's famous Texas sheet cake. It was tax day for everyone but us, Mother said. We had no money so we didn't have to worry about Uncle Sam. She had decided against calling Father and asking for money. Said we'd have to make do.

Barbara had been hinting for days that she knew about Ouija, and she wanted to talk to it. On my birthday, she just couldn't resist anymore and flat-out asked, "Aunt Mary, I know you been talking to a Ouija board." She flung the dish towel over her shoulder and continued, "I wanna ask it some questions, too."

Mother had been sitting at the table snapping peas while we cleared the dishes. As soon as Barbara mentioned Ouija, she dropped her head and let the handful of peas drop into the colander. She folded her hands on her lap and looked up determinedly, "Barbara, I don't know what Edith's been telling you."

"Oh, I know, Mary," Barbara apologized. "Momma told me it said it was God. If it's God, then it'll surely have the right answers. I just need to know some things."

"It's not that easy, Barb," Mother was shaking her head. "Sometimes people learn things that they don't want to know, and then they get mad at me and Tricia."

"Well, that's not a happening, fo' sure," Barbara said emphatically as she squeezed both of Mother's shoulders. "Come on, Mary. Please. Please," she begged.

Tricia was behind Barbara at the kitchen sink. She was doing a great impression of a silent film star. Shaking her head emphatically behind Barbara's back and motioning wildly for Mother to say no. Mother gave in to Barbara. "Timmy, get the Ouija board. It's under my bed."

Tricia was not happy and neither was I. It would have been better if Barbara didn't talk to the Ouija board. I was sure something terrible would come of this session. Where would we go if Barbara kicked us out? I was frantic. I didn't like sleeping in cars.

After the board was placed between them on the table, Tricia and Mother placed their fingers on the indicator, and it started moving, "H-E-L-L-O B-A-R-B-A-R-A"

Barbara sat down next to Tricia and answered tentatively, "Hello, uh. What do I call it?"

"You can just call it Ouija, if you want," Mother said.

Barbara conversed easily with the board, asking questions about her mountain and her kids' future. She asked if Dee was ok and was comforted to hear that he was just fine.

Then she asked, "Lord, what will I be doin' in a couple of years?"

"G-E-T-T-I-N-G M-A-R-R-I-E-D"

I had taken over snapping peas from Mother. When I realized what the board had spelled, I stopped and turned my gaze toward Barbara to see her reaction. Her mouth hung open, and she was trying to speak, but no sounds escaped her throat. She gained her voice after what seemed like an eternity and finally asked, "What did you say?"

'Y-O-U W-I-L-L B-E G-E-T-T-I-N-G M-A-R-R-I-E-D"

"But I'm already married," she answered incredulously. "Will I *re*marry Dee?"

The indicator moved slowly to NO.

"What's going to happen to Dee?" she asked. "Are we getting divorced?"

Again Ouija answered NO.

Barbara stood suddenly and her chair crashed to the floor. She turned to leave, but then rounded on Mother and demanded, "What's it saying?" and then louder, "What's it saying?"

Mother stood up and reached out to hug Barbara, but Barbara wrenched herself free and began sobbing uncontrollably. Friend, who was let in the house to eat, was immediately on his feet and barking viciously at Barbara. Timmy held Friend back and tried to stop the barking, to no avail.

The noise was unbearable—Barbara crying, Mother trying to calm her, Friend barking, and Timmy yelling. All the while, Tricia's fingers hadn't left the indicator. It was as if they were glued to it. She seemed above the hysteria.

"Barbara," Mother was calm. "The Ouija board didn't say Dee was going to die. There's no reason for you to be this upset—"

"Don't tell me not to be upset," Barbara yelled. "What else could it be, Mary? We ain't remarrying and we ain't divorcing," she counted on her fingers. "It's telling me that he's going to be dead. They're all right," she said backing away from the table. "This board is evil."

"Barbara, please don't," Mother pleaded.

"So you didn't think I'd be mad hearin' that?" Barbara said, looking suspiciously from Mother to Tricia. "It's one of you, ain't it?"

"Don't be silly, Barbara. Do you think we could have predicted the things that it has told us about? It's God, and you need to be more respectful, for your own good," Mother warned.

"Are you threatening me, Mary?"

"I'm just warning you for your own good and the good of your children. Things have happened to people who question this board," Mother pleaded for the second time.

"That's it," Barbara flashed. "I want you and the board out of my house right this instant." She turned to Timmy and the dog and screamed, "And shut that stupid dog up!" She walked to her room and before slamming the door, yelled, "You won't be leeching off me anymore!"

Mother signaled for us to gather our belongings. We hurriedly threw our things into our worn suitcases and left Barbara's mountain within fifteen minutes. The Plymouth wound its way slowly off the mountain in pitch black. I wept silently inside and pressed my head hard against the window to try and erase this memory from my mind.

Mother stopped at the junction of Route 15 and lowered her forehead onto the steering wheel. She sat like that for a few minutes. None of us spoke. She suddenly raised her head and said stoically, "It was time to move on, anyway." She dabbed at the tears running down her cheek. "We need to get back to the Lord's work."

Chapter 15

Jeane Dixon

"Man, that's so cool," Ramie said admiringly as he took another drag on his Marlboro. "Sure wish I didn't have to go to no school." He tipped his cigarette pack towards Mike, "Want one?" He tossed his head back in a futile attempt to shake his straight black bangs from his eyes. Ramie reminded me a lot of cousin Aubrey—tall, lanky and Indian-straight hair.

Mike grinned broadly and accepted, "Sure."

"Hey, how about us?" Timmy whined as he pointed to me.

Ramie lit the cigarette for Mike and drawled, "Nah, yer too little." Mike drew in the first breath of smoke and coughed until I thought for sure his lungs would explode all over us. He seemed to get the hang of it after the second cigarette, though. Timmy and I watched enviously as the two lanky teenagers leaned on the rocks and enjoyed their cigs.

Ramie was the only child of Mother's first cousin, Francis Griffin, who was Uncle Price and Aunt Bertha's daughter. Francis had married J.R. Abernath at about the same time as our parents married, and the cousins had stayed in touch over the years. Unlike her cousin, Francis hadn't left her home on Harper Road since Ramie was born.

The four of us had escaped to the woods after breakfast. We sat in Ramie's old play fort and compared California schools to Mississippi schools. While the boys talked excitedly, my mind returned to our sudden departure the night before from Barbara's and our current state of homelessness.

Mother had instinctively turned south onto Highway 45 after we left Barbara's. Just across the Tennessee line, she pulled the Plymouth into a closed gas station and told us to wait in the car while she made a phone call.

"Who's she calling?" Tricia had asked as Mother closed the phone booth door. The booth was lit eerily in the mist.

"Maybe Granddaddy Furtick," I yawned, glancing over at my brothers. Mike was sound asleep with his head resting on the window. Timmy's head was on Mike's shoulder and drool was hanging precariously from his lower lip, poised perfectly to drip onto Mike's shirt. Friend was snoring loudly behind my head.

"I don't think that would be such a good idea," Tricia was alarmed.

"He'll let us stay with him," I said. "We're his grand kids. Besides, Doshie won't let him turn us away. She likes us."

Truth be told, I liked Doshie better than granddaddy, even though she was just a step-grandmother. She'd had Parkinson's disease since forever, and when she talked, I was reminded of a needle skipping on an LP record. "Marr-yy," she'd say, "We're soo glaa-ad to see-ee y'allll." If I closed my eyes, she sounded just like Kathryn Hepburn in the *African Queen*.

"You don't know anything," Tricia snapped. "Have you forgotten that Aunt Edith told granddaddy about the Ouija board. He used to be a preacher. He's not going to let this "devil" into *his* house, no matter what Doshie says." I rolled my eyes dramatically and turned my head to stare out the window.

We watched in silence as Mother talked animatedly for a minute, then listened to the other person, and finally hung up the phone. I sure hoped she had found someone to take us in. Once she was settled back in the front seat, she sighed heavily. "I just wanted to call daddy and see if he'd offer to let us stay there. He doesn't want to see us."

"Where are we going then?" I asked furtively.

"Cousin Francis lives about fifteen miles from here," Mother turned the ignition key and backed the car out onto 45 again. "She'll take us in for a couple of days."

With no money and nowhere else to go, we headed to Francis' house in Alcorn County, just north of Corinth. We traveled the last two miles on a gravel road surrounded by crowded pine trees, bending claustrophobically above the road in the circular light of our high beams. As we pulled into the driveway at a small unlit house, Mother turned off the headlamps.

"I can't wake them," she said, frowning. "We'll wait 'til morning."

"Oh, great, we get to sleep in the car again," I mumbled before closing my eyes and pushing Timmy's head off my shoulder. I slept fitfully in the backseat for the next few hours and was awakened by a rooster crowing just before dawn. My joints were stiff from sleeping upright. I quietly opened the car door and stood, stretching my legs and neck. The pine trees' sweet smell nearly gagged me as I slowly turned, surveying my new surroundings. We were definitely in the backwoods—not a house in sight other than Francis'.

As the sun rose behind the trees I could make out that this house was even smaller than Barbara's. Two bedrooms at the most, I worried. A rusted can with dried peach paint dripping down the side sat on the porch near the steps. A paint-caked brush lay near it, left there months ago I judged from the dust. The porch banister was freshly painted peach, but the rails were a mud-caked brown. Green shutters lay willy-nilly on the grass next to a garden hose and on the clothesline hung stiff, grey-tinged boxers and undershirts waiting to be rescued from the morning dew.

Just then, a woman's head appeared from behind a curtain in one of the dusty windows. I waved timidly and she smiled in return. The door creaked open, and Francis appeared in the doorway, holding her robe closed with one hand. J.R. followed close behind, suspenders flapping and hopping on one foot. The other foot he held in his right hand as he waved and smiled from the doorway. I was shocked to see the detached foot and then remembered that he had lost his left leg below the knee during World War II.

"Lordy mercy," Francis exclaimed as she shaded her eyes with one hand and squinted at the early morning sun. "Is that you Mary Frances?" She and Mother reached each other and embraced tightly. I lost sight of Francis in the embrace. She was stick thin and grey-haired.

"Francis, it's been too long," Mother smiled. "We was just passing through and thought it'd be mighty nice to see you," she half-lied.

Tricia opened the passenger car door and stood slowly, still rubbing her eyes. As soon as Francis caught sight of Tricia's face, she froze. Mother looked from Francis to Tricia and back. "What's wrong? You look like you seen a ghost," she laughed.

"Well, might near," Francis stood transfixed, staring at Tricia. "I dreamt 'bout her last night," she said without taking her eyes off Tricia.

"What?" Mother asked. "Are you sure it was her?"

"Aww, never you mind. I jest recognized her is all," Francis said, finally tearing her eyes away from Tricia and ushering everyone into the house. "It don't mean nothin', Mary Frances. I swear, yer a sight for sore eyes," she said rubbing my back as I passed. "I'll bet you boys is hungry."

I couldn't wait to hear about the dream, but Francis became preoccupied with breakfast. Mother grilled her relentlessly about the Horns—Les and Hoyt, in particular. We couldn't get a word in edgewise. That's when we headed for the woods and our smoking club.

"So, what's this here Ouija board I been hearin' 'bout?" Ramie asked me out of the blue. I instinctively avoided eye contact with him and turned to Mike.

"How'd you know about that?" Mike was ready for a fight. "Who told you?"

Before Ramie could answer, we heard Francis' voice in the distance calling us back to the house.

Inside, J.R. was sprawled on the sofa with both feet attached, thankfully, and a deck of cards spread in piles on the coffee table in front of him. Mother, Tricia and Francis were finishing the breakfast dishes at the kitchen sink.

"Are you playing solitaire?" Timmy asked. Timmy was always up for any game.

"Naw, this here's a game that has no name. It's mathematical," J.R. laughed. The half-chewed cigar hung from his lip and his big belly shook under a grey-tinged beater shirt. "You want me to teach it to y'all?" he asked, gathering the cards in his left hand.

He turned the cards over in his hand with the card faces where he could see them. "Just start counting from the first card you see. This is a ten, so you take that card and put it against your palm, like this, face out. Then you add more cards to it, counting from that card—ten, eleven, twelve, thirteen. You count to thirteen cuz there's thirteen cards in each house," he paused.

"Then you put that pile of cards face down on the table." He continued counting out other piles of cards using that method until he had ten or more piles of cards on the table, all facing down.

"Timmy, take away all but three of the piles," he said confidently. Timmy did as he was told and held the cards in his hand. "Ok, now turn the top card over on two of the piles you got left." Again, Timmy did it. "Add the two cards together—that's an eight and a seven. So, that's fifteen. Then you add ten to whatever number you get. That's twenty-five."

He took the cards from Timmy's hand and counted out twenty-five cards. "Now, the number of cards left in my hand will equal the card on the top of the last pile. That's seven cards left and so that card is a seven." Timmy turned the top card over and it was indeed a seven of clubs.

"Wow." we said in unison. "Show us the card trick again."

"It ain't no card trick. It's a mathematical game," Ramie teased Timmy, laughing. We spent the next half hour trying to duplicate J.R.'s results. After consistent success, I tired of the card challenge and joined the women at the kitchen table, hoping to hear more about this dream of Francis'.

I got there just in time. "Francis, tell me 'bout your dream," Mother said as she folded her hands on the table and gave Francis her full attention.

Francis closed her eyes and raised her head toward the ceiling, "Let me see," she said, struggling to recall all the details.

"This here dream was two nights ago. I was in an amazing church. It was so long that I couldn't see the end and it were taller than a 30 story skyscraper. There was windows on both sides. I counted 'em—twelve on each side. They were tall as the building," Francis paused. "Mary Frances, you all right?"

Mother's face turned ashen in front of my eyes. My heart skipped a beat as Tricia and I exchanged wide-eyed stares. "Oh, my god," Mother said from behind her hand.

"What's the matter?" Francis prodded.

"No, no, you finish your story, then I'll tell you," Mother said.

"Ok," Francis was shaken, but continued retelling her dream. "I was walking through the church staring up at the roof and the mountains outside the windows, and when I looked back in front of me, suddenly there was a dark-haired girl walking in front of me." She looked at Tricia and nodded, "It was you, Tricia. That's why I stared at you when you got outta yer car."

"Go on, Francis," Mother urged.

"Well, I was follering behind Tricia here, and she was wearing a purple flowing robe with gold trim," Francis pursed her lips and frowned. "And I leaned 'round her to see what was ahead of us. I was worried we was going to run inter somethin'. That's when I seen the gold crown sitting on a white pedestal near a round fountain. A ray of light was shining down on it from above."

Francis shook her head slowly and squinted her eyes at something in the distance, "I looked up at the ceiling, but there weren't no light bulbs above the crown. I don't know where that light came from, Mary Frances. It's got me stymied."

"It must have been God's light," Mother whispered to no one.

"Must've been," Francis repeated, nodding her head. "I kept follering Tricia, amazed at everything, and then I heard a rumbling sound, almost like the earth was rolling under my feet. Tricia fell to the side, and I could see the crown falling off the pedestal. It crashed onto the floor and broke into a million pieces." Francis shrugged her shoulders and concluded, "And that's the end of the dream. I don't know what it means."

"Francis, you just described the church that we are supposed to build in Afghanistan," Mother said flatly.

"Shut yer mouth." Francis shoved Mother's shoulder for emphasis, and then she surprised us, "Is that what the Ouija board told y'all?"

"So you know about the Ouija board?" Mother asked suspiciously. "Who told you?"

Francis shook her head vigorously, anticipating Mother's reaction to what she would say next. "Edith told me, Mary Frances. But wait a minute 'for yo get yer blood aboiling, you know I don't hold with nothin' Edith says.

I believe that spirits talks to us all the time," she stopped. "We just gotta be listening is all. Gotta keep an open mind, ya know."

She looked around the table at the three of us in turn. "And it sounds like yer spirit wants you to do good things, so it ain't no bad spirit."

"It was a spirit at first," Mother corrected Francis solemnly. "Now it's God."

"You jest got to tell me the whole story," Francis insisted.

I suddenly noticed that J.R. and Ramie were intently listening to our conversation. Mother motioned for them to join us at the table, and then she related the entire story from beginning to ending up at their house. We sat like that at the kitchen table for three hours, with Francis asking pointed questions about the spirit and offering confirmation that spirits do indeed walk the earth, giving advice and guidance to humans.

Mother finished the story just before dinnertime. After Francis had put away the last cleaned and dried dish, she pleaded with Mother, "Please let me talk to yer spirit."

Mother couldn't refuse her and asked Tricia to get the board from the car.

"Do you think it'll talk to me?" Francis asked as she gnawed relentlessly on her left nail cuticle. Just then ashes fell from her cigarette onto the floor, but she ignored them.

"Ouija talks to everyone," Tricia consoled her as she placed her fingertips on the indicator.

"H-E-L-L-O"

"Is it talkin' to me?" Francis squeaked.

The indicator slid to YES.

"Was my dream about this here girl?" she asked, gently rubbing Tricia's upper arm.

The indicator slid quietly to YES and continued, "I S-P-E-A-K I-N D-R-E-A-M-S," Ouija paused. "R-E-M-E-M-B-E-R J-O-S-E-P-H"

"What were you trying to tell her?" Mother interrupted.

"S-H-E   S-A-W   A-F-G-H-A-N-I-S-T-A-N   A-N-D T-E-M-P-L-E"

"But why did the crown fall?" Mother was very curious. "I mean, why would the crown fall when Patricia came down the aisle?" She looked at Tricia suspiciously.

"E-A-R-T-H-Q-U-A-K-E"

"But why would you let it fall?" Francis asked. "Isn't it your son's crown?"

The indicator slid slowly to NO.

"Whose crown is it?" Mother asked.

"T-H-I-N-K A-B-O-U-T I-T"

The hair on my arms stood up as I murmured, "The crown is the antichrist?"

The indicator slid quickly to YES.

"The antichrist will be destroyed before the thousand years of peace," Francis murmured, eyes glued to the indicator. She looked up at Mother then, "That's when Christ will rule the earth."

"He's going to rule it in Afghanistan," Mother finished for her. "In the church we build."

Francis suddenly stood, hands covering her mouth. She was trying desperately to hold back her next words. "Is Christ coming in the flesh?"

The indicator moved to YES.

"And was he born on February 5, 1962?" she asked frantically. "At 7:17 am?

My head jerked around to face Francis. What?

Again, the indicator moved to YES.

Mother must have been just as shocked as I was by the exchange between Francis and Ouija. Regaining her power of speech quickly, she asked, "Francis, what are you talking about?"

"Mary Frances, it was Jeane Dixon what predicted a child was born in the Middle East on February 5, 1962 who would revolutionize the world," she answered bravely.

"How do you know this?" Mother squinted at her cousin, fingers still glued to the indicator.

"Let me get the book," Francis said as she rose and dug feverishly through a stack of worn books on her end table. "Here 'tis," she read, "*A Gift of Prophecy—The Phenomenal Jeane Dixon.*" She started reading from the back cover of the book, "Jeane Dixon predicted the assassination of President Kennedy and Marilyn Monroe's suicide."

Francis flipped through the last pages in the book and read, "Mankind, Jeane Dixon has said, will begin to feel the great force of this man about 1980, and his power "will grow mightily" until 1999, when there will be peace on earth to all men of good will."

Francis clapped the book closed between her hands and proclaimed, "Yer talking to God almighty, Mary Frances."

Chapter 16

The Extortion

The old farmhouse looked smaller from this side of the road, I decided. I slowly shook my head in disgust at the millions of acorns that had fallen over the past two autumns. No one cared enough to gather them, and there was not a squirrel in sight. Did they all die or something?

The farm's giant oak tree—the acorn mess culprit—hid the afternoon sun from my eyes as I peered out the window of our duplex. On a whim, Mother had called Miss Mattie to inquire about her health last week. She learned that the other half of Miss Mattie's duplex was vacant. Within minutes Mother had convinced Miss Mattie to let us live in it rent free until we left for Afghanistan.

I opened the lace curtains slightly so I could see our old farmhouse better—the one we lived in for seven months the year before. The wrap-around porch was sagging awfully and a tangle of vines had overgrown the dingy white siding. It looked almost the same now as it had when we moved *into* it, but Mother said it was a bargain at twenty-five dollars a month.

Mother called it Tara II after the O'Hara's plantation in *Gone with the Wind*. Just as Scarlett had saved Tara, Mother was determined to save Tara II. So, after a lot of scrubbing, cleaning, raking, hammering, and bonfires fueled by burning junk, the house was transformed from a shack into a real six-bedroom farmhouse. Four fireplaces warmed the house at the turn of the century, but we had only enough money to buy wood for the rusted pot-bellied stove in the living room.

I sighed as I remembered our time at the house across the street from Miss Mattie. Tired of having nothing in the house to eat, and despite Father's protests, Mother went to the government for help. She said she wasn't too proud to ask for handouts. We were excited when she brought the bags of groceries in the kitchen; that is, until we saw what they contained. Canned pork brains, cow tongue, pigs feet, and evaporated milk. The can of Spam was a welcome sight.

Mother bought twenty chickens and a rooster, and we soon had fresh eggs to go with the pork brains. Our milk came straight from a cow down the road. After the cream rose to the top, we skimmed it off and churned it in a mayonnaise jar until it turned into creamy butter.

I had my very own bedroom for the first time in that house. My room was just off the dining room and had its own fireplace and separate door to the wraparound porch. I remember how grown-up I felt because of the bedroom.

A shiver ran down my spine as I remembered that when the pot-bellied stove's embers died at night in winter, the cold would begin its sinister attack on my bedroom. One morning, it left a half-frozen glass of water in its wake, which sent Mother scrambling to the attic for a musty featherbed. She claimed some bricks from the barn and wrapped them in flannel and laid them next to the pot-bellied stove all day. She slipped one under my covers at the foot of the bed that night. Warm indeed.

After the house he was building had been completed, Father wanted to move back to Avondale. Barbara and Dee visited a week after Christmas in '67. That's when Mother asked them for money to get back to Arizona—against Father's wishes.

I was sad to see how quickly the house and its apple orchards, chicken coops and pigpens had been swallowed up by the vines and weeds.

Our work had been in vain. The house had lost the battle with nature after we left.

"Diana, get over here right now," Mother's voice echoed sharply through the empty apartment. I turned away from the window and let the lace curtains swing gracefully closed on my memories.

Mother and Tricia shifted on the folding metal chairs that Miss Mattie had loaned us. The Ouija board was balanced between them on a small, rusted patio table. Their backs were bent uncomfortably as they stretched for the indicator. I plopped down on the wood floor beside them and listened, half-heartedly.

A stream of sunlight began angling through the window, beckoning me to join it outdoors. I wanted desperately to leave the small, empty living room and play outside. Timmy and I had dug a big hole in the dirt under the Southern Magnolia tree the day before—a city with roads and everything—for his Matchbox cars. I knew that if I didn't get out there soon, Mike would destroy our city just like he destroyed everything. Mother was determined to keep me inside.

"Lord," Mother said to Ouija. "We have to pay for the airplane tickets in five weeks, and I don't even have enough money for food. Hoyt told me we won't have the money for at least three months." She paused, "What are we going to—"

Ouija interrupted, "F-A-I-T-H"

Mother sat sullenly for a full minute, lips pursed tightly as she chose her words with care, "Lord, our passports should've been back by now from the Afghan embassy."

"Y-O-U W-I-L-L H-A-V-E S-O-O-N"

Tricia and I exchanged worried glances. What if Mother stopped believing again, and we were stuck in Mississippi for the rest of our lives?

"W-H-A-T I-S N-E-E-D-E-D T-O G-E-T M-O-N-E-Y"

Ouija must be talking about praying, but we prayed all the time and nothing improved with this money thing. Maybe the airline would let us pay for our tickets later was all I could think.

Mother looked confused, "What do you mean?" she asked.

"C-O-N-V-I-N-C-E H-O-Y-T T-O G-I-V-E M-O-N-E-Y N-O-W"

"You want me to beg?" she asked.

The indicator slid sharply to NO. "Y-O-U K-N-O-W"

Suddenly, Mother understood. "You want me to blackmail Hoyt," she said matter-of-factly.

"N-O-T B-L-A-C-K-M-A-I-L," the indicator paused. "P-E-R-S-U-A-D-E"

I had no idea what Ouija was talking about, but Tricia smiled knowingly. What did she know that I didn't?

Ouija told Mother to get to work on the plan and said GOODBYE.

"I gotta talk to Francis," Mother mumbled, slamming the front door behind her. She pounded on Miss Mattie's door. Once she was safely out of sight, I slipped out the back and within seconds, Timmy and I were arguing over matchbox cars.

* * *

With no television, books, church, or school, we nearly died from boredom during our sojourn at Mattie's. For entertainment, I decided to memorize the Book of Matthew. I methodically recited each verse over and over until I knew it by heart, and then I'd go to the next verse. Then I'd recite that verse and the earlier verses.

I was very proud of myself as I recited the last two verses: "Go ye therefore, and teach all nations, baptizing them in the name of the Father, and of the Son, and of the Holy Ghost; Teaching them to observe all things whatsoever I have commanded you: and, lo, I am with you always, even unto the end of the world."

"Miss Walking Book of Matthew," Mike sneered as he slugged my arm randomly. "I'm getting sick of you doing this."

Tricia said I should ignore him and go on and memorize the Book of Mark. I decided that one book was enough. I became convinced though that I had run out of brain cells to store any more words. I'd have to dump some if I wanted to memorize more.

On June 1st, right after breakfast, Mother announced, "Today's the day." She had procrastinated visiting Les and Hoyt's office for almost two weeks. During the two weeks, she talked to Francis two or three times a day on Miss Mattie's phone. Now we had only five days 'til we had to pay for the plane tickets. She changed from her housecoat to her traveling suit and fussed with her hair for way too long in front of the mirror. I was sure she was trying to bolster her courage for the planned extortion.

Mother insisted that the four of us go with her to Hoyt's office. "He might feel sorry for me with the four of you there," she said hopefully.

At ten o'clock, Francis pulled her '54 Hudson Hornet in front of the duplex and beeped her horn. "Mary Frances," she yelled from the street. "Let's git going 'fore you chicken out."

"I ain't gonna chicken out, Francis," Mother said breathlessly as we stuffed ourselves into the small car. "I gotta go through with this. I've got no choice."

"I passed Hoyt's and seen him sitting on the park bench outside his office. He was jest starin' into the sun," she chuckled as she maneuvered the Hornet back onto the road, tires squealing and gravel flying behind us. "He's got no idea what's fixin' to happen to him. Blame ignorant weasel."

"Momma always said he had about as much sense as a cracked piss ant," Mother cackled. "Blame fool, don't know lookin' at the sun will make you go blind."

"That and masturbating," Francis giggled.

Mother laughed and then frowned, embarrassed as she sideways glanced at us kids in the backseat.

She changed the subject suddenly, "Is Les there or just Hoyt? I don't want to do this with both of them there."

"I didn't see Les' car. Besides he don't get in the office this early," she said as she glanced at her watch. "Hoyt is the only one yer gonna face, Mary Frances."

The Hornet sneaked up the alley behind Les and Hoyt's office, and Francis shut off the engine. She said she didn't want them to see us coming. We froze. "Maybe he'll give me the money, and I won't have to persuade him," Mother crossed her fingers as she reached for the door handle.

"I'll be waitin' fer ya here," Francis whispered. "Go ahead kids, get out."

Mother led the way around the building and into the glass doors with "Law Offices" painted in gold. She nodded her head toward the row of wooden chairs outside the office. "Sit down there and wait for me," she said. We didn't argue with her.

Through the door's clean glass pane, I could see a woman typing. I admired her graceful hands moving across the keys. Her eyes never left the paper on the typing stand at her left. She said hello to Mother and picked up the phone to let Hoyt know we were there. "He'll see you now," she said curtly and turned back to the typewriter. Mother turned and looked back at us for courage. Just then, an inner door opened and out of it popped a bald head.

Hoyt stepped out of the doorway and grinned at Mother warily, "Why come on in, Mary Frances." He glimpsed us in the hallway and waved.

He ushered Mother through the door and left it slightly ajar. I strained to hear bits and pieces of their conversation.

"Now, Mary Frances," he blustered, "you know the answer to your question before you even ask it. I ain't givin' you no money. You'll have to wait with the other heirs until the estate is settled. Why, I haven't even sold Dolmer's farm—" And then his voice trailed off. Drat.

"Hoyt, I think you're going to reconsider that," Mother began. "Do you remember when Aunt Nove died?"

"What's that got to do with anything?" Hoyt sounded puzzled.

Mother lowered her voice and I couldn't make out what she was saying. She talked for a good minute before Hoyt exclaimed, "Are you trying to blackmail me?"

The woman stopped typing and looked in our direction nervously. She rose stiffly and gingerly pulled the door closed. She nodded to us and her eyes said, "There'll be no more eavesdropping."

Five minutes passed, and we heard no sounds coming from Hoyt's office. Mike and Timmy couldn't take it anymore and headed toward the front door. Just then, Hoyt's door opened and Mother strode out, brazenly waving a small piece of paper and smiling smugly.

Hoyt followed her and stopped next to the woman's desk. "Mary Frances, I think I liked you better as a sinner. Christianity doesn't become you."

"Sticks and stones, Hoyt," Mother retorted without looking back. "Sticks and stones."

Back in the Hornet, Mother waved the check in the air, "Four thousand six hundred dollars," she clucked. "That's enough to get us to Afghanistan and have some money left for a place and food. There'll be more money coming when the estate settles."

"By God, it worked," Francis was amazed. "He jest wrote you a check?"

"He just took out his pen and wrote me a check," Mother said, "What do ya say we get some ice cream on the way back to the house?" She smiled sheepishly, "I'm buying."

"Well, hallelujah," Francis rejoined.

Chapter 17

Destination Kabul

June 24, 1969

"Get ready to say goodbye to the USA, Diana," Mother said as she leaned over me and peered out my window. "You'll never set foot on American soil again." She smiled, settled her large self into the small seat, and turned her attention back to the stewardess who was demonstrating a flotation device.

Gravity clutched at my body as the wheels of the Pan Am jet left the runway at John F. Kennedy International Airport. I wasn't sure if the sinking feeling in my stomach had to do with gravity or what Mother had just said.

As our plane ascended, the twinkling lights of New York City grew fainter and fainter in my window until they were gone and replaced by the stars above. My stomach finally settled as the plane leveled off. I could see only pitch black below. The dark waters of the Atlantic Ocean, I guessed.

I leaned my head against the window of the plane and recalled what Ouija had said the night before we left Corinth and drove to Memphis to catch the first leg of what we thought would be a two-day journey to Kabul.

"L-E-A-V-E T-H-E B-O-A-R-D W-I-T-H F-R-A-N-C-I-S," Ouija had commanded out of the blue.

Mother stared at the board and grimaced at Francis, "No, Lord. How will I talk to you?"

"T-H-R-O-U-G-H P-R-A-Y-E-R"

Francis rose quickly and tried to rub Mother's back. Mother would not be consoled. She angrily pushed Francis' hand away and continued,

"Why can't we take the Ouija board? I don't understand." Tears welled in her eyes, and she pleaded wildly with Tricia, who just stared at the indicator and left her hands poised lightly on it.

Mother pressed her hands against her chest and rocked back and forth. She wailed, "My husband abandoned me, and now God has abandoned me. I can't do this alone." Beads of sweat magically appeared on her forehead and upper lip as she rose from her folding metal chair. "I'm calling Levoy."

It was clear to me that Mother was about to back out. What would happen to us then? Where would we go?

Tricia broke her silence and gave Mother the evil eye—a trick we all had learned from Mother. She scolded her, "You're not alone. We're with you.'

"Yeah, we're with you," I said, my arms outstretched in a symbolic embrace.

"And which of you is going to support this family?" Mother hissed sullenly.

We stared at her, unable to respond. Finally, Mike said what was slowly dawning on me too, "You're scared. You're a deserter—you got us this far and now you're backing out—just like you always do."

"Look who's talking," she retorted. A minute passed. None of us said a word. Mother took turns glowering at each of us—looking for weakness in our resolve, I was sure. Realizing that we were determined to stand up to her, she slowly placed her fingers back on the indicator.

"Y-E O-F L-I-T-T-L-E F-A-I-T-H," Ouija spelled slowly. "I W-I-L-L P-R-O-V-I-D-E"

"But how can I build a temple without Levoy?" Mother shook her head sadly.

"L-E-V-O-Y W-I-L-L C-O-M-E" Ouija paused. "L-A-T-E-R"

"See, Mary," Francis was still standing next to Mother. She repeated, "Levoy's coming later."

"But the money *will* run out, Lord," Mother said ignoring Francis. "What will I do then?"

"F-E-A-R   N-O-T," Ouija commanded harshly and then said something Mother was completely unprepared for, "R-E-V-O-K-E P-O-W-E-R O-F A-T-T-O-R-N-E-Y"

"What?" Mother couldn't believe her ears. "Won't that put a stop to the probate of the estate? I mean, I'll never get the rest of my money. How will we live?"

"T-R-U-S-T I-N M-E"

Mother closed her eyes and bowed her head in submission, "Yes, Lord."

"I-T   I-S   T-I-M-E" Ouija paused and then spelled, "R-E-V-E-L-A-T-I-O-N-S 2-2 V-E-R-S-E-S 2-0 A-N-D 2-1"

I reached for the Bible we kept on the TV tray and opened it to the last page of Revelations. "He which testifieth these things saith, 'Surely I come quickly.' Amen, Even so, come Lord Jesus. The grace of our Lord Jesus Christ be with you all, Amen." I finished reading the final words in the Bible and closed it gently.

"G-O F-O-R-T-H"

* * *

Mother said God abandoned us in New York City.

We left Memphis on Friday, June 21, with only a promise from the Afghan Embassy that our passport and visa would be waiting for us at the American Airlines counter at JFK. For the first few hours after we arrived at that airport, Mother was unusually calm. As the hours passed—and no package arrived for us—hysteria overtook first her and then the rest of us. Pan Am would not take our trunk and luggage since we couldn't board their plane. So, a porter brought the bags, along with Friend's kennel over to American Airlines.

The nightmare continued. Friend barked hysterically from his kennel by the window while Mother stood, hands on hips, screaming and swearing at the poor ticketing agent. She seemed oblivious to the travelers around us who were pointing at her and whispering. I lowered my head, crossed by ankles in as ladylike a pose as I could muster, and intently studied my folded hands on my lap. If I sat there quietly, maybe people wouldn't think I was with her.

We had been sitting in the chairs near the American Airlines counter for nearly 12 hours. If I was to grow old and die in these chairs, I was glad to be wearing my favorite suit. I admired the gold threads running through the heavy fabric. I had optimistically purchased it from Goodwill in Vallejo and hadn't worn it once. I was saving it for this flight. Suddenly, the pain of the garter belt digging into my right thigh became unbearable, so I nonchalantly unclipped it. I looked up when the ticket agent announced the final boarding call for *our* Pan Am flight and watched, horrified, as the last passenger ran for the gate. *Our* gate.

Mother was sitting across from me now. She must have accepted our situation at that point. Her eyes were closed—to pray or to sleep, I wasn't sure. I noticed that the ticket agent had called a black porter over to the counter and was explaining our situation to him. He nodded his head slowly as he listened and then picked up the phone and made a call. When he was finished, he strode over to where Mother was sitting. She jerked awake and eyed him blearily.

"I found you a hotel room, ma'am," he said kindly. "It's after midnight, and you really got no options but to leave the airport."

Mother nodded absently as she began to gather her purse and jacket. "Come on kids."

Once we were settled in the hotel room, Mother said, "Thank the Lord for that nigger feller. If it hadn't been for him, I don't know what we would've done." I cringed again. When was she going to stop saying that?

For the next 24 hours, we waited anxiously at the Skyway Hotel for word that a special delivery package with our passport and visa had been delivered to someone—anyone. But, word never arrived and neither did the package.

On Sunday morning, Mother reached the Afghan Embassy on the phone. Apparently, the person on the other end was telling Mother that the Embassy had been closed on Friday because it was a Muslim holy day. As Mother listened intently, she covered the mouthpiece and whispered to us, "He says he personally handed the package to the Postal carrier on Thursday. It was marked for special delivery to American Airlines." She thanked him and hung up the phone.

"We should call the Post Office," Tricia urged Mother.

Mother ignored her. "They're closed today. I'm going to try American Airlines again," Mother said and immediately dialed the American Airlines ticket counter. "I'm getting tired of you people," she said angrily into the phone. "Your damned stupidity is costing me money. The Afghan Embassy said the package was delivered to your counter. So, you had better damn well find it."

For the rest of the day, Mother frantically and intermittently called American, Pan Am, and even airport administrators. With no one left to call, she agreed to let us ride the subway into the city and take in a few sights, including the skating rink at Rockefeller Center and Battery Park, where we saw the Statue of Liberty for the first time.

On Monday morning, Tricia again suggested that Mother call the post office. With no ideas of her own, Mother finally agreed and found the number for general delivery in the phone book.

"Thank God, you called us," the government employee said as Mother and I stood at the post office counter downtown. "We had almost given up hope of ever finding you. We knew the package had important travel documents, but no one at American would accept it." He smiled as he handed it to Mother, "Here you go. Enjoy your trip."

With our visa and passports in hand on Tuesday morning we took our final taxi ride back to JFK. After a desperate and last minute search for a kennel for Friend, we boarded the plane at 11:30 p.m.

I leaned forward in my seat and smiled gratefully at Tricia in the aisle seat in front of us. We would probably *still* be sitting in that hotel room if it wasn't for her. Or, worse yet, flying back to San Francisco.

* * *

Mother's voice carried above the whirring sound of the air conditioning vents over my head. I listened as she talked animatedly with a young woman across the aisle from her. I was still thinking about what she had confided to me after we boarded the plane. "I tore up the Revocation of Power of Attorney," she whispered. "I just can't make this harder for Edith and James, and besides, I'm going to need the rest of the money soon." God would just have to understand, she had said.

Our wheels touched down in Paris nearly ten hours later. Sleeping was impossible for me. Mother's body was overflowing into my seat, which required that I lean to the left for the whole flight. To make matters worse, we weren't allowed to leave the plane in Paris or Rome. But, at least I could say we had been in those cities. Way more than anyone else from Avondale could say.

Finally, we were told to deplane in Beirut. Mother said we'd be flying Ariana the rest of the way to Kabul. I was just thinking how good it felt to stand upright after 12 hours, when I spotted the machine gun wielding soldiers. As I stepped off the portable stairs, a soldier shouted at me in a language I did not understand. He motioned me to move behind Mother and I readily complied. I had never had a gun pointed at me.

We were led into a small terminal where we waited for our flight to Teheran. Right before I fell asleep in my chair, I heard a man tell Mother that we should stay at the Spinzar Hotel in Kabul. "Unfortunately, it's the only hotel in Kabul that Americans can abide," he paused. "At least until the Intercontinental Hotel is finished."

"This isn't a very big airplane," Mother said uncomfortably as she looked around the Ariana airplane. She waved to the young woman she had been talking to on the Pan Am flights.

"Melene's going to Kabul, too," Mother said. "Her Father works for some international agricultural group. She's been on vacation, and now she's going home," Mother smiled. "See, the Lord is taking care of us. He's given us another guardian angel." Melene's dark culy hair did look angelic, I thought.

We boarded a twin-propeller Ariana plane in Teheran. "These are getting more and more primitive," Mother said squeamishly to the stewardess. We couldn't talk over the roar of the engines.

"Lord, please keep us safe," Mother prayed, eyes closed tightly.

I had maneuvered into a window seat again. I watched the desert expand until tan was all I could see in every direction. Here and there were thin ribbons of green. I took off my garter and stockings in the bathroom in Teheran because it was so hot. And now this airplane didn't have air conditioning. As I took my jacket off, my own B.O. assaulted my nostrils. Yuck, I thought.

The plane began its descent into Kabul, and I grabbed Timmy's arm and shook it excitedly. We had not seen many photos of Kabul, so it was still mysterious for me. All we knew was that some of the people had cars, electricity, and running water.

The mountains below reminded me of the White Tank Mountains west of Litchfield. "Home," I said out loud as the wheels touched down on the runway. Exactly halfway around the world and a year after we started our journey, we arrived at our destiny.

June 26, 1969, 8:30 in the morning.

Chapter 18

Kabul

Melene Tippets lightly touched Mother's elbow to guide her toward her parents outside the Ariana gate at Kabul airport. She let go abruptly to hug her parents.

"Welcome home," they chimed together.

"We've missed you." Mrs. Tippets said sweetly, and then she looked over her shoulder at my Mother. "And you brought some friends with you?" she asked as she spied the five of us, our dog, and our disheveled pile of bags.

"Oh, I'm sorry," Melene turned away from her parents and put her arm back around Mother's shoulders. She squeezed tightly. "Mommy and Daddy," she started, "I'd like to introduce you to Mrs. Cain and her children."

"Salaam alaykum," her Father said in Farsi, thrusting his hand out to Mother. "How are you?"

Mother shook his hand and replied, "Salaam alaykum to you too," she said half in English. "We're fine, tired after traveling for two days."

"Well, that's understandable. You'll probably have jet leg for awhile," Mr. Tippets smiled. "Kosh-amad goftan," he said. "That means welcome."

"Thank you," Mother said. "We sure are glad to be here."

"Mrs. Cain is a journalist. She's writing a story about Afghanistan," Melene said enthusiastically. I cringed at the lie.

"Wonderful," Mr. Tippets smiled. "Bringing four children and a dog along is brave, I've got to admit. Is your husband with you?"

Mother must not have been prepared for that question, so Tricia answered, "He stayed in San Francisco. We'll be here for a few months."

"You're going to love the people of this country," Mr. Tippets said as he jerked Melene's bag from the sidewalk and started for the curb. "I lead the Wyoming team at the University Farm of Darulaman," he yelled over his shoulder. After shoving the bag in the small trunk, he turned to Mother, "Where are you staying in Kabul?"

"The Spinzar," she replied confidently. "At least for a day."

"That's probably the best hotel in Kabul right now."

"Do you have any suggestions about where we might live?" Mother asked, trying to siphon as much information as she could from the poor man's brain.

"Well, we live in Karte Char," he smiled and nodded knowingly at Mother's puzzled look. "It's a great area. Just tell the taxi driver to take you there. Do you speak Farsi?"

"Enough to get by, I guess."

"Well, taxi drivers will steal you blind, if they think you're a tourist," he cautioned. "You shouldn't pay any more than 200 afghanis for a taxi ride to the Spinzar."

"How much is that in dollars?"

"Umm, that's about four American dollars," he smiled at Mother's surprised look. "Everything's much cheaper here than in the U.S."

He shook hands with each of us and asked, "So, you'll be registering for school in the fall?"

Mother looked at him blankly.

Mr. Tippets tilted his head slightly and explained. "There's a private school for Americans and other internationals who speak English, called the

American International School of Kabul—that's AISK. It's on Darulaman Avenue—maybe four miles from the edge of Karte Char," he paused. "For your youngest here, there's Ahlmund Academy, a Christian elementary school that goes through eighth grade."

They talked for a few more minutes. Mr. Tippets wrote his phone number and address on a piece of paper and handed it to Mother. She clutched it to her chest like it was gold. And, then the Tippets were gone.

Mother eyed first our belongings and then the line of cabs. "We're never gonna get our suitcases in one taxi," she said as she waved to the line of cars.

"Salaam alaykum," the first driver said as he bounced out of the cab.

"Salaam alaykum," Mother replied. "Engelisi?" she asked, hopefully. The driver shook his head.

She held up two fingers, "Do taksi," she said confidently. He nodded and waved to the other car to pull forward.

"Baham?" she said uncertainly. "Together."

"Baham," The two drivers nodded to each other and picked up our bags. Mother motioned to me and Timmy to get into her taxi. Mike and Tricia were to follow in a second taxi with Friend, who took his time relieving himself on the tires before jumping into the cab.

I watched as the driver crammed our footlocker into the trunk and tried valiantly to close it. He pulled a length of kite string from his pocket and used it to tie the lid down. He smiled at me as he kneeled behind the car to tie the string to the tailpipe. "He's missing a bunch of teeth," I observed as I turned back around in the seat. He slid behind the steering wheel and adjusted the turban that had slid off his head. "Koja?" he asked.

I was hoping Mother understood that word—it wasn't one of mine. She nodded and pointed in front of the car. "Spinzar," she said. He nodded and yelled "Spinzar" out the window to the other driver.

That was the beginning of our "ride from hell," as Mother later dubbed it. The bumpy and frightening propeller plane that brought us from Teheran to Kabul didn't even compare to what came next.

The tires squealed as we pulled away from the airport terminal. It was then that I caught my first glimpse of the mountains from ground level. The Koh I Azamai mountain range rose high above the city to the west and to the south was the Koh I Sher Darwaza range. Although much taller than the Estrella and White Tank Mountains near Avondale, they were just as barren and just as rocky.

"Khiaban nam?" Timmy said, flaunting his mastery of Farsi.

"Bebe Mahro," the driver replied.

"It's the Bebe Mahro road," Timmy interpreted smugly.

"Yeah, thanks. I would never have guessed," I said.

Within seconds, dust had blanketed the car and my lungs. Mother hacked and fanned herself, but there was nothing we could do. The car had no air conditioning, and it was approaching 100 degrees. I closed my eyes and tried to imagine I was back in Avondale, wind ripping through my hair as we drove to Pugh's Grocery for a much-anticipated ice cold Coca-Cola. The sitar music scratching over the radio made that almost impossible to visualize, though.

My eyes jerked open as I felt the taxi swerve first to the left and then again sharply to the right. I watched in horror as he weaved in and out of traffic, missing cars and buses by only inches. Our driver only pretended to slow down for stop signs. As we neared the outskirts of Kabul, camels and donkey carts were added to the traffic mix.

I screamed as the driver nearly hit a young boy who had run across the street to chase a stray goat. Our driver flipped a bird and cursed the boy. As the driver turned his attention back to the road in front of him, he realized that the overloaded bus in front of us had stopped to pick up more passengers.

"He's got no brakes." Mother screamed, as she clamped her eyes shut and braced against the dashboard. We swerved quickly to avoid the bus's rear end, barely avoiding the taxi that had been following us. Just as we passed the bus, a giant bale of cotton fell from the roof rack and bounced fortuitously across the two-lane road.

"We're going to die," Timmy said calmly as he pushed me off his shoulder, where centrifugal force had landed me.

Just then, I saw it.

"Look." I yelled. There on the side of the road was a small dust-covered sign that I had wanted to see for more than a year.

تا کابل خوشامد بگو.
Welcome to Kabul

"We made it." Mother exhaled. "Thank the Lord,"

"We made it," I whispered.

The taxi driver jammed on his brakes, causing my body to smash into the back of his seat. As I pulled myself up from the floorboard, the dust cloud cleared, and I realized a caravan of camels, sheep, and goats surrounded us.

A young boy, maybe eight years old, stared suspiciously at me. I was hanging out the window and clapping for joy at the sight before me on the road. A black and white dog barked sharply as it nipped at the heels of the sheep it was responsible for herding across the road. The sheep baaed and bells on their collars clanged loudly with each step. Following the sheep were the overburdened camels who snorted angrily at the sheep in front of them.

"It's just like in James Michener's book," Mother cried in astonishment. When Timmy and I ignored her, she prompted, "*Caravans*. I swear, you two don't read anything."

"It's like it was two thousand years ago," I said quietly. A camel had stopped, legs spread-eagled right in front of our car. Its master encouraged it to keep moving with a small whip. Its load swayed precariously, and I was sure the bundle would cause it to fall over. Once the caravan was safely past, we continued the journey alongside the murky Chan Chamast River that flows through all of Kabul.

When the taxi skidded to a stop in front of the Spinzar Hotel, we fell out of the doors with welcome relief. I wanted to kiss the ground. Tricia and Mike were laughing as they approached our car. They dragged Friend behind them on his leash.

"Oh my God," Mike laughed. "Do you believe that ride?"

"Yek otaq," Mother said holding up one finger to the desk clerk once we were inside the hotel. One room? I dreaded staying in one room again with four other people and a dog. "Do takhtekhab?" she added, holding up two fingers. *Two beds?* The desk clerk nodded enthusiastically.

It didn't escape my attention that the desk clerk looked just like the taxi drivers. In fact, as I turned and surveyed the hotel lobby, I noticed that they all looked like the taxi drivers. Short, thin, dark-skinned—heads topped off with turbans—and long-sleeved tunics over flowing pants. We were the only women in sight.

"Qaza?" Mother said, motioning as if she were eating with her fingers.

"Baleh," he nodded and held up five fingers to indicate that the restaurant was on the fifth floor.

Mother finished checking in, and a turbaned bellman followed us with our bags and trunk to the room. Two beds was a generous description for what we found to sleep on in the tiny room.

Mother had no patience for our barrage of complaints and settled it quickly. "Mike and Timmy, you sleep on the floor."

Mike held his tongue and headed for the bathroom. He emerged after a few minutes with a small square of paper held between his fingers. "At least we have toilet *paper*," he laughed.

It was ten thirty in the morning and Mother was determined to find a house by dinner time. "We don't need to eat until then," she said, grabbing her purse. "Mike and Timmy, you stay here with Friend until we get back. And don't forget to take him out."

"Engelisi?" Mother asked the taxi driver desperately, to which he slowly shook his head. "It's ok, Tricia. How do you say 'American embassy, please'? We need to register there right away."

"American sefarat khaneh, khoshnud kardan," Tricia pronounced each word carefully. The taxi driver shook his head.

"Ok," Tricia thought about it a second. "How about Ayalat-e mot ahedeh? That's United States."

"Ahh, baleh," the driver understood.

We waited in the car as Mother registered at the embassy. The driver tapped rhythmically against the steering wheel and sang along to the sitar music playing on the car's radio. I couldn't tell the difference between this music and what I had heard in the other cab.

When Mother returned from the embassy half an hour later, she instructed the driver in broken Farsi and English, "Karte Char, khaneh, to let." He nodded understanding and turned the car around to head out of the Shar-I-Nau district, where most of the embassies were located. We skirted the Koh I Azamai mountains on our right and headed out the Sher Shar Mina avenue, passing Darulaman, towards Karte Char.

"Karte Char," the driver said eagerly as we entered a small street. He drove up and down the small dirt roads. We couldn't see the houses because of the high concrete fences, or compounds as we later learned they were called. The driver slowly pulled up to a gate with a "To Let" sign on it. He turned off the motor.

"Ejareh-I," he motioned for Mother to get out of the car. He pointed at the sign, "To let."

We could only see the top floor of the house above the fence. Mother shook her head and turned in her seat to talk to me and Tricia. "This ain't the house Ouija described."

"What?" I was horrified. It was a miracle that we could communicate with a taxi driver in a different language, live through horrific taxi rides, and find a house that was for rent. How could Mother hesitate now? I could see a home in sight. Our home—not a car, or a floor, or a tiny hotel room.

"I don't think it matters what the house looks like," I said defiantly.

"Of course it matters, Diana," Mother scorned. She shook her head and motioned for the driver to pull away from the house. "Nah, digar, another," she said.

The driver patiently drove the tiny streets of Karte Char, with Mother agreeing to look at only one or two of the houses with 'To Let' signs. I looked at my Timex for the umpteenth time. It was two o'clock and we still didn't have a house. My stomach growled loudly. I just wanted a house and food, of course.

"Mother, look," Tricia shouted, pointing to a cantaloupe-colored house through an open gate. It was two stories high and next to the front door was what looked like a store window with a statue of a man on a horse. Two men were bent over pulling out shards of broken glass from the window pane around the statue.

"This is it," Mother yelled to the driver. "Stop. Ist."

"Nah to let," he said, shaking his head and shrugging his shoulders.

"Ist." she repeated.

The house was exactly as Ouija had described it to us in Vallejo. As we walked up the sidewalk to the front door, I looked longingly at the grassy front yard and flowers. A small building sat beside the walkway—perhaps guest quarters, Mother said.

The driver walked ahead of us and spoke for a minute with the two men. He nodded and then disappeared around the rear of the house. He reappeared with a middle-aged Afghan woman wearing western clothes following close behind him.

"Salaam alaykum," the woman bowed her head slightly and smiled, "You want to rent?"

"Thank God, you speak English," Mother said. "Yes, how much?"

"Five thousand afghanis," she replied. She smiled when she saw that Mother didn't understand that number. "One hundred ten American dollars."

Mother didn't hesitate. "I'll take it. Can we move in tomorrow?"

"Yes," she replied, astonished at how easy this was. "You pay me two months," she said holding up two fingers. Mother nodded.

"Do you want to see house?"

At that point, I was so happy to have a place to call home that I really didn't care what it looked like.

The landlady motioned for us to follow her. The kitchen was small and had no refrigerator. Next to the kitchen was an L-shaped living and dining room area, with a small powder room near the front door. Just off the kitchen was a door to the 'servant's quarters' as the woman explained. Tricia and I giggled as we thought of having a servant. Up the open stairs were three bedrooms and a full bathroom.

"This is the best house we've ever lived in," Tricia smiled. I hugged the statue as I passed it. "Home at last," I whispered to it.

Mother counted out ten thousand afghanis and placed them in the landlady's hand, who then instructed the driver to drive us to a furniture store and gave us our new address.

"We need a couch and dining room furniture," Mother announced as we entered the store. "That's all I can afford." Mother somehow negotiated the purchase of a brown leather couch and chair, with a matching dining room set. The driver provided delivery instructions to the store owner. Before we left, Mother asked for a glass of water and was handed a glass of warm, brownish water to quench her thirst.

It was six o'clock when we got back to the hotel. We filled Mike and Timmy in on the day's accomplishments.

That's when Mother fell apart.

"I can't breathe," she gasped. Her hands shook furiously and sweat poured off of her chin and forehead. "I can't do this," she repeated over and over.

"What are we going to do?" she pleaded to the sky. "We're gonna run out of money, and we won't have any food." She slid off the bed and fell to all fours, back heaving, forehead touching the cold concrete floor.

"Oh, God. Oh, God." she kept saying.

Her eyes glazed over and she wouldn't respond to our questions. Tricia knelt next to her and held her shoulders loosely. They cried together.

I stepped back, horrified. What was happening to my Mother? I too fell to my knees. Their tears were contagious—soon I was crying and then Timmy. Mike refused to cry. "What is wrong with you people?" he demanded harshly.

Mother's face had contorted horribly and her glasses steamed over from the tears and humidity in the room. She looked scared to death, I thought. She reminded me of our old Tom cat, who used to sleep on the car's engine to keep warm, which was a huge mistake on his part. I'll never forget the sound of the motor running and the cat's howls. As Tom bled to death on the concrete drive, I stayed by his side. As life retreated from his eyes, they became fixed and hollow—just like my Mother's eyes now. She was begging me for help just like he had.

Mother screamed and moaned for more than an hour in that small room. The guests in the next room pounded on the wall and screamed, "Would you shut that up?"

We shushed Mother, but she didn't respond.

Suddenly, I was eight-years old again. I was the only child at home during a vicious fight between my parents. Mother accused Father of flirting with Ila Dee at a party the night before and she threw a coffee cup at him. "There are plenty of men out there who want me. I don't have to put up with your shit," she yelled.

Father punched the wall right next to her head at that, and I screamed uncontrollably. I had tried to push their voices out of my head with my hands over my ears. Daddy had told her to "get the fuck out" and stubbornly sat down in his recliner.

Mother pulled me onto the back porch, nervously glancing over my shoulder, "Get your piggy bank and meet me at the side of the house."

I did as I was told and waited for her outside for at least five minutes. I squished a pyracantha berry in my palm to see if it was ripe. It was. Just then, Mommy tiptoed around the end of the house—car keys jangling in her skirt pocket.

"How much money do you have?" she asked. Then she wrenched the piggy bank out of my hand and threw it to the ground, where it broke, spilling my hard-earned ironing money into the Bermuda grass. She scooped up my money and counted seven dollars.

"Good girl," she said sweetly to me.

I shook uncontrollably at the thought of her leaving "Take me with you," I begged, not caring about my brothers and sisters.

She laughed. "Baby, seven dollars will barely pay for gas," she paused.

"Then stay, Mommy," I cried, pointing to the ripe pyracantha berries. "It's time to make jelly."

"Your Daddy will take care of you. I'll see you when I get on my feet." She turned and left me standing there, alone.

"But you left your other three kids and you never saw them again," I screamed as she drove away. "You never saw them again." I repeated. I cried into my small hands, smearing the sticky crimson pyracantha juice on my face.

She came back after a few months. She always returned and Father always took her back, for some unexplained reason.

I felt no pity for her heaving mass at my feet now. I forced myself to stop sobbing and clenched my jaw purposefully. She wasn't going to ditch us now. Not here. Not now. I wouldn't let her.

"No!" I screamed awkwardly.

Chapter 19

Ouija's Back

"What?" Mother asked feebly, tears streaming down her cheeks.

"I'm hungry," I surprised myself by the hardness in my voice. I didn't know what else to say. I just knew that Mother needed to snap out of this.

She stared at me for several seconds and then a slow, small smile crept across her face. She straightened her back and rose from the floor.

"Well," she said weakly, "So am I."

"Let's go eat," Tricia said, lifting Mother by her elbow.

We climbed the stairs to the Spinzar Restaurant. Mother surveyed the room and commented, "Hmm, not many people here." The waiter led us to a table close to the large windows that overlooked the river and the mountains beyond.

"Ab?" Mother asked quickly. "Yakh. Khahesh mikonam." Yes, please give us ice water. I was tired of drinking warm water from the bathroom faucet.

"I can't read the menu," Mike said, shaking his head. "It's in some foreign language."

We laughed, and Mother couldn't help chiding Mike, "See, Mike, you should have been studying Farsi like the rest of us. I really don't know how you're gonna make it."

"Don't worry 'bout me," he said sharply. "I can fend for myself."

"I think that's lamb," Timmy said, ignoring Mike and pointing to a word he understood—"Bareh."

"Yuck," Mike shuddered as he said the word. "I don't eat sheep."

When the waiter returned, Tricia asked for beef, "Gushte gav?"

"Nah," the waiter replied.

"Looks like lamb, or nothing," Mother proclaimed.

When we had finished our lamb and rice, Mother gave us the room key and told us to go back to our room. She said she wanted to ask the waiter some questions. I was suspicious. When I glanced back over my shoulder, I saw that she had returned to the table. She carefully folded a white placemat and slid it into her open purse.

"What's she up to?" I wondered as the stairwell door closed behind me, and she disappeared from sight.

Not long after we were back in the room, Mother revealed her plan. "I'm making a Ouija board," she grinned like an impish five-year old.

I couldn't believe my ears.

Tricia was aghast, "Mother, God told us to talk to him through prayer."

"You don't understand, Patricia," Mother warned. "I'm not going to be able to do this without Ouija. If I can't do it, none of us can do it."

"Mother, you can do it," Tricia encouraged. "Let's pray together."

"I have a thick skull, Patricia. I can't hear God talking without the Ouija board," she replied. "Do you have any idea what I'm up against here?" Mother looked at each of us, in turn. "I'm in a foreign land, with no money, no husband and four kids and a dog. I'm being told that I am going to build the church for the second coming of Christ. This is outlandish!"

When she put it like that, it did sound overwhelming.

The sweat beaded on Mother's forehead again. Why was she always sweating?

"I'm not talking to Ouija anymore," Tricia said defiantly. "I want to be a kid again."

Mother moved closer to Tricia. They were toe-to-toe. "You're fifteen-years old, Patricia. I was married when I was just six months older than you."

"I'm not you." Tricia screamed.

"No, you're not, and you're not a kid either."

Tricia stepped back, almost like she was going to shove Mother. Seeing her, Mother raised her hand and slapped Tricia square across the face. "What happened to your commitment to God?" she demanded.

Tricia rubbed her cheek and stood her ground then. "I'm committed, but I'm not talking to a Ouija board anymore."

"Oh, yes you are, young lady." Mother screamed again. "What you fail to understand here is that we could die. Do you understand how goddamned serious this is?"

"Yes, I understand," Tricia said flatly. She sat on the edge of the bed and continued rubbing her cheek. She glared at Mother, but didn't say another word.

"How are you going to make a board?" I interjected. It was time to change this subject.

Mother stared at Tricia for a second and then stepped away. She pulled the placemat out of her purse and unfolded it on the bed.

"Mike, go downstairs and see if you can get a piece of cardboard and some scotch tape."

"I'm not helping you do this," Mike said.

"Do as I tell you or you can go back to Vallejo this instant," she threatened.

"I don't even know how to ask for that stuff in Farsi," Mike refused.

Timmy raised his hand for some reason. "I'll go with him. I know what the words are for those things."

Mother nodded to Timmy, "Good boy. Go with your brother."

Tricia shook her head sadly and moved to the window seat to get as far away from Mother as possible. She pulled her knees to her chest and rested her head on them. She stared out the window.

Mike and Timmy returned after fifteen minutes. "Mission accomplished," Timmy said secretively as he pushed the door closed behind him. Mother meticulously wrote the letters and numbers on the placemat from memory.

When we had taped the placemat to the cardboard, Tricia finally spoke, "I don't know why you're doing that."

"So we can talk to God, Patricia," Mother said.

"You don't have the most important part," Tricia said smugly. "Did you think about the indicator, Mother?"

Just then, Timmy emerged from the bathroom, holding the empty toilet paper roll. "We're out of toilet paper. How do we get more?"

"Aha," Mother shrieked. "Who has scissors?"

"What are you doing?" Tricia asked as Mother used the scissors from Mike's manicure kit to cut the toilet paper roll in half. "That's not going to work."

Mother ignored Tricia and continued cutting a hole in the middle of the open roll. She placed the contraption on the board and motioned to Tricia to join her.

"I can't believe this," Tricia said.

"You'd better believe it. Now, get over here," Mother commanded. "I need to talk to God."

They touched the toilet paper roll gingerly and waited for it to move. We waited. And then it scratched its way slowly across the placemat.

"H-E-L-L-O M-A-R-Y"

As the mountains are round about...
so the Lord is round about His people.
Ps. 125:2

The Community Christian Church of Kabul
Phone : 42224

Chapter 20

Settling In

Mother's hands trembled as they hovered above the indicator. "Lord," she started, and then she urgently covered her mouth with her hand and ran to the bathroom.

"She's throwing up," Mike said.

"Yuck," Timmy said. "That's disgusting."

"Did she drink alcohol at dinner?" Tricia asked suspiciously.

"No," Mike said. "She's hurling that lamb. I hope I don't get sick."

We listened to her gagging for another fifteen minutes, and then she emerged, sweat-soaked and trembling.

"I don't know what's wrong with me," she said as she wiped her forehead and then her mouth with the hand towel. "It must be jet lag, or nerves, or maybe bad food." She settled onto the bed across from Tricia and placed her shaking fingers on the toilet paper roll again.

"G-O T-O B-E-D B-E-T-T-E-R T-O-M-O-R-R-O-W" Then Ouija said GOODBYE.

"Well, that was short and sweet," Mother complained. "It doesn't matter. I'm too sick to stay up and talk anyway. Let's get to bed."

I awoke in the middle of the night with an urge to vomit and poop at the same time. Mike had beaten me to the bathroom. As I slammed my fist against the door, he groaned.

"Hurry up," I said. "I'm going to throw up all over this room if you don't get out of there." I was dancing wildly outside the door.

"You're just going to have to wait," he hissed before he vomited again. The door opened right before I heaved. I thrust my body at the foot of the commode and hurled my insides into it. Then I turned to sit on it and continued heaving into the sink, which thankfully was close enough to the toilet. My head, now too heavy for my neck, collapsed onto my outstretched forearms. I groaned with each dreadful pang of diarrhea. I barely flinched when Timmy pounded on the door.

"Get out of there," he screamed. "I've got to go *now*."

We took turns in the bathroom throughout that first night at the Spinzar and, although weakened, I was optimistic I'd be better by morning. After only a few hours of real sleep, I was awakened by Mother's groaning. She sat up weakly and glanced at her wristwatch on the nightstand.

"It's eight o'clock," she announced, a little too loud for my tender ears. I groaned.

"Everyone up," she said. "We'll feel better once we're in our house."

"I told you we shouldn't have eaten the sheep," Mike complained.

After we repacked our suitcases, Mother mentioned breakfast, a thought none of us could bear at that point. "You kids have never turned down food," she said. "You must be sick."

Within an hour, we were moved into our house in Karte Char. Fortunately, the house had two bathrooms, because despite my optimism, the symptoms continued throughout the day. Our new furniture was delivered midmorning, easing our discomfort somewhat.

"I feel like I'm going to die," Mother complained. "Will we be ok, Lord?"

"Y-O-U W-I-L-L S-U-R-V-I-V-E"

"But what's causing us to be so sick?" Mother asked.

"D-I-F-F-E-R-E-N-T D-I-E-T"

"Will we get better soon?"

"O-H Y-E-S"

We were too weak to sit up and talk to Ouija for the rest of the day. So, Mother told us to inflate the air mattresses and lay down in our bedrooms until we felt better. Tricia and I shared a room on the second floor at the front of the house; Mike and Timmy shared the middle room, and Mother had her own room at the back.

After vomiting my insides out throughout the day, I became lightheaded and by two o'clock, my mouth tasted like sewage. I felt an urgent need to brush my teeth.

I turned the bathroom faucet on and opened the medicine cabinet to retrieve my toothbrush. Out of the corner of my eye, I caught sight of a green slimy material oozing from the faucet. I yelled hysterically, "Come quick. Somebody."

Tricia reached the bathroom first. We stared at the green ooze as it fell from the faucet and slimed down the drain.

"What *is* it?" I asked, squeezing it between my fingers.

"It's like cooked spinach," Tricia answered squeamishly. She reached her hand under the faucet to experience the green goo personally. "I have no idea what it is."

Mother heard our discussion and stepped into the bathroom. Staring at the sludge coming from the faucet, she said, "Let the water run for a few minutes. The pipes are probably just stagnant from not being used."

"We *did* let it run," I answered wide-eyed.

"Are we supposed to *drink* this?" Tricia asked.

Mother held her forehead for a second and answered sarcastically. "Patricia, do you see any other water here?" she motioned around the bathroom with her hands. "Unless you want to die of thirst, then I guess you'll be drinking this water." We didn't react to her sarcasm. We were too fixated on the frightening sight of green drinking water oozing from the faucet.

"I'm not drinking this stuff," I said.

"Me either."

Mother must have had a spurt of energy after that. She yelled from the bottom of the stairs, "Mike, get down here right now. I'm going to need your muscles to help me get a stove home." She scratched her head and continued, "Lord knows how far we will have to walk to find an appliance store."

Tricia, Timmy and I had nothing to do but lie on our air mattresses and take turns running to the bathroom. Just as the sun was starting to set, we heard a car pull up in front of our house. I looked out the window and was amazed to see Mother and Mike getting out of the car. And there was Mr. Tippets.

Oh, thank God. We were saved. I ran down the stairs as fast as I could and threw open the front gates of the compound.

"Look who we found," Mother laughed. "The Tippets live just around the corner from us. I'll tell you what," she said smiling admiringly at Mr. Tippets, "you sure were a sight for sore eyes."

Mr. Tippets smiled as he turned his attention to untying the string that held the trunk lid down on his black Ford. He and Mike heaved a two-burner electric stove out of the trunk. It was the smallest stove I had ever seen. Mother took him up on his offer to help set up the stove.

"We've all been so sick," Mother moaned after returning from the bathroom. "I don't know what's wrong with us."

Mr. Tippets smiled, knowingly. "You have the Kabul trots, I'm afraid."

"The Kabul trots?" Tricia asked.

"The water here is like poison to foreigners," he said. "The natives can drink it and not get sick like us; but they don't live long. The average life expectancy for an Afghan is only forty years."

Mother inhaled sharply, "Oh my God. What are we going to do for water? We can't be this sick," she paused, suddenly realizing the brevity of the situation, "We could die."

"Oh, most certainly, you can die," Mr. Tippets nodded urgently. "The Kabul trots are from the amoebae in the water. It's a form of dysentery and people do die from it."

What? I couldn't help thinking that Ouija should have told us about that little detail. We wouldn't have been sick if we'd known not to drink the water. I glanced at my brothers, who were obviously thinking the same thing.

"What causes the dysentery?" Tricia asked.

"Afghans dig their wells right next to their septic tanks," he said sympathetically. "They don't have city water or sewage systems like we do in America."

"What are we supposed to do for water then?" Mother asked. "And why aren't you sick?"

"I'm not sick because I get my water from the American well. It's more than 110 feet deep," he said as he looked at our sick faces. "Mrs. Cain, I'll take you to the well tomorrow. I have an extra ten-gallon can you can use."

"God bless you."

"What can we do with the water from the faucet?" Timmy asked.

"You can only use the faucet water for bathing. Don't even brush your teeth with it."

"Oh my God," Mother said. "We need water now. What should we do until tomorrow?"

"Boil your water for 20 minutes. That should kill any amoebae. Oh, and don't eat fresh vegetables unless you've washed them with chlorinated water." When Mother didn't understand, he continued, "Mix one cup of bleach with a gallon of water and wash the vegetables in it."

"Where can we get a television?" Mike interrupted.

Mr. Tippets laughed heartily. "You might be able to buy one, but there are no television stations here. There's a radio station that plays western music once a week," he paused, "if you can find a radio."

Mike was crestfallen. "Man, I hate this place already."

We gave Mr. Tippets a tour of our house, and he cringed when he saw the air mattresses we were sleeping on. "Mrs. Cain, please tell me you're not going to sleep on the floor."

"Well," Mother began.

"You can buy a native bed called a chor poi for very little afghanis. It's made with woven rope. You could put your air mattresses on top of it."

Mother was relieved, "To tell you the truth, I can get down on the floor all right, but getting back up is a whole 'nother matter."

"The chor poi will make a big difference for you."

"Tell me, Mr. Tippets, do you know where I can get a refrigerator?" she asked.

"Sure, but they aren't the kind of refrigerators you're used to," he laughed. I loved his laugh. "They are very small, and they cost a fortune."

"The fridge will have to wait then," Mother said. "We'll just get some Kool-Aid to make the water taste better. They do have Kool-Aid at the bazaars, don't they?

"I've never seen it," he thought for a second. "Most people use orange Tang to add flavor."

"We could always buy pop, I guess," Mother said.

"I wouldn't do that if I were you," he said. "The Afghans take American pop, open it, dilute it with their water, and then put the cap back on. Same with ketchup."

"Man, I really don't like this place," Mike said.

Mr. Tippets told Mother he'd pick her up first thing in the morning to help her with water and beds. After he left, Mother boiled water in the one pan she had bought at the bazaar. It was warm, but at least it refreshed us. After a dinner consisting of water and canned soup, she insisted that we talk to Ouija.

"Why didn't you tell us about the Kabul trots?" she demanded.

"D-I-D N-O-T W-A-N-T T-O S-C-A-R-E Y-O-U"

"So, getting sick is better than getting scared?"

Ouija answered YES.

"After we got to the Spinzar, why didn't you tell us?"

"I D-I-D"

"When?"

"Y-O-U D-I-D N-O-T L-I-S-T-E-N"

"I couldn't listen, because I had no board. You told us to leave it with Francis."

"Y-O-U W-E-R-E S-U-P-P-O-S-E-D T-O L-I-S-T-EN I-N P-R-A-Y-E-R"

I think it irritated Mother that she had no comeback.

"A-L-L F-O-R-E-I-G-N-E-R-S G-E-T T-H-E T-R-O-T-S"

"It would have been nice if you'd warned us, is all I'm saying," Mother conceded.

"L-I-S-T-E-N N-E-X-T T-I-M-E"

The next morning, Mother served orange Tang and nan for breakfast. "It's bread," she said as she tore the tan snowshoe-shaped bread apart. "It's kind of like Navajo bread, huh?"

The next few days were a blur for me. Even with little to eat, the diarrhea and vomiting didn't stop. Would it ever end?

Mr. Tippets turned out to be a loyal friend to our family. He, or someone else in his family, would check on us every day and take Mother to the bazaar or anywhere else that Ouija wanted her to go.

"I noticed the Bible on your table," he commented one day. "There is an English speaking church here."

Mother smiled. "Really?"

"It's the Community Christian Church of Kabul."

"Oh," Mother said. She must have been struggling with whether it would be polite to ask the denomination. After all, we were evangelicals.

"It's Episcopalian," he offered. "Dr. Christy Wilson is the pastor. He's a friend of mine." He pulled a card from his coat pocket and handed it to Mother. "The church is just a few blocks from here. You could easily walk."

"Thanks, I'll think about it," Mother said. "During all this travel, we've missed attending church."

"If you want to meet other Americans, you should also go to the Fourth of July celebration at AISK," Mr. Tippets said before he left. "Ambassador Newman is paying for fireworks. We're all very excited about it. You should join us."

"I've lost track of time—is that next Friday?" Mother asked, to which Mr. Tippets nodded his head. "I don't know how we'd get there."

"Why don't I pick you up after I drop off my family?" Mr. Tippets offered.

Friend nuzzled his pant leg just then and he reached down to pat his head. "What do you feed your dog?"

"We've been feeding him table scraps. I haven't seen any canned or dry dog food here."

"Most Afghan dogs are working dogs, you know, herding dogs," Mr. Tippets said. "Not a lot of house dogs." He thought for a second, "Why don't you ask the butcher at the bazaar for bones and meat scraps? I'm sure they will sell them to you for a few afghanis."

"That reminds me," Mother said. "Timmy, let the dog out." Timmy slowly pulled himself up from the couch where he had been sprawled for several hours. As soon as he stood up, he fell in a heap to the floor. Mother and Mr. Tippets were immediately at his side, slapping his face and calling to him.

Slowly, he opened his eyes, "What happened?"

"You passed out," Mother responded. "Are you ok?"

"I don't feel so good," he said as he rolled over and crawled on all fours back to the couch.

"Mrs. Cain, he looks deathly ill. You should probably take him to the doctor if he doesn't get better soon," Mr. Tippets warned.

"I will," Mother promised.

For the next few days, we took turns laying around the house and going on daily shopping trips with Mother to buy produce. I was weak, but I seemed to turn the corner after a week. Timmy didn't. He was sicker longer than the rest of us. Mother did go easier on him though. She let him stay in bed as much as possible because he kept passing out.

Our diet for that first week included soup and nan and, of course, warm Tang. The sight of the Tang jar made my stomach turn after a few days. I noticed my clothes were hanging on me by the end of the second week. Mother had lost a lot of weight and had to start pinning her skirts.

We just had to buy a refrigerator soon if we were going to live through this. I anxiously checked the mailbox each day—hoping for that estate check to come.

* * *

On July 4th I pretended we were back in Avondale as I lay on the soft grass at AISK. With my arms folded behind my head, I gazed serenely at the blanket of stars above me. I had never seen so many stars, crowding each other and pressing down on me, fighting for my attention. I was sure God was up there, looking down on us, protecting us. Just then, the fireworks began and my private star show ended.

In between bursts of fireworks, Mike and another boy strolled over to where we were sitting. It struck me as odd that Mike had found a friend who looked like his twin—skinny, with glasses and curly hair. They plopped down next to me without saying a word.

When Mike didn't introduce his friend, Mother asked, "And you are?"

"I'm Greg Newman—Ambassador Newman is my father," he said pointing to a man walking towards us.

Mother remained seated on the grass and reached her hand up to the ambassador, "It's so nice to meet you," she said, a little too syrupy, I thought. "Thank you so much for the fireworks."

"It almost makes you feel like you're home, doesn't it?" the ambassador said with pride.

Mother went on to introduce her other three kids.

"So, you will be starting at AISK in a few weeks?" he said to Tricia and Mike. "Greg is a senior this year. He really likes the school."

"We don't have any plans for them to go to school while we're here," Mother said. "It's expensive, and we really don't have the money."

Mr. Newman had the same look that Mr. Tippets had when he asked Mother this question. "You should apply for scholarships, ma'am. The children need to be in school."

Mother's response was short. "Well, we aren't going to be here that long. I'm writing a book, you see. They can be out of school for a few months, and it won't hurt them none."

"Well, if the school will give them scholarships, you really wouldn't have a problem with that, would you?" he pressed.

"I would feel better if they weren't in school for so short a time. It would be hard for them to say goodbye to their new friends again, after we just left another school."

"You are their mother," he said just as the fireworks started. "It was a pleasure meeting you, Mrs. Cain, children."

"Why can't we go to school?" I asked.

The Invitation for Kargha Lake

Since you're a Hi-teen, YOU are specially invited to a weekend "cruise" at the attractive chalets beside Karga Lake. We're planning a Hi-Seas Adventure which promises fun and a real change of pace.

From: Friday, August 15 at noon
Through: Sunday, August 17 after supper

** For teenagers in grades 9 – 12 **

Sponsored by
The Community Christian Church

Chapter 21

Kargha Lake

"What's she doing?" Tricia muttered from the window of our second floor bedroom. She pointed to the front yard. "Mother's been pacing for almost an hour, back and forth, screaming and pointing," Tricia turned to look at me and lifted her eyebrows meaningfully, "And there's *nobody* there."

I stepped next to her at the window and squinted at the blinding sun streaming through the dusty glass. "She does that," I said matter-of-factly as I shielded my eyes with one hand.

"She's done this before?"

"Sure."

"When?"

"Last year. When we lived in Corinth."

She was flabbergasted. "Why didn't you tell me?"

"'Cause you'd think she was crazy." How could she not understand why I didn't tell her?

"Diana, maybe she *is* crazy."

"I don't know, maybe." Then I related what had happened when I came home sick from school one day. As I stepped onto the front porch of the old farmhouse, I was met with screaming and cursing coming from inside. I knew better than to get in the middle of a fight between my parents, so I decided to wait out the fight on the porch.

After fifteen minutes, I grew cold and impatient. I crawled across the porch to the picture window and pulled myself up to peek inside. As my eyes adjusted to the dark room behind the glass, I realized that Mother was alone. I pressed my nose harder against the glass, hoping that someone else was in the shadowy interior with her. There was no one.

I watched as she pounded both fists against the living room wall and screamed "God help me" over and over. My knees buckled, and I fell into a heap. I rocked back and forth, hands tightly covering my mouth, as she ranted for another hour. When the screaming subsided, I entered the house and found her at the kitchen sink washing the dishes. It was as if nothing had happened.

"I thought it was a one-time thing," I said, turning away from the window.

Right now, I was far more interested in cutting out the pattern for my new dress. Mother had bought a used sewing machine for fifty afghanis at the bazaar. When the taxi driver unloaded it from his car's trunk, Tricia asked where the electrical cord was.

"There's no cord," Mother laughed. "You pump this peddle underneath to make the machine sew. See?" I was anxious to try out the sewing machine, so I had bought salmon-colored chintz fabric at the bazaar. It was laid out neatly on the floor in front of me, a dress pattern pinned loosely to it.

"She's coming back in the house," Tricia exhaled breathlessly as she ducked away from the window.

Just then, Mother yelled from the first floor. "Patricia, I need to talk to Ouija. Now." She insisted that all four of us be there for the session with Ouija, because it was important.

"Lord," she began. "The money's running out."

"Y-E-S M-A-R-Y"

"What am I going to do?"

"I W-I-L-L P-R-O-V-I-D-E"

"How?"

"H-A-V-E F-A-I-T-H"

"I have three thousand afghanis left, Lord. That's not even enough to pay next month's rent."

The toilet paper indicator scratched across the paper as Ouija changed the subject abruptly.

"C-H-I-L-D-R-E-N W-I-L-L S-T-A-R-T S-C-H-O-O-L"

Mr. Tippets had been by earlier in the week to tell us that there were two scholarships available at AISK and that Ahlmund Academy had an opening for an eighth grader. Mother had thanked Mr. Tippets for going to all the trouble of looking into this for us, but she repeated that her children did not need to go to school.

"Lord, there are only three openings at the schools. I have four children."

"P-A-T-R-I-C-I-A A-N-D M-I-K-E G-O T-O A-I-S-K," and then the indicator got hung up on the edge of the paper. We waited as Mother dislodged it.

"T-I-M G-O-E-S T-O A-H-L-M-U-N-D"

"What about me?" I shouted in disbelief.

"AISK has only two scholarships available," Tricia explained calmly. "It makes sense for me and Mike to go there because we're upper classmen."

"And Ahlmund Academy only goes to eighth grade," Timmy finished. "You're in ninth, in case you forgot."

Before I could say anything, Mother shrieked, "Shut up. No one's going to school, do you hear me? How would I talk to Ouija if Patricia is at school? How would we build the temple?"

"D-O N-O-T F-E-A-R," Ouija commanded "L-E-V-O-Y W-I-L-L C-O-M-E I-N D-E-C-E-M-B-E-R"

Mother's eyes lit up when she heard this good news.

"S-C-H-O-O-L U-N-T-I-L T-H-E-N"

"But I still think Diana should go to school, and Patricia should—"

The indicator slid to NO.

Just then a sharp knock interrupted our session. "Hide the board," Mother whispered hurriedly as she walked slowly to the front door. When she opened the door, an Afghan man of slight build, barely taller than me, bowed slightly and began speaking in stiff and faltering English.

"Hello, Mistress. My name Boostan."

Mother smiled. "Yes?"

"My mistress lived here house," his brown eyes smiled as he pointed to our bare windows. "She has—how you say—drapes. You want to buy?"

"How much?" Mother asked.

"One hundred fifty afghanis," he looked from Mother to Tricia, bobbed his head and smiled foolishly. "Good deal, yes?"

"Good deal," Mother repeated, nodding her head. "I'll take them."

"You wait. I bring back."

He returned within five minutes with the blue curtains draped over his outstretched arms.

"Very nice," Mother complimented him. "Wait here."

I watched Boostan as Mother went to fetch her purse. He stood quietly with his hands clutched behind his back. He said nothing and stared at the floor in front of me. He wore a dingy white dress that went to his ankles. He kept reaching into a pocket on his tattered vest, making sure that whatever he put there had not fallen out. He could have been 15 or 40. I couldn't tell. But I liked him.

* * *

July 20, 1969

"Mrs. Cain, we're so glad you could join us," Dr. Wilson opened both his arms as if he was going to hug Mother and then stopped himself and clasped her right hand instead. Holding her hand with both of his, he continued, "I've heard so much about you from some of our parishioners. They tell me you're a writer—I'm sorry, a journalist."

"That's right, Dr. Wilson," Mother said guardedly.

"Are you writing for the Christian Monitor, by any chance?" he asked hopefully. "I think that's a wonderful publication."

"No, not yet," Mother lied. "I'm writing articles about life in Afghanistan, and I'm doing research for a novel over the next few months."

"That's wonderful. I understand your husband will be joining you soon."

"Yes sir, he's working in San Francisco, while I do my research."

"You don't find many husbands like that, do you?" a slim man interrupted their conversation.

"Hi, I'm John Strackan," he said as he clasped Mother's hand in his. "It's so good to have someone who wants to write about these wonderful people and share their stories with the world."

"Dr. Wilson," Tricia interrupted. "Are there any Afghans who attend church here?

"Oh, no, no," he shook his head. "If we allow Afghans to attend, the Afghan government will burn our church and kick us out of their country."

We talked with Dr. Wilson and Mr. Strackan for a few more minutes about how wonderful the Afghan people were. In the midst of the conversation, Mr. Strackan gazed up into the night sky and pointed to the bright moon amid a field of twinkling stars.

"Can you believe it?" he asked.

"Believe what?" Dr. Wilson asked, gazing upward himself.

"Neil Armstrong is walking on the moon right now," he said in wonder. "Do you believe it?" I looked at the moon too, hoping to see Armstrong.

"Is it today?" Mother asked, mirroring our gazes.

"Yes, today."

Dr. Wilson turned his attention back to Mother. "Mrs. Cain, would you consider allowing your children to help out with vacation Bible school? We could really use their assistance over the next few weeks."

He grabbed a program book from the small table in the vestibule and pointed at it, "Our phone number is 42224. Please call me this afternoon, and I'll give you all the details."

Mother took the paper, and said offhandedly, "What time does vacation Bible school start tomorrow? I'll just send them over." She didn't offer that we had no phone.

"Sure, have them come here at nine o'clock in the morning." He clapped his hands loudly. "This is wonderful." As we opened the door to leave, he shouted, "After vacation Bible school is over, we take the hi-teens to Kargha Lake for a weekend retreat. Lots of fun."

For the next few weeks, I talked to Ouija less and less, because I was teaching a Bible school class and had to prepare for it in the afternoons. On weekends, Tricia and I babysat for a couple of American families from the church.

Boostan wanted to be our servant very badly. He came by every day to help with cleaning, shopping and cooking. He didn't ask for any money, but Mother gave him a couple of afghanis every couple of days.

Mother and Tricia usually talked to Ouija late into the night, trying to figure out how to stretch our babysitting money to pay for food first and then rent. Towards the end of July, Mother declared that if we didn't get our final check from the estate soon, we'd have to find a cheaper place to live.

When we received the invitation for the weekend "cruise" at Kargha Lake on August 15th, Mother hit the roof. "There is barely enough money for food. Do you *really* think I'm going to let you go on a vacation that costs five dollars apiece?"

"But we earned enough babysitting money to pay our own way," Tricia retorted tearfully. "And it's *not* a vacation—it's a retreat. We're going to be singing and having Bible discussions."

"I can't believe what I'm hearing, Patricia. You, of all people, know that babysitting money is all the income we've got," Mother sniped as she pointed her finger at Tricia's nose. "There is no money for anything other than food. So, you can just forget it, young lady, you're not going to Kargha Lake and that's final."

"It's our money." I shouted rebelliously as I ran up the stairs before Mother could say anything. I just wanted to be a kid and use my money for me. In my heart I knew that was selfish of me, but sometimes a kid just has to be selfish. Mother constantly told us that feeding our family and keeping the lights on was way more important than a weekend away with other teenagers.

Dr. Wilson was disappointed when we told him that we wouldn't be going on the trip. "May I ask why?" he asked of Mike near the end of Bible school.

"Because we don't have enough money to pay for it," Mike blurted out angrily.

"Oh, I'm sure we can figure out a way for you to go," Dr. Wilson replied. "Let me work on that, ok? I'll speak to your Mother."

Mother had been avoiding the Ouija board the whole weekend before the Kargha Lake trip, even though Tricia was pestering her to talk to Ouija. Her excuse was that she was too busy cleaning and shopping for food to take time out and talk to Ouija.

After Sunday services on August 10th, Dr. Wilson and the Strackans showed up on our doorstep. Mother was all sweet molasses as she opened the door to our guests.

"Mrs. Cain," he motioned between himself and the Strackans. "We were wondering if you might be in need of money to tide you over until funds arrive from America. We'd like to help out with a scholarship for the three older children to go on our trip next weekend."

"Dr. Wilson, whatever made you think that we don't have any money?" she said, shaking her head warily and squinting suspiciously at Tricia.

"Well, the children did mention that they couldn't go on the Kargha Lake trip because funds were low right now."

"It's true that our funds are low, and we can't afford to spend any unnecessary money. So, I'm sure you can understand why I said they can't go," she emphasized. "I assure you, Dr. Wilson, we'll be just fine." Then she shut the door in their faces. Oh, my God. How could she have been so rude to people who were trying to help us?

Finally, late on Sunday night, Mother agreed to talk to the Ouija board. Tricia barely sat the indicator on the board before it spelled out, "T-H-E-Y W-I-L-L G-O T-O K-A-R-G-H-A"

I could hear my heartbeat inside my head. Finally, I could get away from all the adult worries in our house.

"Lord, I don't think they should go," Mother tried to stare into Tricia's eyes, but Tricia had lowered them and was focused on the board. Mother insisted, "We do *not* have the money."

"A C-H-E-C-K I-S O-N W-A-Y"

Mother thought for a few seconds and then conceded, "All right, Lord, if you insist."

We rode a school bus to Kargha Lake—just us and 20 other teenagers from around the world. The weekend went too fast, but we enjoyed it immensely—as much food as we could eat. After weeks of what felt like near starvation, it was good to go to bed with a full belly. Each night by the campfire, we sang along with Jim Hunter, a youth minister from Pakistan, who strummed Irish folk songs on his guitar late into the night.

Jim told us a couple of ghost stories after he finished, and then he told us about gruesome murders in Los Angeles that had happened the previous weekend. A pregnant actress named Sharon Tate and her friends were killed on Saturday and then on Sunday, the LaBiancas were murdered. Jim eerily recounted how "Helter Skelter" and "Death to Pigs" was written in blood on the walls.

"These are the end times," he warned ominously. "We all need to have our souls ready to meet God."

I nodded in complete agreement.

258   *Ouija: For the Record*

*The Nabirs with me
(at the Noon cannon)*

Chapter 22

The Gift of the Nabirs

"Boostan?" Mother said cautiously, a few days after the Kargha Lake trip.

"Baleh, ma`shuqeh?" he replied, not looking up from the nan he was kneading. "Yes, mistress?"

"Have you ever heard of Jesus?" she continued.

I drew in my breath sharply. We weren't supposed to proselytize to Afghans. We could be deported—or worse yet, killed. I kept my head down and listened intently to their conversation as I pretended to do my homework at the dining table.

"Jesus, baleh," he nodded. "Isa."

"His name is 'Isa'?" she asked curiously.

"Baleh, in Qur'an, Isa."

"What does the Qur'an say about Isa?"

Boostan stopped kneading, wiped his hands on a dish towel, and turned to Mother. He didn't answer, taking his time to translate his thoughts from Farsi into English.

"Qur'an say Isa Prophet of Allah," Boostan paused. "How you say *messenger*."

Boostan thought for another minute and then continued. "Isa come before Muhammed—Peace Be Upon Him. Isa say Muhammed—Peace Be Upon Him—come later." He nodded reverently with each "peace be upon him."

"Do you have to say that after you say Muhammed?" Mother asked innocently.

Boostan nodded anxiously, "Baleh, ma`shuqeh, yes." He continued, "Isa say Muhammed—Peace Be Upon Him—will come after. He last prophet. Allah send angel to tell last prophet."

"What was angel's name?" Mother asked.

"Name ... Gabriel."

Mother clasped her hands together, "Praise God." Boostan didn't understand her actions, but I did. Gabriel came to us too.

"So the Qur'an talks about Jesus?" Mother prompted Boostan to finish the story. "Does Qur'an say Jesus is Son of God who was killed—she stabbed at the air with an invisible sword—on a cross—she made the sign of the cross with her index fingers."

Boostan didn't understand at first, then suddenly his face brightened and he smiled, "Isa son of Allah? Nah, son of Maryam," Boostan said, shaking his head. "Qur'an say Isa prophet holy man. Isa not die on cross—Isa in behesht—how you say heaven?"

"Isa didn't die?"

"Nah, Allah take Isa to heaven."

"Is he there now?"

"Baleh," Boostan nodded and pointed toward the ceiling. "Isa come back."

"When?" Mother asked excitedly.

"Ulema say Isa come before Qiyamat," Boostan said. "Hadith say too."

"Ulema is?" Mother asked.

"Ulema—big teachers."

"And Hadith is?"

"Holy story about Muhammed—Peace Be Upon Him," Boostan said.

"And Qiyamat—is that Judgment Day?" Mother guessed.

"Baleh, Judgment Day." Boostan nodded and continued, "Isa come, end jihad, make peace."

"Boostan, the Bible says the same thing," Mother said in amazement. "Christians read the Bible—it's our holy book from God. It says the same thing in a book called Revelations."

Boostan shook his head and insisted, "Nah, Qur'an word of Allah. All Muslims know this," he said. "Isa say Muhammed—Peace Be Upon Him—is comforter to come after Isa and Isa say we to obey comforter laws in Qur'an."

"Well, I guess you could interpret it that way," Mother acquiesced. "Who will Isa come to—Who will be his people—on Qiyamat?"

Boostan thought for another minute. "He come to Jamaat—right people who jihad against Dajjal."

"Oh my—" Mother caught herself. "Dajjal—is this a devil? A very bad person?"

"Baleh," Boostan nodded. "Isa come with do (he held up two fingers) angels on cloud after Fajr Salaat—is prayer time. Isa open door—Dajjal behind it with many Yahudis."

"Yahudis are?" Mother prompted.

"Israel peoples."

"Jews?" she asked.

"Baleh. All kuffaars will die," Boostan stopped abruptly, realizing that what he had said had made Mother wince.

"Kuffaars—no believe Qur'an," he offered. Then he continued carefully, "Muslim and Isa kill Dajjal and Yahudis. All peoples be Islam, and we have good life for long days—Isa king for many year."

"What happens to people who aren't believers?" Mother asked incredulously.

"No more," Boostan shook his head sadly. "Only Islam."

"Well, except for that *tiny* detail, we have more in common than you know, Boostan," Mother finished the conversation and turned back to the cabbage she had been washing with chlorine bleach. "Apparently, we've got the same God and stories. They're just topsy turvy from each other."

"Whew," I thought to myself. At least Mother didn't preach to poor Boostan.

* * *

"Lord, Muslims have the story backwards," Mother chuckled when we talked to Ouija that night.

"N-O M-A-R-Y" Ouija said sternly. "J-U-S-T D-I-F-F-E-R-E-N-T"

"But how can it be different and still true?" Mother asked.

"N-O-T U-P T-O H-U-M-A-N-S T-O S-A-Y W-H-O I-S S-A-V-E-D" Ouija stopped. "U-P T-O M-E"

"I don't understand," Mother shrugged her shoulders.

"S-O-M-E P-E-O-P-L-E U-S-E H-O-L-Y B-O-O-K-S A-G-A-I-N-S-T E-A-C-H O-T-H-E-R," Ouija paused. "W-I-L-L E-N-D S-O-O-N"

Tricia and I looked at each other without saying a word.

Ouija continued, "R-E-A-D M-A-T-T-H-E-W 1-3 1-0 T-O 1-7"

I reached for the Bible on the table and read aloud. When I came to Verse 16, I hesitated and began reading slower, "But blessed are your eyes, for they see; and your ears, for they hear. For verily I say unto you, that many prophets and righteous men have desired to see those things which ye see, and have not seen them; and to hear those things which ye hear; and have not heard them."

"We are special," Mother said reverently. "But shouldn't I tell Boostan he's got the story wrong?"

Ouija slid quickly to NO.

* * *

Over the next week, food was scarcer at our house. Tricia and I had both lost twenty pounds since arriving in Kabul. Mother thought she had lost at least fifty pounds. Timmy was *still* sick with the Kabul Trots. Only Mike didn't seem to lose weight.

Mike had been hanging out with the Ambassador's son, Greg—Mike bragged that they had plenty of food at their house. After we returned from Kargha Lake, Greg invited all of us to his house—they had a movie theater.

Mike and Greg talked about rock music throughout the movie. Something called the Woodstock festival had just happened in New York. Greg said that half a million people gathered on a farm for a three-day concert.

"Why do I have to be stuck in a place where there's no TV and every radio station plays stupid sitar music?" Mike complained. He was growing bored of the five cassette tapes he had brought with him so he started a cassette exchange program with Greg.

Somewhere around the middle of August, Mother was told to look for a new house to rent—one that was cheaper. "T-H-I-R-D H-O-U-S-E I-S T-H-E O-N-E" Ouija said.

The rest of the inheritance hadn't arrived and Father hadn't written one letter to us in two months despite Mother having written him, so I couldn't figure out where we were going to get rent money. I had my answer shortly after Kargha Lake when Dr. Wilson showed up at our front gate and handed Mother a wad of money. Ouija had provided.

With money in hand, Mother set out to find our new home. The realtor showed us two houses, but we didn't pay too much attention because we knew we were waiting for the third, which was in Karte Sei. Unlike Karte Char, it was a mostly Afghan neighborhood and closer to school.

The third house was smaller than the one we were in, but it had a floor to ceiling living room window that overlooked the compound's small front yard. A beautiful tree shaded the yard from the hot summer sun. It was also near a bazaar, which would make bringing food home in our cart a lot easier. We all loved it and Mother signed the lease right then and there.

The realtor told us the landlords lived in the house behind ours. "A very nice family with seven children—from 24 down to 7, I think," he said. "Their name is Nabir—a very educated and westernized family."

* * *

The inheritance check arrived unexpectedly on August 29th.

We were ecstatic, and Mother immediately bought a mustard yellow '59 Volkswagen bus that Boostan told her about. It came in handy during the move on Sunday the 31st. Mother offered Boostan some extra afghanis if he would help us move into the new place. When he saw the house, he laughed hysterically.

"What's so funny?" Mike asked.

"This house where mistress was lived," he laughed. "She have drapes for here to sell too," he said, pointing vigorously at the windows.

"Well, I'll be." Mother laughed as she shot a quick and knowing look at Tricia that said, "So, that's why Ouija wanted us to take the third house." Tricia was laughing now too.

The next day, school started—for everyone but me. When Mother and I registered Timmy at Ahlmund Academy, the headmaster asked if I was going to AISK.

"No, there's no room for her there," Mother said simply.

The headmaster looked at Mother quizzically and then thought for a minute. He asked, "What would you say, Mrs. Cain, if we let Diana be our school's bus monitor and in exchange we give her a classroom of her very own where she can read and study?"

"What would she study?" Mother asked incredulously.

"Well, we have an eighth grade teacher who can give her ninth grade assignments and then check her work. She wouldn't get a report card, but I'm sure we can agree that it's important her education not be interrupted any more than it has to be."

I turned immediately to Mother and pleaded, "Please, please, please let me go here." I really didn't want to spend my days alone with Mother. She might make me sit at the Ouija board with her.

"Sure, that works," Mother said.

The headmaster walked us out to the "classroom" I'd be using. It was a small shed with dusty stacks of books and school supplies.

"Of course, we'll put a desk in here with a lamp and clean it up a bit," he smiled. "You should ride the bus with your brother tomorrow and come directly to this room. We'll have it set up for you. Mr. Thomas will come by to talk to you before he starts each day. Does that sound good?"

"Yes, sir," I beamed. Oh, thank God, I thought to myself.

The three oldest Nabir children dropped by to welcome us shortly after we moved in.

"Salaam alaykum," Mother said politely. She asked them to join us for fresh lemonade. "I'm sorry we have no ice," she apologized. "We only have a small refrigerator."

"Yes, ees same for us," the oldest boy said. He really wasn't a boy. We learned that Abdul Wassy was 24 and the oldest of the clan. He was a handsome and charismatic First Lieutenant in the Eighth Division Infantry. He told us to call him Wassy.

With him was his sister, Fowzia, a pharmacist with the General Medical Department. She was a few years younger than Wassy and I liked her immediately. Her face was still scarred from teenage acne and her blue-black hair was styled in a short bouffant.

Nafiesa was the youngest of the adult children who visited us that day. She sat quietly and tried to pick up what was being said. The other children, Surria and Nazia, attended Rabee-Balkhi High. Abdul Sammie went to Ghazi High and Richard was at Nezat. Their Father was a Royal Secretary in the Petition Department. He was also Abdul and their Mother was called Habibi.

"You don't wear chadres?" Mother asked abruptly as she covered her eyes with her hands. "All the women we have seen on the streets wear chadres."

Fowzia nodded and answered in broken English, "We be teached modern—no wear chadre. Peoples wear chadre—how you say—not teached peoples?"

It was difficult to communicate with each other during our first meeting, but we agreed to teach each other English and Farsi.

Later that night, Ouija agreed.

The Khyber Pass

Chapter 23

Abdul Wassy

The letter was postmarked July 21st and was sent from Corinth, Mississippi. It had taken more than six weeks for the letter from Francis to reach us in Afghanistan. Mother ripped it out of my hand as I opened the front door. She tore open the par avion envelope and salivated over the delectably written English words. We gathered anxiously around her to hear the news from home.

"Oh, thank God. A letter from the outside world," she said as she pressed the letter to her heart and beamed. Then she read,

Dear Mary –

I been waiting nigh onto a month for yall to write, but I gues you aint got no stamps over their. JR and me's been busy in the garden. We's got lots of tomatos and onions. Right nice harvest.

The reason I's writin is that I got some bad news today from Edith. I knows you don't talk to her, so I thought I should tell yall. Barbara's husband was killed on his motorcycle on July 19. He was so tore up that they kept the coffin closed at the funeral.

I knowed you said the Ouija Board told Barbara that something was goin to happen to Dee. Just thought you should know that one more thing Ouija said come true.

God bless yall. Right soon.

Love, Francis

"Oh, my God," Tricia groaned as the color drained from her face.

"Patricia," Mother patted her back and tried to console her. "You had nothing to do with this. Ouija just predicted it."

"Dee's dead?" Mike said.

"Mike, I'm sure he went to heaven," Mother said. I wasn't so sure about that, but I wasn't about to ask Ouija that question.

The weekends after the letter arrived were filled with Sunday services at the church and Saturday trips to the Shor Bazaar, where Mother began exchanging her inherited American dollars for afghanis on the black market.

Mother bought a beautiful Persian rug for our living room from a Koochi man. He peeled back the rugs that were piled atop his camel with great pride, and Mother haggled with him over the price, to his great amusement.

Tricia and I nibbled on freshly baked nan and kabobs as we shopped the outdoor market in search of Afghan coats. Fowzia had told us the light coats we brought from Phoenix would not be warm enough for Kabul winters. She sent us to the bazaar for fleece-lined and embroidered sheepskin coats and told us not to pay more than one thousand afghanis.

We later learned from the Magnums that Afghan coats—like Afghan hashish—were very popular with the hippies who passed through Kabul year-round. I sure hope the hashish smelled better than the coats did after a few months.

Thankfully, school started at the beginning of September. School days started earlier for me as a bus monitor. My sole duty was to make sure the children stayed in their seats throughout the bus ride to school. Once at school, I went straight to my classroom and waited for my teacher.

Mr. Thomas gave me my very own math, English, and social study books. Each morning he stopped by my classroom to return my graded quizzes and make new reading and writing assignments. I'd work on my assignments throughout the day and at three thirty, I'd gather my books and head for the bus, where I waited for my charges.

Soon after school started, Wassy came for another visit. "My Mother wish you and daughters join for tea—hala—now," Wassy said politely.

"We'd be happy to join her," Mother responded equally politely. The three of us followed Wassy to the Nabir's front gate, which was no more than fifteen feet from our own. We were immediately greeted by Mrs. Nabir, Fowzia and Sammie.

"Salaam alaykum," his Mother said as she bowed slightly. Their servant showed me to my very own table for tea. In the center of our individual tables was a larger one with baked goods, a steaming teapot, and fine Istalif china.

Avoiding my eyes, the servant pulled my chair out and placed an embroidered napkin on my lap. Without a word from Mrs. Nabir, he poured hot chai tea into our delicate teacups. He carefully placed small cakes on our plates with shiny silver tongs. He bowed and backed away. A bright yellow canary sang cheerfully from his wooden cage on the porch. It was a perfect day for a tea party.

Wassy translated for Mother as she exchanged pleasantries with Mrs. Nabir. After awhile, Mother turned to Sammie and asked in English, "What do you do?"

"He no speak English well," Fowzia answered and then interpreted for her brother.

"Man danesh-amuz," Sammie replied, nodding his head at Fowzia and smiling happily.

"He is a student," Wassy interpreted. "A very good student."

"You have such wonderful children," Mother said to Mrs. Nabir. Wassy interpreted and Mrs. Nabir seemed very pleased to hear good reports about her children.

Just as I finished my first cake, the servant stepped up and placed another on my plate. He refilled my cup and backed away again. When I had finished another cake, he placed another on my plate before I could say anything. I tried to catch Tricia's eye, but she was staring at Wassy, as if the rest of us didn't exist.

When the servant started at me with the tongs again, I shook my head and thanked him, "nah moteshakeram," but he ignored me. I didn't want to seem rude, but I had to stop this man soon. I leaned over to Mother and whispered, "What should I do?"

"Leave a piece of cake on your plate," she whispered back. "Then he'll know you're full."

"Ohhh," I nodded, comprehending. It worked.

We stayed and talked with Mrs. Nabir and Fowzia for more than an hour. Wassy was such a gentleman, interpreting precisely and courteously for both his Mother and ours—knowing instinctively that it was a woman's occasion, and that he was just there to interpret.

As the last cup of tea was sipped, Wassy told us about a friend of his who owned a vineyard in Kalia Farrat in the Kodaman District. "You enjoy go there, yes?" he asked.

My ears perked up when I heard we might be taking a trip to see something other than Kabul. "Please, Mother, please," I begged.

"We can take our bus, if you want," Mother nodded. "Your family is welcome to join us," she said magnanimously and foolishly.

Wassy talked to Fowzia and Mrs. Nabir for a minute and then turned back to Mother. "We all go. Do weeks?"

"Yes, two weeks," Mother agreed.

After we were back in our house, Mother counted on her fingers, "There are five of us and nine of them. That's fourteen people in one VW bus. I don't know how that's going to work." Then she thought a little longer, "What if the bus breaks down?"

Ouija encouraged us to go on the trip, "E-N-J-O-Y T-R-I-P Y-O-U W-I-L-L N-O-T H-A-V-E P-R-O-B-L-E-M-S"

* * *

The next morning, as I descended the stairs early for the bus, I heard the tapping of manual typewriter keys from the dining room. Mother was sitting at the table with Father's old Remington in front of her. She paused to look at me, "It's time I started writing," she said.

"What are you writing?"

"I'm writing stories about my experiences in Afghanistan. I think I'll call myself the roving reporter. Mrs. Rasmussen told me that the Kabul Times is looking for someone to write articles in English."

Mother had struck up a conversation with Ellen Rasmussen at church last Sunday. She had tried to immigrate to Afghanistan when King Aman Ullah came to power. She was turning seventy on Saturday, September 20th —the same day as Timmy's birthday. She had tried to immigrate to Afghanistan from Denmark in 1933, but wasn't allowed entry until 1963. She was so determined to work among the Afghans that she never went back to Denmark, but stayed on the Pakistan border until she was given a visa. Her story reminded me of Moses. For the past six years, Mrs. Rasmussen had been a nurse at Wazir Akbar Khan Hospital and then at Avicenna Hospital, and finally at the American Embassy Dispensary.

"My first story is going to be about her," Mother said confidently as she put her head down and laboriously typed with two index fingers. She was having lunch with Mrs. Rasmussen at Chihilsatoon Gardens to finish the interview and then she was going to take it to the editor at the Kabul Times.

* * *

On Saturday, September 27th, we crammed fourteen people into our VW bus. Wassy told us that Kodaman valley of the Shamali Plain was about two hours north of Kabul. We passed the Royal Palace and then continued on Shar Ra Road past Shar I Nau and the Indian Embassy. We turned north onto the Istalif road towards the Kodaman Valley. Once outside the city, the road took us through valley after valley of lush vineyards, snuggled between snow-capped mountains.

Occasionally, I sneaked a glance at Tricia and Wassy. Somehow they had maneuvered it so that they sat next to each other on the back seat with me and Timmy. As we bounced along the bumpy road, I noticed that when their forearms touched, they'd exchange shy glances and smile. I was disgusted. I preferred to turn my attention to the breathtaking views rolling by and, of course, the sumptuous aroma emanating from the pots of food the Nabirs had brought for our host.

Finally, we turned onto a rutted dirt road that led to our final destination. A rotund Afghan man stood smiling and waving at the gate of the compound. Our host, Saide Abdul Majeet greeted each of us warmly as he helped us out of the bus, and he shouted for his servants to go ahead of us with the pots of food we had brought.

"Salaam alaykum," he said proudly. "Sobh bekheyr."

"Good morning," Mother replied.

Mr. Majeet and the Nabirs spoke familiarly and kissed each other on their cheeks. As I half-listened to their conversation, I heard music coming from the vineyard. Not sitar music, but American music from the '40s that

I recognized—they were playing a scratched album of "Sentimental Journey."

Mother clutched her chest and tears welled up in her eyes. "Can you believe it?" she sighed. "It's American music in the middle of Afghanistan."

We followed Mr. Majeet down a path between rows of grapevines that led to a grassy clearing circled by weeping willows. In the center of the clearing, a dining area had been set up for our visit with long and low wooden tables, surrounded by colorful floor pillows. My eyes finally found the source of the music. There between the roots of a willow was a portable crank phonograph sitting on the ground. A servant stood next to it, at the ready to crank or replace the album.

We settled at the table and enjoyed a feast of lamb with a sumptuous dish of rice sautéed with carrots and raisins. Then our host asked us to try his grapes, fourteen varieties in all, he said. Wassy explained that Mr. Majeet employed more than five thousand nomadic workers at his vineyard. Tricia asked why none were here now.

"They harvest in morning—when grapes are tazeh kardan—how you say?—fresh," Wassy explained.

After lunch, Mr. Majeet offered to give us a tour of the vineyard, starting with the creek that ran through his property. As we walked along the creek bank, he stooped down to pull a string from the water. At the end of the string was a stone crock filled with something white. He handed a spoon to Mother and encouraged her to taste the crock's contents.

"It ees yogurt," Wassy told her.

Mother hesitated, but took the spoon and tasted Mr. Majeet's yogurt, "Tell him it's delicious," she lied excitedly. Mother hated yogurt.

"Khoshmazeh," Wassy interpreted.

"Khub," he said, nodding his head. *Good.*

We continued our tour through the buildings where his workers made raisins and red and white wine. He stopped intermittently to respond to workers, and then he returned us to the clearing, where we had afternoon tea. I enjoyed the warm sun flickering through the trees and listened contentedly to the hum of young voices and the quiet conversation of the elders. Wassy leaned over to Mother and whispered, pointing to Mr. Majeet, "He is descend from Mohammed. You know Mohammed?"

"Of course," Mother replied. "So, Mr. Majeet is royal or holy?"

"Baleh," Wassy nodded. "Very religious."

Mother wanted to get back to Kabul before dark, so we took our leave at three o'clock. Mr. Majeet thanked us profusely for coming and gave us a large box of grapes for our journey home.

A week later, Mother sold two stories about Mrs. Rasmussen and Mr. Majeet to the editor of the Kabul Times. He told her he had been trying to find a journalist who would be willing to travel Afghanistan and write stories for the weekly English edition. He agreed to pay her one thousand afghanis for each story she submitted—a little more than twenty dollars.

Now that she was a legitimate journalist, she was determined to take weekend trips for stories to sell to the Kabul Times.

Her next story was about Mr. Tippets. He had invited Mother and me to the University Farm of Darulaman, where he worked with a team of Americans—the Wyoming team—on an experimental Afghan farm.

"Welcome to our farm," Mr. Tippets said. He introduced us to Abdul Rasul Akar, a young Afghan farm worker.

Mother reached for Rasul's hand and shook it vigorously. "This farm reminds me of the Goodyear Farm in Litchfield Park. It's also an experimental farm. In fact, the weather and topography here remind me of Phoenix."

Mr. Tippets nodded excitedly. "Yes, exactly. That's why we sent Rasul to Phoenix last year. We wanted him to learn about the Goodyear Farm project."

"Don, do you mind if I write an article about the farm?" Mother asked. Mr. Tippets nodded. "Yes, that would be very good."

"Tell me, Don, how did your family come to Kabul?" Mother asked as she flipped her tablet open and started writing.

"Well, I was an employee of Wyoming University for 22 years. We came here with nine other families who were a part of the Wyoming team. There had been other teams before us, though. I'm going to retire from the university soon, but before I do, I wanted to help the Afghans learn how to farm more efficiently," he said proudly. "We work with professors and students from Kabul University. We're going to build dorms for them to live in during the harvest in the summer."

Mr. Tippets went on to show us more than eight hundred trees they had planted—pears, apples, peaches, cherries and more.

Mother sold her third story about the Wyoming team to the Kabul Times that following Monday. Then she wrote a letter to the editor of the Arizona Republic to offer her services as an "on the spot" reporter in Afghanistan for that newspaper.

She was traveling or writing all the time after that, which meant a lot less time with the Ouija board. We really had nothing to do until Father came to Kabul anyway. Ouija promised Father would surprise us on December 26th. In one of mother's weekly letters to Father, she said that AISK was asking for some money and she found out he had sent some directly to the school—but no letter to her. Mother said that was a good sign.

At church the next Sunday, Mother mentioned to Dr. Freesen and his wife that we would be taking a trip to Djallalabad or even as far as Peshawar the following weekend.

"Mrs. Cain, I would advise against that," Dr. Freesen cautioned. "You will have to go through the Khyber Pass and Kabul Canyon to get there. It is a winding, narrow, and very dangerous road. I don't think your van will make the trip."

"Dr. Freesen, I don't know why you'd say that," Mother replied loudly. "My van has never broken down, and I've been all over Kabul." Besides, Ouija wanted us to go to Peshawar and had assured us that the van wouldn't break down. Of course, Mother wasn't about to say that to the church people.

At about that time, Dr. Wilson joined the conversation, "Where are you going?" he asked innocently. I noticed that others had stopped talking and were eavesdropping on Mother's conversation.

"Dr. Wilson, she's going to take that old van of hers to Peshawar next weekend," Dr. Freesen repeated, chuckling and shaking his head.

"Mrs. Cain, he's right. It's a dangerous road even with a new car," Dr. Wilson said quietly. "I agree. It's a bad idea."

"Thanks for the advice, but I think I'll take my chances," Mother sniped. "And, I'll thank you to m—"

"Mother, we have to get going," Tricia interrupted and gently took Mother's elbow to pull her away. "The Nabirs are coming for lunch."

* * *

The yellow and gold leaves were clinging desperately to the trees, trying to survive the downpour we encountered in the Tange Gharro Gorge. We reached Sarobi at lunch time after driving through pouring rain for nearly three hours. There were nine of us in the van, including Wassy and Fowzia and another Peace Corps couple Mother had met—Grace and Gordon Magnum.

We stopped at the Khyber Restaurant and enjoyed a warm Afghan meal. Afterwards, Grace wanted to gather pine cones for her Christmas decorations, so we tramped through a small, muddy forest to collect them for her.

By then it was too late to make it to Djallalabad, so we decided to trek as far as the Mahee-Par and Sarobi dams and turn around. On the way back, we stopped again at Sarobi to buy melons from a roadside vendor, and we ate them leisurely on the side of the road.

Torrential rains started right after that and a mudslide had oozed its way down the steep canyon walls in front of us. We twisted our way slowly around the slide and continued through the canyon. The air-cooled VW motor was having a hard time catching its breath on the steep inclines at that altitude.

Around one particularly sharp curve, we almost ran into a tourist bus that had partially slid off the road. It now had one tire precariously hanging off the edge of the highway. The driver assured Wassy that he and his passengers could get it back on the road without our help.

Several miles from the stranded bus the VW finally gave up the ghost and died. As it grew darker, Mother's mental state rounded the corner from ill-tempered to frantic. Wassy and Gordon felt obligated to open the engine door and touch various parts of the engine, but both confessed they had no idea what they were looking for. Mike was frustrated with their mechanical ineptness and crossed the road with Timmy to go exploring.

Looking upward at the darkening sky, Mother insisted that we start flagging down passing cars. "We have to get out of here and soon," she cried.

Unfortunately, none of the drivers we flagged knew any more about Volkswagen buses than we did.

As it grew almost dark, Timmy and Mike returned and told us about a cave we could sleep in if we had to.

That vision was too much for Mother. She said we needed a tow out of that canyon immediately. Fortunately, no sooner had she said that than a heavily-laden lorry pulled up behind us and stopped. Wassy conversed with the driver for a few minutes in the downpour and finally convinced him of something. He walked back to the VW with the good news.

"This driver—umm, be-donbal keshidan. How you say?—pull us." Wassy interpreted. "He have rope."

After Wassy and the lorry driver tied the rope securely to the undercarriage of both vehicles, Wassy opened the door and signaled for Mother to get in quickly because the lorry driver was revving his engine.

"I don't think I'm strong enough to steer a car with a dead engine behind a racing lorry," Mother confessed. "What if the brakes give out? We'll go over the side of the canyon, and we'll all die."

I looked at Fowzia and Wassy, who didn't seem to understand the gravity of the situation. Just as well, I thought. They can be blissfully unaware when they die.

Gordon guided Mother to the passenger side of the car. "Mary, let me drive," he said confidently.

Gordon had barely gotten the door shut when the lorry pulled quickly onto the road. The tow strap was fifteen feet long and snapped taut between the two vehicles. Gordon had his foot firmly planted near the brake and both white-knuckled hands clenched the steering wheel.

The lorry quickly got up to what Mother considered a dangerously fast speed. "God help us." she screamed as the lorry swerved around mudslides and then swerved back into our lane, tires squealing on both vehicles.

"It's all downhill from here, and I don't think he's got any brakes," Gordon yelled, not taking his eyes off the rope. "Without headlamps, I can't see if the rope is taut or not. And he's got no brake lights. I don't even know when to brake."

"Oh, this is just getting better all the time," Mike chuckled nervously.

I turned to give him my best evil eye and mouthed, "You're scaring them."

He mouthed back, "We're going to die."

Mother's hands were braced against the front dash in anticipation of the inevitable crash into the bed of the lorry. She prayed over and over, "Please God, save us."

Wassy grasped our dire situation at that point and closed his eyes tightly. He reached instinctively for Tricia's hand. She hid her face in his shoulder. Timmy was in the seat with them and clutched his arm rest for dear life. His eyes were closed, and he chanted "I don't want to die" over and over.

I was sandwiched between Fowzia and Grace. We desperately clung to each other's shoulders and hands as we squealed around each corner in this downhill race to death.

We lived in that purgatory between life and death for more than an hour. Then, slowly, the curves disappeared, and we had only flat roads into Kabul. Just as quickly as he started, the lorry driver stopped and jumped out of his truck. He began untying the rope from the VW. Gordon and Wassy got out of the van and walked weak-kneed to help him.

"He can't take us to your house, Mary," Gordon translated. "He's going to the Shor Bazaar."

Luckily, we were near the military hospital. From there, Mother used the phone to call Dr. Freesen to ask for a tow home, which he was glad to do. He didn't even say, "I told you so."

Even though it was past midnight when we got home, Mother insisted we talk to Ouija. She wanted to know how Ouija could have put our lives in such peril. Mother was righteously angry, "Lord, I've got to know why you wanted us to go on this trip with a van that was going to break down. Surely, you knew it was going to die on us."

The indicator didn't move and Mother gave up.

The next morning, before Sunday services, Mother tried again. This time she was nicer. "Lord, why did you let that happen to us?"

"W-A-S N-O-T F-O-R Y-O-U" Ouija spelled slowly.

"What?" Mother was astounded.

"W-A-S-S-Y A-N-D F-O-W-Z-I-A N-E-E-D T-O B-E S-A-V-E-D"

"So why did you nearly kill them?" Mother asked.

"S-E-E T-H-E-I-R O-W-N M-O-R-T-A-L-I-T-Y"

"But why did you put us in harm's way?" Mother asked.

"Y-O-U W-E-R-E S-A-F-E"

"I really don't want to go through that again," Mother said firmly. "I don't know what we would have done without Gordon and Wassy."

"Wassy is so nice," I said.

"A-S-K W-A-S-S-Y T-O C-H-U-R-C-H N-E-X-T W-E-E-K"

"Lord, that's forbidden," Mother countered.

"N-O-T B-Y M-E"

The indicator moved to GOODBYE.

After Sunday services, Mother went up to Dr. Freesen to thank him again for towing us home. Mrs. Freesen didn't let Mother get off that easy. "Mrs. Cain, my husband is not at your beck and call. He warned you not to go on this trip, and you ignored him. I would advise you to call someone else next time."

"How dare you?" Mother declared. "I've never asked you for anything and now you're getting all huffy with me. And just for the record, there won't be a next time."

She pulled Dr. Wilson aside to tell him what Mrs. Freesen had said to her, but Dr. Wilson really didn't want to hear about it. "Surely, you can understand her concern, Mrs. Cain? You could have killed your children."

"Dr. Wilson, my children were perfectly safe, but I thank you for caring about us," she hesitated. "What I really wanted to talk to you about was our friend, Wassy. He wants to come to church with us next week—"

Dr. Wilson cut her off, "Mrs. Cain, do *not* bring an Afghan to this church." He continued, "Please take this seriously. We could lose everything. I will not have you endanger our church because of your fool-hardy behavior."

Mother stared at him for a moment, then blinked, turned and walked away. "I'll bring him to church if I goddamn want to," she cursed under her breath the rest of the way home.

* * *

Boostan found an Afghan mechanic who said he could repair the Volkswagen. He had the car running by Wednesday and by Thursday, Mother had a trip planned to the King's Dairy.

Wassy and his two eldest sisters piled into the VW on the 18th, a warm and balmy day. The weather was a good omen. We talked excitedly for the first hour of the trip. Then Mother noticed people were staring at us as they passed our bus. One look in the rearview mirror, and she knew why. "For God's sake, there's black smoke billowing from the engine."

We stopped immediately to let the engine cool, and we were standing by the car when a VW beetle crashed into a city bus. Within minutes, two other Afghans showed up with a Karachi wagon pulled by a mule. We watched in amazement as the now four Afghans tried to load the VW onto the cart. We laughed hysterically as more and more Afghans came upon the accident and offered their loud advice.

Wassy humorously interpreted their instructions to the original four Afghans. Finally, after thirty minutes a group of men physically picked up the car and loaded it onto the mule cart that hauled it off.

Mother got back in the bus, crossed her fingers, and turned the key. It started, and we were back on the road to Carriz-Mirr. After another fifteen minutes she stopped and let the engine cool again. We were very near the King's property.

"Here comes a guard," Timmy warned as he slid down the seat.

Before Mother could speak, Fowzia spoke in Farsi to the guard. She seemed to be explaining something to him about us, and then he walked away, turning to wave to her after a few feet.

"What did you tell him?" I asked.

"I said we cousin to King," she laughed and shrugged happily. "We not."

Waiting for the motor to cool didn't work this time. The van was dead. Mike suggested we push it and told Mother to pop the clutch. So, the seven of us jumped out and pushed the van until it reached about ten miles per hour. Suddenly, it jerked, and the motor sputtered to life.

"Hurry, get in," Mother yelled as she slowed down to wait for us.

We arrived at the King's Dairy at noon, a little delayed, but still intact. The dairy belonged to King Mohammad Zahir Shah who had been on the throne for nearly forty years. We heated our lunch on a small camp stove and spread a blanket to sit on. After lunch we roamed the diary and even visited the King's barn, where the huge Holstein presented by President Kennedy was boarded.

We watched as Afghans milked cows with ingenious one-legged stools strapped to their waists. They moved from one cow to the next with their buckets, wasting no time. We stumbled on the King's prize bull in the last stall. He stood at least six feet high and had a gold ring in his nose. He bellowed and snorted loudly at us as he stubbornly dug a deep pit with his front hooves.

At the end of the day we approached the bus warily. "Don't look into its eyes," Mike said as he passed its nefarious headlights, his hands serving as blinders. Mother carefully inserted the key into the ignition and closed her eyes. "Please God, please." The engine didn't even turn over.

"Everybody out," she said. "Start pushing."

Luckily, the VW started, and we jumped in, only to stall again a mile from the dairy. Wassy and Tricia walked back to the dairy and returned fifteen minutes later with a friend of Wassy's who had agreed to tow us home.

His friend towed us uphill and then disconnected the two cars at the crest of each hill. He thought it was safer if we rolled freely to the bottom, where he would pick us up again. Mother drove the van, but told us she had no brakes on the downhill side, so we whizzed wildly past lorries and buses. Mother blasted our horn to warn them we were coming.

On the outskirts of Kabul, a taxi pulled up next to the van, and Wassy recognized the driver. He convinced him to tow us back to the house, free of charge.

It was well after dark when we pushed the van back into the garage. Wassy and Tricia stayed back a minute talking. I went in the house, but suspected something was going on between them. So, I spied on them from our bedroom window.

"I want to kiss you, Patricia jon," Wassy said to her as he cradled her face in his hands. "But I wait until is proper." They held hands briefly, and then he left through the front gate, looking back at her longingly.

Yuck, I thought. She's only fifteen, and he's so old. I don't care if he was good looking. He was way too old for her. Mother didn't share my disgust. I heard her and Tricia talking the next morning about a girl's first kiss, which meant they must have talked about Wassy.

"It's an exciting time for you," Mother agreed. "But Wassy is much older. He's focused on his career, and you need to focus on high school. I think he's kind, but you come from different worlds. I don't think it could work out. Think about all we have to do for the Lord."

"Wassy would help us with our mission. I know he would," Tricia said. "School's not that important. Look at you. You didn't finish the ninth grade, and you're a journalist. What does school matter with the end times coming? Wouldn't it be more important for me to find a husband than go to school?"

"I'm not discussing this anymore," Mother said suddenly angry. "We'll talk about this when your Father gets here."

Chapter 24

The Fleece

Ouija continued to insist that we take weekend trips. One such trip was our excursion to Istalif with Fowzia and Wassy. It was a beautiful fall day when we started out on Saturday morning. We had no trouble with the van all the way to the village.

We shopped the bazaars and had afternoon tea at the Istalif hotel, where we ventured onto the rooftop for a panoramic view of the mountains. Wassy pointed to a white airstrip in the distance. "President Eisenhower come to Istalif there and go to Chihilsatoon to see our King many year ago. I be teenager, but I remember."

After tea, I came out of the restaurant to find Mother standing in front of the VW with her hands on her hips. "This car is a homebody," she said. "It won't start." Even pushing it didn't work this time. We tried for over an hour to find an Afghan brave enough to tow us back to Kabul. We came prepared nowadays with our own cable and flashlight.

A friend of Wassy's family kindly offered to tow us back to the Kabul city limits. This tow seemed uneventful. Either we were getting better at being towed or we had become immune to the trauma. In any event, we got as far as the Indian Embassy and then had to call Dr. Freesen to tow us back to our house again.

We all wanted answers from Ouija after we got the van back in the garage that night.

"G-O   T-O   B-E-D" Ouija commanded.

"That thing is not my boss." Mike screamed as he paced back and forth, pointing to the board. "I'm going to do whatever I want to from now on. I'm not talking to it anymore."

"Michael Levoy Cain," Mother started, but Mike shoved his face right in front of hers and yelled, "Don't you get it, Mother? It's not God. It's Tricia."

"That's blasphemy, Mike," Mother cried. "Please don't. You know what happens to people who say things like that about Ouija."

"Everything's been a coincidence," he laughed. "Tricia says it, and then it just happens. How stupid can you be?"

Mother slapped Mike hard on his face. "Don't you ever talk to me like that again, you ingrate."

Mike clenched his fists, ready to punch Mother, but he held back. "I'm writing to Father. I'm getting away from you and Tricia. I'm going home."

"Why don't you just do that?" Mother secretly flipped Mike the bird as he ran up the stairs. "Your Father's coming here," she laughed. "Don't *you* get it?"

Mother didn't speak to Mike that Sunday morning. She said she wasn't going to make him do anything, including go to church. He was in charge of his own soul, she said, throwing her hands up in the air.

As we sat on the pews in church the next day, I couldn't think about anything but what Mike had said the night before. What if it was all just a coincidence? What if it was Tricia, or Mother, all along?

My mind replayed and listed the events that led us to where we were. All the things that Ouija had predicted and that had come true. I thought back to the beginning when Ouija told us about Bobby Kennedy not becoming president. How about Uncle Dolmer dying without a will within two weeks after Ouija told us he would give us the money? What about the pastor? What about Dee? What about Jeane Dixon's predictions?

I mean, for God's sake, we were in Afghanistan, exactly where the Ouija board told us we needed to be for the second coming—even though none of us had ever heard of Afghanistan. We were told it was where the end times would begin.

What about all the things that hadn't come true, I asked myself. Whenever a prediction didn't come true, Ouija said we were being tested, just like Job. Father had lost the faith, Ouija said, but he would get it back and join us shortly.

My mind turned over each past event and looked at it from a different angle, despite my fear of what I'd find. If what Mike said was true, and everything was just a coincidence, then what was behind Ouija?

If it was Tricia, then I was sure I could assemble enough evidence against her. She always seemed to get her way. Ouija always backed her up. Sometimes she would tell me things, and then the Ouija board would say the same thing later. But, why would she do it? How could she think she'd get away with it? Maybe it was her, sometimes.

Could it have been Mother all along? How could that be? I kept reliving the moment in my bedroom when Ouija told us it was God. Mother wasn't even sitting at the Ouija board. It was Father and Tricia that time. So, how could it be Mother? Maybe it was her, sometimes.

What if Tricia or Mother was possessed by a demon? Oh, my God. That was a scary thought. I didn't even want to think about that one.

What if it was the devil or an evil spirit? That would explain why people kept dying, but it wouldn't explain why we were told to do good things. But, then again, we were told to do bad things too. Things I didn't want to do, like hanging the key in the house when we sold it. Or, how about when we blackmailed the executor of the estate? None of those things seemed very Christian to me.

What if it really was God? The Bible is full of stories about how God was really cruel to people. How about when Abraham was told to kill his son? Or, when he let Moses wander in the desert for forty years just because he lost the faith for a moment? Or, how about Job? God can be pretty mean, I thought to myself.

Just then, I realized where I was. I'd better shut up with these thoughts. I was pretty sure it was blasphemy to be doing this in church. After all, God can read my mind.

The pastor closed the service with the Lord's Prayer, and we rose to leave. Mother turned to say hello to Mrs. Freesen, who had been seated behind us. Mrs. Freesen glowered at Mother for a few seconds without saying a word and then turned rudely away to talk to someone else.

"Well, I'll be damned," Mother muttered. I was behind her as she waved to the D'Antonios who were two rows back. They saw her wave and then purposely turned to exit the other way so they wouldn't have to talk to her.

Oh, no, it's happened again, I thought.

Just then I saw Dr. Wilson at the front door, receiving people as usual. We're ok. He's going to talk to us.

"Dr. Wilson, that was a wonderful sermon," Mother said cheerfully as she extended her hand to shake his.

"Mrs. Cain," he said, avoiding her eyes. He reached past her extended hand and grabbed the hand of the next person in line. "Hello, Mrs. Wiley, how are you? Did you enjoy the sermon?"

I backed out of the reception line when I saw that. I didn't want him to treat me that way too. My eyes burned, and I fought a familiar tightness in my throat.

Once outside, Mother walked stubbornly away from the church without looking back. She wiped a lone tear from her cheek and swore, "I'll never step foot in that place again." She turned mid-stride to face Tricia and warned, "And don't you try to make me, Patricia."

I looked back just as we turned the corner. The Freesens and Wileys stood together outside the church, shaking their heads in unison at our retreat. Less than five months in Kabul, and they hated us already. How did that happen? I was glad Mother didn't look back.

Mother ranted and raved the entire walk back to our house. "What did I ever do to them? And they call themselves Christians. I'll be damned if I ever become like them."

Fortunately, a few people still considered us their friends. On November 9th, the Magnums drove me, Tricia and Timmy to see a group of American Christian singers called the "Teen Team" perform at the Intercontinental and Khyber Restaurant.

After a happy rendition of *Up, Up and Away*, the group took a break, and we stood to stretch our legs.

"This is great, isn't it?" Gordon said. "Hey, did you kids hear about the Peace Day march next week in Washington, D.C.? A half million people are protesting the war in Vietnam. I sure wish I could be there."

I had little interest in politics, so I half listened as he and Grace talked about the march and the upcoming Apollo 12 mission. Then Tricia surprised us all.

"I'm going to work at the *Kabul Times*," she said randomly.

"What?" I was shocked.

"That's wonderful, Patricia. Are you going to work part-time?" Grace asked.

"No, I'm quitting school, and I'm going to work as a copy editor on the English edition," Tricia replied proudly.

"You're quitting school?" I was shocked.

Tricia punched my arm and said, "Shut up, Dinie."

"Is your Mother okay with you quitting school and going to work?" Gordon asked, obviously concerned. "Maybe she should take the job, instead. I mean, she is writing for them already. It makes sense."

"No, the job's for me, not her," Tricia replied, folding her arms stubbornly.

"But you need an education," they countered kindly.

"AISK is too expensive, and we need the money, so I'm going to work." She nodded towards me then, "Diana will take my place at AISK. She doesn't even go to school, but no one's been concerned about her." She turned away from us and clapped as the Teen Team came back onstage.

Grace and Gordon shared concerned looks, but said nothing else about it for the rest of the night.

I found out later that night that Ouija said Tricia was supposed to take the job at the *Kabul Times*. Mother didn't even question Ouija about it. "We need the money," she said to me later. "And I don't argue with Ouija."

The very next day, I was enrolled at AISK, and Tricia had started working. I relished having a real classroom and real schoolmates. By lunch on my first day, I had made a new friend—an Indian girl named Lopamunda Gura.

Tricia loved her job. A week after she started, she proudly pointed out her story in the paper. She had edited a story about women who worked at the Bagrami Textile Company. The article said that women had been emancipated in Afghanistan in 1959. The women in the article earned between two and nine afghanis an hour; but they were also given a free lunch and two outfits a year, and they rode a free bus to and from work.

Mother told us later that week that the inheritance money had run out. She said that we could get by between Tricia's job, her articles, and my babysitting money. But we didn't have enough money to pay for any extras, like fixing the van or buying new glasses for Mike who had broken them in a freak school bus door accident. They were almost beyond electrical tape repair this time.

Tricia and Wassy officially announced that they were dating after she started at the paper. Wassy's parents approved of Tricia, and their relationship was now considered proper in the Afghan culture—as long as the two were chaperoned when on dates.

Thanksgiving came and went without a special dinner. Mother wanted to conserve our money for when Father arrived the day after Christmas. Thanks to Wassy, we had a Christmas tree that we decorated with homemade decorations. Mother had put a pair of socks for each of us under the tree just so we had something.

On the 26th, I woke up even more excited than on Christmas day. Timmy and I couldn't sit still, so Mother told us to go outside and play ping-pong.

Suddenly, Friend began barking ferociously and attacked the front gate. We ran after him and grabbed his collar so he wouldn't hurt Dr. Wilson and another parishioner, who had just stepped inside our compound. We knelt next to Friend and muzzled him so we could hear the conversation taking place between Mother and the church people.

At first, Mother was pleasantly surprised to see the two men. Her demeanor quickly turned icy as she remembered their last encounter at the church.

"Dr. Wilson," she said coldly.

"Mrs. Cain," he answered politely, extending his hand. She didn't take it. "Can we come in? We'd like to talk to you."

"I'm not sure we have anything to say to each other." Mother added dramatically, "after the way you treated me and my children." She barred them from entering with her arm.

"All right, then," Dr. Wilson said. "Please hear us out."

Mother nodded, and he continued. "Let me just say that we have been praying for your family. The church members are very concerned. The reason for our visit is two-fold. First, we understand that Patricia has quit school and is now working full-time. Is that true?"

Mother glared at them, but said nothing.

"Why didn't you take the job, and let Patricia continue with her studies?" the other parishioner interjected coldly. "What kind of Mother are you?"

"That is none of *your* business," Mother yelled at him. She started to close the door, but Dr. Wilson grabbed it with his hand.

"Mrs. Cain, the other reason we are here is to encourage you to go home to your husband. It is apparent to us that he is not coming to Afghanistan, and we know you are running out of money. We think it best you leave Kabul immediately."

"As I told you before, this is none of your business," Mother's voice was shaky. "My family will be just fine."

"Mrs. Cain, your souls *are* our business, and your finances are our business, as long as we are the ones who bail you out financially and tow you back to Kabul every time your van breaks down."

"I don't believe what I'm hearing," Mother said in disbelief. "You can bet your ass I will never ask you for help again. And just so you know, my husband is arriving here *today*."

Mother slammed the door in their faces. They stood stunned in front of our door for a minute and then turned to leave.

Mother immediately wanted to talk to Ouija. "Lord, please promise that Levoy is coming tonight," she begged.

"H-E W-I-L-L B-E H-E-R-E F-O-R D-I-N-N-E-R"

Mother was busy the rest of the day getting ready for dinner. The huge chicken she bought had been roasting for at least an hour in our tiny oven. The bread stuffing smelled delicious, and I was ready to eat it now. Mother was making the lemon icebox pie when they had interrupted her. The house smelled like America to me.

Father didn't arrive by six o'clock, so Mother left the bird in the oven to keep it warm. At six-thirty, she said it was getting overcooked, so she told us to go ahead and dig in. At eight o'clock, Mother instructed us to clean up the dishes. Obviously, Father wasn't coming.

Mother ceremoniously brought the Ouija board to the dining room table. She waited for Ouija to speak first. Mike and Timmy refused to talk to Ouija and went upstairs to play cards. I wanted to hear what God had to say about this.

"M-Y D-E-A-R F-A-M-I-L-Y"

"I'm going home," Mother said. Tears welled up in her eyes, and she sobbed uncontrollably. Tricia sat across from her, hands glued to the indicator. After a minute or so, Mother calmed down enough to put her hands back on the indicator.

"W-H-A-T G-I-F-T D-I-D I G-I-V-E T-O H-U-M-A-N-S"

Tricia responded, "The gift of free will."

Mother looked up at Tricia through teary eyes.

"L-E-V-O-Y D-O-E-S N-O-T P-R-A-Y," the indicator spelled slowly. "H-E H-A-S A-B-A-N-D-O-N-E-D M-E"

"He has abandoned *us*," Mother moaned.

"H-E U-S-E-D H-I-S G-I-F-T O-F F-R-E-E W-I-L-L"

"I can't do this alone," Mother's shoulders were heaving. "Mike and Timmy have asked their Father for plane tickets home. They want to leave as soon as school's out. It will be me and the girls. How can we possibly do what you want us to do?"

"Y-O-U A-R-E N-O-T A-L-O-N-E"

"But we can't see you, Lord," Mother closed her eyes. "If we could just see evidence that you are here, it would help."

"I A-M H-E-R-E"

"Where?" Mother asked. I looked around for something visible, but there was nothing.

"L-O-O-K A-T T-H-E L-E-A-T-H-E-R C-H-A-I-R"

We turned our heads simultaneously towards the chair. There was a depression in it as if someone had sat down and then the depression was gone—as if the person had risen.

"Oh, my God." we cried in unison.

The indicator moved to YES.

"Lord, you are with us," Mother whispered to herself.

"R-E-A-D 1 S-A-M-U-E-L 1-7"

"It's the story of David and Goliath," I said, without opening the Bible. I knew it well. I read the whole chapter as Mother and Tricia listened intently. We were looking for inspiration.

"L-E-V-O-Y M-A-Y Y-E-T C-O-M-E"

"Thank you," Mother said just as the indicator moved slowly to GOODBYE.

I was relieved when the Shillaks stopped by the next morning to ask if I could babysit on New Year's Eve. I jumped at the chance.

I wanted to get away from my life and enjoy the comforts at their house. The Shillaks' fridge was always full of food, and they had a record player. Their music selection was limited, but I was desperate for American music. After putting the kids to bed on New Year's Eve, I listened to "Somewhere Over the Rainbow" several times and then "Oh What a Beautiful World." I lay on my stomach on the living room floor and slowly flipped through the Sears catalog, absently singing along with Louis Armstrong.

I lowered my head onto my folded arms as the song ended. The needle skipped over the label as I lay there. Why did I want to cry? Come on, I told myself, get a grip. You're almost fifteen. You're not a kid anymore. After I pulled myself together, I opened the 1970 Unicef Calendar I bought at school and jotted down a poem that I'd had in my head for a few days:

> While once I walked upon the snow
> I heard a voice so sweet and low.
> It seemed to say my friend, look back
> For where you were is now a track.
>
> Suddenly, I heard a word.
> It had an edge as if a sword.
> Whispered harshly in my ear,
> I ran, but still the voice was near.
>
> Twas fear, I fear, prevented me
> from looking back so readily.
> I stopped, but still the voice was near.
> I heard it singing in my ear.
>
> Suddenly, I felt a tap
> Upon my shoulder, tilt my cap.
> I turned, but saw no face save mine.
> My words and footsteps intertwined.

The cold weeks after New Year's were filled with school and babysitting for me. Tricia worked long hours at the paper and Mother was always typing. The boys had their friends and school and were just biding their time until they went back to Vallejo.

On February 1st, Mother asked Tricia why she looked so nervous. "What's the matter with you?" she questioned her that night. "If you have something to say, spit it out."

"Wassy wants me to go skiing with him in the Salang Pass." Before Mother could say no, Tricia continued, "It would be overnight, but we would have chaperones."

"You are out of your mind, child," Mother said. "That's not happening."

"It's for my birthday," Tricia pleaded. "You know you can trust me."

"No," Mother replied. "You're a girl, and he's a boy. You can't be trusted. I won't allow this."

"Why don't we ask Ouija, then?" Tricia said. "I'll go along with whatever Ouija says. Maybe you're right." I had a feeling that Tricia was going to get her way, but I didn't say anything.

"L-E-T H-E-R G-O" was all Ouija said when Mother finally agreed to talk to the board.

"But, Lord, this isn't right," Mother countered.

"C-H-A-P-E-R-O-N-E-S A-R-E O-K"

Mother finally agreed to let Tricia go on the overnight with Wassy. I didn't know why, but Tricia seemed different after that trip, almost like she didn't need us anymore.

The highlight of February was when Vice President Spiro Agnew visited Kabul. The principal closed the school so we could stand on Darulaman to wave to Agnew's motorcade. Agnew surprised everyone by getting out of his car to shake hands and talk to students.

He came to me and stopped. He smiled and shook my hand. "Where are you from?" he asked politely.

"I'm from Avondale, Arizona," was my proud reply.

"Well, you're certainly a long way from home," he said as he moved on to the next student.

Since we weren't welcome at church anymore, Mother told us we'd be holding Sunday services at home. We read the Bible and sang hymns accompanied by me on the concertina and Tricia on the accordion. Mother didn't make Mike and Timmy participate because she "was finished with those two ingrates."

I was losing interest in school by mid-February, going to school one day and skipping the next, because of stomach aches. Mother didn't seem to care. I missed my Father, and I knew he wasn't coming to Afghanistan, no matter what the Ouija board said.

Money matters continued to worsen. I heard Mother and Tricia talking in low voices one night about the Nabirs wanting their rent money. If we didn't pay the two months we owed soon, they wanted us to move. That didn't seem right to me, though, since Tricia was his girlfriend.

By the beginning of March, Ouija often cut our sessions short by sending Tricia and Mother on various errands, like finding a cheaper house or a new mechanic, that kind of stuff. It was about that time that Mother asked Ouija for a sign that Father was coming.

"Please give me a sign before our wedding anniversary," she pleaded. That would have been March 31st.

"A-L-L R-I-G-H-T" Ouija said.

On March 10th, Mother got her sign.

A large envelope arrived from the states. "It's from Levoy," she exclaimed, tearing open the letter and reading the papers silently. She dropped the papers and ran upstairs, slamming her bedroom door behind her.

Tricia picked up the papers and read out loud to the rest of us, "It's a Petition for Divorce," she said solemnly. "Father filed for divorce."

"He's divorcing us?" I asked. "What do we do now?"

Mother stayed in her bedroom for the next two days, and Tricia and I took turns bringing food to her. We left the tray outside her locked door, and when we'd come back only the glass of water was gone. At night, she argued with the voices—that's what she called them when we asked who she was talking to.

We really didn't need Ouija to tell us that Father was not coming at that point. Mother had lost all hope. On the third day, she came out of her bedroom and told Tricia she wanted to talk to the Ouija board.

Ouija told her this was her mission all along, because God knew from the beginning that Levoy wouldn't come.

"R-E-M-E-M-B-E-R M-A-R-Y M-A-G-D-A-L-E-N-E"

"Lord, I don't want to think about that," Mother rubbed her forehead and then placed her fingers back on the indicator. "I owe two months' rent to the Nabirs, and they want their money. If we don't give it to them, we have to move."

"Y-O-U W-I-L-L R-E-C-E-I-V-E S-O-O-N"

Just then, Mike threw open the front door and interrupted angrily, "Dr. Wilson wrote Father and told him about us." he shouted, throwing his books on the chair. "And Father told him about the Ouija Board. It's all over the school."

"They're going to want to talk to Ouija," Tricia moaned.

"D-O N-O-T H-A-V-E T-O P-R-O-V-E A-N-Y-T-H-I-N-G" Ouija answered.

* * *

On Saint Patrick's Day, we received a letter from Dr. Wilson with two thousand afghanis.

"Why did he send us money?" Tricia questioned Mother.

"I don't care why," she said. "We need the money. It's the funds we were waiting for," she fanned her face with the money. "Two thousand afghanis."

"Thank you, Lord," Mother said gratefully to Ouija.

"D-O N-O-T T-A-K-E M-O-N-E-Y" Ouija warned.

"But isn't this the money you were talking about?" Mother asked.

The indicator slid to NO.

"But where is money coming from?" Mother asked.

"T-R-U-S-T M-E"

Mother returned the money to Dr. Wilson the next day with a note that said, "No thanks."

* * *

On Thursday, March 19, Ouija told Mother to fast and pray.

"Why?" Mother asked.

"V-A-N W-I-L-L S-T-A-R-T Y-O-U M-U-S-T B-E-L-I-E-V-E"

"The van has been weighing heavy on my mind, but I didn't want to beat a dead horse," she quipped.

Mike had been sprawled on the couch, and when he heard the conversation, he laughed. "That van needs a crank shaft. If it starts, it will definitely be a miracle."

Mother fasted and prayed as she was told to do. On Friday morning, she got up before we went to school. "I believe. I believe. I believe," she repeated over and over as she searched desperately for the key to the van.

"Where in hell are the keys?" she asked angrily. Mike remembered that he put them in a kitchen drawer when we got home from the last tow. He dropped them into Mother's waiting hand and shook his head as he bounded up the stairs two at a time.

"I believe. I believe. I believe," she said all the way into the garage. "I believe. I believe. I believe."

I watched excitedly from the window as Mother climbed into the van, pumped the gas, and turned the key. I was praying too.

D. Lynn Cain

Our Guardian Angel in Kabul (see Window)

Chapter 25

A Question of Faith

Nothing.

Mother took the key out of the ignition and inspected it, as if maybe she had the wrong key. She blew on it and wiped it on her sleeve. Then she pushed it gingerly back into the ignition, pumped the gas, and mouthed, "I believe. I believe." She closed her eyes. This time there was a clicking noise, but still no fire. She tried again desperately. Nothing.

She surrendered. She hit the steering wheel hard with her clenched right fist in retaliation. She pounded it again. I was sure it would break. Then she laid her forehead against the steering wheel and stayed like that for several minutes, shoulders heaving all the while.

I thought I could help her believe if I was outside, so I slipped out the front door onto the porch.

Suddenly, she flung the door open and slid out of the seat. "Get out of my way, Diana," she said as she pushed past me.

It was Good Friday, and we were having services that night. "Stupid van," I shouted as I kicked the tire too. "You're the devil." Why couldn't it just start? Why didn't God answer Mother's prayers? My eyes blurred as I backed slowly away from Mother's nemesis.

Mother stood at the bottom of the staircase, hand resting on the rail, shoulders still heaving. She hissed when she saw me. "Diana, stop right there if you know what's good for you." I froze. She heaved one last sigh, "This is between me and Patricia."

She marched determinedly up the stairs, slammed open our bedroom door, and screamed, "Patricia, your jig is up. Get out of bed and follow me."

After a few moments, Tricia passed me on the steps and mouthed, "What's going on?"

"The van won't start," I warned. She rolled her eyes and followed Mother to the dining room table, where the makeshift board lay.

Mike and Timmy were up by now and had joined me on the stairs.

"Why won't the car start?" Mother asked Ouija bluntly.

"B-E-C-A-U-S-E Y-O-U D-O-N-T B-E-L-I-E-V-E"

"But you made me a promise. I kept my end of the bargain, you didn't," she said through clenched teeth, struggling against her angry tears.

"I-T W-O-U-L-D S-T-A-R-T I-F Y-O-U B-E-L-I-E-V-E-D"

"I believed with all my heart," Mother cried, eyes fixed on Tricia. "Don't tell me I didn't believe."

Ouija didn't budge.

"I've had enough. I don't know who you are, but you're not *my* God."

Ouija still didn't budge.

"I'm at my wit's end," Mother said to Tricia. "I'm calling John. This spirit will have to prove to him that it's God."

The indicator scraped over the tattered paper to NO.

"If you won't talk to him," Mother threatened, "then I won't talk to you."

"O-K"

Just like that— it was over.

"The veil has been lifted from my eyes," Mother said dramatically, still staring at Tricia. "It's over." She removed her hands from the indicator for the last time and sat back in her chair. What did she mean—the veil has been lifted? You either believe or you don't, what's a veil got to do with it?

"Good," Tricia said, scooting her chair away from the table. "I'm tired of this anyway."

Mother stared at Tricia's departing back. Then she closed her eyes and shook her head slowly from side to side, a stream of tears was slowly giving in to gravity and sliding off her cheek.

* * *

"John, I want to show you the way God contacted us," Mother said when Mr. Strackan arrived twenty minutes later. "You asked how we got specific instructions from God. Well, it wasn't through prayer. It was a spirit leading us."

"Mary, we've suspected all along that it was not prayer," John answered. "I just didn't know what medium you were using. If it's all right with you, I'd like to call Dr. Wilson."

"Don't you want to talk to it first?" Mother offered.

"No. I'd be afraid for my soul. He's more experienced at these kinds of things than me."

Mr. Strackan left and returned thirty minutes later with Dr. Wilson, who immediately asked to see the Ouija board. Mother insisted that all of us be in the room when Mr. Strackan returned.

She placed the tattered board and toilet paper roll on the table in front of Dr. Wilson. "Here it is," she said apologetically. "We gave away the real board in Mississippi. But when we got here, we were so scared," she motioned to the board helplessly as her voice trailed off.

Dr. Wilson didn't touch the board, but motioned for Tricia and Mother to sit. "Please sit down at the board," he said kindly. "I want to speak to the spirit."

Tricia retreated back into the hallway, "No. I'm afraid of it. I don't want to talk anymore." Then, defiantly, she said she wanted to talk to Wassy.

"You won't see him," Mother threatened. "Not until we get some answers, young lady."

"Please, Patricia," Dr. Wilson urged, taking her elbow and gently pushing her to the chair across from Mother. Tricia looked at him for a minute, and then her eyes flickered. She must have realized her choices involved running away or sitting at the board one more time. She sat down stiffly and placed her fingers on the indicator.

I held my breath.

"Speak to me," Dr. Wilson commanded the spirit.

Nothing happened.

"I command you demon to speak to me," he repeated.

Still nothing.

"There's no vibration," Mother said weakly. "I think the spirit's gone."

Dr. Wilson nodded his head. "Yes, I have no doubt. Would you please tell me how this communication with the spirit world began?" He looked from Mother to Tricia. "Please tell me the whole story, from the beginning." He settled himself comfortably in the leather chair that the spirit had sat in the day before. I drew in my breath to warn him, but changed my mind.

Mother told him our story over the next hour, stopping at various points to cry and recount all she had lost—her husband, her home, her friends, everything. After she tearfully concluded with the final chapter of the story, about how she had made a fleece with God, she stopped to think and finally said. "That's it."

Dr. Wilson insisted that Mother burn the board and the indicator, right then and there. She acquiesced quickly and tore them up. She threw them into the fireplace, followed by a lit match. The board resisted momentarily and then burst into flames. I was mesmerized by Ouija disappearing before my eyes. I held my breath as the flames erased GOODBYE. Ouija ceased to exist in the physical world.

Mother remembered, "What about the plans for the temple? Shouldn't we burn them too?"

"You have plans for a temple?" Mr. Strackan asked curiously.

"Yes, the one that must be built for the second coming of Christ," Mother said matter-of-factly.

She had left out that detail when she told them our story. "Armageddon is going to begin in Afghanistan."

"Afghanistan?" Dr. Wilson laughed, "Really?"

"Yes," Mother replied suspiciously.

"You didn't think it odd that the end of the world was going to start in a country that most people have never even heard of?" he chuckled. "Afghanistan doesn't have nuclear bombs."

"I didn't question it because so many other things that Ouija predicted came true," she retorted.

Oh no.

"I'm sorry, I didn't mean to insinuate anything," he apologized instantly, to my great relief. "May I see the plans for this temple?"

Mother signaled for me to fetch the plans from my room. I was the only person who knew where they were, hidden in a shoebox in my closet. When I returned, Dr. Wilson reached for the box cautiously, as if it was a poisonous python.

Mr. Strackan tried to intercept the box. "I'd like to read these," he said.

Dr. Wilson pulled the box from Mr. Strackan's hands. "No, John, I don't even want to look at these." He removed my meticulously written notes from the box and threw the pages, two at a time, into the fire with Ouija. I held my breath until the last page of the record succumbed to the flames.

My face flushed as the record burned, and I felt as if I was purified by the flames. My mind suddenly leapt into the future—a future without Ouija making every decision for me. In a flash, Dr. Wilson's words brought me back to the present.

"If the spirit told you to get the dog, then it is possessed," he said, eyeing Friend who had been snoring loudly by the front window. "I'm sure you must realize by now that he is not your guardian angel. He is no doubt possessed by a demon or an evil spirit."

What?

"Yes, I've become afraid of him," Mother whispered so that Friend couldn't hear her. "He's been acting strange lately. He follows me from room to room and stares at me. I think he's watching me to make sure I don't disobey Ouija. Now that I think about it, when I sit down to read my Bible, he barks at me until I have to stop and let him outside. Then he immediately scratches on the window to come back in the house."

Mike, sitting on the step above me, whispered, "They have got to be joking." Timmy and I exchanged worried glances and turned our attention back to the conversation in the other room.

Mother took a quick breath as she continued to build her case against our dog. "And two nights ago, I was sleeping in my bed when I felt him jump in the bed with me. I don't let the dog in my room at night, so I kicked at him to make him leave. He snarled at me, and I sat up."

She stopped, for effect, and then, "At the same time, I heard him barking outside. I got up and yelled, "Where's Friend?" Diana heard me and jumped out of bed. She said she had let him out a half hour before and forgot to let him back in." Mother stopped and then whispered conspiratorially, "So, how could the dog be outside *and* inside at the same time?"

Dr. Wilson stared at her for a moment and then shook his head. "I'm sorry to say, but the dog will have to be put down. There is no way to exorcise a demon from an animal." He caught sight of our frightened faces and apologized, "I know this will be painful for the children, but it must be done right away."

"Yes, yes," Mother hissed. "We have to be rid of everything having to do with that infernal Ouija board."

"I'll take care of it for you," he offered.

Mike could restrain himself no longer and jumped up from his perch, "This is insane. You can't kill our dog. He's a good dog."

"He's *just* a dog," Timmy cried. "He's not possessed."

"No, please, don't kill him," I cried. "He's not a demon. He's a *dog*."

"He won't feel a thing," Dr. Wilson said, now standing between Mike and the dog. "You can't take him back to the states with you, anyway. He has to stay in Afghanistan. He has *nowhere* to go here."

Mother had retrieved Friend's leash and handed it to the pastor. "John, please take the dog to my car," Dr. Wilson said, handing the leash to Mr. Strackan, who quickly attached it to Friend's collar.

"I can't believe you're doing this," Tricia was incredulous. She turned on Mother and screamed in her face, "You'll be sorry you did this."

"No, young lady," Mother said, slapping Tricia across the face. "You'll be sorry *you* did this."

For a second, my focus was turned from the impending doom of our dog to my sister's retreating back up the stairs. So now Mother intended for Tricia to take the blame, my mind whispered.

Just then, Mr. Strackan jerked our dog towards the front door. Friend dug his claws into the rug and whined and snarled as he was dragged through the door. I ran to the window just in time to see him being dragged towards the front gate.

Friend twisted on the leash and looked back at me—eyes begging for help—help that I couldn't give. Tears ran down my face and fell from my chin onto the floor. I pressed my hands hard against the cold window pane. Then he was gone.

"No, no," I cried as my knees buckled, and I dropped to the floor next to Timmy and Mike, who had already collapsed. The familiar tightness in my throat started, and I labored to breathe. I pulled my knees to my chest and dropped my head onto my folded arms.

Dr. Wilson watched sympathetically for a moment and then returned to the business at hand. "Mrs. Cain, we need to pray for the spirits to quit your home." He pulled a small book from his breast pocket. "Please walk with me as I cleanse each room. You must repeat the Lord's Prayer the whole time. Do you know it?" Mother nodded.

I watched through a glaze of tears as he and Mother cleansed our home of demons.

"I cast you out, unclean spirit, along with every satanic power of the enemy, every scepter from hell, and all your fallen companions; in the name of our Lord Jesus Christ.

He motioned for Mother to recite the Lord's prayer. She chanted the words over and over, clutching her Bible to her chest, as he continued, "Be gone and stay far from this family. For it is God who commands you, it is God who flung you headlong from the heights of heaven into the depths of hell."

"Hearken, therefore, and tremble in fear, Satan, you enemy of the faith, you foe of the human race, you begetter of death, you robber of life, you corrupter of justice, you root of all evil and vice; seducer of men, betrayer of the nations, instigator of envy, font of avarice, fomenter of discord, and author of pain and sorrow. Be gone, then, in the name of the Father, and of the Son, and of the Holy Spirit.

By the time they returned to the living room, my grief had turned to anger. Timmy, Mike and I sat by the window, clutching our knees, scowling at Mother and listening as these strangers decided *our* fate.

"Mrs. Cain, what will you do now?" Mr. Strackan asked kindly.

"What?" Mother's voice was weak. "I don't know. We've been buying food with Diana's babysitting money and Tricia's job. We owe two months' rent to the Nabirs. She inhaled sharply and dropped her gaze to her lap. "We're destitute." She dropped her head onto her clasped hands.

Dr. Wilson touched Mother's shoulder sympathetically, and she blurted out, "My husband filed for divorce. I have no home—here or in America."

The direness of our situation took my breath away. A minute ago, I was worried about the dog being taken from us, and now I realized my life was in danger because of *this* woman. We were stranded in Afghanistan with a Mother who was stupid and probably crazy. How could I have believed for two years? Why had I ignored the voice inside my head that warned me every step of the way? I finally understood what Mother meant by the veil being lifted.

Dr. Wilson and Mr. Strackan exchanged glances. "Mrs. Cain, we'd like to help your family," Dr. Wilson said.

"Please help," Mother begged in her most contrite voice.

"First, I'm going to send a telegram to your husband that you want to come home," Dr. Wilson said. "Then, I will talk to Ambassador Newman to make arrangements for your family to return to San Francisco as soon as possible."

"Yes, yes," Mother cried. "But I can't pay you back."

Dr. Wilson smiled, "Mrs. Cain, the United States government does not leave Americans stranded in other countries. I will go to Ambassador Newman with your story, and he will make sure the government pays for your plane tickets."

"But that's nearly three thousand dollars!" Mother exclaimed. "Won't they want it back?"

"Eventually," Mr. Strackan confirmed.

"Levoy won't pay it," Mother shook her head as she bit a finger nail. "And they won't get blood from this turnip." She laughed nervously.

"I'm sure they'll let you pay whenever you can," Dr. Wilson consoled her.

They didn't know my Mother like I did. She had no intention of paying back the citizens of the United States for bringing us home.

Mike moaned and dropped his head onto his folded arms. Now that our story was known all over school, we couldn't show our faces there again. I rubbed Mike's shoulder and tried to comfort him, "It's okay, Mike. We'll never see these people again."

Tricia's curiosity got the best of her, and she had returned to the doorway and heard what was being said. When she saw me, she mouthed, "I'm not going back."

* * *

"Give it back to me," I slapped at Mike's face as he held my gold necklace with the crucifix high above my head.

"Give her the necklace," Mother screamed from upstairs. "I swear to God, I will kill you if I have to come down these stairs."

"You think this cross is going to protect you from the devil?" Mike teased me, laughing. "I'm going to flush it down the toilet."

"No, don't." I shouted even louder. I kicked him in the shin, and when he bent over in pain, I grabbed the necklace out of his hand.

"Screw you." I screamed as I placed it safely around my neck.

I couldn't remember who gave me the crucifix, but I somehow felt safer with it on my body at that point.

Chapter 26

The Exorcist

We were still mad at Mother about letting them take Friend, but we were more afraid to stay home alone. So, when Mother said she was going to the church for services that night, with or without us, we quickly offered to go with her. When we returned home after services, the house was eerily quiet without our dog to greet us.

Boostan stopped by shortly after we got home to ask if Mother needed help with baking or cleaning on Saturday.

"Boostan, we are leaving for America next week." When Boostan didn't respond, Mother continued, "I'll find you a job with another American family before we leave, ok?" she hugged him. "You've been a good friend."

"Moteshakeram, ma'shuqeh," he finally answered. "Be safe. Afghanistan miss you."

"We will miss you too," she smiled. "Come by tomorrow, and I'll give you some of our things to sell until you get another job."

"Moteshakeram." he said gratefully.

At midnight, we were still huddled in the living room together.

"I don't want to go to bed," Timmy whispered. "I'm afraid."

"Me, too." Mike admitted.

"Why don't we all sleep in my room?" Mother offered. When we eagerly nodded in agreement, she told us to bring our air mattresses to her room.

"I don't need to sleep in your room," Tricia said belligerently. "I'm not worried about spirits getting *me* in the middle of the night."

"Patricia, of all people, you should be the most worried," Mother snapped back. "I'm not letting you out of my sight, young lady. You bring your mattress to my room, too."

After the four of us had settled into our beds on the floor and Mother was in her chor poi, she turned off the light. Within minutes, I was asleep. I awoke in the middle of the night to Mother's screaming.

"Who's in bed with me?" she screamed. She flipped on the light and was now standing in the middle of her bed—pillow over her head. "Someone was in bed with me. I thought it was you, Timmy."

"What?" he said sleepily.

"Some*thing* was in bed with me."

As we realized what Mother was implying, we huddled closer together on the floor and screamed if one of us touched the other one.

"Shut up. You're scaring me even more," Mother yelled. "Go back to sleep. I'll stay awake and keep watch."

With that reassurance, I slipped back into a deep sleep. I was awakened again by Mother's hissing, "Patricia, just where do you think you're going?" I could see Tricia's silhouette in the moonlight.

"Why are *you* awake?" Tricia hissed back.

"You're not going anywhere," Mother snapped. "Get back in that bed right now."

"I have to go to the bathroom."

"You can wait 'til morning," Mother said harshly.

Tricia had always been a sleepwalker, but tonight it could be dangerous. I stayed awake as long as possible to watch over her. Finally, as the first rays of sunlight streamed into the room, I fell asleep. Shortly after that, Mother woke me again.

"Oh, my God." she screamed. She was standing next to her bed, pointing to a razor blade on the nightstand. "Where did this come from?" she said accusingly.

When no one responded, she picked up the razor and held it up to Tricia's face. "Were you hoping I'd kill myself with this, Patricia?"

Tricia stared at the razor blade.

"What have you got to say for yourself?" Mother wouldn't let it go.

"I didn't put that there," Tricia said softly.

"You were the only person trying to get up in the middle of the night," Mother yelled. "By God, I've had enough of this. Get out of my bedroom."

* * *

Dr. Wilson was sitting in our living room an hour after Mother called him. We were to stay in our bedrooms until she called for us. They talked in hushed voices for quite awhile, and I couldn't make out what they were saying.

Mother called us after he left and said, "We're going home."

"When?" we asked.

"I've got the tickets in my hand. It's finally over," she fanned herself with the tickets. "We're leaving on Tuesday, March 31st at seven o'clock in the morning." She read the tickets, "Pan Am Flight 205 to New York and then TWA #47 to San Francisco. We're going home."

"That's your anniversary," I commented. "You and Father can be together on your anniversary."

"What a nice anniversary gift?" Mother was giddy. "Dr. Wilson sent a telegram to your Father to let him know we're coming home."

Tricia did not share our excitement. "I'm not leaving Wassy," she said.

"Oh, yes, you are." Mother paused and continued, "Did you honestly think you could manipulate Wassy into marrying you? Do you think you can con him like you did us?"

Tricia was paralyzed by Mother's venom. "Why are you saying this? He already asked me to marry him," Tricia ran up the stairs.

"You are not marrying him," Mother yelled as she followed Tricia upstairs. "He's going to throw you away as soon as I'm out of this country. He's going to marry an Afghan girl. You're used goods."

Mother locked the bedroom door behind Tricia.

Mother turned as I walked up behind her, "She's not running this house anymore." She raised her hand threatening me, "And don't you let her out of that bedroom. Do you understand me?"

I nodded vigorously and backed away from the door.

* * *

An unsuspecting Wassy showed up on our doorstep that afternoon to take Tricia to the bazaar. He wasn't expecting what he got. Mother stopped him before he even got to the front porch. I watched and listened from behind the tree, where I'd been crying for the past hour.

"Patricia is not feeling well," Mother said snidely. She spotted me behind the tree and looked back to Wassy. "I have to be honest with you, Wassy. Your family has been good to us, and I really appreciate that."

Wassy didn't respond.

"We are leaving for the United States on Tuesday. I don't have the money to pay your parents, but please tell them they can keep whatever we leave in the house to pay our debt."

Wassy looked past Mother into the dark house. "I must speak with Patricia," he insisted.

"I'm afraid not, Wassy," Mother held him back by his arm. "Your relationship with my daughter is over. She's barely sixteen—too young for you."

"I must," Wassy cried.

"No, Wassy, go home and don't come back," Mother said finally. "It's over."

Wassy was stunned.

"I have nothing else to say." Mother was standing between Wassy and the front door, arms crossed defiantly. "Please leave now."

Wassy backed away from her and then turned to leave. He looked back up to our bedroom and waved to Tricia in the window.

Throughout the rest of the day, Tricia slammed things against the wall and intermittently screamed at Mother and begged me to release her. I felt sorry for her, but I didn't dare touch that door knob.

That night, we slept uninterrupted in Mother's bedroom.

* * *

Tricia and Mother reached a truce the next morning and Mother released her from the bedroom so we could all go to Easter services at the church.

Shortly after we returned home, there was a loud knock on the front door. When I opened it, I was surprised to see Dr. Wilson and his wife Betty at our door. Behind them was another older woman, whom I didn't recognize. John Strackan and Gordon Magnum were behind her.

"Dr. Wilson?" I asked. Mother came to the door and pushed me aside abruptly.

"Thank you so much for coming pastor," she said.

"Mrs. Cain—Mrs. Mitchell," he motioned an introduction to the older woman.

Mother laughed, "Oh, what a coincidence, Mitchell was my former married name."

Mother invited them inside and Dr. Wilson continued the introduction, "Mrs. Mitchell and her husband are the founders of Go-Ye Fellowship, an evangelical worldwide mission group," Dr. Wilson continued. "She is very experienced with exorcising demons—"

"What?" I was shocked.

"Diana, go to your room," Mother commanded, pointing up the stairs. She turned her attention back to Mrs. Mitchell.

"I've just come from Pakistan, where I was asked to conduct several exorcisms similar to this." She nodded calmly to Mother, "Both were possessed teenagers and both were successfully exorcised of their demons."

Oh my God. I backed up the staircase as the group continued into the living room. Which *teenager* was getting exorcised in our family? Mother had already told them that Ouija called me the *recorder*. What if they were here for me?

I burst into the boys' room and shouted, "There's an exorcist here."

"A real exorcist?" Timmy asked innocently.

"She's here to exorcise a *teenager*," I said meaningfully.

"It's got to be Tricia," Mike said, shrugging his shoulders. "Me and Timmy weren't even involved. I've been saying all along that it was Tricia." They didn't move off their beds.

"Don't you want to watch?"

"Nope." Mike said. He shoved me out of their room and slammed the door.

"You're just afraid it might come into you," I whispered to the door.

Just then, Mother yelled, "Patricia, come down here, please."

Thank God, it's not me.

Our door opened and Tricia emerged, not even suspecting what was waiting for her downstairs. I opened my mouth to warn her and thought better of it.

After she was in the room, and everyone's attention was on her, I sneaked down the stairs and found a good hiding spot under the stairs. From there, I could see everything.

Mother grabbed Tricia's elbow tightly and held onto her. Dr. Wilson and Mr. Strackan positioned themselves near her in case she tried to bolt from the room.

"I'm Jennie Mitchell. Your Mother asked me to come here today and help you."

"Help me?" Tricia was clueless.

"Yes, your Mother feels you may be possessed by a demon. I am a trained exorcist," she finished.

"What?" Tricia panicked and stepped away from Mother. The two men grabbed her—one on each side—and held her in front of them. She struggled as Mother slipped back among the others who had formed a circle around Tricia and the exorcist.

"I'm not possessed, she is." Tricia pointed to Mother, wild-eyed. "Let go of me."

"If we let go of you, will you stand here in the middle?" Mrs. Mitchell asked. "Will you stand in the middle of the circle and not try to get away?"

Tricia thought for a second and then nodded her head. The men released her.

"What is your full name?"

Mother answered quickly, "Patricia Faith."

"Please join hands everyone," the exorcist motioned to the adults.

"I doubt that any of you have been in an exorcism, so let me tell you what's involved," she patted Tricia on the shoulder. "This will not hurt you, my dear. In fact, you will feel better after we've finished."

She lifted a small vial on a necklace from her bosom and held it in front of them. "This is holy water from Jerusalem. I will use it to banish the demons. I will command the demons to leave Patricia in the name of God."

"If there is an evil spirit in Patricia, it may become hostile. It is crucial to understand that the devil has power to injure or harm Patricia, both physically and psychologically. We must be careful."

"If there is one characteristic of the evil spirit, it is his hatred of Christ. For that reason, I have brought a crucifix—" She thrust a large gold cross into Tricia's face. Tricia recoiled.

The exorcist lowered the crucifix and continued, "The Book of Revelations says that the Apocalypse predicts the operation of the evil spirit as the anti-Christ until the end of time. It also reassures us that we will overcome Satan provided we trust in the Savior's power and are submissive to His divine will. Jesus told his apostles, "These signs shall attend those who believe: in my name they shall cast out devils."

"Patricia, possession is the result of internal influence by the devil without, however, depriving a person the use of free will. As an exorcist, I cannot believe too readily that you are possessed by an evil spirit." She moved closer to Tricia. "I must ascertain the signs of one possessed from one who is suffering from mental illness."

Tricia's eyes grew wide with fear.

I thought to myself that it would be better for Tricia to be possessed. At least they could rid you of the evil spirit. If you're crazy, they'll lock you up like they did Aunt Loraine and you won't get out until you're too old to care.

"There are signs of possession—the ability to speak in a strange tongue or to understand it when spoken by another," Mrs. Mitchell stopped and turned to Mother. "Does Patricia do this?"

"She has spoken in tongues at the church in Vallejo," Mother said carefully. But Mother didn't mention that lots of people spoke in tongues.

"Does she have the ability to see the future?" Mrs. Mitchell continued.

"Yes," Mother replied emphatically. "The Ouija board predicts what will happen, and she's the only one it works for."

Tricia looked at Mother as if she was Judas Iscariot and had betrayed her in her final hour. Then a shadow of fear fell on Tricia's face as the exorcist continued.

"We must be on our guard against the arts and subterfuges which the evil spirits will use to deceive us, for often they give deceptive answers and make it difficult to understand them. Once in a while, after they are recognized, they conceal themselves and leave the body practically free so that the possessed believes herself completely delivered," she paused dramatically. "But I *cannot stop* until I see the signs of deliverance."

She lowered her chin and looked at Tricia over her glasses. "The evil spirit doesn't want you to submit to exorcism, Patricia. It will try to convince you that your affliction is a natural one. The demon may cause you to fall asleep with an illusory dream and hide from you—so that you appear to be freed. But, we cannot let that happen."

She moved back from Tricia and said to the others, "I want you to chant the Twenty Third Psalm quietly throughout the exorcism," she said turning and looking at each person in the circle. "I will be the only person who speaks to the demon. You are not to ask any questions nor look at Patricia."

"The demon may try to harm her. If I see that she is experiencing a disturbance in some part of her body or an acute pain or a swelling appears in some part, I will trace the sign of the cross over that place." She crossed herself.

"Do you understand what we are facing, Mrs. Cain?" she asked.

"Yes, I do."

"Good, we will start now. Please turn down the lights." The exorcist opened the vial of holy water. "Are you ready, Patricia Faith?"

"I am *not* possessed," Tricia cried and then turned to Mother, "How could you do this to me? Tell them. Tell them it was you."

Mother shook her head and looked away.

The exorcist began by dipping her finger in the holy water and making the sign of the cross on Tricia's forehead. Tricia stared straight ahead and didn't move.

"How many spirits inhabit Patricia Faith? How many of you are there? What are your names?"

Tricia didn't respond, so Mother answered, "She told us she was my dead grandfather, Elijah, Gabriel, and God."

The exorcist nodded and continued, "We drive you from us, whoever you may be, unclean spirits, all satanic powers, all infernal invaders, all wicked legions, assemblies and sects; in the Name and by the power of our Lord Jesus Christ."

She reached for the ceiling with both arms outstretched, "The Most High God commands you, He with whom, in your great insolence, you still claim to be equal; He who wants all men to be saved and to come to the knowledge of the truth. God the Father commands you. God the Son commands you. God the Holy Ghost commands you. Christ, God's Word made flesh, commands you; the faith of the Holy Apostles Peter, Paul, and the other Apostles command you."

She screamed at Tricia, "Begone, Satan, inventor and master of all deceit, enemy of man's salvation. Stoop beneath the all-powerful Hand of God; tremble and flee when we invoke the Holy and Terrible Name of Jesus."

She stopped and joined hands with those in the circle who were still chanting the Twenty Third Psalm. She said a prayer for Tricia and then, "Please chant louder now," she urged. She rocked back and forth with closed eyes. I began chanting with them.

The exorcist continued, "Let your mighty hand cast this demon out of your servant, so he may no longer hold captive Patricia Faith, whom it pleased you to make in your image, and to redeem through your Son, who lives and reigns with you, in the unity of the Holy Spirit.

With one hand pressed hard against Tricia's forehead, the exorcist held the back of her head and proclaimed, "I command you, unclean spirit, whoever you are, along with all your minions now attacking this servant of God, Patricia Faith, by the mysteries of the incarnation, passion, resurrection, and ascension of our Lord Jesus Christ, by the descent of the Holy Spirit, by the coming of our Lord for judgment, that you tell me by some sign your name, and the day and hour of your departure." She pushed Tricia backwards.

And then Mother fell to the floor and writhed uncontrollably. *Oh my God!*

All eyes were on Mother for several seconds, but I watched Tricia. She smiled, but did not move. The exorcism came to a screeching halt. Mrs. Mitchell looked from Tricia to Mother and back again. Then she continued as if Mother was not lying on the floor at her feet.

"Oh, evil serpent, do not think you have fooled me. Do you think you could divert our attention to the mother? I command you to obey me to the letter, I who am a minister of God despite my unworthiness. Release her."

The exorcist crossed herself and then crossed Tricia on the brow, lips, and breast. She continued, "When time began, the Word was there, and the Word was face to face with God, and the Word was God. May the blessing of almighty God, Father, Son, and Holy Spirit, come upon you Patricia Faith and remain with you forever." Then she sprinkled Tricia with holy water from her vial again.

She read from the Book of Mark and paused to signal the others to move Mother out of the circle. She continued when they finished, "I humbly call on your holy name in fear and trembling, asking that you grant me, your unworthy servant, pardon for all my sins, steadfast faith, and the power—supported by your mighty arm—to confront with confidence and resolution this cruel demon. I ask this through you, Jesus Christ, our Lord and God, who are coming to judge both the living and the dead and the world by fire."

She crossed herself and Tricia and then pressed her right hand to Tricia's forehead and proclaimed, "See the cross of the Lord; be gone, you hostile powers. Lord, heed my prayer. I appeal to your holy name, humbly begging your kindness, that you graciously grant me help against this and every unclean spirit now tormenting this creature of yours." Seeing that Mother was awake and upright, the exorcist motioned for her to rejoin the circle. Then she continued, "I cast you out of Patricia Faith, you unclean spirit along with every Satanic power of the enemy and all your fell companions; in the name of our Lord Jesus Christ. Be gone and stay far from this creature of God."

Tricia did not flinch.

The exorcist continued angrily, "Why then do you stand and resist, knowing as you must that Christ the Lord brings your plans to nothing? Fear Him, oh evil spirit, who in Isaac was offered in sacrifice, in Joseph sold into bondage, slain as the paschal lamb, crucified as man, yet triumphed over the powers of hell."

She hit Tricia on the forehead hard this time, "Be gone, then, in the name of the Father, and of the Son, and of the Holy Spirit. Give place to the Holy Spirit by this sign of the holy cross of our Lord Jesus Christ, who lives and reigns with the Father and the Holy Spirit.

The exorcist stopped and drank from the vial of holy water.

"I will conclude now," she said solemnly. "I adjure you, ancient serpent, by the judge of the living and the dead, by your creator, by the creator of the whole universe, by Him who has the power to consign you to hell, to depart forthwith in fear, along with your savage minions, from this servant of God.

She was frustrated by my sister, "To what purpose do you insolently resist? To what purpose do you brazenly refuse? And now as I adjure you in His name, be gone from this young girl who is his creature. It is futile to resist his will. Lord, heed my prayer and let my cry be heard by you. I humbly entreat your glorious majesty to deliver this servant of yours from the unclean spirits; through Christ our Lord. Amen."

"Be gone, now. Be gone, seducer."

I looked at my watch. Two hours had passed. The exorcist said hoarsely, "Let us pray. Lord God almighty, bless this home, and under its shelter let there be health, chastity, self-conquest, humility, goodness, mildness, obedience to your commandments, and thanksgiving to God the Father, Son, and Holy Spirit. May your blessing remain always in this home and on those who live here; through Christ our Lord. Amen."

"We are finished," the exorcist said quietly. The others stopped chanting and looked up at Tricia, who stood with crossed arms in front of them.

"Can I please go to my room now?" she asked flatly.

"Yes, Patricia Faith, go in peace," Mrs. Mitchell nodded as she motioned for Tricia to leave the room.

The adults talked quietly for a few more minutes about the results of the exorcism. I heard the exorcist say, "We've done all we can," and then she picked up her purse off the couch. "God be with you and yours," she said to Mother.

Dr. Wilson and Mr. Strackan saw me behind the stairs and waved goodbye. Having been found out, I had no choice but to come out of hiding. Mother stayed behind in the living room, and I followed the group to the door.

Gordon and Mr. Strackan hugged me as they left. Dr. Wilson smiled and smoothed my hair. I nodded to Mrs. Mitchell, trying to avoid her eyes. I didn't want her to think I needed exorcising too.

She smiled at me and then stepped out onto the porch into the afternoon sunshine. She stopped suddenly and turned to face me. "What is your name?" she asked.

"Diana," I said.

"And how old are you?" she continued to probe.

"I'll be fifteen in two weeks," I replied uncomfortably. I didn't want to talk to this woman at all. She brought her blue-eyed gaze back solidly onto me and spoke words that pierced my soul.

"Diana, you are going to write this story, and it will be known around the world." Then she turned and walked out the gate.

The end of the record.

Epilogue

When I was sure she was gone, I closed the door and leaned against it. I pressed my fingertips against my temples in an attempt to stop a flood of memories. I watched from the sidelines as my mind tried frantically to rewrite the past two years from a new perspective.

What did I know for certain? Sadly, nothing.

If I was going to survive this odyssey, I would have to abandon any hope of knowing "for certain" who or what was behind Ouija. Whether it was God or the Devil—or even mental illness—was not a conclusion I had to reach.

Sure, I'd remember the story—I'd *be* the record, but I was not about to be stuck at that door for the rest of *my* life.

I took a step.

* * *

Kabul's majestic mountains were barely visible through the foggy airplane window. I knew I would never forget Boostan, the Nabirs, and the Afghans and Americans who had come to our aid.

When I could no longer see the city beneath us, I leaned back in my seat and surveyed my family. Mike and Timmy seemed unaffected by any of this. Mother and Tricia had come to an uneasy peace and could carry on simple conversations again. Father had telegrammed that we could come back to Vallejo, and that he had stopped the divorce proceedings.

I smiled with satisfaction, knowing at least one thing for certain. Ouija was wrong—Armageddon would not start in Afghanistan.

Printed in Great Britain
by Amazon